Love,
Dad

A NOVEL

EVAN HUNTER

Crown Publishers, Inc.   New York

Library of Congress Cataloging in Publication Data
Hunter, Evan, 1926–
Love, Dad.
I. Title.
PS3515.U585L6 1981   813'.54   80–27565
ISBN: 0-517-544113

Book Design: Deborah B. Kerner
10 9 8 7 6 5 4 3 2 1
First Edition

THIS IS FOR
ALL THE SONS AND DAUGHTERS,
ALL THE MOTHERS AND FATHERS

MacArthur Park is melting in the dark
All the sweet green icing flowing down
Someone left the cake out in the rain
And I don't think that I can take it
'Cause it took so long to bake it
And I'll never have the recipe again
Oh no
Oh no.

JIMMY WEBB

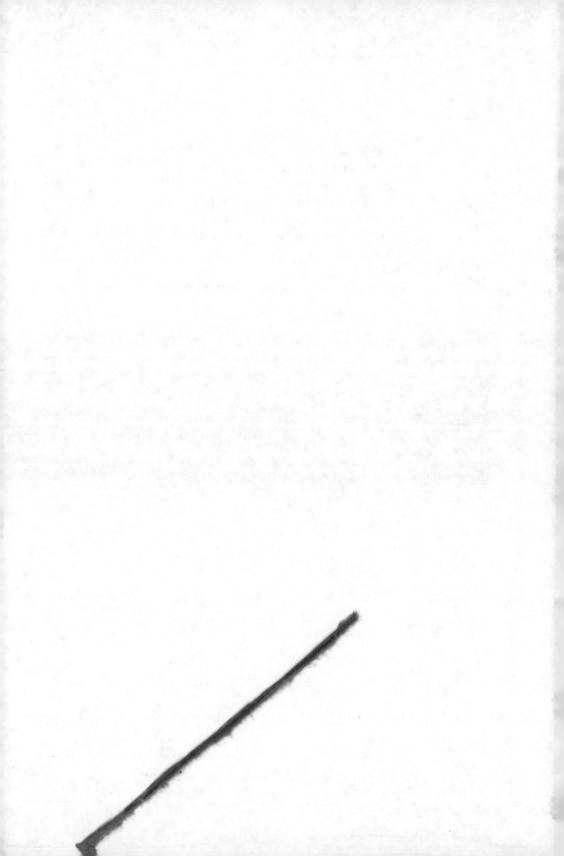

1968

1

Jamie was still working at midnight, hanging the matted enlargements on every available inch of wall space, using double-faced Scotch tape for the plaster surfaces and pushpins for the old wooden beams. His daughter had gone to bed at ten-thirty, serene in the knowledge that the birthday tradition would be honored yet another time—but he alone knew that *this* year the shared secret would carry with it a true surprise.

He had started putting up his photographs of her when she was a year old and couldn't possibly have understood that all those black-and-white enlargements on the walls were pictures of herself, taken over the past year. *See the baby, Lissie? Who's the pretty baby?* Holding her in his arms, her chubby little hand reaching out, one stubby forefinger touching the nose of the baby on the wall. *Yes, darling, that's you, darling.* But not understanding at all. The pictures hadn't even been matted that first year; there simply hadn't been enough extra cash to buy mats for the four dozen enlargements he'd hung all over the living room. That was in 1952, a year before he'd broken through with the photographic essay for *Life.*

On December 18, 1953, the night before Lissie's *second* birthday, he hung the enlargements he'd been working on all that week. Tradition—it had become tradition in the short space of two

3

years—demanded that he perform the task alone, without assistance from Connie, unlike their annual Christmas Eve efforts. *That* year, the enlargements were matted. He had trimmed off the white margins left by the enlarger easel, and then had mounted the pictures with rubber cement—he'd ordered a hot mounting press, but it had not yet been delivered—cutting the mats himself from a lightweight but pure rag stock of Bristol board. He cut most of the mats to accommodate eight-by-tens, but there were several larger pictures as well—at least a dozen eleven-by-fourteens, and one poster-size picture he'd had blown up and printed commercially, the best picture he'd taken of Lissie that year. It showed her looking down in consternation at a sand-covered lollipop, her blue eyes squinted, her blond hair catching the sun for a dazzling halo effect. He'd taken it with the Leica on a bright August day at Jones Beach using Kodak Plus-X and shooting with an f:8 opening at $\frac{1}{250}$ of a second.

That year, she knew who she was. She stood puzzled in the center of the living room, wearing damp Dr. Denton's—she still wasn't toilet-trained and Connie's constant joke was that one day she'd have a college-girl daughter who still wet her pants—and then she waddled from picture to picture, beginning to get the message, her eyes sparking with intelligence; these were pictures Daddy had taken; this was her birthday, and on her birthday, Daddy put up pictures of her. When she saw the poster-size shot of her squinting at the lollipop, she squealed with glee, remembering, and ran to him and hugged his knees. He lifted her into his arms and kissed her plump little cheeks and whispered into her hair, "Daddy loves you."

This year, Lissie would be seventeen—and Jamie was breaking with tradition. The unspoken codicil dictated that the pictures he hung were to be only those taken of her in the previous year. But tomorrow she would be seventeen, and surely seventeen demanded something a bit more earthshaking. He should have done this *last* year, in fact, when she'd turned sixteen; sixteen was a milestone year. But they had just moved into the Rutledge house then, and the place was in total chaos, and there was no time for something as grandiose as what he was doing tonight. He had over the past several weeks gone back through his files for the last sixteen years, selecting three representative photographs for each year, and had added to them a dozen new pictures taken since the beginning of 1968, for a total of sixty pictures of various sizes, five of them the same poster size as the one of Lissie when she was twenty months

4

old and squinting askance at a sandy lollipop. The problem now was where to hang them all.

The living room in the Connecticut house was nowhere near as large as the one on Central Park West had been. They'd discovered the converted sawmill completely by chance a little more than a year ago, on a visit to Rutledge to see a television producer named Lester Blair. This was in October, and fifteen-year-old Lissie—almost sixteen, in fact—was away at school suffering through what was officially called an academic weekend, but which she and her roommate referred to as an "anemic weekend." The suffering had, in fact, been more imaginary than real. Jamie and Connie had driven up from New York on Saturday to take her to dinner, had spent the night in a motel outside New Haven, and had taken her to lunch that afternoon before driving down to Rutledge. The Henderson School was in a Connecticut town called Shottsville (which all the kids at school called Shitsville, naturally) only some twenty minutes beyond New Haven on the Merritt Parkway, but Lissie nonetheless complained constantly that she never got to come home except on so-called long weekends, which official terminology she maintained was a prime example of hyperbole, a figure of speech she'd picked up in her sophomore English class.

The initial choice had been to send her to a public middle school in the city—dread thought—or to any one of several good private schools within busing distance. But the two schools they were seriously considering had long waiting lists, and they learned from a friend that the third contender was really mediocre. They were suddenly confronted with the previously unthinkable possibility of having to send Lissie away from home in order to guarantee the education they felt she should have. They made their decision premised on a map of New York City and its environs, drawing on it a circle with a 150-mile radius, and finally settling on the Henderson School, which was little more than two hours away by car, and which had an excellent record of college placement and a reputedly fine speech and dramatics department. Lissie had till then shown neither the talent nor the inclination to pursue a theatrical career, but Connie—admittedly biased—insisted that good speech was the hallmark of a good education. Not for nothing had she herself been a speech and dramatics major at Vassar; neither for nothing had she finally obtained her master's degree in speech pathology at Columbia University.

They arrived in Rutledge after lunch that fall Sunday to discuss the possibility of doing a half-hour Christmas special utilizing a portfolio of stills Jamie had shot on Fifth Avenue the Christmas before. A dozen of these had appeared in *Life* under the title "White Christmas in a Gray City," and his agent, Lew Barker, had sold another four to *Ladies' Home Journal,* but Jamie had shot eight full rolls of film, which he felt, immodestly, captured the very essence of the city at the peak of the holiday season. It was Lester Blair's opinion that the pictures wouldn't need an accompanying story: a simple connecting monologue would suffice. Of the 288 pictures Jamie had developed and printed—he still did all his own developing, though he knew many professional photographers who preferred leaving the donkey work to labs like Modern Age and Compo—half of them were superb (in his own estimation), a quarter of them were excellent, and the rest were junk. Blair wanted to pace the pictures some ten seconds apart, six shots to a minute, for a total of 180 pictures in the half-hour. He told Jamie he would try to get somebody like Gregory Peck or Charlton Heston to do the connecting monologue, which he himself wanted to take a shot at writing, but that they'd probably end up with some very good New York actor instead, since there wasn't much money involved in public television. But he felt this was something well worth doing, and he ended his pitch by saying he thought the prestige value to Jamie would be enormous.

They took a stroll through the town of Rutledge late that afternoon. Diana Blair was a good deal younger than her husband ("Younger by at *least* twenty years," Connie later suggested), an attractive, shapely brunette who prattled on brainlessly about how much she envied their living in the city, where a person could step out of his front door and drop into a Broadway show, or a concert, or an opera, or a gallery opening, or a first-run movie—the usual suburban-dweller's plaint. Jamie was surprised to hear Connie, his wife of almost seventeen years at the time, his wife whom he thought he knew better than anyone else on earth, saying *she* would much prefer living out here in the country, with all these glorious fall leaves overhead and underfoot, and the joy of a snow-clad winter (her actual words), the promise of daffodils in the spring, the subsequent sounds of summer insects chirping in the tall grass— the usual city-rat's plaint, delivered in what Jamie secretly called Connie's "Vassar Asshole" voice, somewhat nasal and entirely unmodulated, except that this time it was accompanied by a flash of green eyes as brilliant as a jungle glade: she actually *meant* what she was saying.

"If you're serious about this . . ." Lester said.

"Oh, I *am*. I would *adore* living in this town," Connie said. "Adore" was one of her favorite words. She rolled it off her tongue lovingly, kissed it breathily onto the air like the promise of those spring daffodils she'd been anticipating three minutes earlier.

"There's a great old house for sale here," Lester said.

"Right on the river," Diana said.

"Would you like to take a look at it? I know the owner, I'm sure he . . ."

"Thanks," Jamie said, "but I think . . ."

"I'd like to see it," Connie said.

The house was owned and occupied by a surgeon and his wife who, now that all their children were grown and married, were planning retirement in Arizona. The surgeon's hands shook as he showed them around; perhaps a better reason for retirement, Jamie thought, than all those grown and married children. The house had been a working sawmill during the Revolution *("Our* Revolution, not the one in Russia," the surgeon said) and had been converted into a residence in 1910 by a portrait painter who'd also renovated the old barn into a studio for himself, complete with a skylight streaming good northern light.

Connie kept marveling at everything. She loved the old beams and posts, the kitchen with its brick countertops and pegged floors, the attic bedroom with its peaked ceiling supported by beams actually sawn at the old mill, the huge living-room fireplace with its barn-siding façade, the large deck overhanging the river, the spacious lawn rolling away to a rock garden the painter's wife had designed herself and planted away back in 1923 (a small bas-relief raven was set as a plaque into the rocks, bearing the chiseled legend MARTHA'S ROCK GARDEN, and the date, and the painter's chiseled signature below it), the stepping-stones across the river, the stand of pines bordering the rock wall that defined the property, and far on the horizon the graceful steeple of the First Presbyterian Church.

"I adore it," Connie said.

In the car on the way back to the city, she first asked how old Jamie thought Diana Blair was, offered her own opinion about the twenty-year gap between her and her husband, and then asked Jamie if he was *seriously* thinking of letting Blair do a special based on his photographs; from what she'd been able to gather by asking a few discreet questions before they drove up here, Blair had produced nothing but utter *crap* on television for the last six years, ever since he'd left his job at NBC in 1961.

7

"Where'd you ask all these discreet questions?" Jamie said.

"I asked Annie Baumgarten, whose husband is in programming at ABC, and I asked Sylvia Janus, who works for William Morris, and they both said—"

"Why didn't you tell me this *before* we came all the way up here?"

"It's not that far up, and besides I wanted to see for myself. Are you going to let him do it?"

"Let's see what he comes up with."

"He certainly came up with a good *house*," Connie said. "Maybe he should go into real estate."

"I didn't think it was all that great," Jamie said.

"Come on, it was only magnificent."

She got off the subject almost at once, asking him what he'd thought of Blair's comment about "prestige," as if Jamie *needed* prestige, asking him what he thought of the idea of Blair writing the monologue, did he have any writing credits at all, and then suddenly—with another flash of these glade-green eyes—saying, "How much do you think they want?"

"How much do I think *who* wants?"

"Old Dr. Gillespie and his wife."

"For the house, do you mean?"

"No, for the fucking rock garden. Of *course* for the house."

"Fucking" was a word Connie had first picked up from her older sister Janet, who was now married to a film editor at Universal and living in Brentwood, and had later heard used with some regularity by her Vassar roommate, a girl who'd grown up on exclusive Lake Shore Drive in Chicago. Connie used the word frequently, but never when she was actually doing what it defined. She called that "screwing."

"So?" she said. "What do you think?"

"Who cares *how* much they want for it?" Jamie said.

"It would be closer to Lissie's school."

They moved into the house on the sixth day of December in 1967, and for Lissie's sixteenth birthday Jamie festooned the living room with pictures he'd taken of her that year, forty-eight of them in all, some of them tacked to the old posts, the rest Scotch-taped to the walls between the paintings he and Connie had collected since 1953, when *Life* had been good enough to launch his career. But forty-eight pictures weren't *sixty* pictures, and tonight he'd run out of wall and post space before he'd hung little more than half of them.

He got his brilliant idea along about midnight, went down to the basement for a spool of fishing line he'd never used, fifteen-pound clear test, and strong enough to land a battling swordfish, or so Kirk Harkins at the hardware store in town had told him. He then cut himself snippets of line which he threaded through the holes he made in the two top corners of each mat. Standing on a ladder, he tacked the steepled lines to the ceiling beams, spacing the pictures some six inches apart, twisting the separate hanging lines around each pushpin till he got a level dangle. The job was going to be painstaking and time-consuming; he began to understand how Michelangelo must have felt in the Sistine Chapel.

When next he looked at his watch, it was twenty minutes to two, and there were still three pictures to hang. One of them was a terrific shot he'd caught of six-year-old Lissie in Central Park one bright spring day, kneeling to pluck a dandelion from the ragged lawn. Another was of her in a flaking and rusting rowboat, the first (and *last*) summer they'd spent at Martha's Vineyard, back in 1965 when she was almost fourteen, long slender arms tugging at the oars, tiny buds of breasts in the tanktop bathing suit. Her breasts, at seventeen—yes, she was already seventeen; she'd been born at 1:27 A.M. on the morning of December 19, 1951—were still somewhat less than spectacular. At school, she and her similarly unendowed roommate had formed a club they called the Itty-Bitty Titty Committee, clandestinely referred to by its dozen or more titless members as the I.B.T.C., lest the Establishment close them down in a wink.

It was close to 2:00 A.M. when he started to hang the final picture: a candid shot of Lissie in a murderous blue funk at the age of eleven. Straining up over his head to hammer the pushpin into one of the ceiling beams, he heard footsteps on the stairs leading down to the entrance hall, and turned, his arms still stretched up over his head, and saw her standing at the bottom of the stairs, looking tentatively into the living room. He thought at first it was Connie—the same long blond hair, the same light eyes, the same lithe slender look. When he realized it was his daughter, he was at first surprised and then annoyed. She *knew* what he was doing down here, she should have realized—

"I'm sorry, Dad," she said.

"Honey, what . . .?"

"I couldn't sleep. I'm sorry," she said again, and burst into tears.

He came down off the ladder and went to her at once, still foolishly holding the hammer in his right hand. She stood in the

9

center of the hallway, her long white flannel nightgown rumpled, her bare feet planted slightly apart on the riotous blues and reds of the Bokhara rug, her arms dangling forlornly at her side, the tears streaming down her face. Still holding the hammer, he took her in his arms, and held her close, stroking her hair with his free hand.

"What is it, Lissie?" he said.

"I don't know," she said, sobbing.

"Well, it must be some—"

"I'm so happy to be home," she said, sobbing.

"Well, that's nothing to cry—"

"I miss being home so *much*. I *hate* that school," she said.

"Darling girl . . ."

"I hate it, Dad," she said, and suddenly it all came out in a rush, breathlessly mingled with the tears. "They work us too hard, all the kids say so, we never get time to do anything we *want* to do, I'm up till midnight, sometimes one o'clock, doing homework, two o'clock sometimes, and my first class is at eight, and I had kitchen last week, I fell asleep in biology, scraping off all the trays, I *know* I failed my math test, I just *know* it, and Jenny's always playing her damn radio when I'm trying to study, and none of the boys like me 'cause I'm too tall, five nine is too tall, it's supposed to be *study* time after ten o'clock, and Miss Fitch in English says I'm not concentrating when I'm concentrating all the *time*, I didn't even make the soccer team, I hate it, Daddy, I *hate* it!"

"Wow," he said.

"Yeah, wow," she said, and a smile tried hopelessly to break through the tears.

"Come on, let's sit down," he said. "Stop crying, you'll wake Mom. Here," he said, and handed her his handkerchief.

"Thanks," she said.

"Come on, no more crying."

"All right," she said, sniffling, and looked at the handkerchief, and then blew her nose, and belatedly asked, "Is it all right to use this?" and laughed at her own absurdity, and began crying again.

"Darling, please . . ."

"Okay," she said, "I'm sorry, Dad, forgive me," and blew her nose again. Drying her eyes, she looked into the living room, and saw the photographs for the first time. "Aw shit," she said, "I blew it."

"Your nose, do you mean?"

"Yeah, sure, my nose. Aw shit, *look* at all this! Dad, you've . . . oh, *gee*, Dad. And I blew it."

"No, you didn't," he said, and spread his arms wide, like a gallery owner welcoming his patrons to an opening. "But try to ignore the ladder."

"Spoils the effect, yeah," she said, and grinned. *"Look* at all this, willya? Dad, you're only supposed to do the ones from . . . this is *all* of them. God, I think I'm going to cry again."

"You'd better not, I'll take them all down."

"Oh, my God, there's the one of me hating the whole world! Dad, how *could* you? And, oh . . . oh, Jesus, look at this one in the snowsuit! And this, oh, I *love* this one in the rowboat. What was I? Thirteen?"

"Almost fourteen."

"Great big bazooms even then," she said. "Oh, wow, look at *this* one! All tangled up in my skis. Is this Bromley? How old was I?"

"Stratton. You were twelve."

"I *love* it! And *this* one! Dad, this is *terrific! I* don't remember you taking this. When was it?"

"In July. At the Jacobsons' Fourth . . ."

"Right, right. Oh, look, isn't this *sweet?* Oh, look at this little cutie-pie. What was I? Three?"

"Three."

"Yeah, wow. Oh, my *God!"* she said, and burst out laughing. "Here's the one with the lollipop! I must've been *some* dumb kid, all right. What'd I *think* was on that lollipop?"

"You weren't even two yet, honey, you were still learning."

"Oh, Dad," she said, her voice suddenly lowering. "Oh, God, look at . . . Dad, this is *gorgeous.* Where'd you . . .?"

"Down by the river, in August."

"Where were you shooting from?"

"The deck."

"You make me look . . ." She hesitated, and then said, almost in a whisper, shyly, "You make me look beautiful."

"You are beautiful," he said.

"Yeah, sure."

"Do you like them, Liss? Are you pleased?"

"I love them, Dad," she said softly. "Thank you."

"Happy birthday, darling," he said, and took her in his arms and kissed her on the cheek.

"Seventeen," she said.

"Seventeen," he said.

There were supposed to be twenty-eight kids at Lissie's party that

11

Saturday night—two days after her actual birthday—but Scarlett Kreuger got grounded for breaking curfew the night before, and Kimmie Randolph had to go down to North Carolina with her parents for Christmas, so that made it only twenty-six. Jamie told his daughter he would miss Scarlett; each and every time she came to the house, he would greet her at the door with, "Oh, lookee heah, it's Missy Scah-lutt, home fum Atlanta!" to which Scarlett only blinked in response, but then again nobody ever claimed Scarlett Kreuger had an ounce of brain tissue in her skull. Lissie had invited her, in fact, only because she was a very close friend of Linda Moore's; everybody in town was saying Linda had gone down to Puerto Rico for an abortion just before Thanksgiving, and Lissie was eager to pump Scarlett about the details.

Without Scarlett and Kimmie, the party divided itself more evenly into fourteen girls and twelve boys, still a bit lopsided, but Lissie didn't know too many boys in Rutledge. It was Rusty Klein, Lissie's closest friend in the whole world, who'd helped her compile the "boy" side of the party list, which included only two jocks—the McGruder twins—but only because they were excellent students as well. When Lissie suggested inviting a boy named Owen Clarke, whom she'd met at the Jacobsons' Fourth of July picnic this past summer, and who she'd thought was kind of cute, Rusty told her that Owen was smoking pot these days, and a party with him around always turned into a sleep-in, with half the boys drifting outside to light up, and then coming back in to sit around grinning like dopes.

At the Henderson School, there were very tough rules against alcohol, marijuana, or any other kind of drug. For smoking pot, shooting dope, or popping pills, you could get kicked out in a minute. The school tended to look the other way when it came to whiskey or beer, but you could still be put on Intermediate Discipline for as long as two whole months if some dance proctor happened to smell booze on your breath, or if—God forbid—you came back to the dorm one night after pizza in town and couldn't pronounce the house mother's demanded "Presbyterian Episcopalian," a test devised by the Dean of Women, who taught romance languages. When Lissie mentioned the test to her father, he told her that during World War II, the G.I. password in the South Pacific had been "Lallapalooza," which the Japs apparently couldn't pronounce. But every kid at Henderson could say "Presbyterian Episcopalian" backward and forward, and Lissie knew at least two girls who'd gone back to their dorm pissed to the ears one night, barely able to walk a straight line, but able to repeat "Presbyterian Episcopalian" flawlessly till dawn.

Like most of the other kids in Rutledge, Rusty went to school at Lafayette in nearby Clayton, an industrial city of some 60,000 people, most of whom were Irish, Italian, black or Puerto Rican— what all the Rutledge kids called greasers. Rusty was a straight-A student ("It doesn't take much to be an A-student at Lafayette High," Lissie's mother often proclaimed in her Vassar Speech and Dramatics Major voice) and, despite her aversion to jocks, was the best cheerleader on the high school's squad. During Lissie's long *(long,* ha!) Thanksgiving Day weekend this year, she'd gone to watch the football game between Lafayette and Norwalk High, and Rusty had been the cutest thing imaginable in her white pleated skirt and sweater, the school's orange *L* plastered on her chest (God, how Lissie envied girls who had *breasts!),* the letter echoing her curly red-orange hair, her bright blue eyes sparkling as she led the "Lafayette, we are here!" cheer. After the game, she'd introduced Lissie to the McGruder twins, two gigantic boys with black hair and brown eyes and teeth Rusty swore had been capped, her father being an orthodontist and all.

The McGruder twins provided the surprise for Lissie's party that night. David McGruder played electric piano, and his brother Danny played bass guitar, and together with a drummer and a lead guitarist they had formed a group called Turtle Bay, so-named for no reason other than that the twins lived on Turtle Pond which was really no reason at all. Turtle Bay, all four of them, arrived at ten minutes past nine, some forty minutes after the scheduled start of the party, the drummer and lead guitarist bracketed by the bookend twins, and promptly began setting up what Jamie later described as $75,000 worth of electronic equipment, another of his wild rock-and-roll estimates. Lissie was totally surprised; Rusty hadn't given her the slightest clue that the twins were in a group, or that the group would be performing here tonight— *live.*

Live, they certainly were.

They turned the volume on their speakers up full, and shook the house to the attic rafters as they bellowed songs of their own composition. Jamie, in the sanctuary of the master bedroom, shouted to Connie that the difference between *his* generation and the present one was that when he was a kid they *danced* to music, whereas nowadays they *listened* to music, though he couldn't understand how they could possibly *hear* anything with the volume turned up so loud. The band played nonstop for almost an hour, and then—miraculously—the house went still.

"What do you suppose they're doing down there?" Jamie asked suspiciously.

What they were doing down there was talking.

Of the fourteen girls at the party—all of them ranging in age from seventeen to nineteen—only two of them were no longer virgins, and *they'd* been going steady with the same boys since the eighth grade. Both Sally Landers and Carolyn Pierce considered themselves as good as engaged; their boyfriends were both graduating seniors who expected to be drafted early in 1969, perhaps to have their asses blown away in Vietnam; their rationale, if any was needed, was as old as time: *Kiss me, my sweet, for tomorrow I die.* But despite the virginal reality of the remaining dozen girls (and at least seven of the boys gathered there in the photograph-hung living room), the conversation centered largely on young Linda Moore, who had committed the unimaginable error of getting herself pregnant.

Linda wasn't what anyone there would have even remotely considered a slut. She was, in fact, the only daughter of a man named Alex Moore, an actor who played a physician on a continuing daytime soap. Linda was fifteen years old, a bright-eyed little thing who'd scarcely outgrown her baby fat. The culprit who'd knocked her up was a boy named Ralph Yancy, son of the town's postmaster, and the kids were speculating now on whether or not they'd been stoned when they'd slipped. "Slipped" was a euphemism Lissie had never heard used in this context before. She listened wide-eyed as Beth Jackson painstakingly tried to reconstruct the events leading to Linda's abortion in Puerto Rico.

"It must've been right after the Soph Hop," she said. "She went with Yancy, didn't she? And that was in September, the first big dance of the year, and she ran down to Puerto Rico in November, right, so that . . ."

"Just before Thanksgiving," Judy Lipscombe said.

"Right, so that makes it . . . September, October, November," Beth said, ticking the months off on her fingers, "that's three months, that'd be about right. It had to be after the Soph Hop."

"Yancy was stoned that night," David McGruder said, nodding. "I saw Owen Clarke handing him a joint in the toilet."

"And they disappeared right after the dance, didn't they?" Roger Bridges said. His father was an attorney in nearby Tal-

14

madge, a man named Matthew Bridges. Roger was the drummer in Turtle Bay and—at nineteen—the oldest person in the room. Lissie thought he played loud and lousy, but she wasn't an expert on drummers. Whenever her father played his scratchy recording of "Sing, Sing, Sing" for her, she was at a loss to comprehend what was so spectacular about Gene Trooper's drumming.

"Driving his old man's Benz," Jimmy Lewis said.

"Have to be a contortionist to do it on the front seat of a 280 SL," Danny McGruder said, and all the boys laughed, and some of the girls giggled.

"Who paid for the abortion?" Rusty asked.

"Well, that's just it," Beth said. "Apparently, Yancy went to his father . . ."

"His *father!*" David said.

"Yeah, and Mr. Yancy called Mr. Moore to explain the situation to him, and to tell him he thought it inadvisable for the pair of them to get married so early in their—"

"Inadvisable! Jesus!" Roger said.

"Yeah, inadvisable," Beth said, grinning, "and offered to pay for an abortion if Linda'd go down to Puerto Rico for it."

"So *did* he pay?" Rusty asked.

"No, they split the bill and the air fare."

"*Her* parents split the bill with Yancy's?"

"Yeah."

"Now that's what I call exceedingly generous," Jimmy said.

"Well, why?" Danny said. "It takes two to tango."

"I never even guessed she was pregnant," Judy said. "Did she look pregnant to you?"

"No," Rusty said.

"The irony of it," David said, "is that her father plays this family doctor, you know . . ."

"Yeah."

". . . who's always handing out advice to everybody . . ."

"Yeah."

". . . but he couldn't find the right advice to give his own daughter."

"Oh, come *on,* David," Rusty said. "What'd you *want* him to tell her?"

"Keep your legs crossed, dearie," Jimmy said, and burst out laughing.

"Hey, come on, guys," Lissie said, and glanced upward toward the ceiling.

"How much do you suppose it cost?" Sally asked.

"Why? Are you thinking of getting one?" Roger asked.

"Knock it off," Sally's boyfriend said, but he was smiling.

"Two, three thousand bucks, I'll bet," David said.

"You think so?"

"Depending on whether she flew first class or tourist," Judy said, and burst out laughing. This time, all the girls laughed with her.

"I think it costs less than that," Danny said.

"How would *you* know?" Carolyn Pierce's boyfriend said, and grinned across the room at him.

"I'm guessing, that's all. I'd say four or five hundred."

"That sounds low."

"Well, not more than *six* hundred, anyway. There are guys in New York who'll do it for five, that's for sure."

"Yeah, on the kitchen table," Rusty said.

"Wherever," Danny said. "My aunt had one done in New York for five hundred. My father's sister."

"That's without anesthesia," Beth said. "And that's with some kind of butcher. I'll bet Linda's cost a lot more than that. Scarlett told me it was in a regular hospital and everything."

"With anesthesia?" Judy asked.

"Sure, with anesthesia."

"I'd rather have the baby," Sally said.

"Me, too," Rusty said.

"At fifteen?" David said. "Come on."

"I would, I mean it."

"Me, too."

"That's like trying to decide whether to burn your draft card or go fight the friggin' war," Roger said.

"I'm gonna burn mine," Jimmy said. "In fact, I may not even go register when I'm eighteen. Hell with 'em."

"They'll throw you in jail," Sally's boyfriend said.

"That's better than getting killed," Danny said.

"Or wounded," Jimmy said. "I think I'd rather get killed than wounded."

"Me, too," David said.

"Can you imagine coming back without legs or something?"

"Or blind?" Roger said. "Jesus, can you imagine coming back blind?"

"I'm not even gonna register," Jimmy said.

"Well," Sally said, mindful of the fact that her boyfriend had already registered and was certain to be called up within the next few months, *"somebody's* gotta go over there."

"Why?" Danny said.

"Well . . . to keep us free," Sally said.

"Free to go to Puerto Rico for abortions," Beth said, and everyone burst out laughing.

Upstairs in the bedroom, Jamie heard the sudden laughter and said, "I wonder what they're talking about."

The party at the Blairs' that New Year's Eve was scheduled to begin at nine-thirty, but Jamie and Connie did not arrive till almost an hour later. Lester Blair, whose proposed television special never *had* got off the ground, despite all his extravagant promises, had asked Jamie to bring along his camera, but Jamie flatly told him he did not take pictures on New Year's Eve. Dressing that night before the party, he'd gotten miffed all over again, and began ranting out loud to Connie about the goddamn amateur photographers of the world who thought all there was to taking pictures was putting the camera to your eye and clicking the shutter release. Connie had heard all this before. "Yes, darling," she said, over and over again as he fumed about the stupidity of someone asking a *professional* to bring along his Brownie, take a few candid snapshots, huh, Jamie, what do you say? I say go fuck yourself, Lester, *that's* what I say. "Yes, darling," Connie said.

Ever since 1954, a year after Jamie sold the Bowery essay to *Life* and was able to afford his own tuxedo, he'd been dressing for New Year's Eve, putting on the enameled Schlumberger cuff links and studs Connie had bought him for his twenty-eighth birthday, tying his own bow tie, passing a cloth over his black patent-leather Gucci slippers, admiring himself in the full-length mirror behind the bedroom closet door, preening, making imaginary acceptance speeches for the A.S.M.P.'s Magazine Photographer of the Year award, and generally considering himself to be the handsomest cat who'd ever come down the pike.

At forty-two, he did in fact look extremely youthful, his somewhat angular face dominated by brown eyes almost as dark as his hair, his six feet two inches neatly contained in a body he kept compact and spare via weekly visits to the New York Athletic Club whenever he was in the city to see his agent. He supposed there wasn't a man on earth who didn't think of himself as devastatingly handsome—he had learned early in his career that it was much more difficult to photograph men than it was women, the male of

17

the species being inordinately vain—but he nonetheless felt that his subjective view of himself was entirely objective, and there was rarely an occasion when he looked into the mirror and was not pleased with the image looking back at him.

He felt enormously attractive tonight, Connie on his arm in a shimmering green gown slit to her navel, a lynx jacket thrown over her shoulders as they negotiated the slippery path to the Blair front door, he himself resplendent in his formal duds, his sense of well-being fortified by the two glasses of champagne he'd drunk in a New Year's Eve toast with Lissie when he and Connie were ready to leave the house, and a quickie shot of Dewar's neat at the wet-sink bar while Connie ran upstairs for a last-minute change of earrings. She was wearing her blond hair loose to the shoulders tonight, her green eyes emphasized by a paler green shadow, the eyes somewhat slanted and lending a faintly Oriental look to her lupine face with its aristocratic Vassar nose and generous mouth, dangling emerald earrings echoing the green of the dress and the brighter green of her eyes.

The oval driveway was crowded with the status symbol of the men and women who used the town as their bedroom community—no flashy Cadillacs here in Rutledge, where the foreign car reigned supreme. Like Jamie himself, many of the men who'd settled here had been raised during the Depression, when the secret vow was to rise triumphant from the ashes of poverty that had diminished and almost destroyed their parents. Self-made men each and every one of them, with the exception of Reynolds McGruder, father of the McGruder twins, whose own father had sold bootleg whiskey in Chicago during the thirties, and who was now chairman of the board and chief stockholder of one of the nation's largest distilleries. Self-made men and proud of the fact that they had clawed their way—or so they remembered it—up America's mythical ladder of success to achieve the comfort and in fact luxury (though somehow they never thought of it as such) of the lives they lived here in woodsy, exclusive Rutledge, Connecticut.

Diana Blair herself opened the front door for them, allowing a flood of music to escape onto the brittle night air, Nelson Riddle's intro to Frank Sinatra's "It Happened in Monterey."

"Oooo, come in quick," she said, "I'll freeze to death."

The prophecy, Jamie decided at once, was not without foundation; Diana stood in the doorway virtually naked, wearing a strapless, braless, flimsy white nylon sheath that recklessly revealed breasts rather more cushiony than his wife's, a creamy white soft expanse against the cooler white of the gown, one pink nipple briefly exposed as she knelt to move aside the bristle doormat that prevented her from fully opening the door. The mat out of the way, the door standing wide, Diana stepped aside to allow them entrance, embracing Connie and kissing her on the cheek, kissing Jamie on the cheek as well ("Ooooo, I can feel the cold on you") and then rubbing off the lipstick smear with her thumb. One of the Blair children, a twelve-year-old son from Lester's previous marriage, materialized soundlessly and spectrally beside his stepmother, waited patiently while Jamie took off his overcoat and Connie shrugged out of the lynx jacket, and then vanished with the garments as ephemerally as he'd appeared.

The party was in full swing.

Jamie estimated there were at least sixty or seventy people in the Blairs' massive stone-and-glass living room, dancing or drinking, standing in familiar clusters near the bar, chatting amiably on the sofas ranged in a lush semicircle around the walk-in fireplace, the fire blazing blues, reds, greens and oranges generated by chemicals sprinkled onto the six-foot-long logs, a magic dust obtainable at Harkins' Hardware. They picked their way casually toward the bar, dispensing the customary handshakes and cheek pecks, "Hello, how are you, nice to see you," the litany repeated over and again, even though most of these people had seen each other half a dozen times at various parties since the holiday season began.

Connie asked the bartender—one of Rutledge's moonlighting policemen—for a vodka martini on the rocks, with a twist, please. Jamie asked for a Dewar's and soda, figuring he'd stay with what he'd been drinking before he left the house, and fully intending to pace his alcoholic consumption. Someone lifted the arm from the record player, and several of the couples on the floor booed and hissed in mock outrage, but only until the rhythms of Herb Alpert's "A Taste of Honey" oozed from the speakers. Men pulled women close. Cheeks caressed cheeks. Someone discreetly dimmed the rheostated lights.

The talk at most Rutledge parties usually centered on the latest Broadway hit, Hollywood extravaganza or best-selling novel (John Updike's *Couples* had dominated the conversation all through May and part of June, presumably because it dealt with the sexual acrobatics of a band of exurbanites not unlike those who lived in Rutledge) with every now and then a question of deep philosophical concern surfacing to be discussed in the most sophomoric terms, despite the fact that many of Rutledge's residents were accom-

19

plished and educated men and women. Tonight, though, as Jamie and Connie wandered drinks in hand through the crowd of celebrants waiting for the countdown that would take them into the bright new year, he thought he detected a somewhat reflective note to the chatter that wafted on the air in competition with the music. It was, after all, New Year's Eve, and a certain amount of ruminating over the past year was to be expected; but as he drifted through the crowd, catching snatches of conversations here and there, he felt as though he were awkwardly trapped in an updated John Dos Passos novel, the headline stories of 1968 threading through the talk like an insistent leitmotif.

It had, everyone seemed to agree, been one hell of a year.

Frank Lipscombe, who was Judy Lipscombe's father and a psychiatrist of some note in Manhattan's Shrink City along Ninety-sixth Street, maintained while stroking his gray Freudian beard that the year had truly started in April with the assassination of Martin Luther King, Jr., an event that could be bracketed in terms of proximity with the subsequent June murder of Robert Kennedy. Frank was generally full of shit, Jamie thought, constantly handing out unsolicited psychiatric advice on the care and feeding of adolescents, and once telling him that a father should never hug or kiss his own daughter lest Electra run wild and incest stain the family sheets. The end result of such a restrictive paternal policy had been Judy Lipscombe, whom Lissie succinctly described as "a bit slutty." But he seemed to be making sense about the *tone* of violence set by the twin murders so soon after the traumatic death of President John Kennedy less than five years earlier, and it was his belief that the Chicago police at the Democratic National Convention in August were merely reacting in a way that had somehow become as American as apple pie, flailing out with billy clubs at antiwar demonstrators in much the same way that James Earl Ray and Sirhan Sirhan had exploded against *their* innocent victims.

In a largely Republican town, the guests tonight were for the most part Democrats, and their dismay over the election of Richard Nixon in November was still keenly felt a month and more after the event. There were those who insisted that if Humphrey had simply walked out of the convention, refusing to conduct business as usual while kids were having their heads broken in the streets and the relentless television cameras kept cutting back and forth from the convention-hall floor to the blue-shirted, blue-helmeted cops firing Mace and tear gas, he might have swung the election. There were others who felt *nothing* would have worked for the Democrats, not with a nation believing, perhaps rightly, that the Vietnam war was Lyndon Johnson's toy, and despite his having bowed out of the presidential race in April with the famous lines, "I shall not seek, and I will not accept, the nomination of my party . . ."

"He waited too damn long to stop the bombing," Jeff Landers said. He was Sally Landers's father, an advertising man who specialized in Broadway shows, his agency handling the ads for perhaps 60 percent of all the plays and musicals that opened in New York. His daughter's boyfriend had already registered for the draft, and he was certain the boy would be called up early next year, a prospect he anticipated with mixed feelings, some of which might have provided the fodder for another Electral discourse from Dr. Frank Lipscombe, the noted psychiatrist and nonhugger. "A week before the damn election! Everybody in America recognized the timing for just what it was—a ploy to swing the vote to his pal Hubert."

Alistair York, the town's network sportscaster, bored with all this hard-news shit, asked Connie to dance, much to the annoyance of his mistress, a dark-eyed redhead who'd earlier been talking to Reynolds McGruder, and who was now drinking a Scotch and soda almost as dark as her loamish eyes. As Alistair led Connie onto the floor, Jamie noticed that his hand was resting on the naked small of her back, the fingers widespread somewhat familiarly close to the base of her spine and the rounded buttocks beneath the shimmering gown. Jamie looked at his watch. It was close to eleven o'clock. He was about to ask the redhead to dance when Marvin Klein, Rusty's father and one of a dozen or more Jews in Rutledge's tight inner circle, beat him to it. The redhead melted into Marvin's arms, flashing a dark look at her sportscaster lover, who was dancing cheek-to-cheek with Connie across the room, near the Blairs' glass-encased collection of antique medals.

"I'd have done the same thing Bucher did," Mike Randolph said. He was Kimmie Randolph's father, a Wall Street stockbroker with perhaps the longest commute of anyone in Rutledge; his daughter had inherited from him her blue eyes and blond hair and an unfortunate eagle's beak. "What was he *supposed* to do? Open fire and start another damn war in Korea?"

"Ah'm talking about the con*fess*ion," Melanie Kreuger said. She was Scarlett's mother, a woman of forty-two who, presumably because of her Atlanta upbringing, affected all the cutsie-poo mannerisms of a southern belle; she was wearing tonight a lavender

21

confection that might have been more appropriate at a Homecoming Queen Cotillion than at a party here in Rutledge, where the women generally looked sleek and sophisticated. Her mother had named her ten years before reading *Gone With the Wind*. Melanie, later delighted to learn that her name had been used for one of the major characters in a best seller, paid homage to the author by naming her own daughter Scarlett. Her husband, Larry, worked as a translator at the U.N. He rarely said very much at parties, apparently too burdened was he with all the woes of the world. "Bucher said he had no excuse what*ever* fuh his crim'nal act," Melanie said. "He told the whole *world* he was *spyin'* on the No'th Koreans."

"Come dance with me," Diana Blair whispered behind him, and Jamie put his drink down on the coffee table, leaning over the back of the sofa and incidentally the back of a man named Byron Lewis, who was Jimmy Lewis's father. Byron published photographic books under his own imprint and a distribution setup; he had approached Jamie only last month about getting together on a project. He now said, "Hey, *hi,* Jamie, nice to see you," and then turned back to Alistair York's redhead, who had abandoned Marvin Klein after their first dance, and who now denounced—with an intensity as flaming as her hair, and with a surprising Middle-European accent—the Russian invasion of Czechoslovakia that August. Someone liked the Herb Alpert record; as Jamie led Diana onto the floor, "A Taste of Honey" started again.

Diana was wearing her dark hair tonight in a feather cut that framed a narrow oval face with high cheekbones, a nose for which any New York model would have killed and pillaged, and a wide mouth with a bee-stung lower lip. She was long-legged and slender, and whereas Connie found her truly spectacular breasts "exaggerated," most of the men in Rutledge appreciated them with an openness bordering on stupefaction. Diana always danced extremely close, as if attempting to flatten and nullify nature's splendid achievement against any partner's cooperative chest.

The moment she was in his arms, she put her cheek against his and whispered, "Walk right into me, baby," an invitation she presumably extended to any man with whom she was dancing. Immediately pressing herself against him, she began pumping at his obliging thigh purposefully and methodically, pulling away once abruptly and only for an instant, to roll her smoky eyes in mock surprise and to register girlish shock, and then slitheringly adjusting the long length of her body to his again.

In the seconds-long interval between "Green Peppers" and "Tangerine," she held him protectively close, her crotch nestled snugly into him, waiting for the music to start again. The moment it did, she began a rhythmic, excruciatingly slow tease, grinding steadily against him, their vertical quasi-fornication hidden by their own paper-thin proximity and the press of other dancers around them. Jamie glanced nervously toward the bar where Connie was now chatting with Perry Lane, a New York literary agent who had a weekend place in Rutledge, and whom Lissie called "Penny Lane" after the Beatles' song. Gently moving Diana away from him, he said, "Let's sit the rest out, okay?" and led her off the floor, and went to join Connie at the bar.

"You okay?" he asked, putting his arm around her.

"Yes, sure," she said, "why *wouldn't* I be okay?"

"Jamie?"

"Mmm?"

"Are you asleep?"

"Mmm."

"What did you think of the party?"

"Nice. Nice party, hon."

"The people from New York added a lot, don't you think?"

"Mm-huh."

"That redhead with Alistair was very pretty."

"Mm-huh."

"Didn't you think so?"

"Yes, very."

"How old do you guess she was?"

"Thirty? I don't know."

"Twenty-three, I'd say."

"Mm-huh. Maybe."

"He picks them very young, doesn't he?"

"Always has."

"You danced with her often enough."

"Three times."

"That's a lot in Rutledge."

"Well, she's a foreigner."

"I didn't know she was a foreigner."

"Didn't you hear her accent?"

"I thought she was putting it on."

"No, she's from someplace in the Balkans."

"You learned a lot about her."

23

"Well, when you dance with someone, you naturally talk to her."

"Do you talk to Diana when you're dancing with her?"

"Not very much."

"You were dancing very close. With Diana, I mean."

"Diana dances very close."

"Do you get a hard-on when you're dancing with Diana?"

"I only get a hard-on with you," he said.

"Oh, sure."

"That's the truth," he said, and put his hand on her thigh.

"Well, don't get any ideas," she said, and moved away from him.

"Why not?"

"My parents are coming tomorrow . . ."

"It's today already."

"What*ever* it is, it's late."

"Never too late," he said, and rolled in against her.

"Jamie, I want to get some sleep. Really. Not now, okay?"

"Give me your hand," he whispered.

"They'll be here at noon," she said.

"Put your hand here on my . . ."

"Will you please cut it *out?*" she said. "Jesus!"

The room went silent.

"Go ahead," she said. "Tell me again how I never want to make love."

"You said it, not me."

"I *do* want to make love. But not now."

"When?"

"Tomorrow."

"Fine, we'll make love tomorrow."

"Save it for tomorrow night, okay? After they're gone."

"Sure."

"I'll take a bath after dinner, and then we can make love. I'll check the calendar in the morning, but I think tomorrow'll be fine."

"Fine, you check the calendar."

"Are you angry?"

"No."

"Don't be angry. It's just that I have to get up early to start the turkey and . . ."

"Fine."

"Do you want me to . . . you know?"

"No."

"Are you sure?"

"Positive," he said. "Happy New Year."

The letter was dated February 10. It was typewritten on Henderson School stationery, with its embossed seal proclaiming EDUCATIO SUPER OMNIA. It read:

Dear Mr. and Mrs. Croft:

I regret the necessity of writing this letter but Melissa's behavior leaves me no choice. I will be blunt. As I am certain you're aware, there is a stringent rule at the Henderson School against the use of marijuana or other harmful drugs. The penalty for such an offense is immediate expulsion. Your daughter, together with her roommate Jennifer Groat and several other boy and girl students, was discovered yesterday at an off-campus party where a great deal of marijuana smoking was in evidence. Even though your daughter, her roommate, and another graduating senior named Rita Cordova have each separately claimed they were only present at the party and had not been indulging in the smoking of marijuana, we have nonetheless felt it necessary to give them each one month of

Intermediate Discipline commencing this date and continuing through March 14.

I feel I should add that this punishment is regarded as lenient considering the suspicious nature of the circumstances and the continuing tendency of your daughter and her roommate to flout the authority of the prefects on their hall and to ignore completely the rights of others living with them in the dormitory unit. I am willing to give them the benefit of the doubt regarding the marijuana incident, but only because they are both excellent students, and expulsion in their senior year might do irreparable damage and might seem cruel and unusual punishment. I doubt there is anything malicious in their dormitory behavior, but they are after all each of them seventeen years old, and one must see that it has been thoughtless and less than considerate to those with whom they live. They have received much guidance from both prefects and dormitory teachers, apparently to little avail.

We are disappointed that this problem has persisted, and has reached its apparent culmination in the flouting of the school's primary rule. Again, we are willing to grant your daughter and the two other girls the benefit of the doubt, but if you can be of any help in reaching Melissa in this situation, we would appreciate it.

Sincerely yours,

Jonathan Holtzer
Headmaster

Jamie stopped at her dorm first, not expecting to find her there so early in the afternoon, and not surprised when he didn't. At the registrar's office, he looked up her program, and then walked across campus toward Radley Hall, where she had an English class. It was just 2:00 P.M., and the old clock in the chapel steeple was chiming the hour. The day was clear and crisp, the campus—except for its shoveled walks—still snow-covered from Sunday's blizzard. He saw her coming out of Radley with two other students, a boy and a girl. Lissie was wearing blue jeans, boots and a pea jacket. The jacket was open, a striped blue-and-orange muffler, the school's colors, hanging loose over her blue crew-neck sweater. She spotted him when he was still some distance away from her, and came running down the walk toward him, her books clutched to her chest.

"Hi, Dad!" she said, and hugged him, and then kissed him on the cheek. He returned the embrace, but he did not kiss her. He hadn't yet decided whether to play the stern father or the understanding pal, but he felt he ought to appear somewhat distant until he had all the facts.

"I got a letter from Mr. Holtzer today," he said.

"Yeah, there was a copy in my box," Lissie said. "Is that why you're here?"

"That's why I'm here."

"You could've called, you know. This isn't such a big deal."

"I think it's a big deal," Jamie said.

"Yeah? Well, maybe we ought to talk about it then."

"That's exactly what I'd like to do."

"Okay, you want to go have some coffee?"

"Sure," he said.

They walked in silence to the student dining room on the boys' end of the campus. The classes at Henderson were co-ed, but the dorms were discreetly separated by a stand of pines through which a single path wound through a deliberate maze. There were two student dining rooms; most of the girls preferred eating in the one near the boys' dorms. The dining room was sparsely populated at a little after two, a handful of students scattered at the long oaken tables, coats and parkas slung over the backs of chairs, sunlight streaming through the leaded windows, books strewn on tabletops. Lissie went to the coffee machine and came back to the table where he was waiting. She put his cup down before him and said, "Okay, let's talk."

"What happened?" he said.

"I hope you know I wasn't smoking pot," she said.

"I would hope not."

"Well, I wasn't. And neither was Rita Cordova, I don't think you know her."

"How about Jenny?"

"Yeah."

"Yeah, what?"

"Yeah, she was smoking."

"Holtzer's letter . . ."

"I know. She lied to him."

"What happened to the ones who *were* smoking?"

"They all got expelled."

"Where was this?"

"At Ulla's house. Her parents got stuck in Hartford, because of the storm."

29

"Who's Ulla?"

"Captain of the soccer team, Ulla Oftedahl, I think I introduced her to you once."

"Big Brunhilde type?"

"Yeah, that's Ulla."

"So you were lucky," Jamie said.

"How do you figure that? I wasn't smoking any damn pot, how do you figure I was lucky? I'm restricted to campus for a month, and I wasn't even . . ."

"What about this problem in the dorm?"

"I don't know about any problem in the dorm."

"Holtzer's letter . . ."

"Holtzer is full of it," Lissie said angrily. "There's no problem in the dorm."

"Then why have the prefects and the dorm teachers been giving you *guidance?*"

"Yeah, that."

"Yeah, *what?*" Jamie said.

"Dad, there isn't any problem, believe me. It's just that Jenny and I get bored out of our minds every now and then, and we try to create a little fun for ourselves, that's all."

"What kind of fun?"

"Though I don't respect her for lying the way she did. She almost got me and Rita in serious trouble. Because Mr. Holtzer *suspected* Jenny was lying, and he thought maybe *we* were lying, too. It's just that Miss Larkin *saw* the other kids smoking, you know, the ones who got expelled, and Jenny had the joint in an ashtray when Miss Larkin walked in, so . . ."

"Who's Miss Larkin?"

"Head of the phys ed department. And coach of the soccer team. If you want my opinion, nobody would have got kicked out if Miss Larkin hadn't been so pissed. Because Ulla was captain of the team, you know, and she didn't expect her to be smoking pot. So everybody suffered because the party was at Ulla's house. One of the guy's fathers—Bobby Brecht's father—donated five thousand dollars to Greenleaf last year . . ."

"Greenleaf?"

"The new arts center. And *he* got kicked out, too, can you imagine? After giving the school five thousand dollars? Boy," Lissie said, and shook her head.

"What about this *fun* in the dorm?"

"Well, it was Jenny and I who named all the dorms."

"What do you mean, named them?"

"Well . . . Abbott Dorm is Attica, and Ogden Dorm is Ossining, and Allister is Alcatraz, and our own dorm . . . those are all prisons, you know."

"Yes, I know."

"And our own dorm—Lorimer—is Leavenworth, and Sutton is San Quentin . . . can you think of anything for Riker Dorm?"

"You're kidding," he said.

"No," she said. "Huh?"

"There's a jail on Rikers Island."

"Where's that?"

"Just off Bruckner Boulevard, in the Bronx."

"Really? Jesus! Rikers *Island!* Wait'll I tell Jenny! Anyway, that's what it was all about."

"Your naming the dorms after prisons."

"Yeah."

"And that's all."

"Yeah. Because it sort of caught on, you know."

"Uh-huh. And that's why the prefects and dorm teachers were giving you guidance."

"Well . . . yeah. I guess."

"What else, Lissie?"

"Nothing. That's all."

"Holtzer's letter said . . ."

"Well, you know him, he's an asshole."

"Lissie . . . what *else?*"

"You're gonna get mad."

"Why? What'd you do?"

"Nothing. But you'll think it was terrible."

"What was it?"

"We poured hot tea all over Hillary Frankel's bed."

"You *what?*" Jamie said.

"See?" Lissie said. "I told you you'd get mad."

"Poured hot tea . . ."

"Well, Hillary wasn't *in* the bed when we did it."

"But why'd you . . .?"

"She's a creep, Dad. She's always writing things on our door slate, *wrong* things, like pretending she's Jenny and writing that I should meet her in the library after eight, or sometimes using boys' names and leaving a dorm number we should call, like that. And whenever we have the extreme unction sign out . . ."

"The what?"

"The extreme unction sign. That's if we're studying, we tack this little red sign to the door, and it means you're not supposed to knock or anything under penalty of extreme unction. But she always knocks anyway, she's a terrifying creep, believe me."

"So you poured tea in her bed."

"Yeah, hot tea," Lissie said, and grinned.

He was tempted to grin with her. Instead, he kept a stern look on his face, and said, "When was this?"

"Just after the Thanksgiving long weekend."

"Was that the end of the episode?"

"Well, no, not exactly."

"How, exactly, *did* it end?"

"We told all the kids on the dorm that Hillary was a marine—you know, a bed-wetter. We told them the tea stains were piss."

"Uh-huh."

"So naturally, Hillary figured it was us who'd done it."

"Naturally."

"And she went to the house mother, and she gave us a little talk."

"Was that the only incident?"

"Well, no."

"What were the *other* incidents?"

"One other incident."

"What was it, Lissie?"

"Well . . . remember when we had that light snow last month?"

"Yes?"

"Well, what we did, me and Jenny, we went on a sort of panty raid, taking panties from all the rooms on our floor, and then carrying them over to Baxter House—that's on the boys' side—and arranging them in the snow so they, you know, spelled out a word."

"Don't tell me what the word was," Jamie said.

"Yeah, that was the word."

"Are we thinking of the same word?"

"If you're thinking of 'fuck,' that's the word," Lissie said.

"I didn't realize that word was in your vocabulary."

"Oh, come on, Dad."

"I'm serious. When did you start using words like . . .?"

"Dad, *all* the kids say fuck."

"Please lower your voice, Lissie."

32

"Well, they do. In fact, 'fuck, shit, piss, cunt' is the favorite dormitory expletive."

"Expletive, huh?"

"Yeah," Lissie said, and grinned. "Cool word, huh?"

"Cooler than the others, that's for sure."

"Yeah, well, mmm."

"So what happened?"

"After we put out the panties? Well, all the panties had name tags in them, we have to sew name tags in all our clothes so when we send them to the laundry—"

"Get to it, Liss."

"Well, the boys in Baxter House considered it a sort of . . . invitation, I guess. They kept the phone ringing off the hook all afternoon, asking for the girls whose names were in the panties." Lissie shrugged. "That's all."

"And did this lead to *another* little talk with the house mother?"

"A *bigger* talk this time. Mrs. Frawley and all the prefects. Because me and Jenny were the only two girls who didn't get phone calls that afternoon—we hadn't put out our *own* panties, naturally—so all the other girls in the dorm figured we were the ones who did it."

"Elementary," Jamie said.

"Yeah, we should've thought of that." Lissie hesitated. She lifted her coffee cup to her lips, took a sip, and then said, "So what do you think?"

"I think I'd better talk to Mr. Holtzer," Jamie said.

His talk with Holtzer had no effect on the sentence the headmaster had meted. For whereas Jamie argued that both incidents might be considered normal preparatory school pranks, especially prevalent during the long winter months, Holtzer maintained that the smoking of marijuana could hardly be considered a preparatory school prank ("But she *wasn't* smoking mari—") and neither did he consider the antisocial activities of Melissa and her roommate the sort of community-oriented behavior the Henderson School expected from its students, and *especially* its graduating seniors. Like a Philadelphia lawyer begging leniency for a client in a heinous ax-murder case, Jamie argued that the punishment did not fit the crime and that the hardship it entailed—

"It will not be a tremendous hardship," Holtzer said.

"My wife and I both work hard during the week, Mr. Holtzer. I'm a photographer, as you may know, and my assignments—"

"Yes, I'm familiar with your work," Holtzer said.

"Thank you," Jamie said, although he wasn't sure he'd been complimented. "The point is that my assignments frequently require working at night, which would mean that we'd have to visit Lissie only on weekends. My wife works with handicapped children three days a week, teaching speech, and by the weekend she's as exhausted as I am. We live in a small town, our weekends are precious to us; they're the only time we have to see our friends, to socialize, to take part in community activities that—"

"I don't see what *your* weekends have to do with Melissa's."

"I'm suggesting that were she allowed to come home as usual on her nonacademic weekends, we could all pursue a more normal—"

"But that's quite impossible, don't you see?" Holtzer said.

"I'm suggesting that your punishment, though intended for Lissie alone, is including her parents as well."

"Mr. Croft," Holtzer said, "we have students here who come from places as far away as Hawaii. They *never* get to see their parents except during school recesses. The disciplinary action we're taking against Melissa might, in fact, prove more salutary were you to plan on *limiting* your visits to her during the month of restriction to campus. She might otherwise consider this a lark rather than the very serious matter it in reality is."

"I can't agree with you that it's quite as serious as you consider it," Jamie said tightly.

"I'm sorry," Holtzer said, "but neither is it you who are responsible for the welfare of the eight hundred and thirty-seven students here at Henderson. Your daughter among them, I might add."

"Thank you then," Jamie said, and rose.

"Thank you for stopping by," Holtzer said.

On the first weekend of what Lissie termed her "solitary confinement," both Jamie and Connie drove up to Shottsville on Friday night, ate dinner with her in the girls' dining room, attended a student production of *I Remember Mama* in the new Merrill Greenleaf Arts Center (toward the construction of which Bobby Brecht's father had contributed five thousand bucks, only to be rewarded with his son's expulsion) and then went back to the town's only hotel, where they watched Johnny Carson till midnight. Jamie said he wanted to make love. Connie told him she'd left her diaphragm at home, and this was a bad time of the month. On

34

Saturday, they watched an ice hockey game between Henderson and Choate (Henderson lost) and then ate dinner again in the girls' dining room, during which second meal on campus Jamie began to appreciate Lissie's constant complaints about the "swill" the students were expected to eat. From the hotel room that night, he called the headmaster at home, apologized for breaking in on his privacy this way, and asked if it might not be possible for him and his wife to take Lissie out to lunch tomorrow.

"Out?" Holtzer said.

"Off campus," Jamie said.

"No," Holtzer said at once, "I'm afraid that would be quite impossible."

"Because you see," Jamie said, "my wife and I have had some meaningful discussions with Lissie in the last two days . . ."

"Ah, have you?"

"Yes, and we thought our . . . constructive therapy, one might call it . . . would stand a much greater chance of success if we were able to see Lissie in surroundings that weren't at such odds with what we're—"

"No," Holtzer said, "I'm sorry."

"I recognize that my suggestion isn't entirely in keeping with the *letter* of the disciplinary action . . ."

"Indeed not," Holtzer said.

"But certainly if the *spirit* can be served . . ."

"How would taking her off campus . . .?"

"I feel her mother and I could better bring about an understanding of the school's aims and hopes by seeing Lissie in an atmosphere more conducive to acceptance."

Holtzer said nothing.

"Acceptance of the nature of the discipline," Jamie said. "And a firm commitment to seeing that such behavior isn't repeated."

"Well . . . perhaps just for lunch," Holtzer said.

"Thank you, sir," Jamie said. "I'll report back to you, and if tomorrow's experiment works, perhaps we can extend it over next weekend's visit."

"Yes, good luck," Holtzer said, sounding somewhat puzzled.

"Thank you again, sir," Jamie said, and hung up.

"You are the world's biggest bullshit artist," Connie said, shaking her head.

For lunch that Sunday, they took her off campus to a place called

Dominick's which had been highly recommended by Lissie's French teacher, but which proved to be the worst Italian restaurant Jamie had ever eaten in. They left her at four-thirty, and were back in Rutledge in time to catch the tail end of a party at the Kreugers'. Young Scarlett Kreuger, dressed for the party in a rather daringly low-cut blouse and a skintight black skirt—daring for a seventeen-year-old, at any rate—asked Jamie how Lissie was coming along, and he told her she was doing just fine.

The second weekend posed some problems.

The Crofts had made plans as long ago as the beginning of January, when the show opened, to go see *Hadrian VII* with Jeff and Junie Landers. They'd bought the sell-out tickets from a scalper, paying through the nose for them, and the seats were for this Friday night, February 21. Moreover, there was a big Washington's Birthday party scheduled at the McGruders' for Saturday night, and a Rutledge painter named Mark Hopwell was opening a one-man exhibit at the Silvermine Guild that Sunday afternoon.

Connie was willing to forsake the New Canaan opening—although she really *was* interested in Hopwell's work—but she damn well wasn't ready to give up either the Broadway tickets or the big Saturday night bash. Their argument about Lissie's detention and Jamie's determination to "make it easier for her" took place on the Monday after their initial visit to school. Junie Landers had just called, asking where they wanted to eat in the city that Friday night, and Connie had told her she'd discuss it with Jamie and get back to her. Jamie, who had completely forgotten about the theater tickets, immediately said, "Well, what about Lissie?"

"What about her?" Connie said.

"We promised we'd go up there this weekend."

"Well, we can't," Connie said simply. "We have theater tickets."

"Then what's she supposed to *do* up there all by herself?"

"Stop it, Jamie, she won't be 'all by herself.' And besides, if she's been acting up, she *deserves* the damn punishment."

"You sound like Holtzer."

"Are *you* so sure she wasn't smoking pot?"

"I'm positive."

"Because *I'm* not."

"She told me she wasn't, and I believe her."

"But she *was* causing a lot of trouble in the dorm."

"Kid stuff. Pranks."

"Pranks, fine. *You* go see her this weekend. *I'm* going to see

Hadrian VII, and *I'm* going to the McGruder party on Saturday night."

"Where maybe Alistair York can dance with his hand on your ass."

"Yes, maybe. Better his hand than nobody's."

"Maybe you can even ask him to join you and the Landerses at the theater this Friday."

"Good idea. And maybe he'd like to take me to Silvermine on Sunday, while you're up there in Shitsville holding your daughter's hand."

"I thought she was *your* daughter, too."

"Jamie, you're being utterly ridiculous about this," Connie said. "If you want my opinion, the restriction . . ."

"I'm only trying to . . ."

". . . will do her a lot of . . ."

". . . make it easier for . . ."

They stopped talking simultaneously. They looked at each other.

"So?" Connie said.

"So I'm going up to see her."

"Without me," she said flatly.

"Fine, without you," he said.

He drove up to the school on Friday at six, an hour after Connie was picked up by the Landerses and *not* Alistair York but a woman named Alice Keyes, whose dentist husband had abandoned her for his nineteen-year-old receptionist two weeks before Christmas. As the Landerses' Jaguar pulled out of their driveway, Jamie could see Connie and Alice sitting stiffly beside each other on the back seat, looking for all the world like a pair of bereaved widows. With Holtzer's blessing, he took Lissie to dinner that night in a restaurant called the Yankee Stonecutter, and later fell asleep watching the eleven o'clock news on New Haven's Channel 8. The headline story was about the explosion of a terrorist bomb in a Jerusalem supermarket. He awakened at 2:00 A.M., surprised to find himself in bed alone, the television still on, a vampire movie unreeling in black and white. He went to the bathroom to pee, got back into bed, watched the movie for another ten minutes, and then switched off the set and the bedlamp.

On Saturday, he ate breakfast alone at the motel, and then picked Lissie up at ten-fifteen. They spent the morning together antiquing, and had a truly superb lunch at a seafood restaurant just outside Wallingford. He was, he admitted to himself, beginning to enjoy Lissie's Intermediate Discipline. Moreover, he suspected *she* was enjoying it as much as he. And whereas he knew his excursions to Shottsville weren't accomplishing what Jonathan Holtzer and the Henderson School *expected* them to accomplish, he doubted the school's trustees would have frowned upon the strengthening of ties between a father and his daughter. Electra aside (you insidious bastard, Lipscombe), he discovered his daughter as a young lady that weekend, a discovery tantamount in importance to his first glimpse of her at Lenox Hill Hospital in New York on the morning of December 19, 1951.

There was, in Lissie at seventeen, something comfortably reminiscent of Connie at eighteen—which was when he'd met her and fallen in love with her. The same good looks were there, of course, transmitted by those strong Harding genes, her mother's nose and cheeks, her mother's flaxen hair, the same lithe slender body, the physical twinship almost complete save for Lissie's poverty-stricken bust and the fact that her eyes were blue whereas Connie's were green. But there was more of Connie there as well: Lissie's outspoken frankness, her obstinate refusal to accept sham of any kind, her fierce pride, her sense of justice, and an innocence he found spookily like her mother's had been.

She had come into his life in October of 1949, a long-legged, full-breasted eighteen-year-old Vassar girl whose reputation as a Snow Queen had preceded her via the Yale grapevine. It was this about her that had attracted him most, perhaps, her reputed inaccessibility, an aloof manner his mother would have called "stuck-up," the knowledge that any of the boys who'd dated her (the Yalies, at least) hadn't got to first base. Jamie had just turned twenty-three that July, and he considered himself a man of the world. He had been discharged from the United States Army in June of 1946, and had bummed around all summer long, going to the beach on good days and the movies on bad ones, and finally entering Yale in the fall. In 1949, when he first spotted Connie at the Vassar mixer, he was a graduating senior and although his roommate—a boy named Maury Atkins—had told him to stay away from Constance Hard-On, also known in the trade as C. T. Harding, Jamie felt he himself might just possibly be the man to crack her icy façade.

"I warned you," Maury said, and shook his head in sympathy as he watched Jamie cross the floor to where Connie was sitting and talking to a girlfriend. Rock-and-roll had still not exploded on the scene; the song the record player was oozing as Jamie crossed the floor was a sweet little number titled "Mona Lisa"; the man singing it was a relatively new recording star named Nat "King" Cole. Fashion that year had just about outgrown the folly of the New Look; it was now possible to see whether a girl had good legs, or in fact *any* legs at all. As Jamie approached the couch where Connie was sitting with her friend and amiably chatting, he was pleased to notice that she had splendid legs indeed and what one might have termed exuberant boobs protruding perkily in the swooping neck of the green dress she was wearing. Green dress, green shoes, and green eyes, too; she acknowledged his approach with a jungle-glade glance and then turned her attention and her chatter back to her girlfriend, a good-looking brunette who seemed utterly bored with the entire universe.

"Hi," Jamie said, "would you care to dance?"

"I'd adore it," Connie said at once, surprising him, and getting to her feet and moving into his arms. He thought surely Maury Atkins had been wrong. She seemed warm and receptive as he asked her all the questions students ask of each other the world over: How do you like Yale, Harvard, Vassar, Sarah Lawrence, Oxford, University of Michigan, Le Sorbonne, C.C.N.Y., the Citadel, all or none of the above; are you a freshman, sophomore, junior, senior or grad student; how do you like your roommate; what is your major, what is your minor, does your mother come from Ireland, and who threw the overalls in Mrs. Murphy's chowder?

He listened to her, enchanted as she supplied the answers to all his questions, fascinated by the lilt of her voice, and its cadence, and the somewhat breathy rush of it, surely not her *own* voice but something acquired here at Vassar, and remembering the old line attributed to Dorothy Parker: "If you laid every Vassar girl end to end, I wouldn't be a bit surprised."

"I *adore* Vassar," Connie said. "I'm in my freshman year, I room with a girl who lives on Lake Shore Drive in Chicago, I'm majoring in speech and dramatics and minoring in psychology, and I, uh, don't really enjoy dancing this close." He backed away from her at once and told her he himself was a graduating senior at Yale ("Well, *sure,* Yale," she said, and he realized how dumb he'd just been; there were *only* Yalies at the mixer) and that he was majoring in political science and minoring in history, but that he had recently and pretty much by accident become interested in photography and had joined—

"By accident?" she said. "What do you mean?"

"Well, I found a camera."

"Found a camera?"

"Uh-huh."

"Where? What kind of camera?"

"On the Commons. In New Haven. On a bench in the park there."

"Well . . . well, whose camera *is* it? I mean, is it an *expensive* camera?"

"Yeah, pretty much. I checked it out, it's worth about three hundred bucks. It's a Leica. Do you know anything about cameras?"

"Nothing."

"Neither did I, until I joined the Photography Club. I figured if I owned a good camera . . ."

"Well, it's not *really* your camera."

"Yes, I think it is. *Now* it is. I put an ad in the paper, you see, the *New Haven Register,* and I asked whoever'd lost a camera to give me a call, and nobody did."

"Did you describe it?"

"No, of course not. Then anyone in the *world* could've claimed it."

"Well, that's right. Mmm. Yeah."

"I even developed the roll of film that was in it, figuring there'd be pictures of *people,* you know, somebody recognizable, but the whole roll was of buildings. Not the *whole* roll because he'd only taken six or seven pictures, but all of buildings."

"Maybe he was an architect."

"Maybe. Anyway, I figure the camera's mine now, and since I've got it, I've been making use of it. Want me to take your picture sometime?" he said, and grinned.

"Sure," she said. "When?"

He looked at her.

"You're kidding," he said.

"Why would I be?"

"I don't know, I just . . . I mean, we've hardly said a dozen words to each other."

"Well, don't you want to?"

"Sure," he said. "Hey, cool."

Connie's reputation, he discovered on their first date ("I told you so," Maury Atkins said), was firmly rooted in fact. Try as hard as

40

he might, Jamie could not convince her to engage in anything more intimate or spirited than the rather expert kissing she'd learned from one of her older sister's boyfriends one night while Janet was at the ballet with a visiting junior from Harvard. "He was some kisser," Connie disclosed after she and Jamie had been kissing for something close to two hours in the front seat (they had not yet graduated to the back seat) of the used Dodge he'd bought three years earlier with the back pay he'd accumulated overseas. Jamie recalled the story told by one of the stand-up comics about the ugly man walking down the street and thinking he had an extremely beautiful mouth because he overheard one girl saying to another, "Did you see the *kisser* on that guy?" He did not tell the joke to Connie that night because she was, in fact, a very good kisser; he was tempted instead to ask her for the name of her sister's long-ago boyfriend so that he might send him a dozen roses and a letter of recommendation. It was a pity, Jamie thought after their *fifth* date, when he was already hopelessly in Connie's thrall, that Janet's boyfriend (whose name had been Archie Halpern, a hell of a name for such a good kisser) hadn't taught Connie the joys of petting as well.

For this oversight, Jamie was obliged to devote much of his energy during the harsh winter of 1950 attempting entry into Connie's laden blouse, the buttons on which were guarded as jealously as had been the gates of Stalingrad during World War II. By spring, he did manage to steal one or the other of his sneaky hot hands onto her sweatered, shirted, bloused or blanketed (this one day when he popped into her unlocked hotel room in New Haven and surprised her naked in bed with nothing but a blanket over her) mounds, but never would she allow him to touch those prized beauties in the flesh. He heard with some surprise, therefore, that Fodderwing Foley had put in his hand, so to speak, during the torrid summer of 1950.

Fodderwing's true name was Frederick; he was only later rebaptized, cruelly and in anger, by Jamie. He was the son of one of Peter Harding's oldest friends, and he was to be here in New York City for two weeks only, visiting from someplace in Iowa (was there such a place as Pomeroy, Iowa?) and enjoying the Hardings' hospitality, *and* the use of their guest room, *and*—as it later turned out—the ample use of their daughter's until-then sacrosanct bosom. Fodderwing was Jamie's identical age—twenty-four in that summer of 1950—and he had been with the infantry in Europe and had suffered frostbite on all the toes of his left foot, which toes were later amputated at an Army field hospital, leaving him with a discernible limp that did much to encourage excessive sympathy for a young man who was exceedingly handsome anyway. Jamie distrusted him from the moment he took his hand and felt its warm, dry clasp, looked into those limpid brown eyes and glimpsed the soul of a seducer within, studied that almost feminine mouth with its pouting lower lip and Cupid's bow upper, and thought at once of Janet's former boyfriend who'd taught Connie to kiss.

As Foley limped his way to the bedroom down the hall, the one next door to Connie's, the one that had been Janet's when she'd been living here in New York before her marriage, Jamie felt a distinct tremor of foreboding. He and Connie had as yet exchanged no formal declarations of enduring love, but it was tacitly understood that they were "going steady" and that one day, perhaps after Connie's graduation in June of 1953, by which time Jamie hoped to have established himself as a working photographer here in the Big Apple, one day they might *consider* getting engaged and then, *maybe,* sometime in the distant future, *think* about getting married. Or at least that was the way *Connie* seemed to consider their relationship. If Jamie had had his way, they'd have been married already. But she was, after all, only nineteen years old in that summer of 1950, and whereas she was a very good kisser, she seemed so terribly—*young.* Certainly too young to even consider marriage at this early stage of her womanhood. Marriage? She had just completed her freshman year, she would only be entering her sophomore year in the fall. Marriage? She was, for Christ's sake, only nineteen years old!

Fodderwing Foley, the prick, thought it might be nice to seduce young Constance Tate Harding. Jamie could forgive him this; he had, after all, begun his relationship with Connie with the same rapierlike thought in mind, nor had its edge been dulled over the intervening nine months. What he could *not* forgive was the fact that the son of a bitch damn near *succeeded!* Whereas Jamie had been toying with Connie's buttons like a safecracker all through the winter, spring and part of the summer, searching for the combination to the vault wherein the treasures lay; whereas Jamie had had his wrists caught and firmly held more times than a trapeze artist doing a double somersault without a net; whereas Jamie had pleaded and persuaded only to be scolded and excoriated; whereas Jamie had exhausted every male wile at his command in an attempt

42

to weaken the resolve of Constance C. T. Hard-On Snow Queen Harding, that son-of-a-bitch son of her father's best friend, that son-of-a-bitch guest in the third bedroom down the hall, the one next *door* to Connie's, had to do nothing more than march in there one night while she was asleep and naked, and fondle her to his heart's content, claiming the twin turrets of her femaleness as though they were cherished hills overlooking some disputed valley to be taken by an invading American army.

That he did not capture the tinier bastion below had been a miracle of self-restraint: Connie's. In August—long after Fodder-wing had once again departed for the more tranquil pastures of Pomeroy, Iowa, or Ohio, or wherever the hell he lived—she told Jamie all about that simmering steamy night in July, Freddie sneaking into her room and playing with her breasts all night long, kissing them and sucking them and stroking them and probing them and patting them, all of which had been excruciatingly nerve-racking for her, even though terribly exciting, the whole strenuous *battle* all night long, you know, to keep from doing what he really *wanted* her to do, and which of course she could not allow herself to do. ("I shouldn't even be lying here on the couch with you," Jamie thought as she told him her perfidious tale.)

He asked her, as well he might have, why she'd allowed Fodderwing into her bed to begin with. She explained that she hadn't *allowed* him in, he'd simply *come* in, the same way Jamie had come into her hotel room that morning in New Haven when she'd accidentally left the door unlocked, and had found her naked in bed with just a blanket over her, which was the way she slept and which was the way Freddie had found her, too. When Jamie pointed out that in New Haven she hadn't allowed *him* to climb between the sheets with her, had in fact raised a fuss that could have been heard in Paris, France, she explained that she hadn't allowed *Freddie* to climb between the sheets, either, he had just *done* it, and she hadn't been able to yell the way she had in New Haven because Mommy and Daddy were sleeping right next door, and this was Daddy's best friend's *son,* so what could she possibly do? It had all been just too impossible, and so she had suffered his advances and had got herself very, well, wet and, well, excited all night, but had nonetheless managed to save herself (except for her breasts) for whoever, you know, she might, you know, one day marry.

"So why the fuck are you telling this to *me?*" Jamie shouted in a rage. "What makes you think *I* want to know about your sordid little . . . your . . . your *breast* job with that . . . that toeless wonder . . . that that that *Fodderwing—*" and this was where Jamie baptized him after the Marjorie Kinnan Rawlings character—"why tell *me,* go tell your *Daddy* whose best friend's *son* that fucking cocksucker . . ."

"Jamie, I don't like that kind of language," Connie said. "I told *you* because if we ever *do* get married . . ."

"No!" he shouted. "No, we're *not* going to get married, Connie! No, we are—"

"Oh, don't be silly," she said. "Of course we are."

It was Jamie's guess (and he was almost right) that his daughter, at seventeen, had never even been kissed, and he found the contradiction of her sophisticated demeanor and her true inexperience completely enchanting. He took her to see a sneak preview of a movie titled *Last Summer* that night, and was appalled by the behavior of the three teenage kids in it, all of them presumably Lissie's age, but none of them even remotely like her. He did not once regret having missed the McGruder party, did not in fact even *remember* it until he was already in bed at eleven-thirty. From his motel room, he asked the information operator for the McGruder number in Rutledge, and then dialed it. Betty McGruder answered the phone on the fourth ring. There was the sound of music, laughter and voices behind her. He visualized her standing at the phone with one finger in her ear.

"Betty," he said, "this is Jamie. Can I talk to Connie, please?"

"Where *are* you, you dirty dog?" Betty said.

"Up here in Shottsville."

"Where the hell is Shottsville?"

"Up here someplace," he said. "Sounds like a good party."

"It's a mag*nif*icent party, I may never speak to you again for missing it. Let me see if I can find her."

He heard the receiver clattering onto the tabletop, heard Betty yelling, "Connie! Jamie's on the phone! Has anyone seen Connie?"

He listened to the background din.

"Hello?" Connie said.

"Hi, honey, how's the party?"

"Terrific," she said flatly. "Parties are always marvelous when your husband's in Nome, Alaska."

"Where were *you?*" he said.

"What do you mean?"

"Took you a long time to get to the phone."

44

"Oh. Some of us are in the den playing Dictionary. How's Lissie?"

"Fine. We went to a movie."

"When are you coming home?"

"After lunch tomorrow."

"Then you'll be able to come to the Guild with me."

"What time is the opening?"

"Three o'clock, I think."

"Yes, sure."

"Where are you now?"

"In bed," Jamie said.

"Alone?"

"No, with two black girls."

"I believe it," Connie said.

"Want to talk to them? Lula Belle, my wife wants to say hello."

"Take pictures," Connie said. "I want to see if I approve of your taste."

"Haven't got my camera with me. Edna Mae, my wife wants to know how I taste."

Connie laughed.

"See you tomorrow, honey," he said, smiling. "How long are you going to be at that party?"

"Oh, I don't know. How would you define 'peculate'?"

"Peculate?" He thought for a moment, and then said, "To rummage aimlessly."

"Good, I'll use it. Give Lissie my love."

"I will. Good night, darling," he said, and hung up.

He recognized at lunch the next day that he and Lissie were collaborators of a sort, recklessly conspiring to nullify the punishment meted by the school. He felt, along with her, that the punishment was absurd, and he firmly believed that it was essential to reduce absurdity of any kind to its lowest level of idiocy. Lissie had *not* been smoking pot, and the rest was utter nonsense. The rest, in fact, had been behavior he considered somewhat creative. Lissie sensed his approval and plundered it like a pirate, teasingly asking him to come up on the following weekend, even though it was an academic weekend when normally she would not have been allowed home. He drew the line there, telling her he'd end up in a divorce court if he left her mother alone at home on yet another weekend. Lissie's face went suddenly sober.

"You'd never even *consider* divorcing Mom, would you?" she asked.

45

"Never in a million years," he said.

He was lying.

Lissie's academic weekend officially started after her fourth-period class on Friday, February 28. Jamie, as he'd promised, did not go up to see her; neither was she allowed to go home, since that would have amounted to a total revocation of the Intermediate Discipline she was allegedly suffering. On Saturday afternoon, she and her roommate Jenny played a vigorous if amateurish game of squash, showered and washed their hair afterward, and were sitting in bras and panties on one of the locker-room benches, waiting for their hair to dry more completely before venturing out into the cold.

Jenny lived in New York City with her mother and her stepfather, and she went to thousands of Broadway shows each year, and had the albums for all of them, not to mention the albums for *another* thousand she'd never seen. She was almost eighteen, six months older than Lissie, and she still used the name Groat, even though her stepfather wanted to adopt her and give her his name. She liked her stepfather a lot, but his name was Fenner, and Jenny could just *feature* calling herself Jenny Fenner! She'd never met her real father, who'd abandoned Jenny's mother the minute he learned she was pregnant; but according to what her mother had told her, she resembled him a lot, with the same black hair and brown eyes, and the same upturned little Irish nose. Groat, she proudly informed Lissie, was an Irish name going all the way back to the days of the widcairns.

Except for the two of them, the locker room was empty. A shower dripped interminably in one of the stalls. They talked ramblingly about their game—Lissie felt that Jenny's backhand was improving—and then about the guest violinist who was scheduled to play that night at the arts center, and then, as it invariably did, the conversation switched to the injustice of their punishment; by then, Jenny had convinced herself she was truly innocent, and that the sentence levied upon the three nonsmoking girls was enormously extravagant. Lissie, who had seen her father more often during the three weeks of restriction than she had in any previous three weeks of the school term, nonetheless agreed that these were hard times, and began toweling her hair again. When she took the towel away from her head, the first thing she saw was the joint in Jenny's hand.

"What the hell is *that?*" she said, knowing full well what it was. "Come on, put that away, are you *crazy?* Where'd you *get* that?"

"From a boy at Rogers House," Jenny said, the joint bobbing between her lips, her dark head bent over her open handbag.

"Hey, come on," Lissie said. "For Christ's sake, we'll get kicked *out!* If somebody walks in here . . ."

"Everybody's over at the rink, watching the Taft game," Jenny said, and found the matchbook she was looking for.

"Then wait till I'm gone, okay?" Lissie said. "I'm getting the fuck out of here, you just wait till—"

"Why?" Jenny said. "You chicken?"

"That's right, I'm chicken, right, that's it," Lissie said, pulling on her jeans.

"You ever try it?"

"Nope, and I don't intend to," Lissie said. She reached for her sweater, pulled it on over her wet hair, and then sat on the bench again to put on her socks and shoes. She left the laces untied, grabbed her squash racket, and was starting for the door when Jenny's voice stopped her.

"Who are you running to tell?" she said.

"What?" Lissie said, turning to her.

"You heard me."

"Nobody. Why would I . . .?"

"Then stay here with me."

"No."

"You don't have to smoke, if you don't want to. Just stay with me and—"

"No. Jenny, you've got to be out of your—"

"Some friend," Jenny said, and struck the match.

"Jesus, are you going to smoke it right here in the *locker* room?" Lissie said.

"The john then, okay?"

"Jenny . . ."

"Come with me, okay? Just to stand watch, okay?"

"Jenny, I'm scared shitless."

"Just to stand watch."

"Okay, but . . ."

"Thanks," Jenny said, and blew out the match, and picked up her handbag.

The toilets were on the other side of the shower room. Jenny went into one of the stalls and closed the door. Lissie heard her striking another match, and then smelled the burning marijuana. *If somebody walks in here,* she thought, *they'll know in a minute . . .*

"Hurry up, will you?" she said.

"It's not something you can hurry," Jenny said. "You want a drag?"

"No."

"Little goody two-shoes," Jenny said from behind the closed door.

"I'm *not,*" Lissie said. "You *know* I'm not."

"Then what are you afraid of?"

"I don't want to become a fucking goddamn drug addict, okay?" Lissie said. "Will you please . . .?"

Behind the closed door, Jenny began laughing. A cloud of smoke was swirling up toward the ceiling. Lissie listened to the gentle laughter and thought again, *She's crazy,* and suddenly the door to the stall opened.

"Here," Jenny said, extending the joint to her. "Have a little toke."

"No."

"For me," Jenny said.

"For *you?* What?"

"For our friendship."

"No."

"Come on."

"No!"

"Fucking little goody two-shoes," Jenny said. She was still wearing only her bra and panties, and Lissie suddenly remembered that the rest of her clothes were out there on the locker-room bench. If somebody came in and saw the clothes, they'd wonder . . .

"Come on, are you finished?" she said.

"Not till *you* try it," Jenny said, and again extended the joint.

"Let's just get out of here, okay?"

"Try it," Jenny said.

"Why?"

"It won't kill you."

"Shit, all I . . ."

"*Try* it," Jenny said.

"Shit, all right, *give* it to me. Let's just . . . Jesus," she said, and took the joint.

"Draw in deep on it," Jenny said.

48

"I know how to do it."

"Keep the smoke in."

Lissie coughed.

"Take another hit."

Lissie sucked on the joint again, swallowing the smoke, holding it back deep in her throat.

"One more toke," Jenny said.

"I'm burning my fingers."

"It's down to the roach," Jenny said. "Let's light a fresh one." She grinned suddenly. "Is it getting to you?"

"I feel . . ."

"Yeah?"

"A little woozy."

"Mm, yeah, baby," Jenny said, and reached for her handbag where it rested on the tiled floor near the toilet bowl.

When they came out onto the campus again at 4:00 P.M., a crowd of students was working its way over the hill from the hockey rink. They all seemed very tiny to Lissie, like little mechanical boy-and-girl dolls dressed in brightly colored teeny-weeny clothes, waving itty-bitty Henderson School pennants. One of the kids said, "We won, Liss!" and Lissie grinned at her foolishly and said, "Terrif," and then floated beside Jenny through the labyrinthine path that separated the girls' side of the campus from the boys', noticing for the first time the thousands upon thousands of pine needles carpeting the forest floor, each separate pine needle clearly etched, noticing too the sculpted beauty of the rocks edging the path, each glistening facet of each rock, the pines standing in sharp silhouette against a sky more vibrantly blue than any she had ever seen. It took them forever to float through the forest, the path winding endlessly toward an Alice-in-Wonderland rabbit hole opening at the farthest end of the forest . . . the world . . . the universe. When at last they got back to their room in Leavenworth Dorm, they closed and locked the door, and collapsed on their separate beds and repeated "Presbyterian Episcopalian" over and over again, giggling furiously all the while.

It was raining on Friday, March 14, the last day of their detention period. Their senior workload was light, they were both through with classes by midmorning, but they could not leave the campus till noon, at which time the Intermediate Discipline officially ended. They played a listless game of squash, dropped in on a choir

49

practice to hear Francie Bowles—a friend of theirs from Ossining Dorm—and then began counting the hours. For reasons neither of them quite understood, and despite the fact that they'd been somewhat reckless about it during their disciplinary period, each of them felt it would be enormously dangerous to smoke anywhere on campus during this last day of their long incarceration.

The hours dragged.

They wandered over to the library to see if there were any boys they knew there, but Pee Wee Rawles was the only one who paid them any attention, and he was a terrifying creep who asked every girl he danced with if she'd like to have oral sex with him. At a little before twelve, they went back to the dorm to dress, both of them putting on blouses, skirts and heels, Jenny sweeping her long black hair up on top of her head in a sophisticated coiffe, and then putting on a pair of dangling gold earrings that had been a birthday present last year. They spent a goodly amount of time putting on eye liner and shadow, touched their lips with gloss and their cheeks with a faint blush of rouge, and were finally ready to go out on the town. Jenny was carrying four joints in her handbag. They signed out on the first-floor hall, did a little jig together out onto the sidewalk, and walked to the main gate where the taxi they'd called was waiting for them.

When the cabdriver saw them lighting up on the back seat, he asked, "Your parents allow you to smoke?"

"Oh, sure," Jenny said, dragging on the joint.

"You sure?" the cabbie said.

"Positive," Lissie said.

"Cigarettes are bad for you," the cabbie said.

Mildly aglow after the grassy ride to the town's only decent restaurant, giggling over the driver's assumption that they'd been smoking *cigarettes,* they took a corner table in the almost deserted room, and each ordered a glass of white wine before lunch. The legal drinking age in Connecticut was twenty-one that year, but the law was rarely enforced except in package stores. Even there, a phony I.D. card was never looked at askance, and most of the Henderson kids had learned that restaurants in Shottsville wouldn't ask for identification if you simply ordered a glass of wine and not any hard liquor. Drinking wasn't a problem at Henderson, anyway. In fact, from what Lissie could gather—dancing at school mixers with boys from Choate or Kent or Taft—drinking wasn't a problem *anywhere.* Marijuana was the big menace, marijuana was the

Brown Gold Peril, marijuana was the evil weed the authorities everywhere were trying to stamp out before it polluted the young, which, of course, she knew was a lot of bullshit. If Lissie had to take a guess, she'd have said that 40 percent of the kids at Henderson were regularly smoking pot, with another 10 percent trying it every now and again. The only thing that amazed her was why she herself had waited so long.

Sipping at their wine, enjoying the supposition that they'd both looked old enough to be served without challenge, toasting their release from bondage, they looked over the menu, gave the waitress their order, and then began commiserating over the fact that they'd be separated from each other for eighteen whole days during the spring break.

"Be great if we could spend some time together," Jenny said.

"Maybe I could come into New York for a few days," Lissie said.

"No, I mean, you know, *more* than just a few days."

"What do you mean?"

"Get in a car, just go *drive* someplace," Jenny said.

"Yeah, that'd be great," Lissie said. "Like where?"

"California," Jenny said.

"Never make it to California and back in eighteen days," Lissie said.

"Sure, we could."

"No, I don't think so."

"Denver then. How about Denver? Catch some spring skiing out there."

"Yeah, that'd be great."

"Are you a good skier?"

"So-so," Lissie said. "My parents used to take me a lot when I was little."

"Where'd you go?"

"Bromley, Stratton, Mount Snow. Like that."

"But never out west."

"No."

"Me, neither," Jenny said. "Be great to do some skiing out there, wouldn't it?"

"Be terrific."

"You think your parents would let you go?"

"Oh, sure," Lissie said.

"Trouble is, we'd need a car."

"My parents have *two* cars."

51

"And somebody to drive it."

"Why couldn't *I* drive?"

"You mean you have a license?"

"Sure."

"Really?"

"Yeah, sure."

"What *kind* of cars?"

"My dad has a Corvette. Mom drives a station wagon."

"Think she'd let us use it?"

"You mean to go to Denver?"

"Yeah. Well, to Aspen. If we're gonna ski, we should go to Aspen."

The waitress came back to the table with their meals.

"Plates are very hot," she said, "be careful. Would you care for more wine?"

"Yes, please," Jenny said.

"Uh-huh," Lissie said, and nodded.

"What we could do," Jenny said, "is you could pick me up in New York, and then we'd take the tunnel to Jersey, and head across through Pennsylvania and Ohio . . ."

"Then Indiana," Lissie said, "and Illinois . . ."

"Like the fuckin' pioneers," Jenny said, and laughed.

"Across Iowa to Nebraska . . ."

"And then into Colorado . . ."

"And on to Denver!"

"We'd have to check out all those states," Jenny said, "make sure your license is good there."

"Oh, sure," Lissie said. "How many miles you think it'll be?"

"Maybe two thousand, something like that."

"How long do you figure? To Aspen, I mean."

"Let's say we average sixty miles an hour, okay?" Jenny said. "You'd need, say, six, seven hours' sleep a night . . ."

"So what does that come to?"

"Seventeen hours of driving every day . . ."

"We'd better make it *six*teen," Lissie said, "just in case I need *eight* hours a night."

"No, you can do it on seven," Jenny said.

"Well, just in case."

"Okay, *six*teen hours a day times sixty miles an hour . . ."

"Better make it fifty," Lissie said. "Let's say we'll average fifty."

"Okay, sixteen times fifty is eight hundred miles a day. Divide that into two thousand miles, and we get . . . let's see . . . about two and a half days to Colorado. Let's say three days to play it safe."

"Three days, right," Lissie said. "So we'd leave when?"

"The twentieth."

"Right, which would get us to Aspen on the twenty-third."

"Jesus, it sounds terrific! You think your mom'll let us have the car?" Jenny asked.

"Oh, sure."

"When will you ask her?"

"When I get home Wednesday."

"The day before we *leave?*"

"Oh. Yeah."

"That's too late, Liss."

"It's just I wanted to ask her face to face."

"Yeah, but we can't wait till the day *before* . . ."

"Yeah."

"Why don't we call her right now?"

"Now?" Lissie said.

"Sure, what's wrong with now?"

"Well . . ."

"Let's," Jenny said.

There were three eight-year-olds in Connie's last class at the rehab center. All three were stutterers ("Experiencing dysfluency problems," as Connie might have put it to a colleague), all of them exhibiting only primary characteristics, none of them having yet been submitted to the terrible advice of teachers or parents to "stop and *think* so it comes out right." She had tested each of the three individually for diagnosis using the Goldman-Fristoe articulation test, and then had asked the center's audiologist to run an audiometer test on each of them. None of the three had any hearing problems.

Today, she was playing with the children a card game in which she'd dealt four picture cards to each of them and herself, the idea—premised on Go Fish—being to call for a card in another player's hand, and if the player could not match that card, to keep drawing cards from the deck until the correct matching card appeared. She was using the So Sorry deck for the game, the cards showing pictures only of words beginning with the *S* sound—sun, saw, seal, sack, soap, sink, sign, socks, suitcase, sailboat, scissors and saddle. She had deliberately chosen this deck from the many Go-Mo speech materials available because both Mercy and Mark sometimes experienced difficulty getting the *S* sound out without a stutter, but primarily because she wanted to encourage Sean to forget the difficulties he was having with his "th" for "s" substitution.

"D-d-d-do you h-h-h-have a soap?" Mercy asked Mark, stumbling on the "d" and the "h" but getting out the "s" without a trace of hesitation.

"So . . . s-s-s-sorry," Mark said.

Mercy fished in the deck until she found the card picturing a bar of soap. It was Mark's turn.

"Do you have a . . . s-s-s-sink?" he asked Sean.

Sean shook his head.

Connie did not press him for an answer. He was avoiding the *N* sound, with which he'd been having surprising difficulty during the last several sessions. Mark fished in the deck until he found a "sink" card. It was now Sean's turn. He looked at Connie.

"Do you have a thailboat?" he asked.

"It's . . . s-s-s-*sailboat,*" Mark said.

"I *know* what it is," Sean said.

"Then say it right," Mark said.

"He's trying to say it, aren't you?" Connie said.

"Yeth," Sean said.

"You mean *yes,*" Mercy said.

"In fact, I *do* have a sailboat," Connie said, and handed Sean the card.

"Thee?" Sean said. "She d-d-did have one."

"She had a *sail* b-b-b-boat," Mercy said, "n-n-not a *thail* b-b-boat."

"Do you h-h-have a thissors, too?" Sean asked.

"I have a scissors, too," Connie said, handing him the card. "Would you like to try saying it again for me?"

"Thissors," Sean said.

"Scissors," Connie said.

"Thissors."

"Well, we'll try it again later, okay? What card would you like next?"

"Why c-c-can't he say s-s-scissors?" Mercy said.

"It's just a word that gives him trouble," Connie said. "We all

have words that give us trouble. I can never say antidisestab . . .
see what I mean? I always trip on it."

"That's not even a *word!*" Mark said, laughing.

"If Mrs. C-C-Croft said it, then it's a w-w-w-word," Mercy said.

"She d-d-didn't say it. She only t-t-*tried* to say it."

"Antidisestablishmentarianism," Connie said in a rush. "There,
I got it!"

"See?" Mercy said. "She g-g-got it."

"That's some . . . w-w-word, all right," Mark said, shaking his
head.

At the end of the session, little Sean came to her and said, "Mrs.
Cwoft, I f-f-feel so b-b-bad I can't get it," and she hugged him close
and said, "No, darling, it'll come in time. I promise you."

At Columbia, where she'd studied for her master's all those years
ago, there'd been a professor who'd once remarked that the prime
requisite of a speech pathologist was patience. He had written the
word on the blackboard in huge block letters: P-A-T-I-E-N-C-E.
She thought about him on the drive back to Rutledge. It was going
to take somewhere between two and three years to successfully
conclude treatment with her three eight-year-olds. She wasn't there
to treat symptoms, no, there were too many therapists who
successfully treated a stuttering problem only to discover that the
client had "voluntarily-involuntarily" replaced the earlier symptom
with a far more serious physical symptom like hysterical aphonia—
the loss of speech entirely. One therapist (not a *pathologist* like
Connie; in the speech rehab game, a therapist qualified for
certification with a B.A., a pathologist with an M.A.) had come to
her in total astonishment when one of her clients lost his stutter
only to become hysterically blind. Symptom migration was a
common result of impatience. Patience, Connie remembered. P-A-
T-I-E-N-C-E.

It would take two years at best with these kids. She sometimes
felt only despair, the end result of immediate gratification constantly postponed. With Jamie's work, it was different. He took a
picture, he developed it and printed it, he realized his goal within
days, sometimes within—

She stepped on the thought before it ballooned into the anger it
normally triggered. It had been too many years. You couldn't get
angry over something that had happened—or *failed* to happen—all
those years ago. Not if you wanted to preserve whatever it was you
already possessed. What do I already possess? she wondered.

55

They were married in February of 1951. Jamie was almost twenty-five, Connie was not yet twenty. She was still a virgin on their wedding night, and she wept the first time they made love. Jamie held her in his arms and comforted her, and told her he would love her till the day he died. Connie wept into his shoulder, the sexy white silk nightgown she'd bought expressly for their honeymoon bunched above her waist and stained with blood.

She was still only nineteen when she got pregnant in March, a month after their wedding. Jamie had by then taken a job with a commercial photographer in Peekskill, some eighty miles from Poughkeepsie and a long commute back and forth every weekday, but the plan was for Connie to finish her sophomore year at Vassar before they moved into the city. She could not understand how she'd become pregnant. She had used the diaphragm religiously and according to the instructions given her at the Margaret Sanger Clinic in New York, and she simply could not understand how it had failed her. In April 1951, when she learned definitely that she was going to have a baby, abortions were illegal in the United States; moreover, they were dangerous and expensive. In the small garden apartment they were renting near the school, they discussed their plans.

It had been understood between them that they would have no children until they were both established in their separate careers. Connie wanted to be an actress; she had, in fact, already applied to both the Actors Studio and the Vodorin Workshop for possible enrollment in the fall. That was before she got pregnant.

"You can still finish out the term," Jamie said.

"You don't think I'll be showing?"

"No, no, this is what? April, right? You're still only a month pregnant . . ."

"Pregnant, Jesus," she said, and shook her head.

"So June'll be three months, that's all. You won't be showing at all."

"I hope not. Because I'd feel like an idiot, you know."

"I know."

"In class, you know."

"Yeah."

"Doing *Voice of the Turtle* or whatever, and having this big *belly* sticking out."

"You won't be showing yet, hon."

"So I'll finish the term, and then what?"

56

"Well . . . I don't think you'd be able to start anyplace else in the fall, do you?"

"No."

"I mean . . ."

"No, it wouldn't be a good idea."

"The baby's coming . . ."

"December."

"Yeah, so."

"Yeah, I'd be in my sixth month by the time classes started, I don't think Igor Vodorin would particularly appreciate . . ."

"But, you know, once the baby's born . . ."

"Yeah, then what?"

"You could, you know . . ."

"Yeah, what?"

"Well . . ."

"I think I can kiss it goodbye, Jamie."

"No, not necess—"

"Yeah, I think so. I don't think they mix, Jamie. Acting and babies."

"You know, by then I may be earning good money as a photographer, we could get someone in to take care of him—or her—and you could . . ."

"I find it difficult to believe there'll really *be* a him or a her, don't you?"

"Yes."

"I mean, there's a *baby* growing inside me, Jamie, do you *realize* that?" she said, and suddenly clutched her belly with both hands. "But I . . . you know . . . I really don't *feel* anything *about* it, or *for* it, or . . . I just feel *annoyed,* I guess. It's just an annoyance, Jamie. I don't *want* a fucking baby, do *you* want a baby?"

"No, but . . . honey, this doesn't . . . it doesn't have to mean the end of all our plans, you know. You can still go to acting school once the baby's old enough to . . ."

"Sure."

"A year or so, I guess would . . ."

"Sure, leave an infant with a stranger."

"Lots of women . . ."

"Sure."

"Honey, I'm sorry. I wish I . . ."

"Aw, shit," she said, "it's not your fault."

But it *was.* In bed that night, she wept. She turned her back to him and wept silently into her pillow. She was only nineteen years old and about to have a baby. *In December,* she thought, *I'll be a mother.* It was April already, and there were crocuses blooming on the patchy lawn outside the apartment complex. But the wind was still strong, and it rattled the windowpanes, and she thought of all those movies where a train was roaring through the night, and the wheels were going clickety-click-clack and the lights were flashing by the window and a girl was looking outside and remembering the past, the past all came back to the girl. The windows in their tiny bedroom rattled with the wind, and Connie lay beside her husband weeping quietly, but no past came back to her, she was almost too young to have had a significant past. A baby coming in December. To Connie, it seemed as if a baby would be the end of her life.

They moved to the city in June, several weeks after Connie had taken her final exams for the semester. Lissie was born six months later, on the nineteenth of December. She weighed seven pounds, twelve ounces. Jamie watched while Connie breast-fed her for the first time. She held the baby in her arms, cradling baby and breast, looking down at the infant's head.

"What does that feel like?" he asked.

"The baby, do you mean? Here?"

"Yes."

"Just a . . . I don't know . . . a little tugging feeling."

"Is it exciting?"

"A little. I don't know. It's not sexual, it's . . . I don't know. It's just very strange."

"I wonder if she likes it."

"My milk?"

"Yes."

"I'm sure she does."

"Can *I* taste it?"

"Well, not here. When we get home maybe."

"I want to take some pictures of you nursing her."

"All right."

"You look beautiful," he said.

"Thank you," she said, and lowered her eyes again, and studied the baby's face as she drank.

She did not later allow him to taste her milk.

She did not later allow him to take pictures of her nursing their daughter.

As she pulled into the driveway of the Rutledge house, she put all of this out of her mind again. Anger was a luxury she could no longer afford. She was thirty-seven years old, she would be thirty-eight next month. Her husband was a successful photographer now, and she was an underpaid pathologist at an understaffed rehabilitation center. So be it, she thought. *Fuck* it, she thought.

She parked her car in the garage, noted that there was still a light burning in the barn, slung her shoulder bag, keys in her hand, and went to the mailbox. The usual—junk mail and bills. Carrying the mail to the kitchen entrance, she twisted the burglar alarm key (the one marked with red tape) in the system plate to the left of the door, unlocked the kitchen door itself, dumped the mail and her bag on the counter just inside the door, and then went to the wet-sink to mix herself a Scotch and water. Jamie had taped a note to the refrigerator door. There was a movie in Westport he wanted to see, could she be ready to go out for dinner by seven? She looked up at the clock. It was already six-fifteen. Sighing, she sat at the kitchen table, sipping her Scotch and listening to the rush of the river below her. In this house, it always sounded as if it were raining outside. She finished her drink, phoned over to the barn to remind Jamie of the time, and then ran a tub of very hot water.

She was still in the tub when the telephone rang. She yelled "Jamie!" thinking he might be back in the house by now, and then muttered "Shit," and got out of the water and ran naked and dripping to the phone in the upstairs hallway.

"I have a collect call for anyone from Melissa Croft," the operator said, " will you accept charges?"

"Yes," Connie said, "sure."

"Mom?" Lissie said. "Hi."

"Just a second, Liss, let me get a towel," Connie said.

In the third floor corridor of Lorimer Dorm, Lissie and Jenny were standing at the wall telephone. "What is it?" Jenny whispered.

"She's getting a towel," Lissie said, her hand covering the mouthpiece.

"Hi, honey," Connie said. "I was in the tub."

"Where's Dad?"

"Over at the barn."

"I've been trying to reach you all afternoon."

"I was at the center. Is something wrong?"

"No, no," Lissie said.

"Ask her," Jenny whispered.

59

"We're looking forward to seeing you on Wednesday," Connie said. "Do you know what time your train'll be in?"

"I thought you were coming up to get me," Lissie said.

"No, I teach on Wednesdays, you know that."

"Well, how about Dad?"

"Wednesday is his day in the city."

"Then how . . .?"

"I thought you'd take a taxi. You have your key, haven't you?"

"Yeah, but I'll be carrying a lot of crap home."

"Jesus, don't *argue* with her!" Jenny whispered.

"I'm sorry, honey," Connie said, "but I don't see any other way."

"Yeah, well, okay," Lissie said. "I guess."

"Is everything all right up there?"

"Yeah, fine."

"Discipline all over and done with?"

"Yeah. Jenny and I went out to lunch. To celebrate."

"Good, darling."

There was a long silence. As often when she spoke to her mother on the telephone, the conversation seemed to drift off into nothingness after they'd exchanged a few pleasantries. She much preferred talking to her father, and she wondered now whether *he* wasn't the one she should ask about the Colorado trip. But Jenny was rolling her eyes and flapping her hands, silently urging her to get *on* with it. She took a deep breath.

"Mom," she said, "Jenny and I had an idea about what we might like to do on our break."

"Yes, honey, what's that?" Connie asked. She sounded distracted. Lissie guessed she was toweling herself with her free hand.

"We thought we might go to Colorado," Lissie said. "To do some skiing."

"Where?" Connie said.

"Aspen," Lissie said. "Colorado."

There was another silence on the line.

"Mom?" Lissie said.

"Yes," Connie said, "I heard you. But Lissie . . . Colorado's a long way off. And you haven't been on skis since you were thirteen. I'm really not sure I'd want you to . . ."

"Jenny already has permission," Lissie said, and hesitated. "We thought we might drive out."

Sighing, Connie said, "You've only been driving since December, Liss. Colorado's . . ."

"But I had Driver's Ed," Lissie said, and again hesitated. "We thought you might let us use the Ford."

"What do you mean? The station wagon?"

"Well, yeah."

"*My* car?"

"Yeah."

"To drive to Colorado?"

"Well . . . yeah."

"What am *I* supposed to drive while you're gone?"

"You could use Dad's car. You could share . . ."

"Lissie, you can't be serious," Connie said.

"I don't see what's so wrong with . . ."

"How could I possibly get to work without . . . how long did you plan on being away?"

"Well . . . we'd be leaving next Thursday."

"The day after you get *home?*"

"And we'd be back on Easter Sunday. Or maybe the day before. The day before, actually."

"That's your entire vacation."

"Not really."

"Yes, *really*. I thought you were looking forward to spending . . ."

"It's just that we've made all these plans, Mom."

"What plans have you made?"

"Figuring it all out, I mean."

"Whose idea was it to use my car?"

"It's just that Jenny's mother doesn't *have* a car, they live in the city, you know. So I thought since we've got *two* cars . . ."

"Yes, because we *need* two cars. The answer is no."

"Well, gee, Mom . . ."

"It's no. I'm sorry."

"Let me talk to Dad, may I please?"

"Dad's working. And when he gets back here—which should be any minute now—we're going to dinner and a movie."

"Can you ask him to call me when you get home?"

"We won't be home till after midnight."

"Tomorrow, then? First thing in the morning?"

"Lissie, we're talking about *my* car here. What*ever* your father may say, the answer is no."

"Will you ask Dad to call me?"

"Yes."

"Mom?"

"I said yes."

"I'm a very good driver, and anyway we've got insurance on the car, haven't we?"

"Lissie, let's end this conversation," Connie said. "The answer is no, and that's that."

"I think you're being unreasonable," Lissie said.

"Do you? Well, when *you* have a seventeen-year-old daughter who wants to drive to Colorado on her school vacation, you give her *your* car, okay? Meanwhile, mine stays right here," Connie said, and hung up.

Lissie looked at the phone.

"She hung up," she said.

"Boy," Jenny said.

"She actually hung up," Lissie said, still amazed, and put the receiver back on the hook.

"I think you were absolutely right," Jenny said. "She *was* being unreasonable."

"I'll talk to Dad tomorrow," Lissie said, nodding.

"You think *he'll* let you?"

"Oh, sure," Lissie said.

On Saturday morning, she called home at seven-thirty, while Connie was eating breakfast and Jamie was still in bed. He padded to the phone, listened to his daughter's plea, and said he would discuss it with her mother. She called again on Sunday night at eight, and he told her they were still discussing it, even though Connie had already given an emphatic "No!" On Monday morning, again at seven-thirty, Lissie called and began crying on the phone, saying she was never allowed to do anything all the other girls were allowed to do, and how could they be so mean, all she was asking for was the use of a car that was anyhow insured, and didn't he *care* about the fact that this was *her* vacation and that she might like to spend it doing something *she* wanted to do for a change, especially after having been cooped up at Henderson for the past month because of a dumb episode she hadn't even been a part of? And what about all the money he'd spent on ski lessons and liftline tickets when she was just a kid, didn't he want to see something beneficial come of all that?

He told her again he would discuss it with her mother, but there was no discussing it further with Connie. Connie left for work in high dudgeon, telling him if she heard one more *word* about that fucking station wagon and Lissie's trip to Aspen, she would *herself* take the car and disappear from the face of the earth. Ten minutes later, he called Lissie back and told her she could neither borrow her mother's car nor go to Colorado in anybody else's car.

When she began to plead again, he hung up.

3

As far as Lissie was concerned, her father's refusal to come to her rescue was an act of rank betrayal. She had always been able to depend on him in her frequent arguments with her mother, but this time he had failed her, and she felt it necessary to let her disappointment and her displeasure be known.

Throughout the entire length of her school vacation, she moved listlessly about the house or sulked silently in her room. She refused to accompany her parents to the opening of *1776* on the ground that the title had been stolen from Lafayette High School's literary-art magazine, for which Scarlett Kreuger was art editor, an accusation patently ridiculous, but one Lissie stubbornly maintained. She refused to go with them to a "First Day of Spring" party at the Lipscombes, even though the invitation had clearly stated "Bring along the kids," on the ground that the first day of spring was Friday, March 21, and *not* Saturday, March 22, and she didn't like to celebrate an occasion *after* the opportunity had passed. She expressed neither joy nor interest in the daffodils and crocuses tentatively blooming on the riverbank behind the house, refused to attend church with her parents on Palm Sunday, and generally behaved like a prisoner in her own home. In the privacy of their bedroom, Connie expressed to Jamie the wish that their daughter would hurry the hell back to school.

The situation was exacerbated in the week before Easter when Lissie received letters from both Vassar and Wellesley, her first and second choice colleges. She had been rejected by both. She blamed this, in ascending order, on Miss Eloise Larkin, head of the phys ed department, coach of the soccer team, and the tight-assed lady who'd blown the whistle after Ulla's little pot party; and Jonathan Holtzer, headmaster of Henderson State Penitentiary, who had written the letter announcing Lissie's Intermediate Discipline, a carbon of which had undoubtedly found its way into the school files and subsequently into the Admissions offices of both Vassar and Wellesley. There was no other explanation. Her grades were good, she had done well on her S.A.T.s, her personal interviews had gone smoothly, she had in fact been virtually certain of admission to *both* schools.

On Good Friday, Rusty Klein called to say she'd been accepted by Bennington, her first choice college. In that same day's mail, Lissie got letters from both Radcliffe and Sarah Lawrence, her third and fourth choice schools, each of them rejecting her. She had been *positive* of Sarah Lawrence as a safety school, but Holtzer's damn letter had done her in there as well. She had applied to only four colleges. She would be graduating in June. She was all dressed up for a party—with no place to go. When her vacation ended on Easter Sunday, she insisted on taking the *train* back to school, refusing even to allow her parents to drive her to the Stamford station, preferring instead to take a taxi. In her room that night, she commiserated with Jenny—who had been turned down by her three first choice colleges and was still awaiting word from her safety school—and together that night they strolled the campus and smoked some very good stuff Jenny had bought from a boy in New York.

It was not until close to the end of May that Lissie found a college. She had fired off a dozen hasty applications to schools all up and down the Eastern Seaboard, had visited eight of them for personal interviews, and had finally been accepted by three: Boston University, Simmons, and Brenner. She rejected B.U. because it was too big, Simmons because it was too small, and finally settled for Brenner, which was also in Boston—where there were more kids between the ages of eighteen and twenty-two than any place else in the nation.

At graduation that year, she sat listening to Jonathan Holtzer's uninspired speech about the challenges awaiting the youth of America, cursed him silently for the scurrilous action that had caused her to be rejected by the only schools she *really* wanted to go to, and vowed never to forgive him. She had, by then, forgiven her father for *his* dastardly behavior—he was, after all, her father—but she couldn't shake the persistent feeling that if only he'd acted . . . well . . . just differently, things might have worked out better for her.

In her mind, the whole damn fiasco was inextricably linked, an opera in five acts: if Miss Larkin hadn't walked in on a party where Lissie hadn't even been smoking, if Horseface Holtzer hadn't taken such a hard-line stand, if her father had more strenuously argued on her behalf and gotten Holtzer to revoke the Intermediate Discipline and then expunge that damning letter from the record, and, finally, if he'd allowed her to go to Colorado like the mature and responsible young lady she was, why then Vassar would have accepted her for registration in the fall, and she'd be going to Poughkeepsie instead of to Brenner, which she supposed was okay but only because it was in Boston.

She wasn't quite able to explain to herself how the Colorado trip had anything at all to do with the inexorable chain of events that had led to her sitting here in the sun, somewhat disconsolate and totally unexcited in cap and gown, "on the brink of life's great adventure," as Holtzer was now putting it, bound for a school that truly didn't interest her. But the Colorado trip *was* somehow a part of it, the culminating example of her father's inability to come to her defense when his strength was most needed.

"It is," Holtzer said, "perhaps the greatest adventure you will ever undertake. I wish you godspeed and fare thee well, I wish you a safe voyage over life's perilous waters, and a snug harbor on the opposite shore. To this graduating class of June, 1969, I extend my heartiest congratulations, my sincere good wishes, and my hopes for a bountiful future."

She waited till her name was called; "Miss Melissa Abigail Croft"—she *detested* her middle name—and rose from the folding chair, and walked in the sunshine to the platform where Holtzer was handing out the graduation certificates and shaking hands. She could feel the eyes of her family upon her—her mother, her father, her grandparents. She walked with her head erect, somewhat fearful she would lose the precariously perched mortarboard, her shoulders back, wondering if the strong sunlight would stream through the gown to outline her legs as she climbed the steps; she was wearing only panties under the gown, no bra or slip. As she approached Holtzer, she thought only *I hate you, you bastard.* The headmaster was smiling. He said her name softly, "Melissa," and handed her the rolled and ribboned certificate. She did not return the smile. She crossed the platform, came down the steps on the opposite side, and quickly returned to her chair.

The graduating boys and girls were seated alphabetically to facilitate an orderly march to and from the platform. Jenny was sitting some two rows behind her; she turned briefly to look at her before taking her seat again. With her hands folded in her lap over her precious certificate, she listened to the graduates' names being called, grinning when she heard "Jennifer Eileen Groat," watching her as she walked to the platform and accepted her certificate— unsmilingly—from old Horseface; Jenny had ended up at Miami U. In the hot sunshine, Lissie sat inside her black gown, sweltering, until the last name was called, the last certificate dispensed. She got up at once then, and ran to meet Jenny, who was rushing down the aisle toward her. The two girls embraced. "Hey, roomie, how *about* that?" Lissie said, and Jenny whispered, "Paroled at last," and the two girls giggled.

Her parents and grandparents were crossing the lawn toward her now, beaming proudly, her father in his "blue confirmation suit" as he called it, but which she knew had been hand-tailored for him at Chipp in New York, camera around his neck, hands extended. Her mother was just beside him, wearing a white dress and white French-heeled pumps, looking more like a bride than the mother of a June graduate, smiling, even white teeth gleaming against her tanned face, all those spring days of sitting on the deck above the river with a reflector under her chin. Behind them were Grand-mother and Grandfather Harding, flanking Grandmother Croft, who clung to their arms for support; Grandmother Croft had arthritis, she walked slowly and painfully. Of all her grandparents, Lissie liked her best, but somehow, today, they *all* looked strange to her. Those faces approaching, those extended hands. Strange somehow.

Her father was the first to reach her.

"Lissie," he said softly, and took her in his arms.

"Well, I guess I made it," Lissie said, grinning.

"Congratulations," he said, and stepped back to take her picture.

Nodding, beaming, she looked into his face while he focused and set, expecting more, waiting for something more. Something clever perhaps, he was always so clever, even something like Jenny's "Paroled at last," not just an embrace and a brief "Congratulations," as if he were shaking hands with Scarlett Kreuger instead of . . . instead of . . . well, *shit,* she was his daughter, there should have been something more. She didn't know what, just . . . something more. Something more intimate. She was his *daughter,* damn it! The camera shutter clicked. He lowered the camera from his face and stood there looking somewhat embarrassed, she couldn't fathom why, and entirely awkward, his eyes squinted against the sun, his head tilted, nodding. She broke away from him to greet her mother.

Her mother was still smiling, but there was something contradictory in her eyes. Censure? Disappointment? Annoyance over the fact that her only daughter would be going to Brenner in the fall, and *not* to Vassar where she could learn to talk like Mommy? Something. The eyes and mouth in conflict, the eyes winning. Her mother hugged her close. "Congratulations, darling," she said. "I'm so very proud of you." Her V.S. and D.M. voice. That and the eyes, Lissie thought. Her voice and her eyes are telling me, never mind the words, *I'm so very proud of you,* bullshit! I'm graduating with a straight-B average from a tough school like Henderson, isn't that enough for you? What did I have to do, Mom? Become president of the senior class? Deliver the valedictory? *What,* Mom? Straight-A's? Would you have let me use your goddamn station wagon *then?*

"Thanks, Mom," she said, and broke away from her.

Grandmother Croft was crying.

"Oh, *Melissa,*" she said, and released her grip on the Hardings' supporting arms, and opened her own arms wide to Lissie. She was the only one of the grandparents who still called her Melissa, and Lissie found this touching somehow, as though to Grandmother Croft she was still a little blond baby with identifying beads on her chubby wrist, MELISSA CROFT in blue letters, all caps, she still had the beads in her jewelry box, one of her gifts when she'd turned sixteen. Grandmother Croft was a frail, tiny woman but she clasped Lissie surprisingly tightly, almost squeezing the breath out of her, and whispered in her ear almost the identical words her mother had spoken a few moments before, but with a slight difference. "You make me so damn *proud,*" she said, and the word "proud" was itself bursting with pride. For the first time that day, Lissie felt something she knew she was supposed to be feeling: a sense of accomplishment and reward, a sense of familial approval and acceptance, and now—from this dear old woman who used to baby-sit her when she was little and her parents couldn't afford to pay anyone, cooing to her as she changed her diapers and wiped her little behind, now from dear sweet Grandmother Croft—love.

Grandfather Harding took her hand, pompously formal as always, never any kisses from him, oh, no, not from this staid pillar of the community, chairman of the board of directors, president of the Chamber of Commerce, wearing his gray flannel suit even on a day when the temperature was in the eighties, white hair combed sideways to hide his baldness, even more suntanned than mother was, just home from a Caribbean cruise.

"Well, well," he said, "it seems I'll have a college-girl grand-daughter in the fall." The word "granddaughter" reverberated, underscoring her father's earlier lapse. "You look beautiful, Liss," he said, further compounding her father's felony. Couldn't her own father have called her "daughter"? Couldn't he have told her how beautiful she looked, the way Granddaddy had just done? No, just the quick embrace—and "Congratulations." Thank you, sir, she'd felt like answering, I'll try to live up to the expectations of the company.

Grandmother Harding, all blue hair and blue eyes, wearing a pastel blue suit—she always wore blue, never any other color—crowded her husband aside with a "Stop monopolizing her, Peter," and hugged Lissie to her ample bosom, the Harding legacy except for Lissie herself, and said, "We bought you something lovely, Liss," good old Grandma, never able to express affection except in terms of gifts, sometimes "accidentally" leaving the price tags on them so you could better appreciate the magnitude of her love. Standing there in her grandmother's embrace, looking over her shoulder to where her mother was still smiling that false, forced smile, Lissie was astonished to realize how closely the three of them resembled each other, three generations in the bright June sun-shine, grandmother, mother and daughter, the youngest of whom was about to begin a hopefully safe voyage across life's perilous waters, with a godspeed and a fare thee well.

She felt suddenly frightened in her grandmother's arms; she did not want to grow up to be her mother, did not want to further age into this blue-haired woman who now whispered in her ear, "A beautiful Longines *wrist*watch," yet the evidence was plain to see and understand, grandmother unto mother unto daughter, the trinity realized. Unless she was very careful, she herself would one day be standing in the sunshine at the age of seventy-five, all dressed in blue perhaps, whispering in her own granddaughter's ear about the lovely graduation gift she'd bought her. She did not want that to happen. She wanted instead . . .

She suddenly wondered *what* she wanted.

Standing there on the brink of life's greatest adventure, she had no answer.

There had been family vacations galore when Lissie was growing up: weekend skiing trips to Bromley, Stratton, Sugarbush and Stowe, and once even to Mont Tremblant in Canada, where she'd been terrified by the trails and frozen stiff besides; cultural excursions to Washington, D.C., New Orleans, Charlestown and Annapolis; strictly fun stuff like the full week they'd spent in Los Angeles, most of it at Disneyland. On her school breaks, her parents usually took her to someplace in the Caribbean, Jamaica one time (where the natives were surly and one man spit at her), Puerto Rico another time, and the Bahamas, and Caneel Bay when she was eight (which she didn't like because there were no *kids* there) and Haiti and St. Vincent, which was close to South America, and, well, all of them—she was willing to bet she'd been to more Caribbean islands than any kid her age.

In the summers, they usually took a house at the beach someplace. One summer it was Fire Island—well, wait, that was *two* summers. Once in Saltair and the second time in the Pines, right, two years. And one summer they took a house on Martha's Vineyard, and another time on Shelter Island and once on Nantucket, always a beach house someplace. The most glorious summer of all was when Lissie was thirteen and the family went to Paris and the Dordogne, where she fell in love for the first time in her life with a French busboy in the town of Les Eyzies, a romance unfortunately short-lived in that they were moving on to Périgueux in the morning. So there'd been plenty of family vacations, and no cause to complain of neglect or abandonment. Even her parents' vacations *alone* together ("To recharge our batteries," as her father put it) were infrequent and usually of short duration—a week, ten days, two weeks at the most—and so, really, there'd never been any reason to raise a fuss.

But this summer, perhaps because she'd just graduated, perhaps because she was looking forward with some trepidation to beginning college in the fall, she resented enormously the trip her parents planned to take without her, especially since she was expected to spend the time they were gone with her grandparents on the Cape. Her father's shopworn remark about recharging batteries consoled her not in the least. She found her mother's familiar "But we always come *back,* darling" less than reassuring. *They* were going to Italy for two weeks, and *she* was going to the goddamn Cape. The imbalance, the *injustice* of such an arrangement infuriated her. She spent an hour on the phone complaining to Rusty Klein about it, and another hour in a long-distance conversation with Jenny in New York. Jenny offered the greater solace. "They wouldn't let *you* go to Colorado," she said, "but *they're* ready to traipse God knows how many miles to Italy!"

The "God knows how many miles" turned out to be four thousand, as her parents informed her, but they assured her there was very good telephone communication from Italy, even from the island of Sardinia, where they planned to be spending most of their time, and they promised they would call her as often as they had when she was at school. Besides, they would only be gone for two weeks, after which they would spend the rest of the summer together doing whatever Lissie *wanted* to do. Lissie wanted to go to Italy, *that's* what Lissie wanted to do. By the last week in June, which was when they broke the news to her—sneaky, oh, how *sneaky*—she was bored silly with the town of Rutledge, Connecticut, and ready to climb the walls. There were only so many trout she could pull from the river behind the house, only so many bicycle rides she could take on the town's tree-shaded lanes, only so many picnics she could go on with kids as bored as she herself was.

Even so, the prospect of spending July and August in Rutledge was positively brilliant when compared to spending two weeks with Grandmother and Grandfather Harding in the creaky old house they rented on the Cape each summer. Her parents told her, nonetheless, that their plans had been made a long time ago (she doubted this; if it was true, why had they held off telling her till almost the end of June, when they were scheduled to leave on July 12?) and they couldn't at this late date hope to get another room for Lissie, especially at the Cala di Volpe, which was the hotel the Aga Khan had built with his triumvirate or his consortium or *whatever* the hell they told her it was called, a hotel *impossible* to get into at the last minute, and even difficult to book if you made your plans far in advance, as they had done (and which she *still* doubted), so that was that.

On the eleventh day of July, while her parents were still packing for their trip abroad the next day, Lissie was shipped off to the Cape. The man who drove her up ran the town's so-called limousine service which, translated from the English, meant a fleet of two, count 'em, *two* Cadillacs. He was not a man noted for generosity of speech. Lissie spent four hours in utter silence with him, he hunched over the wheel, she sprawled on the back seat of his best car (the blue one), watching the landscape roll by, and dreaming of Tuscany, where her parents planned to spend a few days before taking the Civitavecchia ferry to Sardinia. It happened to be raining, which did nothing to alleviate her dark mood.

The house her grandparents had been renting for the past seven summers, ever since Lissie was ten, was a gray-shingled structure perched on the edge of the beach, gabled and turreted, with a genuine widow's walk on the uppermost story and a reputed ghost in the basement. Lissie would have welcomed the ghost. She kept looking for the goddamn ghost. It rained for the first four days of her stay, the weather denying her even a tentative dip in the frigid ocean, which she wouldn't have relished much anyway. Granddaddy kept asking if she'd seen the poltergeist yet. "Seen the poltergeist yet, Liss?" Grandmother kept saying there was a difference between a poltergeist and a ghost, but she never seemed able to explain the difference satisfactorily. Poltergeist or ghost, Grandmother never went down to the basement alone.

Lissie read, or almost read, four books in the first four days of a confinement worse than her Intermediate Discipline had been. On the first day, she started a paperback edition of Harold Robbins's *The Carpetbaggers,* put it aside as utter trash after the second chapter, and that same day started and finished reading Philip Roth's latest novel, *Portnoy's Complaint,* which she found in a spanking clean dust jacket on Grandmother's bookshelf, and which she was later certain Grandmother had not read. Thus inspired, she masturbated herself to sleep that night, and continued to masturbate on and off for the next two days, between finishing a paperback edition of Saul Bellow's *Seize the Day* (which she found less compelling than her own restless fingers) and a clothbound, unjacketed edition of an old novel titled *Magnificent Obsession* by someone named Lloyd C. Douglas, whose name sounded familiar, but only because she later realized there'd been a kid named Lloyd

72

Rogers in her French class at Henderson. She spent all of the fourth rainy day in her room, refusing to budge from her bed, making a long-distance call to Jenny to tell her she'd read the grooviest dirty book, and then, remembering, masturbating for the better part of the afternoon and evening, her fingers frantically willing away the time. On the fifth day, the sun came out.

"Feeling better, darling?" her grandmother asked when she came down for breakfast.

"Uh-huh," Lissie said. She had eaten only a sandwich for lunch yesterday afternoon, her grandmother carrying it on a tray, together with a glass of milk, to her room. She was ravenously hungry now and she devoured her eggs, bacon and toast with scarcely a word, and then went upstairs to dress, eager to get out of the house. Her parents had still not called from Italy, though they'd left on the twelfth, and this was already the sixteenth. She dressed swiftly, putting on a peasant blouse, a green mini, and a pair of beat-up sandals. She liked miniskirts because they showed her long legs to good advantage. God knew she had little else worth showing . . . well, her behind maybe, her behind wasn't too bad. But her legs were terrific, she thought, and she firmly believed that someone somewhere should one day erect a monument to Mary Quant. She did not feel the same way about whoever had invented the bikini. As president and co-founder of the Itty-Bitty Titty Committee, she would not have been caught dead on a beach with nothing but a strip of cloth covering her nonexistent breasts. She favored tanksuits or maillots instead, cut rather high on the thigh to emphasize her legginess and hopefully to detract from whatever she was lacking elsewhere, giving her a long coltish look she considered somewhat sexy.

She left the house at about eleven, telling her grandmother she'd be back sometime that afternoon, and not to worry about lunch, she'd get something to eat in town. She was familiar with the town, knew all the teenage haunts, and headed for the nearest one now, a lobster-roll joint called Marty's, on the beach a mile or so from her grandparents' house. The town was crowded with its usual share of tourists: fat red-faced men in Hawaiian print shirts; women in halters, shorts and high-heeled wedgies; runny-nosed little kids eating ice cream cones or chocolate bars; all of them thronging the boardwalk and the shops selling silver, scrimshaw, leather goods and touristy crap like ashtrays in the shape of lobsters. She was walking past one of the new art galleries, had in fact stopped to look in the window at a painting of an old house, obviously derivative of Andrew Wyeth's *Christina's World*—which she *adored* because somehow it reminded her so much of herself—when she saw Pee Wee Rawles standing alongside a bicycle outside the five and ten.

Pee Wee was a Henderson student like herself—or like what she *had* been before this June—a red-headed feisty-looking kid with freckles all over his face and his arms, a good foot and a half shorter than Lissie and not particularly liked by any of Henderson's girl students because his sexual preferences, as he frequently proclaimed, were entirely oral. He'd been a junior this past trimester, which would make him a graduating senior when he went back to school in the fall.

Lissie guessed he was sixteen going on seventeen. He was wearing cut-offs and a T-shirt stenciled with the words KISS ME, I'M IRISH. He was barefooted, and his feet were dirty. He had not seen her yet, he was in fact fiddling with something on the rack behind the bicycle seat when she first spotted him. Normally, she'd have avoided him like the plague he was. But just *seeing* a Hendy like herself up here in the boondocks filled her with a sense of camaraderie, the old school tie, all that shit, that completely negated the awful fact of Pee Wee himself. Pee Wee was first a Hendy and only next a terrifying creep.

"Hey!" she yelled. "Pee Wee!"

He looked up sharply, squinting into the sun, frowning, and finally recognizing her. He had settled to his satisfaction whatever had been troubling him on the rack, and he swung one leg up over the bicycle seat as she walked over to him. The first thing he said was, "It's Warren."

"What?" she said.

"My name is Warren."

"Oh," she said. "Sorry."

He nodded curtly, driving the point home, and then immediately said, "What are *you* doing here?" and grinned broadly.

"I'm visiting my grandparents," she said.

"Yeah, no kidding?" he said. "How long'll you be here."

"Till the twenty-sixth. How about you?"

"My folks have a place for the summer," he said.

His voice seemed a bit deeper than when she'd last talked to him, and he also seemed somewhat taller, but maybe that was because he was sitting on a bicycle. In any event, she could understand why he no longer chose to be called Pee Wee. For the longest time—and only because one of her playmates in the building they'd lived in on Central Park West couldn't pronounce the name Melissa—she herself had been called Missie, a nickname she'd detested. Pondering all this, wondering if Pee Wee had changed his personality along with his name, she realized they had both fallen silent, end of conversation, nothing more to say, nice to've seen you.

"Where you headed?" he said.

"Marty's," she said.

"Out of business," he said.

"Oh, yeah?"

"Yeah."

Silence again.

"Why?" he said. "You want something to eat?"

Well, here we go, she thought, some things *never* change. Call me Warren, call me Ishmael, I'm still good old Sixty-nine Rawles.

"Because there's a new place near the lighthouse, makes better lobster rolls than Marty's used to," he said.

"I'm not really hungry," she said. "I just had breakfast. I thought some of the kids might be there."

"Most of the kids hang out on the beach behind the Dunes," he said. "You ever been up there?"

"I thought that was a private beach."

"Yeah," Warren said, grinning, "but we've sort of requisitioned a corner of it. You want a ride up there?"

"You going there?"

"In a minute. I've got to drop this off at the house first," he said, indicating the package he'd fastened to the rack. If you want a ride . . ."

"Sure," she said.

"Well, hop on," he said.

The house his parents were renting was several blocks from town, not on the beach itself, as her grandparents' house was, but on a tree-shaded side street called Sea Grape Lane. Riding through town on the crossbar of the bike, Lissie found it difficult to keep her skirt down, and found herself frowning back at the men trying to see up under it. Never kids. Kids just didn't seem to give a damn about such things, it was all so free and easy with kids. Only *men.* Men her father's age or older, all of them trying to catch a glimpse of her panties.

She couldn't possibly imagine what was so fascinating about her panties. Or *anybody's* panties, for that matter. Walk down the main street, you could see as many panties as you cared to in any of the lingerie shops. But here were grown men, some of them ancient, in fact, craning for a look up her skirt, and it bothered her. Even some of her parents' friends, whose own *daughters* wore minis, for Christ's sake, would sometimes openly stare at her legs whenever she sat down, hoping for a glimpse of those cherished panties of hers. She was sometimes tempted to put on a mini with nothing at *all* under it, surprise hell out of them.

She laughed aloud, and when Warren asked her what was so funny, she said, "Nothing."

"Is it me?" he asked. "Did I do something?"

"No, no," she said, and wondered if Warren *had* changed more than his name, after all. "Nothing you did or said."

"Well, good," he said, sounding tremendously relieved.

He dropped off the package at his house, and then pedaled the bike a mile or so out of town, along a road crawling with automobiles, the men glancing covertly at her legs as they rode past, *annoying* her, damn it. She was relieved when she spotted the hotel ahead, a huge Victorian monster squatting in shingled bygone splendor on the ocean's edge. Warren pedaled the bike past it and onto an access road that rapidly deteriorated into nothing more than a sandy lane. When he could pedal no further, Lissie climbed down onto the sand and immediately took off her sandals. Warren pushed the bike, with some difficulty, to a patch of swaying beach grass, laid it on its side, and then padlocked the front wheel to the crossbar. "They're usually over this way," he said, and began climbing the dune.

They had not, as Warren had indicated, requisitioned a corner of the private beach for themselves, but rather had set up an enclave just beyond the PRIVATE BEACH—HOTEL PATRONS ONLY sign. There were, Lissie estimated at first glance, close to forty kids sprawled there on the sand, or standing in tight little clusters, or sitting around a dark-haired girl who was wearing a minuscule bikini that threatened her huge breasts and earth-mother hips, strumming a guitar and singing the song Joan Baez had dedicated to her husband on a CBS show this past March, a ballad praising draft-resisters. Lissie had caught the show during her detention period, had heard the dedication to Baez's husband, and the words, "He is going to prison for three years." She later read in the *New York Times* that CBS had cut the rest of her speech: "The reason is that he resisted Selective Service and the draft and militarism in general."

The kids, Lissie guessed, ranged in age from seventeen to twenty-two; one of the boys was wearing a Princeton sweatshirt; another had on a T-shirt almost certainly hand-lettered: the front of the shirt read FUCK VIETNAM! Warren seemed a little young for this crowd, but he *did* appear taller even now that he was off his bicycle, and at least three of the kids greeted him by name (Warren and not Pee Wee) as they approached. He introduced Lissie to the boy in the Princeton sweatshirt, whose name was Pete Turner, and who seemed to lose interest in her the moment he scanned the peasant blouse and the scant treasures it held, preferring instead to turn his gaze back to the folksinger's more obvious charms. She finished the Baez tune, and then began singing Dylan's "Like a Rolling Stone." A quarter of the kids were listening to her, the rest were talking or clowning around in the sand, or tossing Frisbees. Along about noon, somebody suggested they all wander up to Sam's—which was the name of the new place near the lighthouse— for lobster rolls. A dozen kids went, the rest of them stayed behind, drinking beer.

At three in the afternoon, the kid with the FUCK VIETNAM! T-shirt broke out some pot, and some of the other kids followed suit, and they all sat smoking openly on the beach, even though they could see Massachusetts State Police cars cruising the road above. Lissie hadn't smoked since her graduation; it was almost impossible to find anything either in Rutledge or in Talmadge, and Rusty Klein, who had begun smoking shortly after the Christmas vacation, said that buying grass from the greasers in Clayton was dangerous. Sitting beside Warren, sharing a joint with him, she felt at peace with herself for the first time in a long time. When he asked if she'd like to go to a cookout with him that Sunday night, the twentieth, she said yes.

The woman was about Connie's age, a redheaded American wearing a Pucci bikini she'd bought in the hotel boutique the day before at a scandalously low price, or so she claimed, because the new line was coming in any day now and the shop was eager to clear its shelves. The woman made her home in Florence, so Jamie figured she qualified as a Pucci comparison shopper. Her name was Lynda, with a y, and she'd been running an art gallery on the Arno for the last fifteen years. She was from Philadelphia originally;

Jamie suspected there was old money in her family. Her cadences were oddly European; she spoke her native English without a trace of accent, and yet her intonation was peculiarly foreign. She had lowered the straps of the bra top and was spreading suntan lotion on the sloping tops of her breasts. She smelled of coconut.

The man's name was Ernesto. He was from Argentina, the owner of a cattle ranch down there, and he visited Italy only sporadically though he claimed to be married to Lynda. He spoke Italian fluently, however, and he told Jamie that the proper way to summon a waiter in Italian was to say *"senta,"* which meant "listen," and not *"cameriere,"* which meant "waiter," a word seldom used by sophisticated Italians, and a word he was sure Jamie, as an American, found enormously difficult to pronounce. Jamie felt that summoning a waiter with the word "listen" was tantamount to snapping your fingers at him. But he watched as Ernesto called to the waiter, the word issuing softly from his lips, *"senta,"* watched as the waiter turned immediately and scurried to where they were sitting by the pool. Ernesto ordered another round of Costa Smeraldas, warning that for all its minty, confectionary taste, the drink could hit you very hard here in the strong Sardinian sun. Lynda lay face down on the lounge and untied the straps of the bra top.

Ernesto's Spanish and Italian were better than his English, but Lynda willingly served as prone translator. Ernesto wanted to know how much you tipped a cabdriver in New York City, and whether or not prostitution was as open there as it was in Hamburg. Lynda was eager to hear all the latest slang, she'd been away from America for such a long time. Did people still say something was a "drag"? Jamie told her the expression was now "a bummer" *("Come?"* Ernesto asked. "Bomber?"), which he guessed had filtered into the vernacular from the jargon of drug-users, a "bum trip" signifying a bad experience with LSD. Ernesto asked if the use of drugs was as widespread in America as all the magazines seemed to claim, and Connie said she guessed maybe 10 percent of the kids smoked marijuana, certainly no more than that. Lynda said she'd read in the overseas edition of *Time* that something like eight million Americans had at least *sampled* marijuana, and Connie said, "Oh, no, nothing *nearly* like that," and then said, "Am I the only one who's suffocating?" and headed for the pool. Ernesto followed her.

"Was it difficult to become a photographer?" Lynda asked.

"Yes," he said.

"Because I have a nephew back home who's considering it. How did you start?"

"Well, you don't really want to hear that, do you?"

"Yes, I do," she said. "Truly." She shifted her position on the lounge. He glimpsed, but only for an instant, a flash of whiter flesh where her tan ended, the briefest glimpse of a pink, erect nipple. In the pool, he heard Connie laughing at something Ernesto had just said.

He found himself telling her easily and unself-consciously about how difficult it had been for him and Connie after the birth of their daughter, both of them so very young and living in a roach-infested rathole on West Seventy-eighth Street, Connie riding the subway each day to Columbia University uptown . . .

"Yes, my brother went to Columbia," Lynda said, nodding.

. . . he himself running all over the city, trying to get newspaper or magazine assignments, the Leica hanging on a battered strap around his neck just in case lightning struck and a Fifth Avenue bus careened onto the sidewalk and into Bonwit's plate-glass window. Developed and printed his film in a bathroom the size of a coat closet. The enlarger he'd used in those days was an old diffusion job without condensers; it sometimes got so hot the negatives would buckle, but it was the only one the school had. He taught photography three nights a week to little old ladies who wanted to become Dorothea Lange, fat chance. Whenever they asked him where they might find samples of his current work, he never knew what the hell to say. Showed them his portfolio instead, the same way he showed it all over town.

By the time he took the breakthrough pictures on the Bowery, he was more or less convinced they would be his last attempt at getting into the big time. He was, after all, a graduate of Yale, and he was certain he could get an honest job someplace that would pay more than he was earning with his "snapshots," as Connie's father used to call them. The Bowery pictures turned out so well, Jamie later realized, only because he so thoroughly identified with the men who'd been his subjects. The derelicts down there were men who had already given up; Jamie was on the verge of giving up. He had, in fact, not come to the Bowery specifically to take pictures, but was there instead to buy a badly needed desk lamp at one of the wholesale electrical houses lining Third Avenue.

As usual, though, his Leica was hanging around his neck, and he had a roll of black-and-white film in the camera and another two, unopened, in his pocket. As he walked from store to store, searching for the bargain he'd come all the way by subway to find, he found instead a shaft of brilliant August sunshine slanting downward from the tracks of the elevated structure overhead to form a ladder pattern on the old cobblestones. He snapped the picture moments before a train rushed past above him, obliterating the light and the image that had been there an instant before.

"I sometimes think all the good things that've happened in my life were a matter of accident," he said now. "Like that shaft of sunlight slanting down from above and reminding me I had a *camera* around my neck, I was still a *photographer*. I took the picture. The train went by, the moment was gone. But I began looking around a bit more carefully."

They slumped in doorways or sat on the low stoops of closed shops, these men who had long ago decided there was no sense pursuing or striving or competing. They scarcely acknowledged Jamie's presence as he took their pictures, continuing whatever conversations they'd been having, their talk the *real* talk of drunks, and not the comic dialogue one read in novels or saw in motion pictures. There was nothing amusing about these men.

He did not develop and print the pictures until the following Tuesday—his teaching evenings were Tuesdays, Wednesdays and Fridays, and the only darkroom he had was the one at the school. He knew even before he'd made any enlargements that he had done some very good work that day on the Bowery. He spent the next several hours working with the old diffusion-job enlarger, blowing up a dozen of the best shots to eight-by-tens, and almost missing his first class. That Friday, he went up to the old Time-Life building at 9 Rockefeller Plaza, carrying his photographs under his arm in a black portfolio, and asked to see the picture editor. The man he talked to was an assistant editor. In his gentle voice he kept saying over and over again, "These are very good," and then picked up the phone and buzzed someone and said, "Charlie, could you come in here a minute? There's some stuff you ought to see."

They offered him $1,600 for the lot. He would have accepted $60. He signed the necessary releases, asked when the pictures would be used, and then asked when he could have his check. They told him the spread (God, it was going to be a *spread!*) would probably appear sometime in late September, early October, and that his check would be vouchered that day and probably mailed by the end of the week. He did not tell Connie he'd sold the pictures until the check arrived. Then he went out to buy a dozen red roses and a bottle of very expensive twelve-year-old Scotch. He had sent the sitter on her way and was waiting in the living room with Lissie on his lap when Connie got home from her summer school classes that day. He had put the flowers in a vase, and had opened the bottle of Scotch—but he had not yet begun drinking it. It sat untouched in the center of the coffee table, the vase of roses and two sparkling clean glasses beside it. When he heard Connie's key in the lock, he whispered, "Here's Mommy."

The moment she opened the door, Connie saw the roses, and the good bottle of Scotch, and the two clean glasses. As she knelt to hug her daughter close, her eyes met Jamie's. Something in them caused her to grin. She knew already. She knew that something marvelous had happened.

"What?" she said.

"I sold some pictures to *Life*," he said.

"Oh, *Jamie*," she said, and burst into tears and ran to him and hugged him close as he came out of the battered easy chair to meet her embrace. Lissie, bewildered, went to where they were standing, and hugged their knees, and began crying along with her mother.

That was the year everything began happening for the Crofts. The calls from the photographers' agents the moment the pictures appeared in *Life*—eight full *pages!*—Christ, the phone wouldn't stop ringing, Black Star, and Globe, and Pix—all the best agencies in New York—calling to ask if they might represent James Croft, the Photographer. He was, at last and suddenly, James Croft the Photographer. He sat alone that night in the tiny living room of the Seventy-eighth Street apartment, Connie feeding the baby in a highchair in the kitchen, and drank a martini, very dry and straight up, and wondered what he had been *before* he became James Croft the Photographer. Had he been any *less* a photographer before the exposure in *Life*?

"Oh, but of course you were," Lynda said.

He told her now, in more detail than he had anticipated (but her gray eyes were fastened to his, and she seemed to be hanging on his every word) how the agent he'd finally settled on was a man named Lewis Barker, of Barker Associates, Inc., on Fifth Avenue. Lew had himself worked for Time-Life, as long ago as the struggle for power between Chiang Kai-shek and Mao Tse-tung, and had barely escaped house arrest in Nanking when, in April of 1949, he watched the People's Liberation Army crossing the flooded Yangtze, and fled with the Kuomintang government to Canton, leaving most of his clothes and two valuable cameras behind, taking with him only a single bag packed with a change of clothing and his model IIc Leica with its 50-mm Summitar lens. He got to Hong Kong by junk, and from there caught a plane to San Francisco via Manila. The pictures he took of the Communist shelling of the British gunboat *Amethyst* appeared in *Life*'s May 20, 1949, issue.

Lew had quit Time-Life in 1950 to start his own agency. The Associates in the agency title were a onetime fashion photographer named Jerry Singer, and a portrait photographer named Abner Pettit, but Lew was the agency's backbone and its drawing power; there wasn't a photographer anywhere in the world who was unaware of his *China Portfolio*—as the collected pictures he'd taken between 1947 and 1949 were titled in the later book version— or his previous coverage of the fighting in Europe during World War II. One picture alone, instantly recognizable everywhere by photographers and laymen alike, would have made his reputation: the infantryman drawing on a cigarette during the Battle of the Bulge, his war-weary eyes scanning the leaden sky in hope of a parachute drop.

"Oh, of course, I know this picture," Lynda said.

Lew was fifty-five in that fall of 1953, when Jamie joined the agency. By December of that year, he'd earned for Jamie five times as much as he'd realized in the ten months preceding the appearance of the Bowery essay in *Life*. Six days before Lissie's second birthday, the Crofts moved to a new apartment on Eighty-ninth and Central Park West. Seven rooms! A darkroom the size of their previous bedroom on Seventy-eighth! A master bedroom overlooking the park, and a room of her own for Lissie, with pale pink wallpaper covered with blooming bluebells, and a new crib with a mobile hanging over it—Donald Duck and his three nephews, Dewey, Dopey, and Doc, or whatever they were called. Seven rooms! A brand new Omega enlarger, with which he blew up all the best shots he'd taken of Lissie in her second year. The huge living room, with its southern exposure, was still largely unfurnished a week before Christmas; they'd moved into it the sofa, floor lamp and single easy chair from the Seventy-eighth Street dump, and the pieces floated there on the new blue broadloom like rafts adrift on a vast uncharted sea.

"And so you have lived happily ever after," Lynda said, and reached behind her to tie the bra straps, rising as she did. Again, he saw the full breasts, naked for an instant before the riotous Pucci fabric covered them.

"Yes," he said.

She was smiling thinly. "And do you still love your wife very much?" she asked, and tossed her long red hair, and looked away from him, toward the pool where Ernesto and Connie were swimming back toward the diving board.

"Yes," Jamie said. "I love her very much."

"How lucky for you," Lynda said, and smiled again. Idly, almost remorsefully, she said, "I've never been made love to in English. I've known only European men."

He said nothing.

Her eyes met his.

She studied him solemnly for a moment, and then said, "I think I'll take a swim. Would you like to swim with me?"

He hesitated. "Connie mentioned something about a nap," he said.

"Ah, yes, then, you must take your nap with Connie," Lynda said, and rose from the lounge and ran to the edge of the pool. He watched as she dove cleanly into the water.

She had been in the bathroom for a very long time.

He lay on the bed in the shuttered room, the voices of waiters calling to each other in Italian below, and far out on the lagoon the sound of a speedboat. He lay with his hands behind his head, waiting for his wife to come to him. The erection tenting the sheet that covered him was a joint enterprise, sponsored by the hot sun (which always made him horny), the promise inherent in Connie's whispered lunchtime suggestion that "a nap later" might be a good idea, and the coconut-scented proximity of a gray-eyed woman who, he admitted, had done much to inspire unbridled passion. Hands behind his head, he lay staring up at the ceiling. Connie had been wearing only her bikini panties and her high-heeled sandals when she'd gone into the bathroom. The bra top to the red bikini lay on the dresser top, where she'd thrown it beside the calendar she normally carried in her cosmetics case. He envisioned taking off the bikini panties and fucking her with just the high-heeled sandals on. He envisioned fucking her tirelessly, all afternoon long. He imagined taking pictures of her with his cock in her mouth, a drop of semen glistening on her lower lip.

He could remember once—this was when they were first married, before she'd got pregnant—when he'd shot four rolls of color film with the camera relentlessly focused on Connie's pert, snub-nosed breasts. *Touch them, honey, make the nipples pop,* Connie turning this way and that, cupping her breasts, stroking the rubescent nipples till they were hard and pouting, basking in the admiration of the camera eye. He had developed an erection of heroic proportions and had finally all but raped her where she lay spread for him on the white shag rug, her hands still clutching her breasts, the nipples bursting through her spread fingers. When he told her later he wanted to try selling the portfolio somewhere, she said, "No way. To you it's a portfolio, to me it's dirty pictures."

When finally she came out of the bathroom, he took one look at her face and knew the afternoon was shot. He didn't even have to ask her. He knew exactly what had happened. The calendar should have been his clue. She must have taken a look at the calendar before going into the bathroom to examine herself.

"What is it?" he asked.

"What do you *think* it is?" she said.

She was naked. She had taken off the bikini panties and the high-heeled sandals, and now she went angrily to the dresser and picked up a hairbrush and began brushing her hair.

"I thought we were going to take a nap," he said.

"That's *just* what we're going to do," she said.

He longed to touch her. He longed for her to steal a sidelong glance at the erection still threatening the white sheet. He longed for her to come to the bed, and pull back the sheet. She kept brushing her hair.

"Why don't you come over here?" he said.

"No."

"I thought we were . . ."

"Shut up," she said, "I'm counting."

"I don't hear you counting."

"In my head."

"Well, stop counting and come over here."

"It's been thirty-two days," she said. "The calendar's right."

"What?"

"I got my period thirty-two days ago."

"Is that what you were counting?"

"Yes."

"I thought you were counting your goddamn *brush* strokes."

"No, I was counting the days. I should have got it four days ago. The calendar's right."

"You've been late before," he said.

"Never four days late. Except when . . ."

"You've been four days late. You've been *five* days late, in fact. In fact, you've been a *week* late, in fact."

"Four days is very late," she said.

"In that case, let's take advantage of it."

"What do you mean?"

"If you're pregnant, let's fuck our brains out," he said, and threw back the sheet.

"Terrific," she said. "Go stick it up your ass."

"How about *your* ass?" he said.

"Don't be disgusting."

"Or your mouth. Is your *mouth* four days late, too?"

"I don't feel like sex right now," she said.

"At lunch, you sounded as if you felt like sex."

"At lunch, I *did* feel like sex. I don't feel like it now."

"Connie . . . it's only four fucking *days*," he said.

"Yes, but we did it at a bad time last month."

"You were wearing your diaphragm," he said.

"Yes, but you came inside me before I went to put it on."

"I did *not* come inside you, damn it! You got up almost the minute we . . ."

"I meant you put it in me."

"So what? If I didn't *come* . . ."

"Men dribble."

"Oh, Jesus," he said.

"They do."

"Okay. Okay, fine."

"It takes only one sperm to . . ."

"Forget it."

"It does. And four days is very late."

"Okay. I said okay, so okay, the hell with it."

"It's not *you* who'd have to march around with a big fucking belly for nine months."

"You don't *know* you're pregnant, it's only been . . ."

"It's not *you* who'd have to give up everything to take care of a goddamn runny-nosed . . ."

"Oh, shit, here we go again."

"Yes, here we go again, you bastard. If you made me pregnant . . ."

"Yes, *what?* What if I made you pregnant?"

"I'd *hate* you," she said.

He was silent for a moment. Then he said, "You already do, don't you?"

She did not answer him. She went into the bathroom instead, and in a little while he heard the shower running. He took his cock in his hand.

In his fantasy, Lynda was wearing black panties, black garter belt, black nylon stockings and black patent-leather, high-heeled shoes. She refused to take off the panties, refused even to allow his caressing hand inside them until the thin fabric covering her crotch was wet with her own juices. Only then did she permit him to ease the panties down over her rounded belly and the flat reddish-brown triangle of her pubic hair, her hips raised to accommodate him, past her thighs and knees, the nylon crackling over the nylon of her stockings, she herself finally pedaling the panties over her shins and kicking them off her ankles and her feet.

In his fantasy, she positioned herself so that her mouth was just above him, and then relentlessly sucked him till he was begging her to make him come. She smiled knowingly and took her questing mouth from him, her unmoving fingers tight around his cock, a ring of flesh that refused either retreat or release, the erection stubbornly maintained, the orgasm denied. She straddled him then and rode him furiously, her breasts bobbing wildly, and then uncannily stopped just as he was about to come, leaning forward to kiss him on the mouth, her breasts flattening against his chest, her cunt as motionless as death, his cock still impaling her, pulsing inside her, his little death denied, the juices subsiding inside his shaft like a thin line of mercury in a thermometer. She started again almost at once, bringing him again to the edge of orgasm, her witch's instinct telling her when to stop, and start again, and stop again, each time just as he was almost there, almost, *almost,* not a word spoken, knowing each time, achieving the effect if not the reality of orgasm with each aborted rush of semen to the base of his shaft.

And then, in his fantasy, she whispered, "Tell me what to say in English," and he said, "Say fuck me," and she repeated the words, "Fuck me," softly at first, whispering them, "Fuck me," and then more loudly, "Fuck me," and finally allowed him to burst inside her, "Fuck me, oh, fuck me," her own screaming orgasm drowning the roar of his blood, his cock mindlessly spurting.

In the bathroom, the shower was still running.

The boys had built a huge bonfire on the sand, digging a hole first and leaving the displaced sand around it in a circle, to facilitate smothering the embers later on. At 3:00 P.M., the day was still suffocatingly hot, and so the kids stayed in the water for at least another half-hour, and then came out onto the sand and briskly toweled themselves by the fire. One of the girls had been swimming without a top; Lissie found this daring and in fact a bit sluttish, and was happy to see her putting on a T-shirt now.

The boys had brought along the hot dogs and the beer, and the girls had contributed all the rest of the food, the way the girls in Rutledge did whenever there was a picnic. Lissie herself had made the potato salad, using a recipe her grandmother had provided, and she was pleased to see that it disappeared almost at once. The girl who'd been swimming topless had made a jelly mold that lost the vote, but the girl folksinger had baked a carrot cake that was positively the most delicious thing Lissie had ever tasted. Everybody kept saying she should go into business. The girl's name was Patty, and when Warren suggested that she call her enterprise "Patty Cakes," he actually got a round of applause.

They sat around the fire on blankets afterward, drinking beer and smoking pot. Warren put his arm around her. She hoped he wouldn't try to kiss her or anything, especially in broad daylight. In all her seventeen years, she'd kissed only four boys, the last of whom had been a kid named Alex Bowles, who'd kissed her openmouthed behind the ice-hockey rink at Henderson State Penitentiary and then immediately began fumbling inside her blouse for her minuscule breasts, scaring her half out of her wits. Her mother kept telling her she was very young for her age. Lissie supposed she was—*maybe*—but she didn't like being told she was immature, which was what her mother was saying despite the euphemism.

It was Pete Turner, the boy from Princeton, who started talking about what had happened at Chappaquiddick, over on the Vineyard, the day before. Well, actually, it had happened two nights ago, but yesterday was when all the papers printed the story, and everybody on the Cape seemed to be talking about nothing else. In fact, Lissie had been surprised last night, when her parents finally called from Sardinia, to discover they knew nothing at all about it. She'd read them the story from the *Boston Globe,* at transatlantic telephone rates, and her father said only, "Something, huh?" There had been the sound of music in the background, and both her parents had sounded very, very distant.

Pete wanted to know what everybody else in America wanted to know: Why the hell had Kennedy driven over that bridge to begin with? "Let's say it's *true* he was taking her to catch the ferry to Edgartown, okay?" he said. "Then why . . .?"

"What was her name, anyway?" one of the girls said.

"Mary something."

"Mary Jo."

"A Polish name."

"Kapachnik or something."

"Kopechne," Warren said.

"Never mind why he drove over the bridge," one of the other boys said. "What *I* want to know is what they were *doing* at that party."

"Well, what do you *think* they were doing?" Pete said.

"He was probably stoned," one of the girls ventured.

"No question," Patty said.

"The road to the ferry was a main road," Pete said.

"Black-topped," another boy said.

"So why'd he make a right turn toward the bridge?"

"He was probably taking her to the beach," Patty said.

"Give her a little Kennedy *shtup*," one of the boys said.

"They're famous for that, the Kennedys."

"Who says?" Lissie asked.

"Oh, come on, John Kennedy was fucking around all the while he was in the White House."

"You don't know that for a fact," Warren said.

"They *all* do," somebody else said, *"all* the presidents. That's the part of history they never tell us about."

"Well, they told us about Harding. Harding had a mistress, didn't he?"

"Oh, sure. But only after he was long dead."

"How can you have a mistress after you're long dead?" someone asked, and everyone laughed.

"My mother's maiden name was Harding," Lissie said, and realized at once how inappropriate her comment had been.

"Kennedy was the worst of them all," Pete said, ignoring her. "He used to send a limo to pick up this actress who was working Off Broadway."

"Who told you that?" the girl who'd been swimming topless said.

"I know people in the theater," Pete said mysteriously. "She used to come out the stage door, and a Secret Service man would drive her straight to where Kennedy was waiting."

"Where was he waiting?"

"Who the hell knows?" Pete said, and shrugged. "The point is it runs in the family. They probably had a few drinks at the party, maybe smoked a little grass . . ."

"You think politicians smoke grass?" Patty asked.

"Sure," one of the boys said. *"Everybody* smokes grass. They just dump on us kids because we're easy targets."

"I'll bet *Nixon* doesn't smoke any fuckin' grass."

"Nixon doesn't even *fuck,"* the topless swimmer said.

"Nixon's a fag, you want my opinion," Patty said.

"Waited a full nine hours to report it," Pete said, getting back to the subject. "Why'd he do that?"

"Because he was taking her to the beach to *shtup* her, and he was stoned, and he drove the fucking car in the water . . ."

"And could only think of saving his own ass."

"He's *still* trying to save his ass," the topless swimmer said. "When's he going to make some kind of public statement?"

"They say he'll be going on TV soon," somebody said.

"Another Checkers speech," Pete said sourly.

"What's that?"

"A speech Nixon made one time. His dog. His dog was named Checkers."

"What?" Patty said, and burst out laughing.

"Well, what's so funny about that?"

"What's his *dog* got to do with anything?"

"You're the big protest singer, you never heard of Nixon's Checkers speech?"

"Never."

"It's only famous, that's all," one of the boys said.

"Who here ever heard of the Checkers speech?" Patty said, and looked around the fire. Pete and the other boy were the only ones who raised their hands. "Very famous," Patty said.

"He's a crook like all the rest of them," somebody said.

"Who, Nixon?"

"No, his fucking dog," somebody said, and they all burst out laughing.

"I'll bet he gets away with it, though," Warren said.

"Kennedy? Sure, he will."

"They *all* get away with it," the topless swimmer said.

"This fucking country," Pete said, and shook his head. "They keep telling *us* what to do, they keep hassling *us* about everything, but meanwhile *they're* cheating on their income tax, and killing off their business competitors, and fucking around outside their marriages, chasing the buck day and night, running in their gray flannel suits to catch their commuter trains, briefcases flying, drinking themselves silly in the bar car on the way home." His voice lowered, he sat staring into the flames. "You sometimes have to *pour* my father off the train," he said.

The fire crackled and spit into the sudden silence.

"I *hate* this fucking country," he said.

In Italy, it was a little after 10:00 P.M.

They had taken their meal in the main dining room, and now they sat on the stone terrace overlooking the lagoon and the spindly dock jutting out jaggedly over the water. Jamie was drinking cognac, Connie was idly sipping an Amaretto. When the bartender wheeled a television set out onto the terrace, neither of them noticed him at first. He spent the next five minutes searching for an extension cord and an outlet, and another five manipulating the rabbit ears on top of the set. None of the people on the terrace knew quite what he was up to. There was still the pleasant hum of conversation as the black-and-white picture came on, the clink of ice in late-night drinks. A woman laughed far too loudly, and someone said "Shhh!" and she answered him in French which Jamie took to be insulting; French always sounded insulting to him. A man across the terrace said, in English, "Oh, look, it's the moon thing," and Jamie looked up over his head and indeed saw a bright crescent moon in a sky laden with brilliant stars, and somebody else said, in Italian, *"Attenzione!"* and the woman who'd insulted (he guessed) the man in French suddenly turned her attention to the picture on the television screen and said, *"Les astronautes,"* which even Jamie understood.

He had not read a newspaper since he'd left the States on the twelfth, but he'd heard other Americans talking about the Apollo-11 blast-off for the moon several days ago. This was the twentieth, he guessed—he had virtually lost all track of time—and he supposed the spaceship was approaching the moon, else why all the elaborate fuss with the television set? The picture was a very bad one, flaked with snow and streaked with vertical lines, but he recognized Houston Control from previous space shots he'd watched on television, and as he turned his attention fully to the set, he heard a voice clearly saying, "Thirty seconds," and another static-ridden voice replied, ". . . drifting right . . . contact light . . .

90

okay, engine stop . . . ACA out of . . . modes control both auto . . . engine arm, off . . . four-thirteen is in." The first voice said, "We copy you down, Eagle."

Jamie caught his breath.

The distant voice, clearly and sharply this time, said, "Houston, Tranquility Base here. The Eagle has landed."

The voice from Houston said, "Roger, Tranquility, we copy you on the ground. You've got a bunch of guys about to turn blue. We're breathing again. Thanks a lot," and suddenly everyone on the terrace was on his feet, Americans and foreigners alike, all of them applauding the television set as the voice from outer space said, "A very smooth touchdown," and Houston replied, "Eagle, you are stay for T-1." Something garbled from up there on the moon in the sky overhead, and then Houston said, "Roger, and we see you venting the ox," and suddenly the foreigners on the terrace turned to those who were obvious Americans and began applauding *them*—Jamie and Connie, and a dentist and his wife from Michigan, and a pair of newlyweds from upstate New York, and an eighty-year-old woman from San Francisco. The Frenchwoman summoned the waiter with a sharp *"Garçon!"* and then shouted, *"Champagne pour tout le monde!"* and everyone applauded again, first the generous Frenchwoman, and then the Americans once more, and finally the screen where Houston was saying, "We have an unofficial time for that touchdown of one hundred and two hours, forty-five minutes, forty-two seconds and we will update that."

As the champagne corks popped, Jamie was surprised to find tears rolling down his cheeks. He guessed it was because he was so goddamn proud of his country's achievement.

No sooner were they home than they were off again.
This time in August. This time for a long weekend with Penny Lane
and his wife on the Vineyard, though in all fairness the Lanes *had*
invited her along as well, an invitation Lissie had politely declined,
thank you. On Friday afternoon, she phoned the Vineyard to say
that she and Rusty had decided to drive up to Woodstock. Her
father asked, "Where's Woodstock?" and she told him it was
upstate New York someplace, they were only going up there to
listen to some rock. Her mother had wanted assurance that Mrs.
Klein knew Rusty was taking the car, and had asked only that
Lissie call the Vineyard again when she got home that night.

It became apparent almost at once that there'd be no getting
home that night, and maybe even no getting to the festival. They
had taken Route 84 west to the Newburgh Bridge, and had crossed
that onto 87 north, heading in the general direction of the Catskills.
There was no index listing for a town called Woodstock on their
Mobil map, nor was there one for either Bethel or White Lake. But
as they got closer to their destination—or at least *assumed* they
were getting closer—they began to see kids. Kids wearing feathers

and cut-offs and open vests and ponchos and T-shirts and minis and capes, kids waving to them from VW buses and campers and cars painted with psychedelic designs, pickup trucks with license plates from California, a dusty Benz with a plate from Colorado, kids on motorcycles and motorbikes, kids crammed into beat-up campus Fords or sleek family Cadillacs, a Chrysler flapping a banner with the words KEEP AMERICA BEAUTIFUL—STAY STONED lettered on it, kids leaning out the windows, waving, kids holding placards that read HEAD POWER, kids clutching guitars, girls with flowers twined in their long flowing hair, boys with beards and beads, a massive army of kids in cars and on foot, thronging the approach road to the festival site.

Overheated cars lined the side of the road, their hoods up, their owners smiling and waving as the line of traffic inched past. A grinning boy flashed a placard lettered THIS IS WHERE IT'S AT, BABY! A tall blond girl, naked from the waist up, a garland of wild flowers around her neck, sat on the fender of a green Chevy and strummed a guitar while her boyfriend fiddled with the cap on the water reservoir. A geyser of steam went up behind her, and she leaped off the fender, grinning, and then sat by the side of the road and serenely resumed her strumming. More and more of the kids were abandoning their cars by the side of the road, cars that were overheated, cars that simply couldn't budge in the traffic jam. They rolled up the windows in defense against the threatening rain clouds overhead, but they left the cars unlocked, heaving knapsacks, sleeping bags and guitars onto their backs, slinging water canteens from their belts as they began walking up the road, threading their way through the stalled cars and the masses of other kids on foot. Rusty swung the car up onto the shoulder in a space between a camper painted with sunbursts and a Dodge with a Michigan license plate. Together, she and Lissie began walking toward where everybody else was going.

It was beginning to rain, gently, but both girls were grinning from ear to ear.

The welcoming party on the Vineyard that Friday night was to have started at six-thirty, in anticipation of the six-fifty-seven sunset, Perry and Laura Lane apparently having come to their vacation paradise fully equipped with an almanac and a stopwatch. The rain began shortly after five, though, and the Vineyard summer people, used to the vagaries of the weather and the uncertainties of promised sunsets, did not begin arriving until almost seven-thirty, by which time the tentative drizzle had turned into a raging downpour. All notions of cocktails on the deck had been abandoned by then, and the score or more invited guests crowded into a living room the size of the one the Crofts had endured on West Seventy-eighth Street before fame and fortune had smiled upon them more beneficently than the weather tonight.

The guests were the usual Martha's Vineyard summer residents (or denizens, as Jamie preferred to call them) with one exception: a dazzling young blonde wearing a gold-link halter top over nothing but skintight black velvet pants and gold slippers that added a good three inches to her already substantial height. She came in on the arm of a frail septuagenarian who seemed bewildered by the noise and the crowd. Immediately behind the mismatched couple was a writer who, for the last twenty years, had been grinding out dull potboilers, but who (on the basis of a single well-received book this year) had landed foursquare in the center of the Literary Establishment. But so it goes, Jamie thought, and studied the blonde's ample naked chest under the gold-link top.

The top had been acquired in Rome, the girl promptly informed her hosts, during the filming of *Cleopatra* seven years before when she was just eighteen and an on-the-spot observer of one of the most publicized romances in the past decade. Jamie politely and dutifully told the literary mafioso how much he'd enjoyed his new novel, and then—being a photographer, after all—said, "You're much taller than I guessed you were from the jacket photo." The writer unblinkingly answered, "I write short," and then immediately turned his back to Jamie and greeted another writer who had written a best seller ten years ago, but nothing since.

There was, Jamie had learned from past experience, something distantly chilling about these "authors," never any plain and simple "writers" in this tight clique of scribblers who had earned the mantle of immortality during their lifetimes. He listened now as the two lionized scribes began comparing notes about how much one of the hand-tooled leatherbound book clubs was offering them for their priceless autographs on their respective novels. The newly elected *capo* had been offered two dollars a signature, the unheard-from-since soldier only a buck and a half. But both had been informed that they could actually *sign* the books anywhere in the world they chose, at the club's expense, and the one who wrote short, and talked the same way, was saying he thought he'd opt for

94

Hong Kong. No one had yet mentioned Jamie's photographs in the current issue of *New York*.

Someone began playing the piano; on the Vineyard, someone *always* began playing the piano. The someone in this case was the composer of a current Off Broadway hit, and he sang without perfection the show's eleven o'clock number, which was presently flooding the airwaves day and night. A woman photographer, who'd been introduced to Jamie as Bertha Somebody-or-other, began playing the bongos along with the composer, and another woman who—ages ago, judging from her appearance—had danced with Martha Graham, took off her shoes and began free-expressing herself all over the small, cramped, tightly packed living room. Two or three hardy souls wandered out onto the deck to watch the gray water, oblivious to the pouring rain. A young girl whose father owned one of New York's biggest imported-wine outlets told the Lanes she'd just signed a singing contract with Capitol Records, and Perry Lane asked her if she wouldn't do some of her own songs for them. The composer of the Off Broadway hit, who had by then run out of his own repertoire of tunes, happily agreed to accompany her. The first song she sang was something titled "Blue Roses," a title which immediately brought to Jamie's mind Tennessee Williams's famous "pleurosis" malapropism, an association apparently lost on the song's nubile creator. Jamie wandered out to the kitchen to mix himself another drink.

The actress in the gold-link top *(was* she an actress? If not, what had she been doing on the *Cleopatra* set?) was standing at the sink, engaged in earnest conversation with Laura Lane. Neither of them even looked at Jamie as he came into the room. He quietly poured two fingers of Scotch into a washed jelly glass, added three ice cubes to it, and was leaving the kitchen when he heard Laura say, somewhat heatedly, "Well, it's *your* business, but *I'd* advise against it." She stormed past Jamie without saying a word to him, and shoved through the swinging door to the living room, where the strains of "Blue Roses" flooded the salt-laden air. The girl in the gold-link top kept staring into the sink.

"You okay?" Jamie asked.

"Fine," she said.

"I'm Jamie Croft," he said.

"Mm," she said, and nodded briefly and walked out of the kitchen past him.

In the living room, the newly signed Capitol Records recording artist had finished "Blue Roses" to a standing ovation, and was resisting the pleas of the crowd for another song. The crowd prevailed. She told the Off Broadway composer which chart to play for the next song, told him what key she sang it in, and hummed a few bars so he'd get the gist of it. Apparently he'd heard her singing the song at another Vineyard party long before she'd got her recording contract; he launched into it familiarly. The title, Jamie gathered from the first few bars, was "Antelope City."

He wandered over to a battered Victorian couch on the far side of the room, away from the piano, and sat next to a man who introduced himself as Alex Namath, "no relation to Joe." Alex was with the *New York Times,* and he immediately began lamenting Nixon's plea to Congress the month before, urging passage of a bill that would stop the flow of drugs at their foreign sources ("Antelope City," the girl sang, "slow-pokey pretty"), provide stringent penalties for violations of federal drug laws ("Dusky-dawn ditty"), and permit federal narcotics agents with search warrants to enter private dwellings unannounced.

In Woodstock, New York, 400,000 kids were openly smoking marijuana in the rain, and listening to the rock star Richie Havens exclaiming into a microphone, "Wow! Phew! I mean like wow! *Phew!"*

She could not have got to a telephone even if she wanted to, but she was so overwhelmed by the sheer *excitement* of it all that long before dusk, she'd completely forgotten the promise to her mother. The festival site had been leased from a dairy farmer named Max Yasgur who by now must have been entertaining second thoughts about the whole idea. He certainly could not have had any notion that his six hundred acres would be turned overnight into the third largest city in New York State, a city without adequate food, shelter, water or sanitation facilities. Nor could he have surmised that a modestly proposed "music and art fair" would become a tribal gathering of such enormous proportions. Then again, neither could anyone else in the United States have reckoned that so *many* damn kids could convene at the drop of a hat to express the ideas and feelings of an entire generation.

The rain had stopped—but who cared about rain? The field was a quagmire—but who gave a damn about mud? On the loudspeaker system, one of the festival's twenty-four-year-old promoters was warning that somebody in the crowd was selling bad acid, but Lissie hadn't seen anyone shooting dope, and the Sullivan County cops weren't even making any marijuana busts. How could they? This was one gigantic smoke-in, one coming together of the Age of Aquarius, one enormous reaffirmation of the *love* people as opposed to the *hate* people. In Vietnam tonight, the airplanes were maybe defoliating the jungles with napalm, and the soldiers were maybe on vill sweeps in the boonies. But here in America, the *heart* of America, the *future* of America, the kids were offering each other food and pot and water and solace and sympathy and Lissie had never in her life felt more a part of something truly important.

At eleven that night, while the party was still in full swing, Jamie learned from the television set in the Lanes' bedroom that the Woodstock Music and Art Fair had mushroomed beyond the wildest expectations of its promoters and that half the kids in the nation (or so it seemed) were crammed onto the upstate New York site, sleeping in the open or in tents, and passing around marijuana as if it were salted peanuts. He had come upstairs to escape a rendition of "Falling in Love Again" by a sixty-year-old lady who began her impression of Marlene Dietrich by straddling a chair and inadvertently showing her lacy black panties to a somewhat startled audience. When she showed her panties a second time, Jamie decided the exhibition was something less than accidental, and he eased his way through the crowd, found the steps leading to the second story of the house, and—drink in hand—climbed stealthily upstairs.

He had nothing more in mind than flopping onto the paisley-covered bed in the guest room, but he'd had a little more to drink than was normally good for him, and as he came down the narrow hallway he felt the familiar buzz that told him he was on the thin edge of inebriation. When he looked into the Lanes' bedroom, he thought it was his own, his own for the *weekend* at any rate, except that he couldn't remember a television set in his room. He went into the room, sat on the floor in front of the set, searched for the on-off volume control, found it, and then scanned the channels for a news report, finally getting one originating in Boston.

In near-intoxicated wonder, he listened while the commentator told all about the appalling lack of toilet facilities at the Woodstock festival, the drenching rain that had turned the festival site into a semblance of a World War I battlefield, the lines of automobiles still backed up for fifteen miles in any direction from White Lake, the half-naked boys and girls romping in the mud. He was calmed somewhat, but only somewhat, when the commentator mentioned that there had been only one short-tempered incident thus far, an argument between two boys, which was promptly squelched when all the kids around them began chanting, "Peace, peace." The festival-goers, in fact, seemed to be in exceptionally high spirits despite the rain (Small wonder, Jamie thought, with all that dope around), helping each other to cope with the elements and inadequate facilities.

"There hasn't been a single fistfight," the commentator said, "and it's impossible to believe that anything like a rape or a stabbing could occur here at Woodstock this weekend. The message here is love. Soggy, but loud and clear nonetheless." The commentator paused, looked at his notes, and then said, "An Australian-American board of inquiry into the June third collision between . . ."

"That's what the message should be *all* the time," a voice behind Jamie said.

He turned from where he was sitting cross-legged before the television set. The blonde in the gold-link top was standing in the doorway to the bedroom, leaning against the jamb, a drink in her hand.

"Love," she said.

". . . and the Australian carrier *Melbourne* in the South China . . ."

"Why don't you turn that off?" she said.

". . . concluded that the American ship . . ."

He snapped off the television set.

"I was rude to you," she said. "I'm Joanna Berkowitz. I should have introduced myself when we talked in the kitchen."

"Well, don't worry about it," he said.

"You're the photographer, aren't you?"

"*A* photographer."

"With the marvelous pictures in *New York* this week."

"Thank you."

"When did you take them?"

"In March."

"The kids all looked cold."

"They *were* cold," Jamie said, and nodded. "Very cold night."

"I loved that one of the old men playing checkers."

"I liked that one, too." He drank from his glass, and looked up at her. "What did you think of Marlene downstairs?"

"Sort of sad. Harrison told me she was a beauty when she was young."

"Who's Harrison?"

"The man I came with."

"Ah, yes, Harrison. Knew her when she was younger, did he?"

"Harrison knew *everybody* when they were younger," she said, and smiled.

"*Was* younger," Jamie said. "When *he* was younger."

"Yes, Harrison."

"No, *everybody*," Jamie said.

"I'm not following you."

"Everybody. Singular. Everybody *was* younger."

"Oh."

"Right." He nodded, swallowed what was left in his glass, and said, "Pain in the ass, right? People who correct your grammar."

"People who correct *one's* grammar," she said.

"Touché," he said, and nodded again. "What are you drinking there, Joanna?"

"Scotch."

"May I have a sip of it? My glass seems to be empty."

She walked into the room and extended her own glass to him. He took it, turned it so that the lipstick stain was away from his lips, and drank from it.

He studied her face, the good cheekbones and generous mouth, the large brown eyes fringed with thick dark lashes, her nose a bit too long for her face, and rather thin and finely sculpted, a Mediterranean nose, he supposed one could say, yes, it could have been Greek or Italian, but of course it was Jewish, a spate of freckles across its bridge and splashing subtly onto one cheek—

"Something?" she asked.

"No, no," he said, and immediately and idiotically added, "I like your top."

She looked at him and said nothing. Turning, she walked out of the room, leaving him with the remainder of her Scotch and little else.

The rain started again shortly after midnight, a downpour that turned the already inundated festival site into a pockmarked morass of shallow pools. Running through the rain, giggling, holding sodden newspapers over their heads, Rusty and Lissie

99

finally found dubious shelter under a huge maple. A girl poked her head out of a tent pitched nearby, glanced briefly and disconsolately at the rain, and then spotted them where they were standing under the tree.

"Hey! Come in out of the rain!" she called.

They hesitated.

"Well, come *on!*" she called again, and disappeared inside the tent.

"You want to?" Rusty asked.

"Sure," Lissie said, "why not?" and both girls ran to the tent and scrambled in under the flap.

"Really coming down again," the girl said. She was wearing only red panties under a blanket that was draped over her shoulders and hanging unevenly to just above her knees. She was a rather plump girl, with marvelous blue eyes and dark hair, the planes of her square face catching light from a kerosene lamp resting on a blanket in the center of the tent. Sitting on the blanket was a bearded boy wearing a Harvard T-shirt and blue jeans, struggling to open a can of sardines with the can-opener blade of a Swiss army knife.

"Lost the key," he said, looking up and grinning, and then getting back to work with the can opener.

"I'm Suzie," the girl said.

"Hi, I'm Rusty."

"Lissie."

"Judd," the boy said.

"You look drowned," Suzie said. "You want a towel?"

"We sure could use one," Rusty said.

Suzie knelt beside one of the knapsacks, the blanket hanging loose over her naked breasts. She rummaged for a towel, found one, and handed it to Rusty, who—immediately and to Lissie's enormous surprise—promptly peeled off her wet T-shirt, and began briskly toweling her back, her shoulders and her breasts.

"That's the only dry one," Suzie said.

"I think there's another one in my knapsack," Judd said, not looking up from the stubborn can of sardines.

"I can use this one," Lissie said, "that's okay."

"Might as well take the dry one," Judd said, and put down the can of sardines and the knife, and rose from his cross-legged position on the blanket to walk to the other side of the tent. She was surprised to see how tall he was, six one, six two, she guessed, a

100

gangly boy with long stringy blond hair and a shaggy beard, all knobby elbows and long legs as he bent over his knapsack and began digging into it.

"I'm *sure* there's one in here," he said, and began tossing rolled clothing onto another blanket partially soaked through from the wet ground under it.

"It's okay, really," Lissie said. "I can use the one Rusty's—"

"No trouble," Judd said, and kept tossing clothes onto the blanket. "Here we go," he said, and rose again, and carried the towel to where Lissie was standing.

"Thanks," she said, and began drying her hair. Rusty was standing some three feet away from her, the other towel draped around her neck now, hanging loosely over her breasts.

"Sure glad we brought the tent," Suzie said.

"Oh, yeah," Judd said, and went to work again on the sardine can. "Where's that cheese?" he asked. "Give these guys some cheese. You had anything to eat today?"

"We grabbed some hot dogs before they ran out," Rusty said.

"Something, huh?" Judd said. "Wouldn't have missed it for the world. Where you guys from?"

"Connecticut," Lissie said.

"We're up in Boston," Suzie said. "You'd better take off that wet shirt."

"Well," Lissie said.

"Catch a cold otherwise," Suzie said.

"Yeah, I guess so," Lissie said. She hesitated a moment, and then pulled the wet T-shirt over her head. Embarrassed, she turned her back at once, and began drying herself.

Suzie was passing around the wedge of cheddar cheese on a paper plate. "What'd you do with the good knife?" she asked Judd.

"Over there someplace," he said, and then—triumphantly as he opened the sardine can—"Ah-*ha!*" He dipped his forefinger into the oil, brought it to his lips, licked at it and said, "Good. Want some sardines, anybody?"

"Mm, thanks, I'm starved," Rusty said.

Lissie still had her back to the others. She hung the towel around her neck, the way Rusty had, and then—before she turned—arranged it so that the folds were covering her breasts.

"There's some bread, too," Suzie said. "Where's the bread, Judd?"

"Right there."

"Listen to that rain."

They sat cross-legged around the kerosene lamp, passing around the cheese and sardines.

"We could use some beer," Judd said.

"All gone," Suzie said.

"Where do you guys go to school?" Judd asked.

"I'll be starting Bennington in the fall," Rusty said.

"How about you?"

"Brenner," Lissie said. "Also in the fall."

"That's near us," Suzie said. "I'm at B.U."

"Boston's a great city," Judd said. "You'll really dig it."

"Brenner's a nice school," Suzie said. "We know lots of kids at Brenner."

"What are you majoring in?" Rusty asked.

"Pot," Judd said.

"Speaking of which," Suzie said, and got to her feet, almost tripping over the tails of the blanket.

"Let's finish off the food first," Judd said.

"Where'd you put it?" Suzie asked.

"Never *can* find anything," Judd said, smiling. "The pocket on my knapsack."

"You guys smoke?" Suzie said.

"Oh, sure," Rusty said.

"Who doesn't?" Judd said.

Lissie hadn't realized until now just how hungry she was. She cut herself another huge wedge of cheese, dipped a sardine out of the oil, put both on a slice of white bread, and unashamedly devoured the open-faced sandwich in what seemed to her like thirty seconds.

"Have some more," Judd said.

"Thanks," she said, and cut herself another wedge of cheese.

"Bread, too," he said. "Plenty of bread. Damn, I *wish* we hadn't run out of beer."

"Maybe we can get some tomorrow," Suzie said, coming back to the blanket with a small plastic bag of marijuana.

"Yeah, but I'd like it *now*," Judd said.

"Everything has to be *now* with him," Suzie said, smiling and shaking her head.

"Better than later, right?" Judd said.

The sand was still wet from the earlier downpour. Behind him, coming from the Lanes' rented house on the dunes, Jamie could hear the muted sound of someone playing a guitar and someone else singing along. He had requisitioned a half-empty bottle of Scotch from the kitchen counter, and a plastic cup from one of the cabinets, and had wandered down the rickety steps leading to the beach, eager for a breath of fresh air and a respite from the noise. He had left his shoes at the foot of the steps, and rolled his trousers midway to his shins. The sand was cool underfoot. The water gently nudged the shore.

He saw, at first, only the gold of her top and the blond of her hair catching whatever faint light filtered to the beach from the house above. She was sitting alone on a black raincoat spread on the sand, smoking, looking out over the water. She seemed engrossed in thought; he almost turned to walk up the beach in the opposite direction—but she had already seen him. He hesitated, and then went to where she was sitting.

"Hello," he said.

"Hello," she answered, and sucked on the cigarette. He realized all at once that it was marijuana.

"Think it's going to clear up?" he asked.

"Who cares?" she said, and shrugged.

"Would you like a drink?" he asked, and extended the plastic cup.

She shook her head. "Would you like a toke?" she asked, and extended the joint.

"I don't smoke," he said, and sat on the raincoat beside her. "Okay to sit?" he asked belatedly.

She nodded, inhaled on the joint again, extended it to him again, and said, "Are you sure?"

"Positive."

"Generation gap," she said, and shrugged again.

"Tell me all about the generation gap," he said, and smiled. "I have a seventeen-year-old daughter."

"Seventeen isn't twenty-five, my generation isn't your daughter's. Anyway, it really doesn't matter, does it?"

"I don't think my daughter smokes pot, either," he said.

"Doesn't she? Well, well."

"*You* think she does."

"I don't know what she does."

"But you *suspect* she does."

"Well, really, who gives a shit?"

They fell silent. He sipped at his Scotch. She dropped the stub of the joint, and then brushed sand over it with her hand. He had the feeling he should leave. He was intruding on her privacy; she obviously wanted to be alone with her thoughts.

"Are you an actress?" he asked.

"An actress? No. What makes you think that?"

"You were talking about being in Rome for *Cleopatra* . . ."

"Oh, that. I was there with my father, he was trying to get a job scoring the film. He's a musician." She paused. "So am I."

"Oh? What do you play?"

"The flute."

"The flute," he said, nodding.

"I'm a flutician, as my teacher would put it." She paused. "Julie Baker."

"Am I supposed to know her?"

"*Him*. And yes. Well, I mean, *most* people who know music know who Julius Baker is."

"Who is he?"

"I gather you don't know music."

"I don't."

"Well, it doesn't matter. Let's just say he's a very good flutist."

"Do you play professionally?"

"Yes, of course."

"Where?"

"I'm with the New York City Opera Orchestra. We start rehearsing next week for the new season."

"I never thought of music as being seasonal."

"Well, of course it is. Come on, you know that. Don't you ever . . . I mean, haven't you ever been to the Philharmonic? Or a ballet? I mean . . . well, of *course* it's seasonal. All of it's seasonal. Well, wait, I take that back. I guess if you're in the pit at *Fiddler*, that isn't seasonal. But most orchestras, sure, they're seasonal."

"And the season starts next week."

"*Rehearsals* for the season, yes."

"When does it end?"

"Sometime in November."

"Then what?"

"I go to Los Angeles for four weeks."

"With the orchestra?"

"Yes. Well, the whole company actually." She paused. "So," she said. "Now you know where I am every minute of the day and night."

"Forgive me," he said, "but . . ."

She looked at him, puzzled.

"I've forgotten your name."

"You're joking," she said. "It's Joanna."

"Your last name, I mean."

"Berkowitz."

"Right. Berkowitz. Right."

"Yes," she said.

"Are you sure you wouldn't like some of this?"

"Well . . . all right. I really shouldn't, though, I've really had enough tonight." She shook her head, and then suddenly laughed. "Last season, one of the fiddlers in the first section got drunk before a performance . . . we were doing *Traviata* . . . not drunk, actually, but a bit high. And he began singing from the pit, I mean actually *singing* out loud along with the coloratura. Do you know the '*fors'è lui*' aria in the first . . .?"

"No, I'm sorry."

"Well, that one. Singing right along with it." She laughed again, and again shook her head. "But I *will* have a sip, thank you."

He poured Scotch into the plastic cup and handed it to her.

"That's yours, isn't it?" she said.

"I'll drink from the bottle."

"Cheers," she said.

"Cheers."

"I can use this, actually. Rough night tonight."

"How so?"

"Endings. I find endings difficult, don't you?"

"Beginnings, too," he said, and smiled.

"How about middles?" she asked, and returned the smile. She sipped again at the Scotch, dug into her handbag for a package of cigarettes, shook one free, and then offered the package to him. "This isn't grass," she said, "you're absolutely safe." He took one of the cigarettes, and struck a match for both of them. She blew out a stream of smoke, and said, "Harrison's married, you see."

"Harrison. The man you came with."

"He's a poet, he teaches a workshop out in Indiana. He wants to divorce his wife and marry me, take me to Indiana with him. There are two children involved, both of them older than I am. Daughters. There must be something about me, all these men working out their oedipal . . ."

"*All* these men?"

105

"Well. . . Harrison primarily. But I've known other men besides Harrison. I mean . . . well . . . I guess you realize that. I was on my own in Rome when I was just eighteen, I guess I *had* to have known at least a few men."

"Yes," he said.

"So," she said and shrugged.

"All of them married?"

"You make it sound like an *army*. There were only three. Two of them were married."

"With daughters?"

"One of them had a daughter, yes," she said, and drained the cup.

"More?" he asked, and extended the bottle.

"I really shouldn't," she said. "I'm really beginning to feel it. The booze, the dope . . . fuck it, let me have some." She held out the cup, and he poured for her. "I told him no. Harrison. I told him I didn't want to go to Indiana. Half an hour ago. Just before I came down here. Told him no." She shook her head. "I guess I did the right thing, who the fuck knows? Fuck it," she said, and drank. "My shrink said it was what I should do. He said . . ."

"You're in analysis, huh?"

"Isn't everyone?" she said. "Ninety-sixth Street is practically my home away from home."

"Is that where he's located?"

"That's where *everybody's* shrink is located. Ninety-sixth, between Madison and Park."

"His name wouldn't be Frank Lipscombe, would it?"

"No. Who's Frank Lipscombe?"

"An analyst I know."

"There must be ten thousand shrinks in New York, maybe on Ninety-sixth alone. Why would *my* shrink be Frank whatever-his-name-is."

"Lipscombe."

"No," she said, and ground her cigarette out in the sand, and sipped at the Scotch again.

"How long have you been seeing him?" he asked.

"Too *damn* long."

"How long is that?"

"Since I met Harrison."

"And when was that?"

"April."

106

"That's not so long ago."

"It's pretty damn long when *you're* twenty-five and *he's* seventy-three. How old are *you?*"

"Forty-two. Well, wait, I just turned forty-three."

"Eighteen years older than I am."

"More or less."

"No, not more or less. Eighteen years is what it is. Which I suppose is an improvement," she said, and shrugged. "How tall are you?"

"Six two. And you?"

"Five ten."

"That's big."

"Yes, I'm a big girl. Tall, anyway. As for mature . . ." She shook her head. "Mandelbaum says I've got to grow up one day."

"Mandelbaum?"

"My shrink. He thinks I'm immature, and a little bit crazy besides."

Suddenly, without realizing he was about to do it, he kissed her. The kiss was brief, it took her as much by surprise as it did him. She looked into his face.

"What was that for?" she asked.

"I'm sorry, forgive me."

"No, that's all right."

"Really, I'm sorry."

She turned away from him and looked out over the sea. They were silent for several moments. Then she said, "Do you do this all the time?"

"No. As a matter of fact . . ." He shook his head.

"Yes, what?"

"Never."

"Uh-huh."

"I'm sorry. Really. I am."

"Never, huh? How long have you been married?"

"Eighteen years."

"And never been tempted."

"Tempted, yes."

"You sound like Jesus in the wilderness."

"Not quite."

"Sorely tempted, but never compromised. Until tonight. Must be my ripe young bod, huh?"

"Joanna . . . I'm sorry. I mean it. Would you like to . . .?"

"Stop being so sorry. It was kind of nice, as a matter of fact. Sort of. Would I like to what?"

"Go back up to the house."

"No. Why? Would you?"

"Not particularly."

"Neither would I." She looked out over the sea again. "I thought you were a jerk, you know. When you said you liked my top. A middle-aged jerk talking euphemistically about my breasts. Well, I do have good breasts, I suppose," she said, and glanced idly down at them. "How'd we get on my breasts, anyway? Maybe we'd *better* go inside."

"If you like."

"Because I hate rushing things, and I get the feeling we're rushing at a headlong pace." She shook her head. "I barely said goodbye to Harrison thirty seconds ago. Are you happily married?"

"Yes."

"Then why'd you kiss me?"

"I guess I wanted to."

"Do you still want to."

"Yes."

"Then kiss me," she said.

He kissed her. The kiss was longer this time. Their lips lingered. When she drew away from him at last, she said, "But that's enough. I've got to be out of my mind. Wait'll Mandelbaum hears this, he'll take a fit."

"Why do you have to tell him?"

"It's costing me fifty dollars an hour, I suppose I *ought* to tell him, don't you? I mean instead of just lying on his couch and looking up at the ceiling. Though he does have a marvelous ceiling. One of those old tin things with curlicues all over it. I can just see Monday. Hey, guess what, doctor? I broke off with Harrison and ten minutes later I was kissing a married stranger on the beach. I've got to be crazy."

He looked at her, studying her face, his eyes accustomed to the semidarkness now, seeing again the freckles he had noticed in the bedroom upstairs, a light dusting on the bridge of her nose and on only one cheek, the high cheekbones and generous mouth—

"Does it meet with your approval?" she asked.

"Yes, it does."

"Nose and all?"

"Especially the nose," he said, and smiled.

"Oh, sure. I *hate* my nose. You don't know how many times I've thought of getting it bobbed."

"Don't."

"Just here," she said, and brought her hand up, exerting the smallest amount of pressure with her forefinger, lifting the tip.

"You're beautiful just the way you are," he said.

"Well . . . thank you," she said, and dropped her hand into her lap again, and looked away shyly.

"Very beautiful," he whispered.

"Thank you." She hesitated and then said, "I find you very attractive, too. But that's just me, I guess. I mean, the older-man thing. And married, of course," she said, and rolled her eyes.

"I guess you've discussed all this with . . ."

"Oh, sure."

"What does he think?"

"He thinks my liaisons, *his* word, are quote dangerous unquote. Do you know you're staring at me?"

"Yes."

"Must be the gorgeous nose."

"Must be."

"If you didn't have a wife inside there . . . you *do* have a wife inside there, don't you?"

"Yes."

"Worse luck, I thought you might have left her home for the weekend. What does she look like?"

"Blond, green eyes, good figure."

"Oh, yes. Pretty."

"If I didn't have a wife inside there . . ." he prompted.

"I'd disgrace myself in the eyes of God and Mandelbaum," she said, and hesitated. "Do you work in the city?"

"Sometimes."

"How often do you come in? God," she said, "I sound like an advertising executive on the make!"

"Once a week, sometimes more often."

"Would you like to call me? I'm in the book, J. Berkowitz on East Sixty-fifth."

"Would you like me to call you?"

"Yes."

He looked at her.

"Call me," she said.

The rain had tapered off, and they stood outside the tent—Judd and Lissie—looking out over the festival site and the myriad small fires that had been started on the sodden ground, glowing against the blackness of the night like blazing galaxies in a distant sky. From where they stood, the ground sloped gently away and they could see across the entire site, could hear the gentle strumming of guitars, the sound of floating laughter, and behind them the patter of leaves dripping raindrops on the forest floor.

"I'll never forget this as long as I live," Judd said.

"Neither will I," Lissie said.

"Want to take a walk down there?"

"Sure."

He lifted the flap of the tent and said, "We're going for a walk, anybody want to come?"

"I'm totaled," Suzie said.

"How about you, Rusty?"

"She's already asleep."

"Okay, see you later," Judd said.

They went down the slope and onto the muddier ground. They were both barefoot, their jeans rolled to their shins. Lissie was wearing a B.U. sweatshirt Suzie had loaned her; Judd had changed from his T-shirt to a plaid flannel shirt as protection against the cool night air.

"Watch out for broken glass," he said.

They walked through the camp, stopping here and there to talk with other kids, all of them still excited from the day's events, all of them eager to trade stories about what for them had been the most thrilling experience in their lives. Scarcely any of them mentioned the performers: the performers were only secondary to this event. Judd and Lissie sat with kids they didn't know, and shared their pot, and warmed themselves by the fires of strangers made friends through a common bond.

They could not have fully explained the bond if they'd tried. It had something to do with being young and being *here* where they were able to express themselves without restraint. It wasn't just being able to smoke pot in the open without fear of arrest or imprisonment, it wasn't just *seeing* all these hundreds of thousands of other kids who looked the way they did, and dressed the way they did, and talked the way they did, all together in one place, stretching from horizon to horizon, some of them acres away from the stage where they could not have seen or even *heard* the performers clearly despite the amplifiers that had blared from eighty-foot-high scaffolds, it wasn't any of that separately, but all of it together. They had got it *together* at last, they had come from everywhere to *do* this thing, to *be* this thing. They *were* the event, a conglomerate entity with a single voice. Us.

As they wandered back leisurely toward the slope upon which the tent was pitched, Judd said, "'A little touch of Harry in the night.'" He saw the puzzled look on her face, and said, "Do you know it?"

"No," she said, "I'm sorry."

"Careful," he said, and extended his hand to help her over a rock ledge. She took his hand. He did not release it when they were on firm ground again.

"Henry the Fifth," he said. "The scene before the battle. When he's walking through the camp, talking to the soldiers. He's in disguise, you know . . . don't you know *Henry the Fifth?"*

She shook her head. She was very much aware of his hand, the fingers gently clasped around her own. The glowing fires were behind them now, they climbed steadily toward where the tent was pitched.

"'Now entertain conjecture of a time,'" Judd said, almost in a whisper, and it took her a moment to realize he was quoting, "'When creeping murmur and the poring dark fills the wide vessel of the universe.' Reminds me of this, I don't know why."

"Don't stop," she said.

"Well . . ."

"Please."

"'From camp to camp, through the foul womb of night, the hum of either army stilly sounds, that the fix'd sentinels almost receive the secret whispers of each other's watch. Fire answers fire; and through their paly flames' . . . well, that's enough," he said, and squeezed her hand.

"Armies?" she said, "This reminds you of armies?"

"Yes, I think so."

"But . . . why?"

"I don't know. It just seems like an army to me."

"And the *other* army?"

"The other army?" He turned to her, and grinned, and again squeezed her hand. "Why, them, Lissie," he said. *"Them."*

When they got back to the tent, the others were asleep, the kerosene lamp was out. He prepared a place for her near where Rusty was sleeping, a blanket on the ground, another to cover her.

They undressed silently in the darkness. She took off the B.U. sweatshirt and her jeans, but she left on her panties. He went to the sleeping bag, and she went to the blankets on the other side of the tent.

"Good night," he said.

"Good night," she answered, and crawled between the blankets. She lay in the darkness, listening to the breathing, Suzie's and Rusty's, trying to isolate Judd's. Her heart was pounding. She lay very still for what seemed like a long time.

"Lissie?" he whispered.

"Yes?"

"Are you asleep?"

"No."

"Why don't you come over here?"

"Well . . ."

"Well what?"

"Well . . . I don't know."

"Come on over."

"No, I don't think so."

"Isn't it cold over there, all alone under that blanket?"

"Well . . ."

"Isn't it?"

"Well . . . I guess so."

"Then come on over here."

"Well . . ."

"Come on."

"Well . . . just for a minute."

"Okay."

"I mean it."

"Okay, just for a minute."

Wearing only her panties, pulling the blanket around her, she moved to his sleeping bag. He had already unzipped it; he opened the flap wide for her, and she crawled in beside him.

"So," he whispered, "hello."

"Hello," she whispered.

They fell silent. Across the tent, she could hear Rusty's gentle breathing and Suzie's light snoring. She was suddenly trembling beside him.

"Still cold?" he whispered.

"Yes, I . . . guess so."

"Here," he said, and put his arms around her.

112

"Listen, don't get any . . ."

"You're very pretty," he said.

"Sure."

"You are."

"Sure."

"How old are you?"

"Seventeen," she said. She was still trembling. She wished she could stop trembling. "How . . . how old are you?" she asked.

"Nineteen," he said.

"I thought you were older . . . no, don't do that," she said.

"Why not?"

"Well . . ."

"Well what?"

"Well, why would you want to?"

"*Want* to?"

"I'm so . . . small," she said.

"So?" he said.

"So . . ."

"Well . . ."

"Be still," he said, and kissed her.

She thought for a moment, *Hey, watch out, Liss,* she thought, *Oh, wow,* as his tongue parted her lips, and moved into her mouth, caressing her own tongue, his hand gently kneading her breast, the nipple rising, she thought *Hey!* and pulled her mouth from his and said, "Hey, come on."

"You said a minute."

"Well . . ."

"It hasn't been thirty seconds."

"Well . . ."

"Be still," he said again.

His lips touched hers, gently, but the hand kneading her breast was insistent.

"You have terrific nipples," he said.

"Sure. Listen . . ."

"Yes?"

"We'd better cut this out."

"Why?"

"Because . . . well, listen, let's just cut it out, okay?"

"No," he said.

"Judd . . ."

"Yes?"

"Listen . . . I . . ."

His hand moved from her breast. She felt it suddenly on her panties, between her legs, touching her there where no one had ever . . .

"Listen," she said.

"Yes?"

"Cut it out, okay?"

"No."

"Listen, take your hand away, okay?" she said, and reached for his wrist, and caught it and said, "Come on now."

"No," he said.

"Well, I'm not about to . . ." she started to say, and he shook her hand loose, and began lowering her panties over her belly, "Hey, listen," she whispered, pulling them down over her nakedness, "Listen, Judd really, this," and suddenly he moved in against her, and she felt his hardness and said, started to say, "Hey, come on . . ." but he took her hand in his own and brought it to him, brought it gently to him, and she said, "Judd, listen" and he opened her hand and then closed her fingers around him.

"Judd," she said.

"Yes?" he said.

"I don't know you."

"You know me."

"No, really, listen," she said, but her hand, her hand was unbiddenly touching him, gliding along his shaft, she could feel him pulsing under her fingers, she thought *Jesus* and she said, "Judd, listen," and his mouth found hers again. She thought *Jesus, this is crazy* while his mouth, while his hand, her mouth, her hand . . .

"Judd . . ."

"Shhh," he said.

"Listen, I'm, you know . . ."

"Shhh," he said, and rolled on top of her.

She felt him inside her, enormous inside her, felt a sharp momentary pain, and gasped, and urgently whispered, "Listen, I'm a *virgin*," recognizing the lie at once, whatever she'd been she no longer was, the hugeness of him swelling inside her own swollen, her own, "Listen," she said, "I wish you'd," his mouth stopping the words, sealing her lips while below he began a steady fierce rhythm. "Listen," she said, pulling her mouth from his, incessantly probing, *Oh, Jesus,* she thought, "Listen," she said, "Shhh," he said, and shoved himself deeper inside her, "They'll hear us," she said,

114

"Shhh," he said, his massive, his, *Jesus,* she thought and his lips found hers again, his mouth more demanding now, biting her lips, thrusting his tongue into her, searching the walls of her mouth while below she began moving with a fierce rhythm of her own, searching for, rubbing against, moving it against him, getting it there *against* him, pushing it there *against* him, swollen and wet, *Jesus,* she thought, *Jesus, I,* "That's the girl," he whispered, "that's it, Lissie, that's it, honey," impaled beneath him, her body moving without conscious will, the roof of the tent, the ground beneath her, *My father'll kill me,* she thought, and said aloud, sharply, "Oh! Oh, *Jesus!"* and felt his hand clamping onto her mouth, and suddenly lost all sense of time or place or being or self or anything but, anything else, anything.

5

He called her the next time he was in the city.

"Hello?" she said.

"Joanna?"

"Yes?"

"Jamie," he said. "Jamie Croft."

"Oh. Hi."

"I said I might call." He hesitated. "I'm in the city."

"How are you?" she said.

"Fine, thanks." He hesitated again. "I thought you might like to have lunch."

He waited.

"Why don't you come here instead?" she said.

"Well . . . sure," he said.

"It's on East Sixty-fifth," she said, and gave him the address.

When she opened the door, she was wearing blue jeans and a man's shirt, the tails hanging loose. Her hair was pulled into a pony tail; Jamie thought it looked rather too young for her. She was wearing no makeup; she looked a bit wan, he thought.

"Well, hello," she said.

"Sorry it took so long," he said. "I had trouble getting a cab."

"Wednesday," she said. "Matinee day."

"Yes," he said.

"Come in," she said.

The apartment was a three-story brownstone, the living room on the first floor, the kitchen, dining room and guest room on the second floor, the master bedroom and a library on the third floor. The living room—Jamie had not yet seen the rest of the house—was furnished with antiques she told him she had purchased at a shop in Brewster. He figured they must have cost her a fortune, but she told him at once that the prices there were very good, he should drop in sometime. She asked him if he would like a drink. He said he thought not. They sat opposite each other in easy chairs covered in red plush velvet. It was close to noon. The light was flat.

"No rehearsal today?" he asked.

"No."

"Do you have a performance tonight?"

"Yes?" There was a slight inflection at the tail end of the single word, as if she still could not believe he was really interested in what she did or when she did it.

"Which opera?"

"*Roberto d'Evereux,*" she said. "Donizetti." She looked at him and smiled. "You don't know it."

"No."

"So," she said. "What are *you* working on?"

"An architectural thing for the *Times Magazine* section."

"New *York* architecture?"

"Yes. Landmark buildings."

"Are you enjoying it?"

"I haven't begun shooting yet. I only got the list yesterday."

"Of buildings?"

"Yes, the buildings they want me to photograph. Twelve in all."

"Sounds exhausting," she said.

"It may turn out to be," he said, and smiled.

There was a long silence.

"Must be twenty to," Joanna said.

"What?"

"Or twenty after."

"I'm sorry, I . . ."

"Long pause in the conversation."

"Oh."

"That's what they say, isn't it?"

"I thought it was *ten* to and *ten* after."

"No, twenty to." She crossed her legs. "You seem nervous," she said. "Have you changed your mind?"

"About what?"

"About making love to me. That's why you're here, isn't it?"

"I'm not sure why I'm here."

"That's why you're here," she said. "Shall we go upstairs?"

"If you want to."

"Yes, I want to."

"All right then," he said.

Her third-floor bedroom was entered through a library that served as a sort of cloistered anteroom lined with floor-to-ceiling shelves of leatherbound books. A tiled Franklin stove was set into one wall, under the bookshelves. There were two wingback chairs, each upholstered in red leather, flanking the fireplace. A brass coal scuttle rested on the slate hearth. There were brass andirons, a brass-handled poker, brass-handled fire tongs. An antique bellows, in faded green and red leather, hung just to the left of the fireplace opening.

A metal music stand with an open manuscript on it was standing near the hearth. On the dark, richly stained floor, a flute lay nestled in its open leather case, silvery bright against the green plush lining. The floor was scattered with Oriental rugs: a Bokhara like the one in the Rutledge living room, an Abadeh, and a smaller Isfahan. He could imagine her sitting in this room practicing her flute, or perhaps reading before she went to bed, the coals of a dwindling fire glowing in the grate, a brandy snifter on the inlaid table beside one of the wingback chairs. The door leading to her bedroom was made of heavy oak, with a massive brass doorknob. He followed her into the room.

She undressed without ceremony or artifice, as if she had taken off her clothes for him a hundred times before. Naked, she was more spectacularly beautiful than he imagined she could possibly be; he caught his breath as she came toward him, her long blond hair falling loosely over her shoulders to mantle the sloping tops of her young breasts, so young, the erect pink nipples circled with wider roseate aureoles. Her waist was narrower than it appeared when she was clothed, her hips flaring below it, the triangle of her pubic hair arrowing downward toward her rounded thighs and long legs.

He was still fully dressed when they kissed. Their kiss was long and passionate. When at last she took her mouth from his, she helped him to disrobe, loosening his tie, unbuttoning his shirt, unfastening the belt around his waist, and at last lowering his zipper and pulling him free of his shorts. She held him only for a moment, tightly, her fist clenched around him, and then she released him, and turned from him abruptly, and went to the bed. She lay on her back watching as he undressed, one leg bent, the other extended, propped against the pillows, her hands behind her head, a faint smile on her lips. He put most of his clothing on the seat of a chair, and hung his jacket over the back of it. Then he went to where she was waiting for him.

He discovered during that first afternoon in bed with her that there were several separate and distinct personalities which, like those of schizophrenic Eve in the Joanne Woodward movie, formed in the conglomerate the single person who was Joanna Berkowitz. The first and foremost of these was someone he labeled Joanna La Flute, who could talk tirelessly and with unbridled passion about the instrument she played and its role in the orchestra. She had grown up in a musical family; her father had been only a so-so pianist but a marvelous arranger who had worked for many of the big bands in the thirties and forties before moving on to score several motion pictures; her uncle played the cello, and it was he, she guessed, certainly not her father, who stimulated her first real response to music.

"I fell in love with the cello the first time I heard it," she told Jamie. "I must have been seven or eight years old. My father took me to hear my Uncle Izzy playing—his name is Israel Berkowitz, he used to play first desk with the Philharmonic, but to me he was Uncle Izzy—and I heard the music he was making, and I simply fell in love with the instrument. It had such a *masculine* sound, do you know? I mean, I was only eight years old, but Jesus, I felt it right down *here,* I mean it, so robust, and gutsy, like a man, do you know? If I had to assign a color to the sound a cello makes, I guess it would be Army green."

But despite her immediate infatuation with the instrument her Uncle Izzy played, her mother decided that Joanna should begin taking piano lessons, which she did indifferently all through her prepubescent years. In 1955, when the motion picture *Blackboard Jungle* exploded onto the screen with an under-the-titles background rendition of "Rock Around the Clock" by Bill Haley and the Comets, Joanna (like millions of *other* eleven-year-old girls) discovered rock-and-roll and immediately began fooling around with the guitar.

"No lessons, you understand, just picking it up and strumming it, you know, like if a friend brought one over. Mostly folksongs, like that. But the important thing was that it got me away from the piano and into strings. So when I went to a music camp the summer I turned twelve—my birthday is June 6, 1944, does that date mean anything to you? Of *course* it does, it's D-Day, I was born on D-Day. Anyway, that summer I went to camp, this was 1956, it was to study cello, not piano. *Cello,* mind you.

"But whereas I still loved the sound of it, I still *do* as a matter of fact, I really wasn't devoting too much time to practicing or anything, I was more interested in boys, I guess. I'd just turned twelve, but I was pretty well developed for my age, and *extremely* horny. So that deep rumbling sound coming up from between my legs—the sound the *cello* was making, not me—was very sexual to me, and it just aggravated my horniness, and instead of practicing I went chasing around after all the boys. That's neither here nor there, right? I mean, nothing happened to me that summer, musically *or* sexually. Sexually, I'd have to wait till I was seventeen. Musically, it happened two years later."

She was a student at Fieldston-Riverdale and still taking cello lessons—this was now the fall of 1958; she was fourteen years old—when her grandmother took her to the Metropolitan Opera one night to hear *Lucia di Lammermoor,* which turned out to be the musical experience that changed Joanna's entire life. When she mentioned the opera, she familiarly called it *Lucia,* and then saw the blank look on Jamie's face (he truly *was* a musical ignoramus) and expanded it to its full, honorable and only world-famous title, drawing another blank, shrugging, and saying, "Anyway, I'd never really dug opera, and I didn't that night, either. I mean, I frankly found it very boring until they got to the Mad Scene, do you know the opera at all? Not at *all?* Well, it's really too complicated to explain, I mean the plot is really very complicated, even for an opera.

"But there's the scene following the murder of Sir Arthur, she kills him, you see, she kills Sir Arthur whom she's just married, and then she goes mad, and there's this marvelous aria for coloratura soprano accompanied by flute, and when I heard that *flute*—oh, my God! I can't tell you what it *felt* like, just hearing that sound. I took my grandmother's glasses—I had to find out where that sound was coming from, who in the orchestra was making that sound—and I zeroed in on the flute. A lovely woman was playing it, I loved the look of her, and I loved the look of the instrument in her hands, and the way she was holding it, the way you have to hold the flute, but most of all, I loved the *sound,* so very different from the cello.

"It was sexy the way a dream is sexy, smooth and turning, like a dream, everything white, like daytime, like a mirror, smooth, like glass, turning, like a dream, like beach glass, do you know? Smooth and swift, like a cat, rainbow soft, like glass, like beach glass, pastels, smooth, God, I *loved* that sound! And I just *knew,* I knew right that minute, as I focused those glasses on that beautiful woman making that rapturous sound, I knew right *then* that what I wanted to play was the flute. I mean, I'd *always* known I wanted to play *something,* play it well, you know, not just fool around with it, but now I knew my instrument would be the flute. That was it. No further debate. The flute. Period.

"I borrowed a C-footed flute from the band room at school, and took it home to assemble the three pieces. There are three pieces, you know, it comes apart. The head-joint with the blow-hole on it—it sounds obscene, I know, but remember I was only fourteen and I didn't know from things like giving head, dollink, or blowjobs, or other such disgusting tings, *nu?* The head-joint, and the middle-joint and then the tail, or the foot-joint, *voilà,* you got a whole *fecockteh* flute, am I right? Anyway, I put it all together, and I put my mouth over the blow-hole, covering about a quarter of it, and holding the flute horizontally, the way I'd seen that lady doing at the Met, and I blew down into the hole, and Jesus Christ, I made a *sound!*

"I was so surprised I almost wet my pants! My father was sitting in the living room, and he looked up at me, and saw the startled look on my face, and misinterpreted it for something else, because it certainly wasn't what I was feeling—all I was feeling was shock at having produced *any* sound at all. My father said, 'Such joy!' and I looked at him, and realized he was looking at my face, studying it with a fondness and an appreciation I'd never seen before, not when I was playing piano, not when I was playing cello, but now, making a dumb *ooonk* sound on the flute, he gives me a look of approval like I've never seen before from him in my life, and he says, 'Such joy' again, softer this time, and that does it. Now I know that not only am I going to play the flute, I am going to be the best fucking flute player who ever lived."

She wasn't quite that ("I'm *still* not that," she told Jamie), but she discovered in the first few months of private lessons with a teacher recommended by her Uncle Izzy that she had, well (and she told this to Jamie reluctantly and with a modesty he found both touching and endearing), well, she had what she supposed was a natural affinity for the instrument, what you might call a *talent*, she supposed. And she was surprised when, after having taken lessons for little more than a year, her teacher arranged a recital at Town Hall for five flutists, two men and three women, and Joanna was chosen to be one of the women. ("I was fifteen years old, not exactly what you'd call a woman, but the others really *were* women.") In such fast company, Joanna was not far enough advanced to play first, but she did play third flute, and she did have several solos in a twenty-minute piece the name of which she could still recall, Boismortier's *Quintet No. 1* for five flutes. There at Town Hall, she made her next important musical decision: not only was it enough to play the flute and to play it well, it was important for her to perform before people who would hear her play and derive from her playing the same enjoyment she herself did. In short, she decided on that thrilling night that she wanted to become a professional musician.

In the summer of 1962, when Joanna was just eighteen, and shortly after she'd graduated from Fieldston-Riverdale, she went with her father to Rome. She had already applied to the Juilliard School, and had been accepted, and was looking forward to beginning her studies there in the fall. "In New York City," she said, "anyone truly interested in becoming a professional musician—a *classical* musician, that is—goes either to Juilliard or Mannes. The Mannes College of Music, do you know? Both very good, but maybe Juilliard's a bit more competitive. Anyway, that's where I went. Juilliard, I mean. This was 1962, the fall of 1962, the school hadn't yet moved to Lincoln Center, it was still uptown on 122nd Street, near Riverside Drive. I used to love that old building. I mean, it doesn't *compare* with the facilities at Lincoln Center, I'm right there at the State Theater, you know, I drop in every now and then to say hello to Julie, he's *still* teaching flute at Juilliard, he's marvelous. I told you about him, do you remember? Julie Baker? He's the first flutist with the Philharmonic.

"Anyway, he was teaching up there at the old Juilliard, and what I did for four years was play flute. Well, not only flute. You have to take piano as your second instrument, all students in the music department do. But flute was my major, and there was L and M, that's literature and materials, and then orchestra—there were only two orchestras then, the Concert Orchestra and the Repertory Orchestra, but now there are four—and music history, and chamber music, if you were assigned to it, though that was mostly for string musicians, still I played a lot of chamber music at Juilliard.

"What it was, if you were a student there, you were supposed to be *serious* about music, so it was music, music, music all day long every day of the week. Either lessons, or else practicing, or else performing with this or that school orchestra or, you know, a friend might be giving a little recital, and he'd ask you to play with him, or you'd get together with some other musicians and just play things you loved, you know, like, oh, God, you know, the Mozart flute concertos or, God, there was a girl there, she was just a lovely harpist, do you know Mozart's *Concerto in C Major for Flute and Harp?* God, I used to *love* playing that with her, we'd spend *hours* on that, I absolutely *adored* it.

"But you see, I loved *all* of it. I mean, even the dumb exercises. *All* of it. Taffanel and Gaubert, or the Andersen exercises, or the Marcel Moyse stuff, all the exercises I use now when I'm warming up before a performance, but which *then*, meant a *lot* to me, when I was developing technique. I'd go to the hearing room, the school had this room with record players and earphones, it still has one at Lincoln Center, with the same person behind the desk, and I'd listen to, oh, God, I don't know, *tons* of stuff—do you know the fourth movement of the Brahms four symphony? There's some beautiful flute stuff in it. Or Prokofiev's *Classical Symphony?* The third movement? There's some very hard stuff there for two flutes, I mean, it's hard for me even *now,* but then it was impossible. Or, you know, the flute solo in *Daphnis and Chloé,* or Strauss, well, Strauss, yes, *everything* in *Till Eulenspiegel.* And there's *L'après-midi,* I'm *sure* you know that one, the flute solo at the beginning, Debussy? No? You don't know Debussy? Oh, well.

"I don't want you to get the impression that all I did was play music all the time, or think about it all the time. I was twenty-two when I got out of Juilliard, and by then, well, you know, I'd, uh, picked up a little experience along the way with this or that man, I'll tell you about that sometime, but not right now. The thing was trying to get a *job* when I got out. You see, if you're a fiddler, I mean a *good* fiddler, you've got a shot at something like thirty, thirty-five chairs in the orchestra—sure, there are what? eighteen fiddles in the first section, another fifteen in the second? That's thirty-three, am I right? Thirty-three chances for a job in any given orchestra. In New York, we haven't *got* that many orchestras, you know. Cultural center of the world, sure, thank you, Mayor Lindsay, but all we've got is the Philharmonic and the American Symphony, which is only so-so, and the National Symphony, which doesn't really count because that's semi-pro, and then the Met and the City Opera, and that's about it.

"Well, wait, you've got your ballet orchestras, but those are mostly pick-up jobs, the Joffrey, you know, and the Harkness, and the New York City Ballet company. There's nothing that says you can't leave New York and get a job with the Chicago Symphony, which, by the way, is the *best* orchestra in America, or the Cleveland, or wherever, but if you *live* here then you want to *stay* here and *work* here, even if it means subbing in a Broadway musical when a musician gets sick. My point is, there are only three flutes in an orchestra. Count 'em. Three. So, if you've got four or five true orchestras here in New York, that's fifteen jobs. And you're not going to get one of those jobs unless a flutist dies or moves to London.

"So there I am in 1966 with my B.M. from Juilliard, and all I want to do is *perform,* and there's not a job anywhere on the horizon. Julie suggested that I call Arthur Aaron, he was contractor for the American Symphony, and Dino Proto who contracts for the State Theater, and he was nice enough to prepare the way for me so that when I called and told them I was a flutist looking for a job they didn't just say, 'Oh, really, how nice, what a surprise!' I auditioned for both of them, and they were very complimentary, but they really didn't have anything at all, and they told me to get back to them in six months or so. Well, Dino said that. Arthur Aaron didn't have anything, and he wasn't *expecting* anything, either. You have to understand that when a musician lands a chair in an orchestra, he stays with it. He doesn't go job hopping, the way you do in advertising or publishing. Jobs are hard to get. So I called Dino back in six months—this was now getting to be 1967—I didn't call him Dino in those days, it was still Mr. Proto. His name is Secondo, anyway, his first name, but everybody who knows him calls him Dino—and he *still* didn't have anything for me.

"I was a trained musician, out of Juilliard since June of 1966, and it was now the spring of 1967, the Beatles had just come out with 'Strawberry Fields,' I remember, and I thought they'd written that

124

one line just for me, do you know the line I mean? The one about how hard it was getting to *be* someone? That one. There were a lot of musicals running that year on Broadway, but I couldn't get a job with any of them. I mean, *really* a lot. *My Fair Lady* and *Oklahoma!* and *South Pacific* and *Dolly* and *Sound of Music,* I mean it, the list just went on and on, *How to Succeed, Fiddler, Kiss Me Kate, Pajama Game,* some really terrific stuff, when you think of it, *Damn Yankees, Guys and Dolls,* wow! But I could not get a job.

"So I found a couple of students who thought they might like to play flute, I charged them ten dollars an hour, but they didn't really *love* the flute, and you've either got to love it or forget it. And then I began working at a drugstore near Carnegie Hall, the proximity had nothing to do with it, I mean I wasn't hoping to get discovered or anything, it was just a job. Then I sold music for a while, at Schirmer's on Forty-ninth, and then a friend of mine, a girl with the Radio City orchestra, she'd gone to Juilliard with me and had landed a job in the second fiddle section, called to say they needed a sub there for a week or so, the third flute was out sick, so I played that for a while. And I did two nights in *King and I,* there's a lot of nice flute stuff in it, but that was just dumb luck, I just stumbled into that one.

"And then I got a call from a friend—you make a lot of friends who are in the music business, you know, music becomes your *life,* can you understand that?—anyway, this friend called, he was a percussionist, and he'd been auditioning for something, I forget what now, and he'd run into a bassoonist who said he'd heard the first chair in the City Opera Orchestra—this is *flute,* did I say *flute?* the first chair in the *flute* section—was desperately ill, he was dying of cancer or something, and they were going to be auditioning flutists all the next week!

"Bang! Like a shot I called Dino, hello, Mr. Proto, do you remember me, this is Joanna Berkowitz, I'm the flutist, I auditioned for you a while back, when I got out of Juilliard, I was recommended by Julie Baker, he suggested that I call you, do you remember me? Not only did he remember me, thank God, but he confirmed the rumor that they'd be hearing flutists at open auditions all the next week, and he set up an audition for me on the following Wednesday at ten A.M. Okay. I get there. This is the State Theater at Lincoln Center. It's been built by then, this is

1967, August of 1967. They've already begun rehearsing the season, in fact, and here's this flutist who's about to drop dead on them.

"I have to tell you something you may not know, Jamie, *despite* your vast knowledge of matters musical and orchestral, and that's if a first chair ever becomes vacant, it's rare that the second or third chairs are promoted. The conductor usually brings in somebody from outside to fill the spot. Okay? Unfair, but who cares when you're twenty-three years old, and a first flutist is about to die, and not only are you a remarkable flutician, as your teacher had told you ten thousand times, but you are also young, and fairly attractive, and *most* important of all—an *outsider*. The attractiveness, maybe it couldn't matter less, dollink. The young, yes, it matters. But the *outsider,* it matters most—provided you're good in the bargain.

"I get there a little before ten, and the people who are holding the audition include the concertmaster—do you know who the concertmaster is? He's the first desk in the first fiddle section. First desk, dollink. The same as first chair. Desk, chair, the same thing. Just like in real life, no, dollink? Sit on your desk and start writing on your chair. Anyway. Concertmaster, plus first chair in the oboe section, plus first chair in the bassoon section—this is a woodwind audition, you follow, the flute is what is known as a woodwind instrument, dollink. And also the conductor, who in that year of 1967 happened to be Julius Rudel. There they are, and there I am.

"They ask me to do a little bit of *Syrinx*—that's the Debussy piece, which of *course* I know you're familiar with, but I thought I'd clarify anyway—and then I thought they'd ask me to do what a flute player might be *expected* to do at an audition, maybe something from the Bach D Minor, or a little bit of the fourth movement from the *Eroica* or maybe the Mozart G Major, but this is an *opera* company orchestra, don't forget, this is people *singing,* my dear. So what they ask me to do, and by now I'm beginning to realize that the Debussy was just a warmup, what they now put in front of me is—vot else?—the Mad Scene from *Lucia*. And when I'm finished fumbling my way through that, they give me something from *Daughter of the Regiment* and then that old standby, if you've been playing opera for fifty years, the prelude to the third act of *Carmen*, the flute-over-harp section, except there is no harp there at the audition, just frightened little Joanna Berkowitz playing her heart

126

out for a lot of old men who are probably tone deaf.

"I played for—I don't even remember now—it must've been twenty minutes, a half-hour, something like that. This wasn't *steady* playing, you understand. I'd do the Mad Scene, and then there'd be a little powwow out there, and then they'd ask me to do the next one, and somebody would bring the music up, this was all sight-reading, you understand, and then there'd be another little pow-wow and so on. When I finished the bit from *Carmen,* they thanked me and told me they'd call me in a day or two. There must've been another twenty flutists waiting outside when I left, all of them looking desperate.

"But, surprise of all surprises, I *did* get a call on Friday, and they told me the job was mine and could I start right away with tomorrow's rehearsal, they're doing *Seraglio,* I think it was, and was I familiar with it? I wasn't familiar with it, I wasn't familiar with too many operas at the time. In those days, this wasn't too very long ago, actually, but back then if the musicians were familiar with a score, I mean if they'd been playing it over and over again for years, they might not even bother rehearsing it before the singers came in. Nowadays, the idea is to have at *least* one rehearsal, even if you know the thing upside down and backward, before your singers start. Anyway, the rehearsal was for two-fifteen that Saturday, and he wanted me there at two, and I said, 'How much are you paying?'

"Now remember, I've been looking for a job with an orchestra for God knows how long, and now I've *got* one, and I want to know how much they're *paying.* He explains to me that the orchestra has contracted to play for *X* numbers of dollars, and the scale for first chair in the flute section is blah, blah, blah—I forget what it was, something like nine thousand dollars, I really don't remember. But what he *neglected* to mention was that the first-chair men are usually guaranteed ten percent more than scale—Julie *Baker* told me this, good old Julie. So I said, 'Well, that's fine, but I want fifteen percent *over* scale, and he said, 'No, that's impossible,' and I said 'Well, then, make it twelve and I'll take the job,' and he *gave* it to me! Can you *imagine* such chutzpa? Twenty-three years old, and I get a job with the New York City *Opera* Orchestra, and I'm haggling over *salary!* Wow!"

The second of her multiple personalities was Joanna Jewish (originally Joanna *Jewess* until she informed him, at once and

127

somewhat heatedly, that the word "Jewess" was derogatory), a combination of Henny Youngman and Barbra Streisand being Brooklyn when she wasn't singing. Joanna told him that there was only one similarity between Streisand and herself, and then turned her face in profile, and said in her Joanna Jewish voice, "The beak, dollink, vot den?" She used this voice and this personality to snap off one-liners and to tell long stories about what had happened to her at rehearsal or while wandering the city (she was a dedicated walker, and spent hours roaming the streets, looking and listening), delivering her *shtik* with all the élan of a stand-up comic, frequently interrupting herself with bursts of self-appreciative laughter. She suddenly became Joanna Jewish after they had made love the first time—"Well, well, vot haff we *here,* dollink? Where'd *this* come from again, all of a sudden, hah?"—but he suspected, and said aloud, that this aspect of her personality was normally reserved for whenever she needed reinforcement from whatever ethnic roots lay deeply buried and half-forgotten in her psyche. "You tink you're Dr. Mandelbaum maybe?" she said.

Joanna Jewish had never eaten pork in her life; the very thought of it turned her stomach. Joanna Jewish still put newspapers on the wet kitchen floor every Friday night, a Shabbes habit picked up from her mother. She celebrated Chanukah, and not Christmas. She peppered her speech with Yiddish expressions like *vontz,* which meant bedbug, and which she used to describe the orchestra's first bassoonist, or *aleha ha-shalom,* which Jamie gathered meant "rest in peace" and which she used whenever she mentioned her mother, who had died in 1962, shortly after Joanna's *Cleopatra* summer. She defined for him the difference between *shmuck* and *putz —* "A *shmuck* is a dope, a *putz* is what's sticking up there between your legs again"—and she told him what *kvelling* meant ("That's what I did when I told Mandelbaum about you"). But contradictorily, Joanna Jewish considered the state of Israel a foreign country, and whereas she had contributed money to plant trees there, she railed unexpectedly against American Jews who seemed to put the well-being of "the homeland" *("That's* their homeland? Then what the fuck is *this?")* above that of America. "If there were *German*-Americans who felt about Germany the way some Jews feel about Israel," she said, "we'd call them subversives and throw them in jail." Jamie disagreed, but he knew better than to argue with her on her own turf.

Professor J. D. Berkowitz was the last of the triumvirate, a learned scholar whom one would not dare call by her first name, no less her hated middle name, Doris. Professor Berkowitz was a pontificator who pronounced her theories and dictums in a voice reminiscent of his own Connie's V.S. and D.M. voice, although the professor was quick to point out that she'd never been to a "genuine" college, in that the Juilliard School paid scant attention to anything but music and, as a result, sometimes turned out people who were virtual illiterates in any other field. She had felt this most keenly in her freshman year there, after the more catholic education at Fieldston-Riverdale. The voice she assumed for Professor J. D., in fact, was the result of that private school education, or so Jamie surmised, a bit nasal, a bit New Canaan corporation wife-ish, culturally affected, totally phony, her teeth clenched, her Gothic nose tilted as though she smelled something recently dead in the room.

She used this voice when she quoted, with presumed accuracy, any psychological premise picked up from the redoubtable Dr. Mandelbaum, the Tweedledee to Frank Lipscombe's Tweedledum. She used it when she told him what her politics were: she voted Democrat and considered herself a liberal, but many of the views she held (about welfare giveaways, for example, or bilingual public notices in New York) seemed conservative if not downright reactionary. She used it when she told him about her father's work or her Uncle Izzy's, but never when she discussed her own; the instrument she played was the secure domain of Joanna La Flute, its borders sealed to either Joanna Jewish or the professor.

At 4:00 P.M., reluctantly, he went into the bathroom to shower. Joanna was leaning nude against the sink, smoking marijuana, watching him as he lathered himself, the outline of his naked body blurred behind the mottled glass door of the shower stall.

"What time is your train?" she asked.

"I can catch an express at five-oh-five."

"To where?"

"Stamford. My car's at Stamford."

"What kind of car do you drive?"

"A Corvette," he said. "Why?"

"Just want to know."

He came out of the shower stall, took a towel from the rack, and began drying himself.

129

"Look at it," she said. "All sweet and clean and soft. Let me dry your back." She took a last drag, threw the roach into the toilet bowl, and then flushed it down. Taking the towel from him, she said, "Turn," and began briskly drying his back. "Will I see you next week?" she asked.

"Yes."

"What time?"

"Same as today? Eleven-thirty, twelve?"

"I'll have to look at my book," she said. "I know we've got *Figaro* next Wednesday night, but I'm not sure whether there's a rehearsal of anything."

"Well, I'll call you."

"No, I'll check it before you leave."

Her hand reached around him.

"Hey," he said. "Train to catch."

"When's the next one?" she asked.

"I really have to get home," he said.

"When's the next train?" she said, and her hand tightened on him.

He turned to her. He took her in his arms. He looked into her face. "Next time," he said. "Okay?"

"No, *this* time," she said, "okay?" and fell to her knees before him, and wrapped her arms around his legs, and took him savagely in her mouth. He placed his hands on top of her head. He closed his eyes. Her mouth was relentless. And suddenly, she pulled away from his erection, her lips sliding free, her hand cradling him rigid and pulsing against her cheek. Looking up at him, she whispered, "When's the next train, Jamie?"

"Six-oh-five," he said.

"An express?"

"Yes."

"You have time," she said, and took his hand and led him back into the bedroom.

He was in New York again that Saturday, scouting the landmark buildings with the *Times* people, and was through with his work by eleven o'clock. On the offchance that Joanna might be home, he called, surprised when she answered the phone. She told him they were performing *Turn of the Screw* that afternoon at two-fifteen, which meant she had to be in her chair at about two or a little after, which further meant she'd have to leave the apartment no later than twenty to. She apologized profusely, explaining that the Britten opera was scored for a sort of miniature orchestra, but that as first flutist she had to be there to play alto and piccolo. Could he . . . would he be willing . . . did he think he might be able to come over for just a little while? He caught a taxi from the Flatiron Building and was uptown in her apartment twenty minutes later.

In bed with her again, the blinds drawn, the blankets hastily thrown back, Jamie learned that she had yet another personality in her multilingual fold, outdoing the schizophrenic Eve by at least one—so far. (Had Mandelbaum discovered over the course of the past several months what Jamie was discovering in a scant four days? He doubted it.) This personality, and the voice accompanying it, emerged only when she was totally relaxed and unguarded, as she seemed to be now. If any of the voices was authentic, if any of the personalities truly reflected the *real* Joanna (whoever *that* might have been, lost in the facelessness of the crowd she was), Jamie considered this to be the one. He dared not label her. She was, simply enough, Joanna.

It was this Joanna who emerged when she told him about the untimely death of her mother, so soon after her return from Rome. It was this Joanna who told him about her first sexual experience, terrifying in that her bedmate (or more appropriately her carmate, since the seduction had taken place in the back seat of a Pontiac convertible) had been a member of the enemy camp, a goy from the tips of his toes to the very ends of his flaming red tresses, worn long in that year of 1961, when Joanna was seventeen and a senior at Fieldston-Riverdale. "My mother, *aleha ha-shalom,* would have died right then if she'd known," Joanna said. "Thank God, she never found out."

David Boyle, for such was the young seducer's name, had fumbled below her waist for almost an hour and a half before achieving penetration. By that time, Joanna was sore in both senses of the word, feeling pain whenever he thrust his less-than-massive (she later realized) penis against her, and angry as hell besides, her ardor diminishing with each new rigorous assault. Her initiation into the mysteries of poke and probe was not helped a whit by the fact that young David ("How'd an Irish mick get a nize Jush name like David?" she asked, reverting to her Joanna Jewish voice) wasn't wearing a condom and came all over her the moment he succeeded in parting her reluctant portals. She had him drive her posthaste to

131

the nearest open grocery store, where she purchased a bottle of Coca-Cola and improvised an on-the-spot Pontiac douche, but she worried for the better part of a month that she would have to tell her mother she'd gotten pregnant by a goy. Boyle was almost as worried as she was. On Christmas Day, when Joanna got her period at last, she called him at home and—because both her parents were within earshot of her end of the conversation—asked, "What goes with green for a merry Christmas?"

Boyle didn't know what the hell she meant. "Huh?" he said.

"Red," she said.

"Does that mean . . .?"

"Yes, I got it," she said.

"Phew," he said.

When she hung up, her mother asked, "Who was that?"

"A boy named David Fein," Joanna said.

"What is it you got?" her father asked.

"He sent me a little Chanukah gift."

Her father went back to reading his copy of *Variety*. Her mother glanced at her a moment longer, and then continued knitting a sweater she'd been working on since July.

Technically no longer a virgin, Joanna nonetheless had to wait till the summer after her graduation for her first *true* sexual experience. She had accompanied her father to Rome for his conferences on the *Cleopatra* score (a job he'd never got), and then had prevailed upon him to let her stay behind for a few weeks after he went back home. She was, after all, eighteen years old now, and her father had many friends there who would take good care of her. One friend who took extremely good care of her was a man named Emmanuel Epstein who, after a champagne dinner in his room at the Hassler, humped her royally and later spanked her "little bottom," as he'd called it, for betraying the trust of her father— "my very best friend in the whole world." Epstein was five inches shorter than she was, a man of fifty-eight, going slightly bald, with a wife and two children in Scarsdale; he was doing publicity work for Fox in Rome. He was, as Joanna recalled, somewhat better hung than young Boyle had been, but she was nonetheless turned off the moment he achieved a second, almost immediate orgasm while spanking her.

It was Epstein who introduced her to the other two men with whom she spent a profligate month—she had promised her father only two weeks—in various bedrooms around the city. One of the men was married; the other was a young Italian auto worker from Turin, who was employed as a spear-carrying extra on the film. His thirty-second scene was later cut from the final print, much to Joanna's dismay; she had gone to the movie when it was released, hoping to see what Antonio would look like on the screen. It was Antonio who'd given her the gold-link top she'd been wearing when Jamie met her on the Vineyard. Her other gentleman friend, the married one, gave her a variety of other things: an elephant-hair bracelet he had purchased on the Via Condotti, a hand-tooled, leatherbound edition of Dante's *Inferno*—and gonorrhea.

She did not realize she was carrying this ("Ahem, social disease," Professor Berkowitz said in a sudden excursion from Joanna's genuine voice) until she had already enrolled at Juilliard that fall. Her ailment, once discovered and properly diagnosed, was treated promptly and effectively but not before, she was certain, she had unwittingly infected a piano student named Vladimir Potemkin (Vlad the Impaler, as she familiarly called him) who was devoted to practicing twelve hours a day and who, she was equally certain had strayed from his piano bench only once that fall, and then only to pick up a dose. She sent him one of her doctor's cards, unsigned, but with the inscription, "Dear Vlad, *please* have a checkup!" He was now doing quite well on the concert circuit, making guest appearances with both the Boston and the Cleveland symphonies. He did not look particularly disease-ridden in his press photos, so Joanna guessed he'd taken her advice.

It was her genuine self who began talking about love that Saturday afternoon.

The only man she'd ever loved, she said, had been Harrison Masters, the aging poet from Indiana. She had met him at an April party given for the composer of a piece for string quartet which had been premiered at the Y on Ninety-second Street. She'd been invited to the event *and* the party following it by one of the fiddlers, who also played with her at the State Theater. Harrison had met the composer the summer before at Spoleto, where Menotti had arranged to have one of his poems set to harpsichord and lute, an experiment that failed because Harrison had insisted on reading the poem himself, and his rather frail voice had been drowned out by even such delicate instruments. There was a young girl on his arm when he arrived at the private party shortly after midnight. Joanna noticed them both the moment they came in.

He was a man with the gangling height of a giraffe, an eagle-like beak that was due to his part-Siouan heritage, and a leonine head of flowing white hair. "A walking menagerie," Joanna said, "but I couldn't take my eyes off him." Hoping against hope that the girl on his arm was his daughter, dismayed to learn that she was instead one of his students, Joanna nonetheless sashayed across the room in the black wool knit dress she was wearing ("Basic black, dollink, mit pearls," Joanna Jewish interjected), boldly intruded upon the conversation Harrison was having with the young composer of the work, and promptly and to the bewilderment of the hayseed student from Elephant Breath, Indiana, gained Harrison's complete and rapt attention as she told him about her own side excursion to Spoleto during the summer of her Roman adventure. The student later went home with the cello player who'd performed brilliantly that night, playing *Landscapes* or *Interiors* or whatever the hell it was called as though it were the Haydn *String Quartet in G*. Joanna took Harrison home with her—to this house, to this bedroom, and on this bed they made love together for the first time.

Hearing this, Jamie felt only anger at first, and was tempted to ask whether she'd changed the sheets since. And then he suddenly realized she wasn't going to give a detailed report on what had transpired in this bed with the poet from Indiana, but was instead only trying to understand *why*, for the first time in her life, she had felt unsparingly and selflessly devoted to a man who, by all reasonable standards, had been so completely wrong for her. Her voice was soft, scarcely more than a whisper. She lay beside him naked, one arm behind her head, staring up at the ceiling, wondering aloud, searching for clues to her own behavior; he suddenly felt as useless as Mandelbaum. But oddly, the feeling that he was neither necessary nor particularly vital to Joanna's rambling monologue dissipated as swiftly as had his anger. Holding her in his arms, he listened without rancor or discomfort.

"He was," she said, "the gentlest man I'd ever known. I'm not talking about when we made love, we did that rarely, in fact. Anyway, no man is *really* gentle in bed, is he? I mean, the very *act* demands that he perform aggressively—I hate the word 'performance,' don't you? But it's what we do actually, isn't it? In bed, I mean. In a sense, I mean. Perform? Utilize our skills to give pleasure. It's a performance, really, similar to a concert, but not as

134

carefully orchestrated or rehearsed."

She took a deep breath, and turned into his arms.

"So gentle . . . in so many different ways," she said. "I think his age had something to do with it, the very fact that we were eons apart, light-years apart, seventy-three and twenty-four, well, almost twenty-five, and earning a living as a musician—first chair with the City Opera, not bad, huh?—and having the time of my life before I met Harrison. So why him? The gentleness, yes, as though he were dealing with a child. So delicate with me. So careful of my feelings. So tolerant of my moods."

Abruptly, she stopped. She was silent for what seemed like a long time. Then she said, "I think what I'm trying to say is I never thought I'd ever fall in love with anybody else ever again, not after Harrison. But now, you see, I have." She smiled wanly, and touched his mouth with her fingertips. "I love you, Jamie," she said.

He had heard these words before, had spoken them himself to countless teenage girls when he was growing up, had even whispered them into the ear of a Yokohama whore after the war, knowing she couldn't possibly understand them, and actually believing he *did* love her, or the comfort of her body, or the safety she represented after months of slogging through the jungle dodging snipers' bullets. He had heard these words before, he had used these words as easy currency in a free market—except with Connie. With Connie he had meant them, he guessed. With Connie he had always been impeccably honest when saying the three cheapest words in the English language.

As he held Joanna in his arms now, he recognized that "I love you" was only another meaningless bit of pillow talk, the puritanical way of softening the sordidness of sex, sanding down the splintery edges of lust, ridding the basic act of its raw physicality. "I love you" was the unguent of American morality, the salve which when gingerly applied beforehand or immediately afterward eased the shock of animal recognition, and thereby separated all those fornicating beasts of the field from their human counterparts. He knew she didn't love him; she hardly even *knew* him.

But then he realized that in the space of—how the hell long had it been since he'd met her on the Vineyard, and who the hell cared *how* long it was?—in the space of *that* short a time, that infinitesimally brief moment in the millennium that had been his life till now, he had come to know her—*all* of her, Joanna La Flute, the professor, Joanna Jewish, each and every one another glittering facet of her unique and singular self—better than he'd known any woman before. Recognizing this, realizing he could never hope to pretend she was merely inconsequential, he made his decision in the form of a fervent wish: *I want this to last.*

But it was a decision nonetheless, conclusive and unalterable. Without surprise, and this was surprising in itself, he said, "I love you, too," and believed (Connie notwithstanding) that this was the first time in his life he'd ever really meant the words.

Brenner University would have been a bummer except for Judd's proximity. She called him the minute she got to school that September, at the number he'd given her for Briggs Hall, but he'd moved since and she wasn't able to make contact till early in October. His new apartment was on Commonwealth Avenue, where he was living with another boy, who, like Judd, had just dropped out of Harvard, the school that kept you till you were eighty once they accepted you, on the assumption that the Harvard Admissions Office never made errors in judgment. The other boy's name was Joshua Steinberg. He and Judd had lasted through two full semesters of Harvard undergraduate bullshit before deciding *they* were the ones who'd made the error in judgment. The boys wanted to be rock stars instead of lawyers. Judd played bass guitar and Joshua played lead. Together, they were going to set the musical world on fire.

When Lissie heard this, she immediately thought of her father, who hated rock with a passion. There were, by his exaggerated estimate, no fewer than 15,000 teenage rock groups in the town of Rutledge, Connecticut, an amazing count considering the town's modest 17,000 population. Moreover, and still according to her father, each of these groups, like the McGruder twins, possessed $75,000 worth of electronic equipment purchased by parents who were being rendered totally *deaf* by the sheer decibels at any living room rehearsal. Judd and Joshua rehearsed in the living room of the Commonwealth Avenue apartment. The first time Lissie and Judd made love in Boston was during a break in rehearsals. The Beatles had just released *Abbey Road* and the boys were trying to learn all the songs on the album. Steinberg kept yelling through the closed bedroom door for Judd to hurry it up in there, meanwhile picking out the chords to "Come Together."

Judd's last name was Gordon, and the boys billed themselves as Gordon and Steinberg. He told Lissie he was of French-English extraction, the pale blue eyes and blond hair comprising the British half of his heritage, he guessed. His parents, a Dr. and Mrs. James Gordon who lived in—

"That's my father's name, too," Lissie said.

"James Gordon? No kidding! We're *siblings!*" Judd said, and kissed her fleetingly on the cheek.

—a Dr. and Mrs. James Gordon who lived in Sarasota, Florida, learned in November that Judd was no longer attending classes at Harvard but was pursuing instead a musical dream of glory with a lead guitarist whose name was Joshua Steinberg. They immediately cut off all funds to him ("A total injustice," Judd said) and told him they would not send him another penny until he began studying again at a qualified institute of higher education. Guitar lessons, they told Judd, did not in their book or on their block constitute higher education. Gordon and Steinberg were currently playing gigs in this or that Boston bar, usually for sandwiches and beer, but sometimes for three or four bucks each a night. They still had their Harvard meal tickets, which would not expire till June, and ate most of their meals at Radcliffe, where the table manners were better and the scenery more pleasant. It was Lissie who suggested that they change the name of the group—

"Do two people even *qualify* as a group?" she asked.

"Oh, sure. A group, sure," Judd said.

—to Joshua and Judd, because Gordon and Steinberg sounded like a law firm. Judd thought maybe she was right, not because he thought it sounded like a law firm, but only because it was too close to Simon and Garfunkel, whom they were frankly imitating. Lissie didn't think Gordon and Steinberg sounded the slightest *bit* like Simon and Garfunkel—

"You mean the way we play?"

"Well, no."

"Then what?"

"The *name.*"

—but if they were considering a name change, anyway, then why *not* use Joshua and Judd which she thought had a nice ring to it. Judd said he would consider it, and maybe mention it to Steinberg. He told her later that he'd never considered it for more than ten seconds, and certainly had never mentioned it to Steinberg, simply because the name Joshua and Judd gave his partner top billing. When Lissie mentioned that the lead guitarist *should* get top billing, Judd said, "But *I* write all the songs." *All* the songs, as it turned out, were half a dozen Judd had composed since leaving Harvard.

Safe from the draft because of a slight heart murmur, Judd had felt no qualms about dropping out of school and losing his student classification. But he identified completely with other kids his own age who were being called up every day to get themselves shot to death in some stupid fucking rice paddy. It was Judd who insisted that Lissie accompany him to Washington for the November 15 Moratorium on Vietnam. She simply went with him, not even telephoning her parents to say she'd be out of Boston that weekend. The following week, when the My Lai stories began getting full-scale treatment in all the Boston papers, Judd organized a protest outside the Mugar Memorial Library, and although only 150 students showed up to march, he felt he had focused something more than media attention on a situation of pressing moral concern to all Americans.

Most of the time, Lissie and Judd had the Commonwealth Avenue apartment to themselves because Steinberg was dating a twenty-one-year-old Catholic girl from Simmons who steadfastly refused to consummate their relationship until they got married, an unlikely prospect in that his widowed mother was an Orthodox Jew and Eileen's parents were practicing Catholics who *still* refused to eat meat on Fridays, although it was now permitted by the church. Steinberg and Eileen spent a lot of time walking along the Charles together, torturing each other with a great deal of hand play.

Judd was rather a marathon lover, quick to climax ("They don't call me Flash Gordon for nothing, lady"), but equally quick to regenerate and begin again after a bottle of beer or a cream cheese sandwich. He loved to eat in bed, and the sheets were littered with cracker crumbs and bits of cheese and salami. Since the apartment

139

was virtually theirs to roam at will, they made love not only in the delicatessen bed, but also on the battered living room couch, and in the old-fashioned claw-footed bathtub, and once on the enamel-topped kitchen table.

She told her parents nothing at all about Judd. One thing she had learned since Woodstock was that you didn't *ask* your parents beforehand and you didn't *tell* them afterward. When she'd called the Vineyard from Rutledge that August day almost three months earlier, she hadn't *asked* if she could go up to Woodstock with Rusty, she'd simply said she was *going,* knowing damn well there wasn't any way they could stop her. And even though her mother had made some feeble noises about making sure Rusty had permission to use the family car, Lissie knew she'd won a major victory that day, and had gained as well an important insight into what was to be her future relationship with her parents.

Besides, she wasn't too sure how long this thing with Judd would last, and she saw no reason for bringing her parents into her personal life if this turned out to be a romance of short duration. She had, by early December, heard Gordon and Steinberg in concert at a bar in West Newton, and had calculated that the odds against their ever achieving success as rock musicians were, generously, about ten million to one; she suspected that before long Judd would pack his guitar case and head home to Sarasota, perhaps to attend the University of South Florida where he could major in basket weaving at his father's expense.

She hadn't even known where Sarasota *was* at first. She'd thought Judd had said Saratoga. "One of these days," Judd told her, "I'm going to write a novel, and there are going to be two hookers in it, a Greek hooker and a Japanese hooker. I'll call the Greek hooker Sara Toga, and the Japanese hooker Sara Sota." Lissie *still* didn't know which was which until she studied an atlas at the school library, and pinpointed each town, and decided she'd never care to live in either, thanks. "One of these days " was one of Judd's favorite expressions. "One of these days, when Steinberg and I get a recording contract . . ." or "One of these days, when I get that little Porsche I've got my eye on . . ." or "One of these days, I'm going to paint this whole apartment red, the floors, the ceiling, the toilet bowl . . ."

One of these days, Lissie thought, you're going to get tired of playing one-night stands in sleazy bars for crackers and beer, and you're going to head south where Mommy and Daddy will welcome you with open arms. I'll press you in my memory book, Judd, together with my senior prom corsage and my autographed picture of Elvis. Had she ever swooned over Elvis? Had she *truly* been to Henderson's senior prom with a pimply-faced boy whose name she couldn't even remember now? David? Daniel? Had she ever really been that *young?*

In just a few weeks, she would be eighteen.

Oddly, the promise of the Christmas break—the return to Rutledge and what she supposed was still her home, the living room hung with her photographs, the lighted tree in the far corner of the room, the familiar rush of the river beyond—left her feeling only indifferent. She imagined herself going back to school again on the fifth of January, and settling once more into a now familiar and, yes, dull routine. The year would have gone by like a whisper, leaving not an echo of itself, and, more depressingly, causing very little real change in the person who was Lissie Croft, a person she no longer thought of as a kid, but could not yet truly consider a woman.

As she packed her duffel to head for home, she wondered bleakly if anything as exciting as Woodstock would ever in her entire life happen to her again.

1970

The name and return address on the envelope were unfamiliar to Jamie. Someone named Carol Steinberg in Chicago, Illinois. He tore open the envelope flap. The handwritten letter read:

March 16, 1970

Dear Mr. Croft:

After failing to reach you by telephone this morning (I'll keep trying), I decided to send the enclosed summons—one copy for you, one for Judd's parents, and one for me. As stated in the court notice, the balance of rent due is $130 for the month of February, but actually it will be an additional $130 after March 31, covering the month of March.

I have been paying Joshua's share of the rent myself and sending it directly to Matheson Realty at 1283 Commonwealth Avenue, Allston, Massachusetts. I did this purposely, not only because I'm the one who signed the new lease, but I also wanted to be certain the rent was paid on time, knowing how unreliable young people are. Joshua is now alone in the apartment and he certainly (or *me* certainly) cannot pay a total of $195 monthly for the apartment.

Joshua is truly upset by all this. He told me he disliked ending his personal and professional relationship with Judd in this distasteful way, especially since they have been roommates since they were still students at Harvard. But he's alone in the apartment now, and he told me in a letter that enclosed the court notice that if you people (you and Judd's father in Sarasota) would pay the $130 for February, he will try to find another roommate to pay for March.

I must tell you that I am in no position to be paying any additional rent on the apartment. I am a widow living on a small pension, and it is enough of a burden to keep myself and my son going. I feel we are all responsible for this together, and I feel it would be fair for you and Judd's father to pay for February *and* March, and if Joshua is able to get a new roommate (who will pay *before* he moves) I will see to it that whatever rent money Joshua receives would be returned to you and to Judd's father in Sarasota—to whom I'm sending a Xerox copy of this letter, which I had made at the bank.

I would appreciate hearing from you as to what decision you come to. I'll keep trying you by telephone up until March 31st. I do hope I'll be successful in reaching you so that I can elaborate further.

Sincerely,

Carol Steinberg
(Mrs. Morris Steinberg)

Puzzled, he read the letter again, and then went back into the barn, past the darkroom door he'd left open when he'd heard the mail truck outside, closing the door as he passed it, and walking directly to his desk. The telephone was surrounded by a clutter of contact sheets, grease pencils, bills from photo suppliers and custom labs, an illuminated magnifier, a stamp pad, a rubber stamp reading PHOTO CREDIT: JAMES CROFT, another reading PHOTOS, DO NOT BEND OR FOLD, several letters from Lew Barker, and half a dozen uncashed checks. He pulled the phone toward him, through the besieging debris, picked up the receiver, dialed the operator, and asked for Chicago information. When he got a listing for Carol Steinberg at the address on her stationery, he dialed the 312 area code and then the number, and waited while the phone rang on the other end.

"Hello?" a woman's voice said.

"Mrs. Steinberg?"

"Yes."

"This is James Croft."

"Yes, Mr. Croft, I've been trying to . . ."

"I have your letter."

"Good, I was hoping . . ."

"What's this about, Mrs. Steinberg?"

"About?" she said. "It's about the rent."

"Yes, I gathered that. But what makes you think I'm responsible for any rent due on an apartment your son is sharing with some other boy?"

"What?" she said.

"I said . . ."

"Yes, I heard you. But I don't know what you mean."

"I mean I don't know any of these people you're talking about."

"Joshua, do you mean? Judd?"

"Yes, Joshua and Judd, this is the first I'm hearing of them."

"Oh," Mrs. Steinberg said.

"So would you mind . . ."

"I'm sorry, I didn't realize. I thought you knew."

"Knew what?"

"I thought your daughter had permission."

"My daughter? Permission for what?"

"Well, to . . . to share the apartment."

"My daughter's sharing an apartment with a girl named Judy Gordon, now perhaps you can explain . . ."

"Is that what she told you?"

"That's not only what she *told* me, that's what happens to be the *fact* of the matter."

"Judy Gordon," Mrs. Steinberg said.

"Yes, Judy Gordon."

"It's *Judd* Gordon. Not Judy."

There was a long silence on the line.

"I'm sorry, Mr. Croft, I . . . so many young people are living together these days, I thought . . . I really thought you knew. The

147

reason I wrote is they've left for California now, you see. Lissie and Judd. Without paying the February rent. And now the March rent is also coming due . . ."

"Lissie will be home before Easter, I'm sure the March rent . . ."

"Well, that's not the impression Joshua got. My son."

"What do you mean? What impression did he get?"

"That it was indefinite."

"*What* was indefinite? I'm sorry, Mrs. Steinberg, but I find this entire situation . . ."

"I can understand . . ."

"*What* did he find indefinite?"

"Whether or not they planned to come back."

"From California, do you mean?"

"Well . . . yes. That's where they went, didn't she tell you she was going to California?"

"*Yes,* she told me, of *course* she told me."

"Then . . . well, I don't know what to say. My son had the distinct impression they planned to . . . well . . . *stay* there."

"Your son is mistaken," Jamie said flatly. "My daughter has every intention of returning to Boston after the spring break."

"Well, if that's what she told you."

"That's what she told me, and I have no reason to doubt her."

"Well," Mrs. Steinberg said, and the single word said all there was to say. Lissie had lied to him about the apartment, she had told him her roommate was a girl named Judy Gordon; how in hell could he believe anything *else* she'd told him! The silence lengthened.

At last, he said, "I'll send you my check for . . . what is it?"

"Her share is sixty-five for February, and sixty-five for March. But if she plans to come back, maybe . . ."

"She plans to come back, but she won't be living in that apartment anymore," Jamie said.

"Then I'd want the sixty-five for March, too."

"I'll send you my check for a hundred and thirty."

"You understand that Joshua will refund the March rent the minute . . ."

"Yes, I understand that."

"Mr. Croft, please forgive me, I had no intention of . . ."

"That's quite all right."

"The way things are nowadays, a parent doesn't know *what* to do. If I've caused any trouble . . ."

148

"No, that's all right."

"I worry about Joshua day and night. I don't know where it'll end, Mr. Croft, I just don't. And I realize how *you*, with a daughter . . ."

"That's all right, Mrs. Steinberg," he said.

"I'm sorry if I've caused any problem between you."

"No, no problem at all," he said.

They had known, of course, that Lissie was headed for California, had in fact argued fruitlessly against the plan from the moment she'd proposed it, astonished when they realized she wasn't asking *permission* to go, but was simply filling them in as a matter of courtesy. It was Connie's contention now that nothing so terribly drastic had happened; their daughter had simply lost her virginity, something that *had* to happen, anyway, sooner or—

"She's been *living* with this guy!" Jamie shouted.

"Yes, so I understand," Connie said.

"How can you take this so *calmly?*"

"I don't think she's committed a crime of heinous proportions. She's . . ."

"When *you* were eighteen . . ."

"When *I* was eighteen, you seemed singularly intent on doing to *me* exactly what *this* boy has done to *her*."

"And never got to first base!"

"The times they are a-changin', dear."

"I don't want you transmitting that attitude to Lissie," Jamie said. "When she calls . . ."

"*If* she calls . . ."

"She'd damn well *better* call."

"My God, you sound positively Victorian," Connie said.

"Oh? Really? My daughter's . . ."

"*Our* daughter."

"*Our* daughter's fucking around with some pimply-faced . . ."

"Jamie, what the hell's the matter with you?" Connie asked flatly. "Would you please tell me?"

"Nothing," he said. "Nothing's the matter with me."

And then, as she found him doing more and more often these days, he turned away from her, ending the conversation, ending whatever brief moment of intimacy had been inspired by his daughter's malfeasance and the revelation of it by the woman in Chicago.

Lissie did not call until that Sunday night, the twenty-second.

149

Jamie picked up the phone in the kitchen, and the moment the operator told him it was a collect call from a Melissa Croft in San Francisco, he yelled to Connie to pick up the extension in the upstairs bedroom. They had barely exchanged hellos when he heard the small click telling him Connie was on the line.

"Lissie," she said, "are you all right?"

"Yes, fine, Mom," Lissie said. "Exhausted, but fine."

"Where are you staying?"

"We crashed with a friend out here. A girl Judy knows."

"Give me the number there," Jamie said at once, "and let's cut the Judy crap."

"Jamie . . ."

"Stay out of this, Connie. What's the number there?"

"Dad?"

"Give me the number."

"It's . . . just a second," she said. "It's 824-7996."

"What's the area code?"

"415."

"Thank you. Why'd you lie to us, Lissie?"

"About what?"

"Lissie . . ." he warned.

"Okay, there's no Judy, okay?"

"No, there's a Judd."

"Yes."

"And a Joshua, and Christ knows how many . . ."

"Just Judd and Joshua."

"Are you sleeping with both of them?"

"Jamie!"

"Or just Judd?"

"Come on, Dad."

"Jamie, you're being . . ."

"*Answer* me, Liss?"

"Dad," she said, slowly and carefully, "I don't think that's any of your business."

"It isn't huh? I get a letter from a woman in Chicago, there's a goddamn *court* order in the letter, she wants to know why my daughter ran off without paying the rent . . ."

"I *didn't* run off! We *forgot*, that's all. Jesus, that fucking Steinberg! He *knows* we . . ."

"I don't appreciate that kind of language," Connie said.

"I'm sorry, Mom, but he *knew* we planned to pay the rent, *Jesus!*

Do you know what this is? It's he's a lousy guitar player, and he knows Judd's about to break up with him . . ."

"He's a musician, is he?" Jamie said. "This Judd Gordon."

"Yes, he's a musician."

"Marvelous," Jamie said.

"He went to Harvard," Lissie said defensively.

"How old is he?"

"Nineteen. Well, he'll be twenty soon."

"And he's already graduated from Harvard?" Connie said.

"No, he didn't graduate."

"What *did* he do?" Jamie asked.

"He left."

"He dropped *out*, you mean."

"Well, yes, if you want to put it that way."

"And now he's a musician."

"Yes."

"What does he play?"

"Guitar."

"Naturally," Jamie said.

"Dad, the harpsichord went out of style in—"

"Lissie, I'm not in the mood for any of your smart-ass—"

"Jamie, calm down," Connie said.

"I want you to come home right this minute," Jamie said, "do you hear me? I want you to get on a plane . . ."

"I haven't got enough money for a plane ticket," Lissie said.

"I'll prepay it on this end."

"Anyway, I don't *want* to come home yet. Jesus, I just *got* here!"

"Lissie, this isn't a question of what *you* want. The minute you started lying to us, you lost the right to . . ."

"Dad, I'm eighteen years old, I don't have to do everything you *want* me to do."

"Would you like me to call the police? I'd hate . . ."

"The *police?* Jesus! You've got to be kidding! What'd I *do*, would you mind telling me?"

"You ran off to California with a boy we don't even . . ."

"You'll meet him when we get back, okay? I'll bring him home the minute we get back. Calm down, Dad, willya?"

"I want you to come home," Jamie said.

"No."

"Lissie, I . . ."

"No," she said, and hung up.

"Lissie?"

"She hung up," Connie said.

Jamie immediately began jiggling the receiver rest.

"Operator," a voice said.

"Operator, could you please get me 824-7996 in San Francisco?"

"You can dial that direct, sir, the area code is . . ."

"I *know* I can dial it direct, this is an emergency."

"Well . . . all right, sir, I'll try it for you."

He waited as she dialed. On the extension, Connie said, "Now calm down, Jamie. Getting excited isn't going to help."

"What number are you calling from?" the operator asked as the phone began ringing on the other end.

"Rutledge 4-8072," Jamie said.

"Hello?" a voice on the other end said. A boy's voice this time.

"Let me speak to Lissie Croft, please."

"Who's this?"

"Her father."

"Oh, hi, Mr. Croft. This is Judd."

"Get my daughter, please," Jamie said.

"Sure, just a sec," Judd said. The phone clattered as he put it down. Jamie heard voices. He waited.

"'Oh, *hi*, Mr. Croft,'" he mimicked, "'this is *Judd*.'"

"Calm down," Connie warned on the extension.

"Hello?" a voice said.

"Who's this?"

"Barbara."

"Barbara who?"

"Barbara Duggan."

"Barbara, may I please speak to my daughter?"

"Well . . . she can't come to the phone just now," Barbara said.

"Why not? I just spoke to her a minute—"

"She'll have to call you back later, Mr. Croft."

"I want to talk to her now."

"Well, yeah, but the thing of it—"

"Would you please get her for me?"

"Mr. Croft . . . she doesn't *want* to talk to you just now."

"What's the address there?" Jamie said. "Is this your apartment?"

"Yes."

"What's the address?"

"Well, Mr. Croft . . ."

"Young lady . . ."

"I'm not sure Lissie wants you to have the address."

"Let me talk to Judd."

"Sure, just a second."

Jamie waited.

"Hello?"

"Judd?"

"Yes, Mr. Croft?"

"Listen to me, you little son of a bitch. If my daughter doesn't come to the phone in three seconds flat, I'm calling the F.B.I. to tell them she's been kidnapped. Now do you want to get her to the phone, or do you want more trouble than you've ever—"

"Hey, take it easy," Judd said.

"Don't *you* tell *me* to take it—"

"I mean, she's not hanging by her thumbs here, okay? Just take it easy."

"I'm counting, Judd. You've got thirty seconds."

"Jesus," Judd said, and again put the phone down. "Lissie!" he shouted. "You'd better come take this."

Jamie and Connie waited.

"Hello?" Lissie said wearily.

"Don't hang up again," Jamie warned. "Don't you *ever* dare . . ."

"Dad, I just don't want to talk to you when you're in this kind of mood."

"Mood? If you think this is just—"

"Let me talk to her alone," Connie said.

"Why? Why can't I . . . ?"

"Jamie, *please*. Get off the phone."

"I want you *home,* miss," Jamie said, and slammed the kitchen receiver down on the cradle rest.

"Boy," Lissie said.

"All right, let me hear it," Connie said.

"Is he gone?"

"He's gone."

"I've never heard him *sound* like that in my—"

"I think you can understand why he's upset," Connie said levelly. "How long have you known this boy?"

"Mom . . ."

"Lissie, I don't think you realize how furious your father is. I suggest . . ."

153

"All right, all right. It's been eight months now."

"You've been living with him for eight *months?*"

"Well, no, only since January when I . . . Mom, I really don't want to discuss this. Not with Dad, and not with you, either."

"I'm afraid you'll *have* to discuss it," Connie said. "This woman Dad spoke to, this Mrs. Steinberg, said that you had no intention of returning to school. Is that true?"

"That is total and absolute bullshit."

"Lissie, I *would* appreciate . . ."

"Okay, okay."

"*Do* you plan to stay in California?"

"No. I told you no. But I'm not turning around tomorrow *morning* if *that's* what Dad thinks."

"When *will* you be home?"

"For Easter."

"Why did Mrs. Steinberg's son think you and Judd . . ."

"Because he's crazy."

"You *didn't* tell him you planned to stay in California?"

"Why would we tell him anything like that? Mom, I'm really very tired. We were hassled halfway across the country, and we're exhausted. So if you don't mind . . ."

"What do you mean, hassled?"

"Hassled. The usual."

"Tell me what you mean."

"Could we please continue this tomorrow? I'd like to get some sleep. Really, we'll talk about it tomorrow, okay? And tell Dad not to worry, I'll be home for Easter."

"You're sure about that."

"I'm positive."

"I'll tell him."

"I'll call tomorrow, okay?"

"When tomorrow?"

"When I get up. It'll be afternoon your time."

"We'll be waiting for your call."

"I promise."

"Is this Steinberg boy Jewish?"

"Yes."

"And Judd? Is he Jewish, too?"

"What difference does *that* make?"

"Is he?"

"No. Since when did you . . . ?"

"I was merely curious."

"It sounded like more than curiosity."

"It wasn't."

"Well, he isn't Jewish, you can relax."

"Lissie . . ."

"I'm sorry, Mom, but I really don't appreciate that sort of question."

"I think we have a right to know who or *what* this boy you've been living with . . ."

"I'm not sure you *do* have that right, but I don't want to discuss it now, okay? Mom, I'll call you tomorrow, we'll have a nice long talk, okay? Is it okay if I go now?"

"Yes."

"Okay then. And Mom? Don't worry, okay?"

"All right."

"Good night, Mom."

"Good night, Lissie."

Connie put the receiver gently back on the cradle. She stood by the bedroom phone for several moments, staring at it, and then went downstairs to the kitchen. Jamie had poured himself a drink. He was pacing back and forth between the pantry bar and the table against the kitchen window.

"What'd she say?"

"Will you make me one, please?"

"Yes, what'd she say?"

"She's coming home, you needn't worry."

"When?"

"She'll be here for Easter."

"I want her . . ."

"It doesn't matter *what* you want, Jamie."

"What?"

"It doesn't matter anymore," Connie said, and took the drink from his hand.

Barbara Duggan was leaving for Europe, and her apartment—in its present barren state—was furnished only with a single mattress in one of the bedrooms, a half-dozen throw-pillows on the living-room floor, and an ancient battered floor lamp, none of which Barbara had been able to sell to the steady stream of bargain hunters who'd traipsed up the stairs to the third floor all through the past month. Her duffel bag was already packed, and she had $3,000 in traveler's checks tucked into a sock in her shoulder bag,

155

but her final destination was still a question mark. The two boys who were crashing with her were Carnegie Tech dropouts who'd come west in search of acting careers, but who were leery about making the big move to L.A. and were using San Francisco as a sort of decompression chamber.

The five of them were sitting on the living-room floor, propped on the throw-pillows, smoking pot and drinking hot chocolate. The apartment was on a street lined with factories, and fumes from their chimneys seeped through the cracks in the old sash windows to mingle with the headier aroma of marijuana. Now and again on the street outside—this was now close to midnight, California time—a horn honked, but for the most part the night was still except for the sound of machinery in the nearby factories. Barbara had sold her record player; otherwise there might have been music. Jerry, the better looking of the two Carnegie dropouts, and therefore presumably the one with the brighter theatrical future, was telling about the cops who'd stopped them in Kansas.

"Middle of a big fucking wheatfield," he said, "not another car in sight, we were doing—what, Michael?—fifty miles an hour?"

"Maybe sixty," the other boy said. "Point is, we were observing the speed limit."

"That doesn't mean anything to them," Barbara said.

She was wearing a brightly printed caftan, her thick black hair pulled into a knot at the back of her head, gold hoop earrings on her ears, sandals on her feet, a string of Indian beads around her neck. She was perhaps Lissie's age, a girl with a flawless, pale, almost porcelain complexion, and slanted brown eyes that gave her a composed and somewhat inscrutable Oriental appearance. She spoke in a very low, well-modulated voice (Mom would *adore* her, Lissie thought), her *A*'s broadened by her Bostonian upbringing, her cadences soft and lilting. Sitting beside her barefooted, in jeans and a scruffy T-shirt, Lissie felt bedraggled by contrast. She wanted nothing more than a hot bath and a good night's sleep. She did not want to hear about the dropouts' trials and tribulations on the road; she and Judd had suffered through enough of their own. But she stifled a yawn and listened.

"Pulled us over to the side of the road," Jerry said.

"Siren blaring, like we'd just held up a bank," Michael said.

"Checked out the driver's license and the registration, then asked us to get out of the car."

"Went over it top to bottom, looking for grass."

"Didn't find any, of course, we're not that fucking dumb."

"But they kept us at least an hour, pulled the seats out, looked through the trunk, the glove compartment, the pockets . . ."

"Even looked under the car, figuring we had a hundred pounds of heroin taped under . . ."

She'd never heard her father sound the way he had tonight. Never. You'd think she was selling herself on the *street,* for Christ's sake! Well, she should have told them about Judd long before this, she guessed, but judging from tonight's performance maybe she'd been right in delaying a confrontation. At least *this* had been on the phone, and it had been bad enough. Awful, in fact. She could just imagine what a face-to-face in the Rutledge living room would have been like. You're living with a *what?* A *boy?* A boy you're *sleeping* with? And then the heart attack, whammo, flat on the living room Bokhara, her mother standing by weeping.

". . . even *serve* us in Utah," Judd was saying. "We went into this greasy spoon, cowboys on the front porch, you know . . ."

"Yeah, cowboys," Michael said.

"Judd, I'm sleepy," Lissie said.

"Bull Durham in their shirt pockets, that little tag hanging, you know . . ."

"Yeah, cowboys," Michael said again.

"Looked Lissie over head to toe, raped her with their eyes."

"No, they didn't," Lissie said.

"You didn't see them."

"Well," she said, and shrugged.

"We went inside to the counter," Judd said, "and this big beefy bastard ambles over and says, 'We don't serve hippies.'"

"What'd you do?" Jerry asked.

"I told him that was against the law. He said I should first go get a haircut, and then we could discuss legalities. I told him what I was going to get was a goddamn *lawyer.*"

"Did you?"

"In Brindleshit, Utah? We just kept driving till we got to Nevada. In Nevada, they served us."

"That's 'cause the Mafia runs Nevada," Michael said.

"Barbara, do you think I could take a bath?" Lissie said.

"Sure, honey," Barbara said, "provided you've got your own towel. I sold all mine except the one in the bathroom."

"I've got one," Lissie said.

She went to her duffel, took a towel and a bottle of shampoo from it, and followed Barbara into the bathroom, across the hall from the largest bedroom. The tub was an old-fashioned monster that reminded her of the one in the Commonwealth Avenue apartment.

"How long will you be in Frisco?" Barbara asked, turning on both water taps.

"I have to be back before Easter," Lissie said, and yawned. "Forgive me, I'm really exhausted."

"Well, it was a long trip," Barbara said, nodding. "So you'll be leaving when?"

"I don't know the exact date, you'll have to ask Judd."

"When are you due back at school?"

"Not till the thirtieth."

"Nice long break."

"Yes, but I have to be home the day before. For Easter."

"That doesn't give you much time here. Easter's only a week away."

"We figure we can make it back in four days."

"That'd be pushing it."

"Judd's a fast driver. Anyway, I promised my father."

"He sounded apoplectic on the phone."

"Yeah, I guess he *was* a little excited."

"A *little,* huh? I'd hate to hear him in a rage."

"He's all right, though. Usually."

"Mm," Barbara said. "How old are you, Liss?"

"Eighteen. You?"

"I was nineteen last month. Where'd you say you were going to school?"

"Brenner. How about you?"

"I dropped out of William and Mary a year ago, in my first semester. Came west on the back seat of a motorcycle with a twerp named Percy. You should never ride a motorcycle with anyone named Percy. You should never, in fact, do *anything* with anyone named Percy. The Percys of the world are superior only to the Bruces of the world. Avoid both, my child, and may God bless you." She made the sign of the cross in the air, much as the Pope might have.

"Are you Catholic?" Lissie asked.

"*Used* to be."

"When did you *stop* being?"

"Rode to church on my bicycle—must have been eight years

158

ago—the day before Easter, full of holy emanations. Got in the confessional, crossed myself, said 'Bless me, father, for I have sinned, this is one year since my last confession.' I was eleven years old, the biggest sin I had to confess was having seen myself naked in the mirror, *horrors!* Silence in the booth. Blackness. The priest finally said, 'And you pick the *busiest* time of the year to come?' I left the confessional, left the church, got on my bike and rode home. How about you?"

"Presbyterian."

"Religious?"

"Hardly."

"We'd make a fine pair," Barbara said and smiled.

After breakfast on Monday morning, they took a bus across the Mission to Castro Street. Barbara was wearing the same brightly colored caftan she'd been wearing the night before, her hair loose now, falling in a black cascade to the middle of her back. The fog had burned off, but the day was gray and chilly.

"The reason I'm going to Europe is I'm fed up with all the bullshit in this country," she said. "You know, like your father giving you all that stuff on the phone last night."

"That was unusual," Lissie said.

"But representative of an attitude. In this country, it's a crime to be young right now. It pisses them off, our being young. The great contradiction, of course, is that *they* spend half their time trying to *look* young, dieting or sunbathing or exercising or having their faces lifted or whatever. But they resent us because we *are* young, that's what we really *are,* and that's what they can't ever be again. Every time I come face to face with one of them, in the street, on a cable car, wherever, every time one of them approaches me from the opposite direction, I see it in their eyes. How *dare* you dress this way, how *dare* you smile your fucking flower-child smile, how *dare* you run around without a bra, how *dare* you wear your hair so long, how *dare* you be so young? A constant challenge. I remember once when I was in L.A., I went to meet this guy in MacArthur Park, he had an ounce of good pot I wanted to buy. And this pregnant lady was walking toward me in the park, giving me that same *look,* you know, and I remember thinking, 'Excuse me for being alive, lady, but this is the way I *am. Young.* So go fuck yourself.' Don't *you* ever feel that way? You *must* feel that way."

"Yes, sometimes," Lissie said, and thought again of the conversation with her father the night before, and began feeling rotten about it all over again. The thing was, you had to keep *fighting* them all the time, you had to keep reminding them you weren't a kid in pigtails anymore, you were *eighteen* now! Well, she supposed she should have told them about Judd the minute she'd moved in with him. Instead, because of Steinberg and his dumb mother, she'd found herself in a defensive position, trying to explain, and having to apologize for—*what?* For doing what every other girl in the world—with the possible exception of Steinberg's Irish sweetheart—was doing? Had her father really thought she was still a virgin? At eighteen? Who on earth would even *want* a daughter like that?

". . . in Europe," Barbara was saying. "They've had more practice there, they know how to deal with anything that comes along. Hippies are nothing compared to invading Turks. *C'est la vie, ma cherie,*" she said, and gave what was supposed to be a Gallic shrug. "I can't wait to get there. Only thing that bothers me is I'm going alone."

They ate lunch in a Japanese restaurant, bought ice cream cones afterward, and walked toward the park on Dolores and Eighteenth. Behind them were the Twin Peaks. Ahead, the Mission spread below them, the sky above it dull and threatening.

"Have you ever been to Europe?" Barbara asked.

"Once," Lissie said. "With my parents."

"Where?" Barbara asked.

"France."

"Paris?"

"Just for a few days. Mostly the Dordogne."

"But you *do* know Paris."

"I was just a kid."

"'Cause I'd sure like somebody with me who knew Paris," Barbara said. "I'll be flying straight to London, but I'll be going from there to Paris."

"When are you leaving?" Lissie asked.

"Soon as I can sell the rest of the junk in the apartment. You think anybody'll want a calendar with nine months left on it?"

"When do you suppose that'll be?"

"I'm planning on the seventeenth. That's a Friday." Barbara paused. "Why don't you come with me?"

"Oh, sure," Lissie said. "Just like that."

The rain drummed against the soot-stained windows. Up the

street, they could hear the factory machinery thrumming through the steady beat of the storm. The room was thick with marijuana smoke. The boys had bought three bottles of wine, but only one of them had any left in it.

"Why don't *I* go with you?" Michael said.

"You don't know Paris," Barbara said.

"I'll *learn* Paris. I'll learn every fucking *sewer* in Paris. Take me with you, Barb."

"Ho-ho," Barbara said.

"Listen to that fucking rain," Jerry said.

"Paris in the Spring!" Barbara said. "Think of it! *Café filtre* on the Champs Élysées! Broiled fish for lunch on the Left Bank! All those cute adorable Frenchmen with their funny mustaches and their . . ."

"Lissie can do without all those cute adorable Frenchmen," Judd said.

"Anyway, I couldn't possibly," Lissie said, but she was thinking, *Why not?*

"She has to stay home so she can take shit from her father," Jerry said.

"That was *some* phone call, all right," Lissie said, shaking her head.

"Your father's very good at long-distance shit," Jerry said.

"You wouldn't have to stay any longer than you wanted to," Barbara said. "I'll be there till my money runs out, but you can come back whenever you like. A week, two weeks, whatever you like."

"It wouldn't be worth going all the way to Europe for just a few weeks," Jerry said. "The fare alone would kill her."

"You'd be better off taking *me*," Michael said. "I've already memorized the entire fifth *arrondissement.*"

"How much *is* the fare?" Lissie asked.

"One-way to London is a hun' ninety-eight dollars and ten cents," Barbara said. "I'm flying Icelandic."

"You could always ask *Daddy* for the bread," Jerry said, grinning.

"Oh, sure."

"It wouldn't cost much, Liss, really," Barbara said. "I've got three thousand bucks and I expect that to last a *long* time, believe me."

"Well, even if I *did* go, it wouldn't be for more than a few weeks. Just to get away for a while, you know."

"Sure."

"That wouldn't bother you, would it, Judd?" Lissie asked.

"There's this redhead I've got my eye on anyway."

"Yeah, sure."

"Two, three weeks, something like that," Barbara said. "Maybe a month. Something like that."

"Well, not a month."

"However long you *felt* like. We'd play it *loose,* Lissie, that's the whole idea."

"It sounds terrific," Lissie said. "But I couldn't possibly."

She knew she wasn't going to Europe; she hardly even *knew* Barbara and besides she wasn't sure she could manage the financial end of it, even if she *did* decide to go, which of course she wouldn't. And yet, the concept of absolute freedom for even just a little while—freedom from her parents, freedom from the grind of schoolwork, freedom (yes, she admitted this to herself) from Judd as well—was enormously appealing. She had close to $500 in her savings account in Boston, the end result of Grandmother Croft's yearly birthday gifts of $50 U.S. Savings Bonds, held in trust for her by her father, but which he'd turned over to her when she'd reached eighteen. She also had some jewelry she could sell, Grandmother Harding's legacy over the years, and she supposed that if push came to shove she could sell her stereo equipment which was still in very good condition and which maybe would bring half what her father had paid for it. So she figured she could raise maybe $1,500 tops, which was just *half* of what Barbara planned to take with her, but of course Barbara planned to stay much longer. And anyway, *if* she decided to go, she'd have to sell all her stuff in a hell of a hurry, go back to Boston, put up some signs at school, she didn't know *quite* how she'd be able to manage it all before April 17. All she could count on, actually, was the $500 in cash, from which she'd have to buy a plane ticket—no, it was impossible.

Late that night, she and Barbara had their first really serious talk about the trip. The girls were lying in nightgowns on the mattress in Barbara's bedroom, smoking. Barbara was saying she wouldn't *dare* take her stash to London with her, the customs officials there were supposed to be murderous, and besides you could get marijuana any place in Europe, even in tight-assed London, where they called it cannabis, "which is a *much* more civilized word for it, don't you think?" she asked. They were silent for several moments, passing the toke between them.

"Liss," Barbara said, "do you think there's *any* chance at all you might come with me?"

"I'd love to, but . . ."

"Is it the money?"

"Yes, that. But mostly . . . well . . . my parents, mostly."

"Why would you have to tell them?"

"That I'm going all the way to *Europe?* Of *course* I'd have to tell them."

"Why?"

"Well . . . don't *your* parents know?"

"My mother does. She and Dad are divorced."

"Well, how does *she* feel about it?"

"She couldn't care less," Barbara said, and shrugged. "She's been living with a real estate broker in Providence, they've got their own thing, they're not worried about mine."

"My parents would take a fit," Lissie said.

"So fuck 'em," Barbara said cheerfully.

"Well, it's . . . you know . . . *Europe.*"

"Can I say something?"

"Sure, what?"

"You won't get offended?"

"No, no."

"You sometimes seem very young for eighteen."

"Yeah, I know."

"You still haven't got any idea what it's like to be on your own, have you?"

"I guess not."

"Just don't give them a *chance* to say no, Liss. Given the opportunity, there isn't a parent on God's green earth who'll say yes when he can just as easily say no."

"Oh, sure, I know that."

"What you do is you tell them *after* you get there."

"Oh, yeah, I wouldn't tell them before."

"How much money do you think you can raise?"

"Maybe fifteen hundred dollars. That's if I can sell some . . ."

"God, that would last you *forever!* You'd *never* have to go home, if you didn't want to."

"I'd have to go back to Boston for it, though. Five hundred is in my savings account there."

"What have you got in checking?"

"Just another hundred or so."

"How's your passport?"

"How *is* it? What do you mean?"

"Well, first of all, *where* is it?"

"In Boston. I use it when I'm cashing checks. Saves a lot of hassle."

"It hasn't expired, has it?"

"It did last year, but I had it renewed. It's good till 1974. That's what they're good for, isn't it? Five years?"

"That's right. So what's bothering you?"

"Nothing. It's just . . ."

"Here's how you work it," Barbara said. "You leave early tomorrow morning, you get home *before* Easter, you understand? That's because you're so fucking contrite. You square it all away with your father, tell him how sorry you are about the hassle on the phone, and then you go back to school. But back to the *dorm.* That's what all the shit was about, your living with Judd. So, okay, you go back to the *dorm,* and you call them every night and tell them how glad you are they saved you from that fucking den of iniquity on Commonwealth Avenue. Meanwhile, you're getting your cash together and packing your things. On April seventeenth, you meet me at Kennedy, and off we go."

"You think I should, huh?"

"I think you should."

"Leave early tomorrow morning, huh?"

"Get home by Saturday, maybe sooner."

"Mm."

"Liss, *please* come with me, okay?"

Lissie was silent for a moment.

"Liss?"

"Yes," she said.

"What?"

"I said yes."

"What?"

"Yes," Lissie said, grinning. *Yes!*"

"Jesus!" Barbara said. "Oh, Jesus! Oh, dear God, thank you so much, oh, *Jesus,* Lissie!" she said, and suddenly hugged her.

They spent their first night in London sleeping in Trafalgar Square, together with what appeared to be a thousand other kids from nations all over the world—Americans, of course, but kids from Germany, France, the Netherlands, and even India and Japan as well. The sense of open camaraderie was akin to what Lissie had felt at Woodstock the summer before. Here was a massive congregation of kids united by their dress, their casual use of drugs, their musical preferences, their seeming poverty, and an attitude that was clearly anti-Establishment and therefore threatening to adults, *despite* the kids' wide smiles and cheerful greetings.

They found lodgings the next day at a rooming house off Bayswater Road (thirty-five shillings for bed and breakfast) convenient to Soho and the theater district, a short walk to Kensington Gardens, and a twenty-minute bus ride to Chelsea. In their exploration of the city that day—they had arrived late the night before, too exhausted to do anything but find a spot to flop in Trafalgar Square—they scrupulously avoided anything they considered to be tourist attractions. The "tourists" were all those Americans who sauntered out of Claridge's or the Ritz on their way to visit the Tower of London or the Houses of Parliament, Westminster Abbey or the British Museum. The tourists were all those faceless American businessmen in gray flannel suits—gabardine, actually, now that the promise of spring sunshine tantalized a populace peering expectantly at the broken cloud cover overhead. The tourists were all those overly madeup American women (to Lissie and Barbara, the tourists were *always* Americans) flaunting precious gems on their fingers and around their throats, emerging on wafting scents of expensive perfume from the Mirabelle or Le Gavroche, their laughter bright but somehow forced.

In the girls' minds, Mr. and Mrs. America Abroad were awakened at eight to be served continental breakfast in their balconied room overlooking a Mayfair square; at nine, they left the hotel for a scheduled outing to the Portobello Road Market (provided it was Saturday); lunch afterward at that quaint little cheese restaurant in an alley off Fleet Street, recommended by Fielding, and Fodor, and perhaps Aunt Martha as well; a brief walk to Dr. Johnson's house in Gough Square, and from there by taxi to the Tate Museum or Madame Tussaud's; drinks at The Bunch of Grapes in Shepherd Market, and then back to the hotel to change out of the low-heeled walking shoes and tweedy skirt, the unmatching slacks and rowdy sports jacket, into something elegant for the theater and dinner-dancing later at the Savoy; home (the hotel was "home," the Americans referred to it as such in Barbara and Lissie's fantasy) before eleven to order cognac from the hall waiter and to sip it while watching the late-night news on BBC-2; and then at last to bed—

"Another big day tomorrow, darling."

"Night-night, sweets."

Tourists.

The London Barbara and Lissie created for themselves was as much a figment of their imagination as the limited, prejudiced (though partially valid) tour-guide fantasy they had created for their adult counterparts. It never occurred to either of the girls that by forsaking St. Paul's Cathedral for a shopping spree in the jeans shops mushrooming along Oxford Street, by preferring a trip to the new Lord Kitchener's Valet rather than to the magnificent Middle Temple Hall where Shakespeare himself first produced *Twelfth Night* in 1601, by fashionably opting for the "in" head shops along King's Road rather than the serene and timeless Albert Memorial in Kensington Gardens, they were in effect reducing the foreign city that surrounded them to something as familiar as New York or New Haven, and thereby nullifying its very existence.

Their quest was to meet other kids like themselves. Toward this end, they accidentally, but *only* accidentally, stumbled upon some of the city's treasures: a glimpse of a trio of street troubadours wending their way around Piccadilly Circus toward Haymarket, caught on the periphery of their vision as they discussed the availability of pot with a girl from Scranton and two boys from Denver who were heading for Greece; an unexpected afternoon concert in the band shell at Hyde Park, where for one and threepence apiece they rented striped deck chairs on the lawn, but only because two "cute guys" were sitting nearby; the argument Barbara got into with one of the speakers at Hyde Park Corner, a lofty debate on world Communism (about which she knew next to nothing), solely to impress a pair of British sailors who stood nearby with their Winston Churchill pudding faces and their stained teeth bared in flirtatious grins.

They later strolled with the sailors along the docks by the Thames, the air redolent with the aromas of tobacco, spices, fruit and timber, but the bustle of activity did little to conjure for them the vast world beyond, from which these various commercial vessels had transported bananas and ginger, teak and madras, wheat and tea, and they preferred instead to ooh-and-ahh over the warship the boys proudly pointed out as their own. Before joining the navy, they had worked in the mills outside Manchester, young men Barbara and Lissie might instantly have told to bug off back in America, but the girls were inordinately fascinated by their droll Lancashire accents and accepted an invitation to tea at Queen Mary's Rose Garden in Regent's Park. The boys took them afterward to a place they thought their visitors from abroad might enjoy, a glorified hamburger joint called The Great American Disaster (It *is*, Lissie thought), and then strolled them through Soho, where they snickeringly pointed out the prostitutes lounging in shadowed doorways. Lissie was suddenly reminded of her father's favorite Eliot poem, which he'd read to her in place of a bedtime story when she was only ten, and the lines "Let us go, through certain half-deserted streets / The muttering retreats / Of restless nights in one-night cheap hotels"—and simultaneously and guiltily remembered that she had not yet called home.

At a tobacconist's shop in Dean Street, the boys showed them the jamb around the entrance door, where typed or handwritten notices in a widely understood (to Londoners) code advertised the sexual specialties of the various "ladies of the night," as Jem, the older of the two sailors, knowingly called them. STRICT TEACHER LOOKING FOR OBEDIENT STUDENT or GOLDEN SHOWERS or FRENCH LESSONS, TEACHER FLUENT or the like, all of them gleefully deciphered by these worldly nineteen-year-old mill-workers from Oldham, who seemed singularly intent on confirming the adage that American "gels" fucked like "rebbits." Their tactical approach was not lost on Lissie and Barbara, who declined a walk through St. James's Park ("But it shuts down in an *hour*," Horace, the other of the sailors urgently protested) and insisted instead that they get back to their lodgings by eleven because Lissie was expecting a call from home. Eleven in London was six in New York, and so the lie was a reasonable one, lost nonetheless on the Lancashire dolts, who were totally unaware of the intricacies of time zones.

They walked the girls back to the rooming house on Leinster Terrace, where, on the front doorstep, they kissed them lingeringly, ever hopeful of finding purchase in foreign waters. Horace, who kissed Lissie, tasted of very strong tobacco, undoubtedly distributed to her loyal seamen through the largess of Her Majesty the Queen. As the sailors wandered off into the crisp April night, Lissie found herself wondering where all that yellow fog was, the stuff that rubbed its back upon the windowpanes.

This was Sunday night, the nineteenth. She had last spoken to her parents on Thursday, from the Brenner dorm, telling them she was going to a Yale mixer for the weekend (she had deliberately chosen Yale, as her father's alma mater) and would call them when she got back to Boston. She assumed she would be safe until tomorrow morning at least, but she knew she could not postpone the call indefinitely. Barbara's alibi to the sailors now provided ample opportunity for her to pick up the phone in the hall downstairs and place a collect, transatlantic call to Connecticut (it was now only 6:30 P.M. there) but she delayed yet another time.

When she fell asleep that night, she was thinking of the World War II, fleece-lined, fighter-pilot's jacket she'd bought at Railway Lost in Piccadilly, and wondering whether she'd ever get to wear it in Europe this summer.

As spring burst ingloriously on the British countryside in a torrent of rain distantly related to a monsoon in the long-lost colonial empire, Barbara and Lissie, wearing her fighter-pilot jacket over a T-shirt and blue jeans, morosely decided upon a hasty exodus from these dewy sceptered isles, and visited a travel agent in Berkeley Street to inquire about the cheapest fare to Spain.

They chose Spain only because the weather in Paris was as shitty as it was here in London, and they had heard it would be sunny and mild on the Costa del Sol. But as they made their inquiries of a pretty little blond girl with a marked Cockney accent and a miniskirt showing lace-edged panties above its precipitous hem, three boys standing at the counter with them quickly disabused them of any notion they'd had of spending a carefree and inexpensive, suntanned two weeks on a beach.

"The weather is fine there," one of the boys told them, "but the Spanish attitude toward hippies absolutely sucks. I know guys who've been kicked off beaches on the Costa Brava only because their *hair's* too long, would you believe it? And if those Fascist bastards catch you smoking pot, you'll languish in a Spanish prison for the rest of your life. Whatever you do," he said, "stay away from that fucking Spain."

The British girl behind the counter, unused to such language in public places, partial to Spain because she'd spent a £50 all-inclusive two-week holiday there the summer before, snippily asked, "Did you wish to book then, or what?"

"We do not wish to book then," Barbara said, and, together with the three boys, she and Lissie walked out into the pouring rain toward the nearest pub.

The boys were Americans, one of them a dropout from the University of North Carolina at Chapel Hill, another the son of a Philadelphia restaurant owner, the third a somewhat mysterious and taciturn young man with a scrubby, red, growing-in beard, a patchy uneven crewcut, and brooding brown eyes, who remained rather vague about where he came from or whither he was bound. His first name was Paul, and he offered his last name only when Lissie asked him what it was. Even then he hesitated before answering. "Gillis," he said, "Paul Gillis." He was wearing a rubberized, camouflaged poncho like the ones she'd seen at Railway Lost the week before, blue jeans, and sandals totally unsuitable to the rain outside. The rain oozed serpentinely along the pub's front plate-glass window. On the jukebox, the Beatles were singing "Let It Be."

The U.N.C. dropout spoke with a thick southern accent modified only when he was using hippie expressions like "far out" or "getting off," national in flavor and therefore impervious to his drawl; he was the one who'd given them the initial information on Spain. His name was Robert Alston Chadwick, and his two friends called him Robby. Tall, blond and blue-eyed, sporting no beard but instead a mustache like a Hussar cavalryman's, wearing a yellow rain slicker and a peaked baseball cap, he advised the girls that they should change their minds and head for Greece instead, via Amsterdam.

"That's where we're heading," he said.

"Cool city," the third boy said.

His name was Tony Giglio and he was here, at his father's insistence, for a pilgrimage to a town northwest of Naples, a hilltop village called Ruvo del Monte from which his grandfather had emigrated in the year 1900, shortly after *la fillossera* struck that country's vineyards and reduced to insignificance its thriving wine industry. Tony was clean-shaven, albeit with shadowy jowls, and he wore his black hair in a slicked-back greaser's style. He told the girls he would be accompanying Robby and Paul only as far as Amsterdam, after which he would board a plane to Naples, and then take a bus to Ruvo del Monte, so he could "hug all the wop *paisans* there and contribute five hundred dollars to the fucking village parish, in honor of the fucking local saint."

Paul Gillis listened to all this without saying a word.

"How long will you be in Amsterdam?" Barbara asked.

"Till it gets boring," Robby said, and grinned.

His smile gave to his already handsome face a widescreen, movie-star radiance. Lissie suspected, from the way Barbara flutteringly batted her lashes in that instant, that she'd fallen madly in love with him at once, a dismaying insight in that she herself had always been partial to blond boys; hadn't her only experience been with blond Judd Gordon?

"So what do you say?" Robby asked.

"Is it expensive there?" Barbara said.

"Cheap as donkey shit," Robby said. "Anyway, we'll be crashing with some girls I know, more the merrier."

"American girls?"

"Dutch."

"Well, how would they feel about . . . ?"

"I told you. More the merrier. The pot flows like wine in

Holland, not like that fuckin' Spain . . . or even *here,* for that matter. You find any choice stuff in little old London Town?"

"We've been grubbing from other Americans," Barbara said.

"Different in Holland," Robby said. "Nobody cares *what* you do there. The Dutch love hippies. Isn't that right, Paul?"

"Mm," Paul said.

"So what do you say?"

"Liss?"

"Sure," Lissie said.

They had made love twice that afternoon. After the first time, Joanna La Flute recounted to him with surprising anger, considering the fact that she hadn't been the recipient of the concertmaster's tirade, what had happened at rehearsal that morning when the first fiddler in the second section was accused of playing over the finger board instead of near the bridge as the rest of the section was doing.

Fillipa, for such was the first fiddler's name, promptly informed the concertmaster that the words *"sur la touche"* were clearly printed on the score beside the suspect passage, and that *she* knew what those words meant even if nobody *else* in the section seemed to know, and even if the concertmaster *himself* didn't seem to know. If he wanted her to play it closer to the bridge, she would most certainly do that, contrary to the composer's wish for a covered, less piercing, more pastellike sound. But if the concertmaster wanted a suggestion (and here Joanna did a fine imitation of sixty-two-year-old Fillipa who had been playing in orchestras since she was nineteen) perhaps he might prefer them not to *bow* the passage at all, but to *pluck* it instead, in which case the concertmaster could go pluck *himself.*

Joanna La Flute laughed when she repeated Fillipa's bon mot, but otherwise she'd told the story with a kind of contained professional fury. It was after they'd made love the second time that Joanna Jewish stole into bed and snuggled up close to Jamie and began telling him in detail of what had been her final session with the redoubtable Marvin Mandelbaum.

"It was surprising to both of us," Joanna said. "I was lying on the couch, studying his tin ceiling and not saying anything as usual, and behind me I could hear the heavy breathing that meant either he was about to make an obscene phone call or else fall asleep, and all at once I said, 'I'd like to quit, Dr. Mandelbaum,' and like a shot, he answered, 'I think you should!'

"I was so surprised by what *I'd* said, and so surprised by the *answer* I got, that I sat up and turned to look at him, and he was sitting there with a surprised look on *his* face, too, everybody in the whole room was surprised. So I said, 'I *mean* it, Doctor,' and now he wipes the glee—Jamie, he looked absolutely *gleeful* after the initial shock wore off—he wipes the glee off his face, the *pisher*, and very solemnly says, 'Do you feel you are now able to cope successfully with your various problems, Joanna?' Since I was already sitting up, and since I was quitting anyway, I dug in my handbag for a cigarette, and I lit it, and got off the couch and began pacing the room while he sat there in his chair watching me and listening to me. I had the feeling this was the first time anything like this had ever happened in his office. I was making medical history there in his office.

"I told him I didn't think I had a problem with married men anymore, not if he thought the problem was that I *chose* married men because I didn't *want* to get married. I told him I'd been talking about nothing else *but* marrying you for the past eight months now, ever since we met on the Vineyard, so if he figured that *talking* about someone all the time was a *problem,* then he was wrong because *I* figured it was *love*. I figured if somebody's in your mind day and night, and you can't get him out, and you can't wait till you see him the next time, can't wait to touch him and kiss him, touch his hair, I love touching your hair, then—what's *that?"* she said, and sat bolt upright.

"What?"

"Listen!"

He listened. The room was silent, the house was silent.

"I don't—"

"Shhh!"

He could hear only the various sounds of the house itself, the ticking of the clock on the dresser (it was precisely 4:00 P.M.), a *click* someplace downstairs and then the hum of the refrigerator as it began its cycle, the *whoosh* of the oil burner as it went on. But nothing else. Joanna was virtually bristling, eyes and nostrils wide, nipples puckered, hands opened like radar antennas hovering on the air before her breasts as though hoping to absorb sound through the palms. She knew the noises in this house, knew which were normal and which were not, and now she listened and tried to sift one from the other, tried to separate the sound that had startled her in the first place. There was suddenly the thin sharp glittery crack of breaking glass.

She grabbed his hand.

He felt the bristles go up at the back of his neck, felt his heart suddenly begin pounding in his chest, felt a rush of adrenaline that propelled him over to the dresser where he picked up Joanna's silver hairbrush and held it by the handle like a hammer. There was the sound of more glass breaking now, but it was a methodical, even sound, the sound of someone chipping away shards before attempting entry, slivers falling to the floor and shattering there. And then silence. He caught his breath. Across the room, Joanna was picking up the bedside phone.

"No!" he whispered.

She looked at him, puzzled for an instant, and then she understood. They could not call the police because when they got here they would discover not only a burglar coming in through the third-floor window where there was a fire escape outside, but also a naked man holding a silver hairbrush in his trembling hand, a man named James Croft who was married to Constance Croft in Rutledge, Connecticut, and who had no more right than the burglar to be here in the apartment of naked, twenty-five-year-old Joanna Berkowitz. She let her hand fall limply from the receiver.

Jamie stood just inside the doorjamb. The door was open, and he could see past the library with its Oriental rugs and Joanna's music stand and her flute case open on one of the wingback chairs, silver against green velvet—he was probably after the flutes. She had three flutes, she had told Jamie how insurance costs were devastating for musicians who owned expensive instruments; Fillipa owned a Strad that was insured for half a million dollars. He was here for the instruments. He had heard her playing one day, figured he'd come in just before dark, before she got home from wherever she worked, grab whatever instrument it was he'd heard up there on the third floor.

Past the study, Jamie could see the flat even light of late afternoon streaming in the hallway, and then he heard footfalls crunching on the broken glass beneath the hall window, and then more footfalls, and something blocked the streaming light for just a moment, caused it to waver for just a moment before the man

173

obviously flattened himself against the corridor wall, and began inching his way down the corridor soundlessly, perhaps sensing someone else in the house, perhaps merely exercising a caution any burglar might, Jamie neither knew nor cared. He was trapped in a nightmare realized.

He had often in the Rutledge house, lying awake at night and listening to the creak of a staircase or the clatter of a raccoon, wondered what he would do if someone entered the house. He always slept naked; he imagined himself at an immediate disadvantage against a fully clothed and possibly armed intruder, a man facing however many years in prison for breaking-and-entering or armed robbery, or whatever the hell the police called it. He had imagined someone creeping up the steps from below, hearing the creak of the treads under a stranger's heavy footfalls, hearing him padding down the hallway toward the bedroom where Jamie stood just inside the doorway, a brass candlestick in his right hand, one of a pair that were a wedding present from Connie's mother, both normally sitting on the ledge of the upstream bedroom windows. Had imagined this scene. And had known he would kill to protect either Lissie or Connie, and had hoped no one ever forced him to do that, no one ever got as far into his house as that bedroom hallway outside, where he would have to swing the heavy brass candlestick hoping merely to stun but knowing he might perhaps kill.

The hall outside was silent now.

The afternoon light filled the open doorframe at the far end of the study, unbroken. On the bed behind him, Joanna sat still and tense, listening. This was not Jamie's house, he did not know what to do here. If he struck this man as he entered the bedroom, if he knocked him unconscious with the hairbrush or God forbid killed him—no, he didn't think the hairbrush would kill him, he wasn't even certain it was heavy enough to knock him out—but *then* what? What did they do then? If he had warned Joanna against calling the police *before* the man posed the threat he now posed, how would the situation have changed *after* he was bleeding and unconscious on the Bokhara outside the bedroom door?

"Anybody here?" a voice called.

Joanna gasped. Jamie felt a shock of electric fear run up his spine and into his skull.

"Hey?" the voice called again. "Anybody here?"

Black. A black man.

"You hear me?" the voice called.

Jamie looked at Joanna. He took a deep breath, and very quietly said, "I'm waiting for you with a shotgun." The lie hung on the suddenly stifling air. He waited for an answer. Nothing came.

"You hear me, you little prick?" he yelled. "I've got a shotgun in my hands, you come one step closer and I'll blow your fucking head off."

"Hey, cool it," the voice said.

"Get the fuck *out* of here!" Jamie shouted.

"Shoot him, shoot him!" Joanna screamed, as if she really believed there *was* a shotgun.

There was another moment of silence in the hall outside, and the frantic beat of footsteps toward the broken window, and the crunch of glass underfoot when he reached the window, and then more glass as he went through, and the sound of his feet on the iron railings of the fire escape and the iron rungs of the ladder, retreating, fading. Jamie went out into the library, still holding the hairbrush in his hand, and peeked around the doorjamb. The hallway was empty.

"He's gone," he whispered.

"I have to pee," Joanna said.

He sat naked in the red leather wingback chair near the tiled Franklin stove, and he heard the sound of Joanna urinating, and he thought, If I don't tell Connie soon, the whole fucking world will know before she does. All the black burglars in Harlem will know, only next time we might not be so lucky, next time the guy out there in the hall may have a shotgun himself, a real shotgun and not a hairbrush posing as one. And he'll come in here blasting, ask the questions later, kill the fucking honkies first, grab the silver flute and all the silver shit on the dresser, fence the stuff uptown, leave it for the cops to later discover that the honkie with his brains on the rug ain't married to the honkie with the big tits and the open windpipe.

He heard the toilet flushing and then heard the sink tap being turned on, Joanna splashing water onto her hands and perhaps her face as well, cold water to wash away the stale sweat caused by that fucking bastard who'd had the *nerve* to break in here, to intrude, to violate, smashing the window and stealing down the hallway, here to steal the silver, here to steal the family jewels, the family, the . . . what do we do now? Today was dangerous, today could have been disastrous. Too damn close today. No cigar, but very goddamn close. So what do we do? What do the big lovers do. The red-hot lovers. The red-hot *burglars,* what do we do? Burglars breaking into that fucking Rutledge house, stealing through its hallways, *intruding,* violating the way that cocksucker violated this house today, *violating!* What do we do?

"Don't go out in the hall without your shoes on," Joanna called.

The airmail letter was waiting in the mailbox when he got home from the city that afternoon. It read:

April 20, 1970

Dear Mom and Dad,

I know this will come as a shock to you both, and I hope you won't take it the wrong way. I know you think I'm in school right now, but instead I'm in London. Before you hit the ceiling, please let me explain. This isn't a flouting of parental authority, or any kind of diminishing of the love I feel for you both. When I went out to California, I did plan on returning to school, I told you the truth about that, and those are still my plans now, nothing has changed. But me and Barbara, she's the girl you spoke to briefly on the telephone, had some very good talks in San Francisco about the direction my life was taking, and I decided to get away for a while to think things out more completely. I know you're probably wondering why I needed *another* break from school when I'd just had one, but what with the hassle of getting across the country, and the subsaquent troubling talks we had with each other, I felt the need for further replenishment of the spirit. So that's why I'm here in London.

Barbara (Duggan) is a girl my age, well actually just a bit older, who plans to stay here in Europe much longer than I. She's a darling person, and she has money of her own, you don't have to worry about her grubbing from me or anything. My own plans indicate that I'll be home in two or three weeks, which is about how long I guess my money will last. I drew the $500 out of my savings account in Boston, and I also sold my stereo to a girl in Davis Hall. I know you'll be pleased to hear I got $400 for it, which I think was cool trading since we only paid $620 for it brand-new at Radio Shack. This will be more than enough to get me to Amsterdam, which is where we'll be heading when we leave here tomorrow

176

morning. I don't know where we'll be staying yet, so I can't give you an address. I'll keep in touch, though, and I don't want you to worry about me.

There are lots of young people like ourselves here in Europe, striving and learning, and I'm sure I'll gain much from the experience of being on my own and discovering things for myself. Please understand that the reason I didn't tell you about my plan was that I was sure you would object to it the way you objected to my taking that trip to Denver with Jenny when I was still at Henderson. Also, the various conversations we had didn't seem to indicate that you'd be receptive to something like this, and so I had to do it on my own and then let you know about it this way. So, again, I'm sorry if this comes as a surprise, but it was something I felt I had to do just now. It is a matter of values, I guess, and finding the right values. I don't know if you can understand that, but I hope you will try. I love you both, and I would never in the world do anything to hurt either one of you.

All my love,

Lissie

He called his agent the moment he read the letter (oddly, the fact that she could not spell the word "subsequent" annoyed him almost as much as her defection) to tell Lew he was sorry as hell to be bothering him with something like this, but he was wondering nonetheless if he could help with a matter that had nothing to do with marketing pictures. Lew listened patiently as Jamie explained that his daughter was presumably in Amsterdam someplace—her letter had been dated the twentieth, and this was now the twenty-fifth—and that he was very worried about her because he knew what the drug scene was like in Holland, and she was an eighteen-year-old girl traveling alone with another girl her age and he wondered if Lew could help by putting him in touch with the Dutch agent he'd met just before Christmas in Lew's office, Evert somebody, who he knew handled work for Lew in Amsterdam, and who had presumably earned commissions selling some of Jamie's pictures there.

He said all of this in a breathless rush, and Lew, on the other end of the line, immediately grasping the urgency of the situation, told him to hold a minute while he got his book, and was back on the phone thirty seconds later to reel off the Dutch agent's name, address and telephone number. He spelled out the last name, G-o-e-d-k-o-o-p, and similarly spelled out the Witte de Withstraat address, and then repeated his office and home numbers twice to make certain Jamie had them. Now, at a quarter to eight in the evening in Connecticut, Jamie listened to the phone ringing in Noordwijk aan Zee, wherever the hell *that* was, a peculiarly urgent sound as compared to the more leisurely American ring, and then the ringing stopped abruptly, and there was the sound of the receiver clattering to a hard surface, and then someone muttering something in Dutch, and then silence, and then *"Hallo?"*

"Mr. Goedkoop?" Jamie said. He wasn't sure of the pronunciation, and he hoped the man wouldn't hang up on him, thinking he was trying to reach someone else entirely.

"Yes?"

"Evert, this is Jamie Croft, we met once in Lew Barker's . . ."

"Yes?"

"I'm calling from America."

Goedkoop was slowly coming awake. "Yes, Jamie," he said, "how are you?"

"Fine, thanks, I'm sorry to be waking you at this hour . . ."

"No, no, *graag gedaan,*" Goedkoop said.

". . . but my daughter is in Amsterdam, she left suddenly to go to Europe . . ."

"Your daughter?" Goedkoop said.

"Yes, my eighteen-year-old daughter."

"Ah, is here in *Amsterdam!* Ah, of course," Goedkoop said, misunderstanding, and wondering why such a call had to be made at two in the morning. "Where is she staying? I'll be certain to ring her up and . . ."

"That's just it. I don't *know* where she is. She's traveling alone with another girl her age, and we'd very much appreciate it if you could—Amsterdam isn't a very large city—if you could ask around and try to get a line on her."

"A line?"

"Try to find out where she's staying. So we can make contact with her."

"Ah," Goedkoop said. He was wide-awake now. "Yes, I will check the various hotels, of course," he said. "But, do you know, not many young people are staying at hotels. Well, I will call on various underground people here . . ."

178

"Underground?" Jamie said, alarmed.

"Pardon?"

"You said . . ."

"Yes, people who are having knowledge of the places these youngsters frequent. Do not worry, Jamie, I quite understand, and will do all I can. What is your daughter's name?"

"Melissa. Melissa Croft. And she's traveling with a girl named Barbara Duggan."

"Would you spell that for me, please?"

Jamie spelled both names for him. On the other end of the line, he heard Goedkoop's labored breathing and remembered him as a man who was exceedingly overweight.

"I have two boys myself," Goedkoop said, "of eighteen and twenty-three, and so I can feel for you and your wife, believe me. Amsterdam seems to be the *middlepunt* for young people from everywhere, do you know, the epicenter? Even Dutch boys and girls. They are coming from all over the Netherlands to Amsterdam. I know Dutch parents who are combing the city for weeks on end. Do you perhaps have a photograph? If you could send me one, it might facilitate . . ."

"Yes, I'll put one in the mail immediately."

"Goed, okay, that will be good. But in the meanwhile, what does she look like, your daughter?"

"She's five nine, and weighs about . . . Connie, what does she weigh?"

"Pardon?" Goedkoop said.

"I'm checking with my wife. Connie?" he said, and impatiently snapped his fingers at her, something he'd never done in his life. "A hundred and twenty," he said into the phone when she'd given him the information. "She has long blond hair, and blue eyes and . . . uh . . . let me see what else might help you. A birthmark on her left shoulder, sort of like a crescent moon."

"Ah, yes," Goedkoop said, "a crescent moon. And you said her height was . . . ?"

"Five nine."

"Yes, what would that be in centimeters?"

"I'm not sure. Do you want me to check? Connie, could you get the dictionary or something? He wants to know what five nine would be in . . ."

"That is five feet nine inches, yes?" Goedkoop said.

"Yes, five . . ."

"I can convert it here, do not worry. And one hundred and twenty pounds? That is *pounds* you are saying."

"Yes, pounds."

"Blond hair, blue eyes," Goedkoop muttered, obviously writing down the information. "And the other girl?"

"I have no idea what she looks like."

"No matter, I will try to find them both for you. In the meanwhile, don't worry, please. I am sure you will hear from your daughter soon. My older son is studying in London, and if he isn't writing for some weeks his mother becomes so upset, not to mention his father," Goedkoop said, and chuckled. "I will do what I can, and I will call you with my results. But as I say, do not worry. I am sure she is fine."

"Thank you, Evert," Jamie said, relieved. "When you call, please make it collect, I don't want you to . . ."

"Nonsense, no, no," Goedkoop said. "I have a long time been an admirer of your work, and it is a pleasure when Lewis sends me your photographs to sell. I saw in a recent issue of *Time* magazine here, the photographs you took of the downtown fire in New York. They are splendid. Has *Time* bought all rights, or would they be free for the Dutch market?"

"You'd have to ask Lew about that."

"Ah? Yes, of course, I will. And I will call you when I have the good news I expect I will soon have."

"Thank you," Jamie said. "And please forgive me for calling at this hour, but . . ."

"No, no, it is quite all right," Goedkoop said, and hung up abruptly, the way Jamie had discovered most foreigners did, without the conversational *pas de deux* Americans used as a terminating shorthand.

Goedkoop did in fact fastidiously explore what he referred to, in his call to Jamie two days later, as "the darkness of Amsterdam," inquiring after the tall blond girl with blue eyes, phoning all the hotels, visiting in person the myriad rooming houses and the several youth hostels, spending a considerable amount of time at Delaurier, the largest of the hostels which—appropriately enough, he felt—had recently opened an annex as a rehabilitation center for drug addicts, and then taking to the streets themselves, roaming through the parks and along the canals during the daytime hours and frequenting at night those dimly lighted *boîtes* off the Rembrandtsplein, wandering into the Seaman's Quarter, searching through the sleazy bars on the Oude Zijds Voorburgwal and around the Oudekerksplein where prostitutes beckoned from cribs over which red lights actually were hanging. He even walked onto the Oude Zijds Achterburgwal, knowing this was dangerous, and hoping against hope he would *not* find James Croft's daughter here.

He found no trace of her anywhere, but he assured Jamie on the telephone that he would try yet another time when the photograph of her was in hand. He told Jamie, again, that he was not to worry; he was certain "young Matilda" (his faulty memory of the name caused Jamie a sudden lurch of despair) would be writing or calling home sooner than he expected. "In the meanwhile," he had also talked to Lewis about those pictures in *Time,* and had learned that only North American rights had been purchased, and that he was free to sell the photographs elsewhere. Lewis was sending him prints forthwith. Again, he hung up abruptly.

Jamie had no way of knowing that Lissie had left Amsterdam on the very day Evert Goedkoop had begun his fruitless search.

Robby's Dutch girlfriends were twenty-two-year-old twins named Elisabeth and Ida Verschoor, who made their home in an apartment off Jan Eversten Straat, within walking distance of Erasmus Park. Both girls spoke fluent English and were, in fact, employed as translators at the American Consulate near the Concertgebouw, to which they took the tram each morning, leaving their guests to enjoy the exuberant hospitality of the city before rejoining them at the apartment along about six each evening.

There were three bedrooms in the apartment. Barbara shared one of them with Robby the very first night they were there. The blond twins, pretty and rather tall by Dutch standards, slept in their own bedroom, side by side in a king-sized bed. Tony Giglio and Paul Gillis slept in the third bedroom at the end of the hall. Lissie slept on a couch in the small but neatly furnished living room; a tiled clock on the mantelpiece chimed the hour and the half-hour, keeping her awake half the night.

The Amsterdam equivalent of the statue of Eros in London was the white stone memorial on the east side of Dam Square, across from the Grand Hotel Krasnapolsky with its orange awnings and fluttering rooftop flags. There, close by a smaller but much fiercer lion than the ones guarding Trafalgar Square, the hippies gathered on the cobblestoned curbs circling the memorial. But here, perhaps because the girls had never before been a part of such a concentrated congregation of similarly minded young people (except, as Lissie recalled and pointed out to Barbara, at Woodstock last year), the girls found themselves more attracted to what they called "the heavy culture" the city had to offer, which many young people like themselves were actively seeking out. The Anne Frank House was especially appealing to many of the visiting American youths, who wrongheadedly equated the young Dutch girl's ordeal during the German occupation with the totally incomparable "hassling" they suffered at the hands of law enforcement officials everywhere, the Dutch cops forming a part of the international brotherhood where it came to loitering or disorderly conduct, but remarkably benign where it concerned the free and easy transfer and open use of drugs of every stripe and color.

In Amsterdam that spring, the visiting kids were of the general opinion that the grass here in Europe was greener than it had been back in the States. Most of the marijuana that found its way into the American market came from Mexico; the stuff in Amsterdam came from Asia, Africa or the Near East, and was stronger than what the Americans were used to smoking. There was a great deal of hashish in Amsterdam. The kids called it hash as though it were as innocuous as a dish of chopped meat and potatoes served over the counter of a greasy spoon restaurant.

And perhaps it was. Marijuana or its various derivatives was the least concern of anyone in Amsterdam. The kids, repeatedly warned by every rock-and-roll disk jockey in the States that "Speed Kills," further warned by insistent wall posters wherever young people gathered, nonetheless seemed to be turning to amphetamines with an avidity that was bewildering and frightening to Lissie. Even Barbara, slightly older and presumably more sophisticated, found sickening the druggies draped around the Dam Memorial.

The streets were littered with dog shit and broken glass, two rather unrelated commodities, but they were also strewn with human debris, the instantly recognizable speed freaks who jabbered like monkeys, their bodies running on a hyperactive double-time, their pupils dilated, their sweat soaking through T-shirts or tent dresses. Pale, invariably thin to the point of emaciation, they raved like lunatics when they were high, and then became enormously depressed when they crashed. A confirmed speed freak could get off for hours on a single shot of Dexedrine or Methedrine, mainlined by syringe, like heroin, which was also prevalent and easily obtainable in Amsterdam that spring. Even before the twins suggested that they might enjoy going to Elysium that night, a place they described as "Woodstock playing in Amsterdam," even before Lissie caught the scene there, she had firmly decided that the one thing she would never in her life do was poke a needle into her body.

Elysium was perhaps as large as the Fillmore East in New York, but unlike its American rock counterpart, there was no extravagant psychedelic light-show accompanying the music here. Instead, the cavernous two-storied hall was dimly lighted and dingy, thronged—when they entered it at midnight—with what Lissie estimated to be 5,000 kids between the ages of thirteen and twenty-five, all of them stoned. There was no furniture in the place, not a chair, a table or a bench anywhere in sight. The kids milled about the big stage at the front of the hall, or sat on the floor below it, listening to a badly amplified, four-piece rock group that billed itself, in American fashion, as The Rocketeers, singing American tunes in a European accent of uncertain origin, the words "Plizz riliss me . . . *lat* me go" blaring from the speakers as the twins-guided party paid their admission fees and pushed their way through into what Lissie immediately equated with a Chinese opium den.

Marijuana smoke hung thickly on the air, its sweet aroma almost sickening in such concentration. ("Just take a deep breath," Barbara said, "and you're high.") To the right of the entrance door, a young blonde wearing a miniskirt with nothing under it, her eyes glazed, her jaw hanging lax, was sitting on the floor in a noxiously fluid pile of her own excrement. Lissie hurried past her, frightened, taking Tony's arm in reflexive defense, watching as Paul Gillis glanced at the girl and turned away. He had said nothing when the twins suggested Elysium; he said nothing now.

On the stage, a gangly young man moved swiftly and erratically toward the lead guitarist, his arms waving jerkily, demanding in a rush that he be allowed to sing. The guitarist began arguing with him, and the kids sitting on the floor or milling around the perimeter of the stage began hissing and booing till the guitarist relinquished the microphone and the spotlight. The new possessor of both said a few words to the kid behind the electric piano,

184

presumably establishing a key, and then launched into a spaced-out, amphetamine-high imitation of Alvin Lee's "I'm Comin' Home," taking particular joy in simulating the dog barks that had been an integral part of that hit record, losing the pianist completely, the lyrics trailing into an a cappella symphony of manic barking, a veritable dog pound unleashed at the microphone, yelping and screeching from the amplified speakers.

The kids crowding the stage began booing and hissing again, and the would-be rock star raised his arms like President Nixon, the index and middle finger of both hands spread in *V*'s for Victory, and grinned appreciatively, mistaking the roar of disapproval for gratified applause and cries of encouragement. He pulled the belt he was wearing free of the loops on his blue jeans, held it up like a prize boa constrictor, and boomed into the microphone, "See this belt? That's one beautiful belt, all right. Does anybody want to buy this gorgeous belt? Do I hear ten guilders? Okay, do I hear *five* guilders? How about two? I'll settle for a single solitary guilder" (the boos louder and more insistent now), "the thinnest part of a dollar, the equivalent" (and here he fell into an imitation of W. C. Fields), "m'friends, of thirty cents American, ah, yes, do I have any takers? No takers? Go fuck yourselves, you fuckin' freaks."

When they left the place at two-thirty in the morning, the kid who'd tried to sell his belt had crashed, and was standing on the sidewalk outside, leaning against a lamppost, muttering morosely to himself. They heard his unintelligible words behind them all the way up the street, and Lissie thought she could still hear them after they had turned the corner onto the Leidseplein.

They did not get back to the apartment until almost three. Tony and the twins, apparently having discovered one another over some good Turkish hash purchased at Elysium from a British kid just back from Algiers, retired to the middle bedroom with the king-sized bed, all thoughts of his pilgrimage to Ruvo del Monte obscured by the prospects of a sexual playground unimagined in his wildest fantasies. Lissie, exhausted and unwilling even to *think* of spending another night trying to maneuver, however craftily, her five feet nine inches into the confines of a couch that was seven inches shorter than her body, readily accepted Barbara's suggestion that she take the now-vacant bed in the third bedroom. Changing into a nightgown in the hall bathroom, she tiptoed past the twins' already acrobatically reverberating room and opened the door onto the utter darkness of the end room. Paul Gillis was already asleep.

Not daring to put on a light, she stumbled across the room, banging her shins against an ottoman, muttering "Shit!" in the inky blackness, turning swiftly to see whether or not she'd awakened him, and then finally finding her bed, and spending another three minutes trying to figure out how these damn Dutch sheets could possibly be tucked in so tight that a person couldn't find where they began or ended. At last yanking back the resistant sheets and blanket, she climbed under the covers on a sigh, pulled the bedclothes to her throat, and heard the toot of a solitary tugboat somewhere on one of the canals. The horn bleated again, echoed, faded. The city, so vibrantly alive in the daylight hours, was still and silent. She fell asleep almost at once.

He came to her bed sometime during the night.

He did not say a word.

She thought of it later as a silent, consensual rape.

She had barely said three sentences to this boy since meeting him in London, and she awoke now to find him beside her. Wordlessly, he spread his right hand on her thigh, the wrist resting lightly on the patch of pubic hair between her legs. His face loomed above hers for an instant, and then he kissed her. She loved beards, she found them a turn-on, perhaps because her one and only experience had been with bearded Judd Gordon, perhaps because they represented to her a statement of male youthfulness, defiant and brave—*This is what I want to look like, take it or leave it.*

As Paul kissed her now, as this boy she didn't know kissed her, she thought instantly of that first night in Woodstock, perhaps mistaking him in that murky instant between sleep and wakefulness for Judd, opening her mouth in automatic response to his kiss, feeling the stiff bristles of his nascent mustache against her upper lip, his hand still grasping her thigh, the wrist lightly resting on her mound below. She knew instantly and instantaneously that she was not dreaming, and that this was not Judd.

Oddly, she felt neither outrage nor indignation over his violation of her turf, but instead a sense of appropriateness. In an apartment where Tony and the twins were fucking their brains out next door, and Barbara and Robby were similarly if not numerically inter-locked farther down the hall, there seemed something fitting, almost preordained, about Paul's silent nocturnal passage across the six feet that separated their beds, his body beside hers, his lips covering hers, his hand on her thigh, the wrist motionless on the bronze triangular shield that protected, she now realized, an entrance cleft already vulnerable to entreaty. Had she been dreaming erotically before he'd slipped into bed beside her? Or was her reaction prompted solely by his sudden wordless presence and lingering kiss, the hand that refused to budge a scant four inches to the right where it would have found her straining toward his questing fingers, still spread and motionless on her thigh?

A single tinny note sounded in the blackness, the small tiled clock on the living room mantel striking the half-hour. The widespread fingers on her thigh, their subtle weight, their warmth, their utter immobility; the insistent urging of his mouth upon hers, his tongue thrusting and exploring now, her own tongue responding; the wrist suspended a millimeter above her crotch, all combined to arouse her more completely than would have a more deliberate assault.

She spread her legs, silently indicating acquiescence, but his mouth remained the sole adventurer, the widespread hand burning its imprint into her thigh, the reluctant wrist motionless even when she lifted herself slightly to engage it flesh to flesh, and felt its strong beating pulse. For the first time in her life—never with Judd—she found herself in the role of active aggressor, reaching over him to find his rigid penis, clutching it in her hand, urging it with bold, hard strokes cunningly calculated to elicit a response that would rocket into his brain and trigger his recalcitrant hand, causing that hand to move from her thigh (where now she felt his fingers trembling) and onto her seething vagina.

When at last the hand moved, with a suddenness as startling as his appearance beside her in bed had been, when at last his fingers parted the seeping folds of her flesh to locate with pinpoint accuracy her throbbing clitoris, when at last he began fondling her there with a touch as wispily tantalizing as his stubborn wrist had been, she felt at once a familiar melting inside, a recognized dissolving of her interior walls, a rush of blood to her head, an unbearable mounting pressure that promised imminent inundation, and tightened her hand on him, pumping him now with an urgency dictated by her dangerously impending tidal wave, pulling him toward her in fitful jerks, crushing him stiff against her belly where he spilled his juices just as she felt herself crumbling helplessly before the torrential, crashing, blindly raging ecstasy of her own orgasm.

And still, they did not speak.

With surprising alacrity, they began again at once, more familiarly this time. His fingers parted and probed, his hands roamed over her belly and her thighs, caressed her minuscule breasts with their all-consuming nipples, her backside, searched out her anal cavity (she had never permitted Judd to do this), again returned to her persistently moist and stubbornly aching vagina, labored her clitoris more forcefully now, abandoned it to reach for her face in the darkness, touching her nose and her lips like a blind man seeking, cupping her cheeks and her chin in both hands, his mouth claiming hers again. Her own hands moved lingeringly over the smooth almost hairless skin on his chest, the flat belly (her finger poking gently into his navel) then down to where his pubic hair began silkenly above his groin and then savagely transformed itself into the coarser red hair that surrounded his tumescent penis, smooth in the circle of her gliding fist, enlarging as she stroked it gently and lowered her mouth to it, insinuating the tip of her tongue into its single blind eye, moistening the engorged shaft and taking it pulsing between her lips.

When he entered her for the first time, she was astonished to find herself coming again at once, gasping in surprise as much as in passion, hearing herself muttering (never before with Judd), "Yes, fuck me, do it," her nails digging into his backside, her trembling legs widespread, the ankles locked somewhere around the small of his muscular back as he pounded at her with a steady, controlled rhythm that brought her to orgasm twice again before at last he shuddered in her embrace and with a fierce final thrust spent himself inside her.

Now they talked—or at least *he* did.

As the first gray light of day broke timidly against the drawn shade on the single window in the room, as the sounds of morning traffic began on the street outside, peculiarly foreign in tone, the horns high and piping as compared to the deeper throated basses of American automobiles, they lay side by side, fingers entwined like those of children idly watching drifting clouds above a sloping summer hillside—and he talked.

Paul was almost nineteen, six months older than Lissie, a New Yorker born and bred who, upon his graduation from high school in June of 1969, had taken a job working as a common laborer for a construction company named Jenkins Contracting, Inc., run by a besotted old Irishman who'd taken to calling him "Gillie" for Gillis, a nickname he'd despised almost as much as he'd hated hauling bricks. He'd never planned on going to college—in high school he'd maintained a risky C-average that sometimes dipped into a C-minus and on occasion a D—and whereas he'd debated joining the Peace Corps, he'd somehow procrastinated, enjoying the lucrative bread he was earning and reasoning that his minor knee injury, a torn cartilage suffered while playing football for Cardinal Hayes High, would keep him forever safe from the draft.

The joke in 1969, however, prevalent among young men all over the United States, was that the Army was drafting even blind men, so long as their seeing-eye dogs could read the chart on the wall. Paul remained blithely unaware until the first of December, when the Selective Service System held its lottery for men who would be drafted in 1970. The newspapers the next day all published charts listing numbers and dates under headlines such as YOUR DRAFT CHANCES or YOUR DRAFT PROSPECTS. The newspapers all agreed that any man whose lottery number, premised on his date of birth, fell between 1 and 120 could be fairly certain he would be drafted in 1970. Men with numbers between 121 and 240 had a fifty-fifty chance of being drafted. Men with numbers higher than that could consider themselves reasonably safe. Paul's birthday was June 10, 1951. His lottery number was 206. He weighed his fifty-fifty chances against the torn cartilage, and began reading the newspapers with an interest bordering on obsession, studying the daily body counts of North Vietnamese soldiers, and wondering what the count on *American* soldiers looked like in the Hanoi papers.

He was certain he would be killed in Vietnam.

Born into a Catholic family (the Gillis was as Irish as the red hair and scratchy beard), he'd been dutifully impressed during the early days of his youth and the attendant thrice-weekly catechism classes in the basement of the church, with the sacrifices Jesus had made for an unrepentant, self-indulging mankind, and became convinced at the age of twelve that his masturbatory expertise would damn him forever in Hell, no matter *how* many Hail Marys or Our Fathers he said in penance. He had recognized in some of his Italian friends, and in the few Jews who did construction work with him, an inordinate sense of guilt that indicated a kinship in spirit if not in any other discernible way. Irish, and therefore presumably immune to the pains of self-flagellation, his own feeling of guilt—exacerbated by the fact that he no longer went to confession or even to church—seemed almost as extravagant as those shared by his ethnic co-workers. He was certain that an ever-watchful God up there someplace had His eye on Paul Michael Gillis, and that a

Vietnamese bullet, or perhaps a bayonet, would serve as the instrument of His vengeance. In short, he had decided to run before he got his fucking "Greeting!" notice and they sent him to some fucking jungle where he would step on an excrement-dipped punji stick that was razor-sharp enough to penetrate the sole of a combat boot, provided some Gook didn't shoot him first.

He told her he had considered running from the moment he'd read those fifty-fifty figures on the morning after the lottery, but what had firmly convinced him that this was the nobler course of action was a book he'd read and subsequently stolen from the New York Public Library—"I still have it in my duffel, in fact, just a second," he said, and rose from the bed with a swift, angular motion, padding across the room as though dodging one of the murderous linebackers who'd injured his knee, pulling the tassle on the shade to flood the room with surprising Amsterdam sunshine, and then stooping over his duffel and rummaging through it, his back to her, the light mantling his shoulders and setting aflame his red hair. When he came back to the bed, he was carrying not one book, but two.

The first was the book he'd just mentioned, a novel, which title he refused to reveal just yet, placing the book face down on the end table near the bed. The second was a black notebook some five inches wide by eight inches long. He explained to her that he had begun keeping a sort of diary after he got out of Cardinal Hayes, in which he recorded everyday events and his reactions to them. He had also begun reading voraciously, a habit he'd never developed in high school, being at the time more interested in football and girls than in literature.

Browsing the shelves of the public library, he borrowed whichever books appealed to him by title or through a scanning of the first few paragraphs. He was, he told her, an expert on first lines and could quote accurately and from memory the first line of any book he'd ever read. It was his opinion that a writer spent a lot of time polishing that first line because this was the initial impression, you know, like meeting somebody for the very first time, and noticing her eyes, or her hair ("You have beautiful eyes and hair, by the way") and deciding right then and there that you either like or dislike what you're seeing.

He had, perhaps because this was in effect his first true encounter with that vast world illuminated between the covers of a book, kept a record of everything he'd read since getting out of Cardinal Hayes last June. The list wasn't quite staggering, but it was prodigious nonetheless. In ten months he had read 141 books, a rather high total for anyone who had not been trained in speed reading. In a small, precise (and proud, it seemed to her) hand, he had listed the titles one below the other. Many of them were unfamiliar to Lissie.

She recognized *The Sun Also Rises,* of course, and *The Good Earth* ("It was Wang Lung's marriage day," Paul said, as her finger traveled down the lined page) and *Freedom Road* and, with a short trill of surprise, *Magnificent Obsession,* which she'd read during those two weeks she'd spent with Grandmother and Grandfather Harding on the Cape. But titles like *Soap Behind the Ears* by Cornelia Otis Skinner, or *Random Harvest* by James Hilton, or *Saratoga Trunk* by Edna Ferber were totally unknown to her. Well, here was another one she'd read—*Black Boy* by Richard Wright— but what on earth was *Low Man on a Totem Pole* by some man named H. Allen Smith, or *Dragonwyck* by Anya Seton? She knew Ngaio Marsh was a mystery writer, but had never read any of his books (Was he Japanese? Was he even a *he,* or was Ngaio a woman's name?) and she'd certainly never heard of *Artists in Crime.* Ah, here were some recent titles: *Slaughterhouse-Five,* which she'd read and liked, and *The Andromeda Strain,* and *Love Story,* which she positively adored.

"Didn't you just *love* it?" she said.

"Yeah, it was good," Paul said briefly, and then immediately quoted the first line, which even Lissie knew by heart, "What can you say about a twenty-five-year-old girl who died?"

But what on earth was *This Above All,* and who was Eric Knight to have so boldly plundered Polonius's speech to his son Laertes?

This Above All, as it turned out, was the novel that had finally convinced Paul to run. *"This* book," he said now, turning it face side up on the bedside table so that Lissie could read the title, and then moving it onto his lap so it rested on his thigh, somewhere between his flaccid, soft, utterly vulnerable and sweet penis, and the minisectomy scar on his left leg, equally vulnerable looking.

"Well, actually this one and two others. *All Quiet on the Western Front,* do you see it listed there? It's by a German writer, and it's about World War I—'We are at rest five miles behind the front,' that's the first line—and *Johnny Got His Gun* by this man named Dalton Trumbo, which is about a guy—it's listed there, do you see it?—who gets his arms and his legs and his face blown away in the war, and he's just this *trunk* now, just this piece of meat lying on the bed with a little bit of gauze over his missing face. Jesus, what a book!

"But *This Above All* is about a British soldier who's in the rear-guard action at Dunkirk during World War II and who later deserts because he's trying to be true to himself, you know, to his own *values,* I mean. When I read it, I was already worried about those figures in the paper, but then I suddenly began worrying about my *values,* you know? Did I *really* want to fight a war that was a bunch of bullshit? I mean, never mind getting killed or coming home a basket case like that guy in *Johnny Got His Gun.* What about the *morality,* do you understand me? What about killing some poor bastard Gook who maybe didn't want to fight this war the same way *I* didn't want to? So I split. Simple as that. And here I am."

There was in Paul Gillis much of the streetwise urchin, the cunning New York City waif (a true waif now that he was a draft dodger) forced to live by his wits in a hostile world, a city-honed attitude that had caused him first to consider and then actively to pursue running as an expedient solution to what, in her reasoning mind, was far from a foregone conclusion but still only an even possibility—his number coming up before the year was out. Herself born and raised in the city, Lissie had nonetheless led the sheltered life of a suburban small-town preppie ever since she was twelve, when her parents shipped her off to Henderson, and she now found this combination of tough urban resiliency and childlike helplessness irresistibly attractive.

She loved the brisk way he moved, as though dodging taxi cabs or pushing his way into a subway train. She loved the clipped cadences of his Bronx speech with its frequently interjected "you know" or "I mean," verbal tics she supposed ran rampant among young people everywhere but which she associated exclusively with New York and, by extension, Paul Gillis. She loved his silly scratchy beard and his dark brooding eyes, and his long, angular body. She loved the swiftness about him, the pace of him, the sheer momentum of him. She loved his hard-edged assertiveness and his surprising vulnerability. But most of all, she loved the way he made love to her.

That spring in Amsterdam, as she succumbed to a passion she had never before experienced, she recognized at once and without question that she would follow Paul Gillis wherever he went, wherever he chose to lead her.

The call from Venice did not come until April 28, the Tuesday

192

before Jamie was scheduled to leave for Louisville on assignment for *Sports Illustrated*. He was nervous about going down there. The job was a plum of sorts; *Sports Illustrated* rarely doled out freelance assignments, preferring instead to use staff photographers for coverage of this sort. But it wasn't this singular recognition that caused his anxiety; he knew the assignment couldn't possibly present any insurmountable professional problems. He was nervous because he and Joanna, after considerable discussion, had decided to risk going down there together.

They had made their decision cautiously and soberly, weighing the opportunity for being alone together against the virtually impossible odds of running into anyone they knew at the Derby. He had wondered aloud, at the time, whether or not his eagerness to get away had anything to do with whatever he was feeling about his daughter. He had not heard from her since her London letter of the twentieth, and Evert Goedkoop's telephone call had done little to reassure him. Not knowing what to do next, Jamie had phoned his lawyer, who repeated essentially what Goedkoop had said: American kids traveling in Europe were safer than they would be in Central Park, and he was sure Lissie would be contacting them soon. She had, after all, been gone for only a few weeks.

When the darkroom phone rang, he half-expected it would be Joanna, calling to finalize their plans.

"Hello?" he said.

"Dad?" the voice on the other end asked.

He was speechless for a moment. Recognizing her voice at once, astonished and relieved, suspecting from the crackling static on the line that she was calling from thousands of miles away, where a collect call would have been difficult if not impossible to place, he stammered, "Hey, hi, Lissie, hi, how are you?" as though she were calling from Boston instead, as though he'd seen her only a few days earlier.

"I'm fine," she said. "I'm sorry I haven't called or written sooner, but things have been sort of hectic here. Barbara and I.. . ."

"Hectic how?" he asked at once. "Where are you? Are you all right?"

"Well, I was getting to that. I don't mean there's been any *problem,* you don't have to worry, I'm fine. I just meant getting to *see* everything over here, and trying to figure out . . ."

"Where? Where's *here?*"

"Well, right now I'm in Venice."

193

"Venice?" he said. "What are you doing in Venice? I thought . . ."

"Well, that's why I'm calling, Dad. How's Mom?"

"Fine," he said. "What are you doing in Venice? It seems to me you're moving *farther* away from . . ."

"Yeah, but I'll be heading home in a few days."

"Good. You have no idea . . ."

"In fact, I'm calling because . . ."

". . . how worried Mom and I have been. This is the best news I've . . ."

"The thing is, I'll need some money, Dad."

"Sure," he said, "certainly."

"To buy a plane ticket back."

"Right, fine."

"I was hoping you could wire me five hundred dollars care of American Express here in Venice, I have the address if you'd like to take it down. It's Melissa Croft—well, you still know my name, I guess," she said, and giggled, "care of American Express, 1261 Bocca de . . ."

"Why do you need five hundred, Liss? I'll send you whatever it takes to get you home, of course, but five hundred sounds . . ."

"Well, just in case," she said.

"In case of what? How much is the fare?"

"Two-seventy-seven. That's one-way tourist from Venice to Kennedy. I'd have to connect either at Heathrow, or else Malpensa in Milan, or Orly in Paris. But the fare is the same either way."

"If it's two-seventy-seven, why do you need five hundred?"

"In case there's a delay or anything. Frankly, Dad, I'm running short of cash. So in case we can't get reservations and have to stay a day or two longer . . ."

"Who's *we?*"

"Me and Barbara."

"Even so, wouldn't it be easier if I bought a prepaid ticket on this end?"

"No, I don't think so. Anyway, I don't want you to go to that kind of trouble. If you'd just send me five hundred care of American Express . . ."

"It wouldn't be any trouble at all," Jamie said. "In fact, it'd save you running around all over Venice trying to . . ."

"American Express is right in the Piazza, I can easily . . ."

194

"Let me prepay the ticket on this end, okay?"

"Why? Don't you trust me?"

"I trust you, Lissie."

"Then just send me the five hundred, okay?"

He hesitated, and then said, "I'd rather prepay it here. I'll call Andrews Travel right away. I'm sure they can arrange to have a ticket waiting for you in Venice tomorrow morning. Maybe even sooner."

"Well . . . where would that be? The ticket, I mean."

"Let's say the main office of Alitalia. I'm sure they have . . ."

"I don't even know where that is. You see, Dad, that's the point. If you sent me the cash, I could just drop by American Express, which is right here on the . . ."

"I'm sure you could find Alitalia's main ticket office."

"I guess so, but it'd be simpler . . ."

"I prefer doing it this way," Jamie said.

There was a silence on the line.

"Okay?" he said.

"Sure," Lissie said.

There was another silence, longer this time.

"I certainly don't want to argue with you," she said.

"Where are you staying?" he asked. "In case I need to reach you."

"Why would you need to reach me? If you're arranging for the ticket . . ."

"Just in case there's any problem."

"What kind of problem could there be?"

"Lissie . . . where are you staying?"

"Well . . . we haven't found a place yet. We just got off the train a little while ago. We had something to eat at a little trattoria, and I called you right afterward."

"What time is it there?"

"Six-thirty."

"Will you find a place for the night?"

"Yes, sure, we're both exhausted."

"Be sure to go to Alitalia first thing tomorrow morning . . ."

"I will."

"The main ticket office."

"Right."

"Find out where it is."

"I will."

"And when you've got the ticket, I'd appreciate it if you called home collect to let us know."

"Collect is a hassle, Dad, but I'll get through to you one way or another."

"We love you, Lissie, and can't wait to see you."

"I love you, too," she said.

"Call us in the morning."

"Yes, Dad."

"Right after you've picked up the ticket."

"I will."

"I love you, Liss."

"I love you, too."

He put the phone back on the wall cradle, and stood standing by the darkroom sink for several moments. Then he shoved open the door to the outer room, blinked against the sunlight, blinding after the amber-light blackness, and crossed at once to the telephone on his desk. He dialed Andrews Travel in White Plains and spoke to a woman named Miss Kirsch there, who told him Alitalia had a flight leaving Venice at 10:30 A.M. every morning—that was flight 189—arriving in Milan at 11:40, and connecting with their flight 626 leaving Malpensa at 1:00 P.M. and arriving at Kennedy at 3:45 local time.

She told him a prepaid ticket could most likely be waiting for his daughter tomorrow morning at Alitalia's main office on the Campo San Moise, but just to play it safe, he might instead consider booking a few days ahead, say Thursday, April 30, just in case any problem arose. Jamie told her to go ahead and book the Thursday morning flight in Melissa Croft's name, and when asked for her local address, had to say he didn't know where she was staying as yet. Miss Kirsch told him that the one-way ticket to Kennedy would cost $277 plus tax, and asked if he would like to put this on a credit card. He charged it to American Express, and after several more assurances from Miss Kirsch that the ticket would be there and waiting for Lissie, he hung up. His heart was pounding. He remembered all at once that he would be in Louisville on the thirtieth, and debated calling Lew Barker to beg off the assignment, get him to contact *Sports Illustrated,* see if they wouldn't settle for another photographer. He didn't know quite what to do. He was picking up the phone to call Joanna when he heard Connie's car turning into the driveway. He went out of the studio, and reached her just as she was opening the door of the station wagon.

Grinning, he said, "Lissie just called from Venice. She's fine, she'll be coming home Thursday."

"Thank God," Connie said.

"I've already arranged for a prepaid ticket."

"Thank God," she said again.

He helped her with the grocery bags in the back of the wagon, carrying them to the house for her, and then—as he put the bags on the kitchen table, his back to her—he said, "What should I do about Louisville?"

"What do you mean?" Connie asked.

He turned to face her.

"I'm supposed to leave tomorrow," he said.

"Yes, I know," she said, and her eyes met his.

"Well . . . what should I do?"

"Do you *want* to go?"

"It's a good assignment."

Her gaze refused to waver. He felt suddenly that she knew he would not be going to Louisville alone, she had learned somehow about him and Joanna, or perhaps only sensed it, but she knew, she *knew*.

"Are you asking *me* whether you should go?" Connie said.

"Well . . . yes, I suppose so."

"That's a decision you have to make for yourself, isn't it?"

"It's just that . . . Lissie has to be picked up, you know. At the airport, you know."

Her eyes were locked into his, her gaze was steady, searching.

"Yes, I know," she said.

"And I'd like to be here when she arrives."

"Well, I could pick her up."

"Yes, but . . ."

"It's not such a big deal."

"Still . . ."

"Can you get out of the assignment at this late date?"

"I'm not sure."

"Or is it something . . . ?" Connie hesitated. "Something you're already deeply committed to?"

"I'd have to check with Lew."

"Yes, check with him," Connie said, and sighed. "I'd like to take a bath, I'm exhausted." She hesitated again. "Would you . . . do you think you might want to come upstairs later? When I'm out of the tub?"

"Yes, sure," he said.

"If you want to," she said. "And you think about Louisville, okay? About whether you really feel you should go, okay?"

"Okay," he said.

Her eyes lingered a moment longer, and then she turned away from him.

In the downstairs bar of the Louisville hotel, Jamie and Joanna struck up a conversation with a sloe-eyed brunette from Mississippi who told him she came up to the Derby each year with her daddy, not because she enjoyed the race itself ("It's aftuh awl, onleh two minutes long") but because she enjoyed all the excitement *before* the race.

They sat beside her listening. They were holding hands. This was the first time they'd been away together. Tonight would be the first time they'd ever made love in any bed but Joanna's.

"When did y'all get here?" the brunette asked.

"Just a little while ago," Jamie said.

"Way-ell, y'just about missed out on all the good fun," she said.

It seemed that a Knights of Columbus dinner had taken place on Monday night, to which she'd been invited with her daddy, not because he was a Catholic ("We'ah both Methodists") but only because he knew a man in Louisville who belonged to that order, and they'd also missed the bicycle and tricycle races out at the Fairgrounds Speedway, and the Pegasus Parade along Broadway ("With all those yew-*mon*-gous, goh-geous floats"), and the Great Steamboat Race between the *Belle of Louisiana* and Cincinnati's *Delta Queen*, "and, oh, just scads of other excitin' thangs."

When Jamie mentioned that he was a photographer on assignment for *Sports Illustrated* and regretted having missed these eminently photographable events, she told him he should have been here *last* night, when the Thoroughbred Breeders of Kentucky gave their big dinner, because lots of sportswriters were invited to it each year, and whereas her daddy didn't *breed* horses ("Though he sure can *bet* 'em"), she was certain he could have arranged for Jamie to have been invited because he knew the Louisville newspaperman who moderated the panel. She said all this in a boozy drawl that was sometimes unintelligible, her meaning sifting through a mist of alcohol fumes and a layer of treacle, and then ordered another martini.

Her daddy, she told them, owned a thousand acres of choice land in Morehouse Parish, Louisiana, if they were familiar with that part of the state, upon which he planted cotton and soybeans. The property had been inherited from his mother, and he gentleman-farmed it together with his three brothers for an annual income she guessed was in the "hah six figgers." Bonnie Ellen herself ("Mah name's Scotch-Irish, but whose *isn't* in the South?") expected to be graduated this June from the University of Mississippi, where she was majoring in business administration, after which she planned to join the family enterprise at its headquarters in Monroe at a beginning salary of $34,000 a year ("Give or take a few pennehs").

Listening to her, Jamie found himself wondering if Lissie was at this moment sitting in a bar someplace in Venice, talking to a pair of strangers, telling them why she had suddenly left home, telling them (perhaps) how much she missed her parents, confiding how eager she was to be flying back to the States again tomorrow. Listening to Bonnie Ellen, contrasting her seeming maturity with his daughter's still childish (to him) behavior—but after all, Bonnie Ellen *was* several years older—he wondered whether Lissie would one day be graduating from a university in June, wondered if she would one day enter a vast and sprawling business enterprise at a salary of $34,000 a year, give or take a few pennies.

Wondering all this, he found himself unburdening to Bonnie Ellen all his fears and doubts, telling her that his eighteen-year-old daughter ("You *surely* don't have an eighteen-year-old daughter!") had been traveling all over Europe for what seemed like forever, even though it had only been since the middle of the month sometime, telling her how they'd heard from her only twice in all that time, once in a letter she'd written from London, and the next time only yesterday, from Venice, a phone call this time, to tell him she'd be coming home. He told Bonnie Ellen he'd arranged for a prepaid ticket to be waiting for his daughter in Venice, and told her too how eager he was to see her again. Bonnie Ellen spread her hand on his thigh and said, "You're really a very genuinely deep nice man, aren't you?"

In the elevator on the way up to their room, Joanna said, "How'd you like her hand?"

"Whose hand?" Jamie said, surprised.

"Bonnie Ellen Cornpone's."

"What hand?"

"The one on your thigh."

"Come on, she didn't have her hand on my thigh."

"Another inch, and it would've been on your *cock,*" Joanna said.

"I didn't even feel it."

"Maybe you're paralyzed, dollink?"

"Are you kidding?"

"Kidding? I wanted to kill her. 'Y'all *are* really a very genuinely deep nahss man, ahn't you?'" Joanna mimicked.

Jamie laughed. "I wasn't even aware, I mean it," he said.

She was silent all the way up to the third floor, silent as he unlocked the door to their room, silent as they undressed for bed. Then, lying beside him, she said, "You know what bothered me more than her fucking restless fingers?"

"Joanna, I really didn't even feel . . ."

"Feel, shmeel. Why'd you spill out your life story to her?"

"Well, she . . . she made me think of Lissie somehow."

"Who do *I* make you think of somehow?"

"Not Lissie, that's for sure."

"How come you never talk to *me* about Lissie?"

"I didn't think you were interested."

"I'm interested in everything about you."

"I just thought . . ."

"Everything," Joanna said, and reached for him. "The next time any woman puts her hand anywhere *close* to this thing," she said, her hand tightening on him, "I'll cut it off."

"Her hand?"

"You'd better *hope* it's only her hand," Joanna said, and rolled on top of him, and looked directly into his face. "I want to share with you, Jamie," she said.

"All right," he said softly.

"Everything."

"All right," he said, and smiled.

He fell asleep content later, thinking his daughter would be home sometime tomorrow night.

He had told Connie where he'd be staying in Louisville, and had cautioned Joanna against answering the phone when the expected call came. It came at 4:30 P.M. the next day. He snatched the phone from the receiver at once.

"Hello?" he said.

"Jamie?"

"Yes, hi, Connie."

"She's not on the plane."

"What?"

"She's not on it. Everyone's been through customs already, she's not on the plane."

"Well, what . . . *what?*"

"Jamie, she's *not* on the fucking plane!"

"Where is she then?" he asked idiotically.

"What?" Connie said. "What do you mean, where?"

"Jesus," he said. "Are you sure you . . . ?"

"I'm trying to get a manifest now. But, Jamie, they've all come through customs already, I'm sure she . . ."

"Jesus," he said again. "All right, look, I . . . let me call Andrews Travel. Where are you, give me the number there, I'll get right back to—"

"What's the good of calling Andrews? If she's not on the plane . . ."

"Well, maybe there was some mixup. Give me the number there, will you?"

"No, let me call you back. I've got Alitalia checking, they may . . ."

"Okay, fine. Give me half an hour or so."

"Jamie . . . what are we going to do?"

"I don't know," he said. "Let's hope . . ." He let the sentence trail.

"I'll call you back," she said.

"Yes, okay. Half an hour," he said, and hung up.

"What is it?" Joanna asked.

"My daughter wasn't on the plane," he said, jiggling the receiver rest. "Come *on,*" he said impatiently.

When the telephone operator came on the line, he told her he needed information for White Plains, New York. She told him he could dial that directly, first a one, and then the area code, and then 555 and then—"All right, thanks," he said abruptly. When he got the information operator, he asked for the number of Andrews Travel in White Plains, and then hastily dialed it. Lionel Andrews himself answered the phone.

Jamie filled him in on what had happened, and Andrews promised to get back to him as soon as he had checked. He did not call back until fifteen minutes later, when he informed Jamie that his daughter's ticket had been exchanged in Venice for a "further transportation" ticket. Jamie wanted to know what that meant.

Andrews explained that it meant further transportation in the amount of the face value of the ticket. "Further transportation to *where?*" Jamie asked. Andrews said he had no way of knowing that just yet, but he would continue checking. Maybe Alitalia would have some additional information. Or perhaps one of the *other* airlines—

"Yes, please keep after it," Jamie said.

He said nothing to Joanna while he waited for Connie to call back. She called at a little past five. She told him Alitalia had checked their manifest, and no one named Melissa Croft had been aboard the airplane. They were now checking to see whether she had been on the connecting flight from Venice. If so, there was a chance she might have decided to stop over in Milan for a few days. Perhaps she was *still* on the way home, perhaps she—

"No," Jamie said softly. "I don't think so."

Connie was silent for a long time. Then she said, "What now, Jamie?"

"I don't know," he said.

"When will you be home?"

"After the race tomorrow."

"Be careful," she said, and hung up.

Joanna didn't know quite what was happening.

Jamie was there to cover the running of the ninety-sixth annual Derby, and so he took his obligatory shots of the blooming tulips at Churchill Downs, the families picnicking on the infield, the college students tossing footballs, the vendors selling mint juleps at a buck and a quarter a throw, the stylishly dressed men and women in the clubhouse, the bettors at the windows, the trainers and owners in the paddock area. He was wearing two cameras around his neck, both Nikons, one with a wide-angle lens and the other with a 200-millimeter. Each time he took a roll of film from a camera to replace it with a fresh one, he marked it with a piece of adhesive tape upon which he inked a number and then jotted into a small notebook the identical number and a few words describing what was on the exposed roll, "So I can later identify the pictures for captioning," he explained to her.

Those were virtually the only words he'd said to her all day long; she might just as well have been back in New York, sitting alone in her apartment. She had made a two-dollar win bet on one of the losers. She tore up her ticket as Jamie took a picture of the victorious jockey holding up his left hand in a *V* for Victory sign.

He took a picture of the winner's trainer, and yet another—a mood shot—of a balding old man staring disconsolately out at the trampled track, clutching a pair of losing tickets in his fist. Joanna kept wishing he would take a picture of her. Joanna kept wishing he would in some way indicate he was aware of her presence, squeeze her hand or throw her a smile, something, *anything*. But he went about his work methodically and efficiently (if a bit bloodlessly, she thought) and seemed glad when it was all over.

"I want to get back home," he said, and she felt her first sense of foreboding, a sudden, secret terror that she was about to lose him. This was the first day of May. They had made love for the first time nine months ago, and now, for reasons she could not fathom, he seemed ready to vanish into that great beyond that swallowed married men once they felt they'd had enough and were in imminent danger of threatening the blissful, loveless arrangements they shared with their wives.

They were in the room packing when at last she said, "What is it, Jamie? What have I suddenly contracted? Halitosis? Leprosy? What?"

He looked up from his valise. He seemed on the edge of tears.

"I'm sorry," he said.

"You've hardly said a word to me all day."

"I'm sorry. Really."

"I know you're upset about your daughter," she said, "but I'm not aware that *I* did anything or said anything to turn you off this way. If there *is* something, I wish you'd . . ."

"I shouldn't have come here," he said.

"What do you mean?"

"I should've been at the airport to meet her."

"Well . . . what difference would *that* have made? If she wasn't on the plane . . ."

"She'd have *been* on the plane."

"Come on, Jamie. You surely don't believe . . . ?"

"I should've been there, that's all."

"But how would that have changed anything? And anyway, forgive me, Jamie, but what have *I* got to do with your daughter's whereabouts? What possible connection . . . ?"

"Joanna . . . please. I'd rather not talk about it. Really."

"Well, I *would,* damn it! *She* decides not to come home, and suddenly *I'm* the one getting punished. What kind of crazy compensatory substitution . . . ?"

"You sound like Mandelbaum," Jamie said.

"And *you* sound like—"

She cut herself short.

She shook her head.

"Jamie," she said, "let's not do this to each other, please."

"Right, let's not," he said. "I certainly don't want to end it with—"

"*End* it?" she said.

"The trip, I mean."

She was staring at him now, a stunned look on her face.

"Let's finish packing," he said.

On the plane back to New York, he busied himself first with sorting out his little containers of exposed film and checking the numbers on them against the shabby little notebook he kept in the inside pocket of his jacket, next with reading *Time* magazine from cover to cover and pointing out in a friendly stranger-on-a-plane way the work of various photographers he knew, and then paying excessive gourmand attention to the virtually inedible "snack" the airline served, and finally—she was sure—flirting with the flight attendant, a bosomy southern belle who looked more like an Eighth Avenue hooker than the real-life ones prancing that stretch of sordid turf.

In the taxi on the way back to the city, he commented on how good it was to be home again in the Big Apple, and then repeated to her a joke he told her he'd overheard at the track, something about a dog learning to talk, something about a dog getting shot, she really wasn't following it, her mind was on the looming possibility that this might be the last time in her life she'd ever see him. When he finished the joke, she laughed politely.

She was certain that she herself had little or nothing to do with his decision to end the relationship. She was being evicted by a person she'd never met, an eighteen-year-old twerp "finding herself," or whatever the fuck she was doing, someplace in Europe, a daughter who, by her irresponsible mindlessness, her adolescent inability to get her immature ass on a goddamn airplane, was somehow causing *this*. She wished she could explore this further with him, probe whatever promises he had made to himself or to God—"Bring my daughter home safely, and I'll never, *never* fuck around again"—investigate the possibility that he was linking his daughter's profligacy to his own, perhaps even accepting as his own the guilt that silly teenage twit *should* have been feeling. But the taxi meter was ticking, the watch on Joanna's wrist was ticking, the minutes were flying past, the opportunities were vanishing second by second.

"Here we are," Jamie said.

He carried her suitcase up to the front door, and waited while she searched for her key, and then unlocked the door. She debated asking him to come in for a drink.

"I'll call you," he said, and kissed her on the cheek.

She watched as he went down the steps to the waiting taxi, watched as the taxi pulled away from the curb, knowing he would not call, knowing he was gone forever, and blaming it on his dumb wandering cunt of a daughter.

Dear Mom and Dad,

I guess I ought to explain first why I wasn't on that plane from Venice, as you thought I would be. I know that must have come as a surprise to you, because when I spoke to you on the phone (you, Dad) I told you I would be coming home. I know you went to a lot of trouble getting that ticket to me, and I really am sorry if you think there was any duplicity or betrayal involved when I cashed it in at the airport in Venice. The problem was we needed money to continue our travels, and I couldn't think of any way to get it except by telling a lie I hope you will forgive.

You'll want to know why I have come here to Greece, I guess, instead of coming home as I promised I would. I can only say that there are some things I must do at this stage of my life, and I can assure you I am in the presence of a very warm and loving person and that no harm can possibly come to me. There are hippies like me and Paul all over Europe, and I'm sure we will find hippies wherever we travel, wherever we go, young people like us who are trying to learn about life by actually experiencing it and savoring it.

I will be staying here on Mykonos for several weeks to learn some Greek. Barbara Duggan plans to stay here indefinitely (she is living with a very nice southern boy named Robby) but Paul and I plan to travel around some of the other islands before settling down someplace. It is impossible to describe the natural splendor of this island. Flowers and green hills, air fresh from the Aegean breezes. I can't give you an address for you to answer until we settle down, but I will write to you from time to time to let you know how I'm doing.

All my love,

Lissie

Secretly, Connie blamed it all on Jamie, tracing it back to that Sunday night in March when he'd delivered his long-distance telephone harangue to Lissie in San Francisco. His violent reaction that night had bewildered her at first, his anger seeming out of all proportion to what had actually happened. But then she'd begun wondering, Oedipus and Frank Lipscombe aside, just what had *really* triggered his rage. Had it truly been the knowledge that Lissie had lied to him, that Lissie was no longer a virgin, that Lissie was living with a boy he didn't know? She wondered.

She had read somewhere—or perhaps Frank had revealed this during one of his learned Rutledge-party discourses—that unusual or unexpected behavior, deviation from set routines or schedules, unexplained absences, long meditative silences and deep sighs, sudden outbursts of anger, excessive apologies or remorseful breast-beating, all added up to trouble right here in River City, sure indicators that the male or female partner in a marriage was philandering. Jamie had over the past several months, certainly— and perhaps longer before she'd detected it—exhibited all of these symptoms, plus what she might have termed a lingering absence, a perpetual removal from the circumstances of their life together. She was, she came to realize, living with an empty cipher these days, and she thought she knew why: Jamie was involved with another woman.

The abiding suspicion that there was certainly someone else, the accompanying anger and indecision led to a helpless sort of despair in which Connie asked herself the same questions over and again:

What should I do once I know for certain? Call his hand? End the marriage? Turn the other cheek? Do I even *want* to stay married to a man who needs other women? Is Diana Blair the other woman? Diana, who had once confided, "The way I look at it, Connie, there are the Titters and the Twatters. The girls who press their, you know, breasts against their partner's chest, and the ones who use the, well, *lower* parts of their anatomies to achieve this . . . uh . . . closeness that makes it easier to dance well together. It becomes a problem for me, since I've been . . . uh . . . unfortunately and . . . uh . . . overabundantly endowed . . . well, Jesus, you know how big my tits are"—and here she'd giggled—"which of course makes it almost impossible for me to dance without *some* sort of frontal contact"—and she'd giggled again. Could he have possibly taken up with Diana Blair, the U.S. Open?

Maybe I should call her, Connie thought, pick up the phone, lay it right on the line: "Diana, are you having an affair with my husband?" An affair! The nice little words we've invented to accommodate the most despicable human behavior. Maybe the kids are right, maybe our values *do* reek, maybe our system *is* rotten and rotting further, maybe they've got the right idea, go out there and live with someone, live with a *dozen* someones on a commune, forget about marriage, forget about nineteen years of marriage— oh, dear God, what should I do?

She could not call Diana, nor could she flatly accuse Jamie of infidelity simply on the grounds that he'd been behaving strangely for the past God knew how many months. Without evidence that he was actually "philandering" (another one of our nice little words; fucking *around* was more like it) she would risk placing herself in an impossibly weak position if she happened to be wrong, become the abject, sniveling wife, "I'm sorry, darling, I'm sorry— you rotten *bastard!*"

The anger.

This was the second week of May, they had at last heard from their daughter, who was living with someone named Paul on a Greek island named Mykonos. ("Are you *someone?*" an autograph hound once asked Connie outside the Helen Hayes Theater on an opening night. When was the last time she and Jamie had attended an opening together? Where had her husband gone? "Are you *someone?*") Sometimes when she called the studio from work, the phone rang and rang with no one there to answer it. And when she discreetly (she hoped) questioned him later about where he'd been on those particular days, he always had a ready reason for his absence: he'd been in the city ordering supplies (*But can't you order supplies on the phone?* she thought) or having some prints made (*Isn't there a darkroom at the studio, darling?*) or interviewing a model or seeing Lew Barker or etcetera, etcetera, etcetera. It was all the etceteras that bothered Connie. She wondered now if he went into the city at *all* on those days when he was away from the studio. Was he spending the time up here in the country instead, frolicking with Diana Blair?

Connie sometimes fantasized that she had a father who was kindly and understanding, generous to a fault, capable of discoursing on lofty subjects beyond her own ken or intelligence, warm and loving, offering advice untainted by prejudice, supportive and wise, entirely objective and uncensoring, a Judge Hardy (Harding?) who would call her into his study for a little chat before the fireplace. But Peter Harding, for all his nominal similarity to the character acted by Lewis Stone, whom she'd adored on the screens of countless movie theaters when she was a young girl (in those days, she had also loved Mickey Rooney with a passion beyond belief) was not the man to help her in the solution of anything more important than the pressing problem of the front doorbell: "You should have had them put a little light on it," he'd once said, "so your company can see it in the dark."

She had longed in these past several months to be able to spill out to him her innumerable fears about Lissie traveling alone through God knew which foreign countries, the dark and forbidding prospect that her daughter might never again return home, the confusion she'd felt about Lissie's inconsiderateness, the unthinkable possibility that she might be injured or even killed while she was thousands of miles away. But no. "She'll call, don't worry," and then dismissal of his granddaughter, as though the offspring of offspring were of absolutely no earthly concern to a man who ran his life with all the stopwatch precision of a time-analyst.

Oh, how she longed to open her heart to him, reveal to him everything that was troubling her about her daughter—and her husband. Who *else* was there to tell? Her mother was more a child than Lissie was, and her sister in Los Angeles had never truly been a confidante. It seemed ironic to her that the one person she had always trusted completely, the one person with whom she had always felt safe in confiding anything at *all,* was now the one person she could not ask for advice. Had Jamie gone alone to Louisville last week, or had he taken a woman with him? *Oh, God,* she thought. *Help me,* she thought. *Help me, Daddy. What should I do?*

Sometimes she found herself trembling with impotent rage, feeling in those moments utterly female, helpless in the grip of a centuries-old conspiracy of bondage and servitude, realizing in a flash as terrifying as an ozone-stinking bolt of lightning just how dependent she was on this man to whom she was married. Perhaps her father was correct in never deigning to honor her own silly occupation, her fiddling with the handicapped, the exalted $16,000-a-year job that would, should Jamie ever leave her, pay for almost none of the things she now shared with him.

Shamed by a glimpse of this selfish person who was herself, revolted by her own lack of courage, disgusted by this quaking fragile view of herself as the end product of a civilization that asked its females to drink sperm and enjoy it besides, knowing she should *say* something, *storm* at Jamie, *insist* on knowing, *demand* apologies, *exact* penance, *force* him to kiss her ass and lick her shoes, *reduce* this . . . this . . . rotten son of a bitch—and the rage would rise again, overwhelming her with its force.

Holding back her tears, refusing to cry, afraid to challenge him, hating him and loving him at the same time, bewildered and helpless in her confusion, she thought *I have to* do *something, I have to* save *it,* and wished with all her heart that her daughter was here by her side, to help remind Jamie that there was something important here they had all shared together and *lived* together—instead of on Mykonos where the green hills were flecked with flowers and the air blew in fresh over the Aegean.

May 20, 1970

Dear Mom and Dad,

Hello! Hello!

Deep breathing and yoga in the first rays of the deep orange sun. A quick cool dip in crystal waters and a walk to town. An argument with some officials who thought I came illegally from Turkey, a brisk retaliation, and the day has begun. Morning tea sings to me a soft song, the second day of fasting.

Paul and I have found a house on Samos which suits our needs and now it's time to live. A small ancient villa overlooking a beautiful beach, mountains, air, food and insects. Paul is a very dear person, and we are trying to live honestly.

We came here via Santorini which is supposed to be the Lost City of Atlantis. Vampire bats, strange superstitious people, and a volcano. Black sand and religious festivals and incredible stars. But here I am in my new home with Paul and many thoughts realized. I'm reading Nietzsche's *Thus Spake Zarathustra,* and I would deeply appreciate it if at some point you could send me any more of his books you may find in the shops there. It is very warm here, now, and I do feel great. My Greek is improving "oreo" and I can handle any situation. Please write to me % Poste Restante, Kokkári, Samos, Greece. All my love to everyone.

Your loving daughter,

Lissie

May 29, 1970

Dear Lissie:

I can't pretend I'm thrilled. It is not enough to lie and to deceive and then apologize for it afterward. The moment we got an address for you, I wanted to fly over there and drag you home by the hair. Your mother advised me that this was not the right thing to do. You are, after all, eighteen years old, you will be nineteen in December. That is supposed to be an adult. But I'm still not sure I wasn't right. I do not like your lying, I do not like your getting money from us under false pretenses, I do not like your dropping out of school, and I *definitely* do not like your living with someone we do not know. Don't any of the kids today have last names? What is Paul's last name? Who *is* he?

Are you deliberately trying to cause anxiety, Liss? Would it have been so difficult for you to drop at least a card between this letter and the one before it? To let us know whether or not you were still on Mykonos, still in good health, still *alive,* for God's sake! Never mind, let it go. Mom says I shouldn't express any anger in my letter to you. All right, I won't express any anger.

We called your grandparents the moment we heard from you, and I expect you'll be getting some mail from them shortly, if you haven't already moved on from the address you gave us. A small ancient villa overlooking the beach sounds very nice. Please fill us in. How many rooms are there, what's the layout, how much is it costing you a month, and so on? What time do you get up, what time do you eat, what do you eat, when do you swim (is it really warm enough there for swimming now), when do you go to sleep, and have you any plans for finding some sort of job while you're there? Please tell us all, as we'd very much like to know.

Mom says she will be writing you separately. I hope she is better able to conceal her anger and frustration than I am. Please keep writing, and stay well and happy.

Love,

Dad

June 10, 1970

Dear Mom and Dad,

I am writing again the very *minute* after reading your letter because I don't want to be accused again of being thoughtless or selfish, as your last letter seemed to indicate. I am fine, happier than ever, stronger than ever, and continually creatively growing. You'll be very happy to know that I've been reading like a fiend, a habit I picked up from Paul, who reads tons of books every week, anything he can get his hands on. As my knowledge of the medium increases, the more stimulated and curious I am. I want to write more and more, and plans are beginning to appear in the direction of my own books which would be based around my travels and new sensitivity to nature and the world.

I am still living on Samos, mainly because it is one of the most beautiful places I've had the opportunity to know. Also, because of my increased sensitivity through daily discipline and yoga. I'm experimenting with pressing flowers, and the infinite array of natural prints and composition which I am learning to control. I have been offered a job working in a tavern here, which I have passed up. I'm sorry I can't tell you anything more about Paul, but that would be betraying a confidence. We'll still be staying here in Kokkári for another little while before leaving for India.

All my love,

Lissie

212

Dear Lissie:

India!

It takes an impossibly long time for your letters to reach us, ten days for the last one, and then only to learn the depressing news that you're planning to move on farther east. Lissie, I hope this decision isn't a firm one. Mom and I truly feel that the best possible thing for you to do is to finish your stay in Greece, stay there for the summer if you like, and then come back in the fall to continue your studies at Brenner. Lissie, I don't understand this. I didn't understand your sudden decision to leave the country in the first place, and now I am totally baffled by what you wrote in your last letter. Why India? For God's sake, Lissie, India is the opposite end of the earth!

I am making this short because I'm eager to seal the envelope and get it off to you, knowing it will take forever to reach you. Please write as soon as you receive it, and *please*, Lissie, tell us your plans have changed!

Love,

Dad

He had spent almost the entire day with a fashion editor named Lucy Katz, a bright New York Jewish girl who'd graduated with a B.A. from Brooklyn College and who was working her way up to *Vogue* via *McCall's*. She was twenty-four years old, a virtually hipless, titless blonde with Joanna's blue eyes and a voice not unlike hers, distinctly New York-sounding, with an added flavor of Bensonhurst. They'd spent ten hours together working with a model who'd learned to walk in Skokie, Illinois, shooting take after take of her in a fall wardrobe, and finally quitting at 9:00 P.M., with the promise, or threat, of an 8:00 A.M. shoot ahead of them tomorrow. He'd called home to tell Connie he'd have to stay in the city that night, and then had accepted Lucy's contrite ("It's the *least McCall's* can do for you") invitation to dinner. Sitting side by side in the restaurant booth, commiserating about the shlock model who was getting seventy-five an hour, he startled himself by calling Lucy Lissie, and then—because the wine was good and the hour was late—he told her all about his daughter's phone call from Venice, and the way he'd mishandled it, sending her a prepaid ticket instead of the money she'd wanted, which was maybe why she'd cashed the ticket in, after all, because he simply hadn't *trusted* her enough with the cash.

"When I was a kid," he said, "this was in September of 1939—I was thirteen years old, my father was still alive—these three older kids and I cooked up a great idea on how to spend our last weekend before going back to school. We wanted to go fishing. We were all city kids, and none of us knew one end of a fishing pole from the other, but this was the end of summer, the Labor Day weekend, and we decided we'd ride our bikes up to City Island, and go fishing from the dock there . . ."

His father had been sitting in the kitchen washtub, taking his nightly bath, when Jamie came home to tell him about the plan. He was a giant of a man, and his knobby knees came to just under his chin as he soaped himself in the narrow boxlike tub and sang at the top of his lungs. He was singing "Now's the Time to Fall in Love," a Depression song about potatoes and tomatoes being cheaper; Jamie could to this day remember the song his father was singing on that September night in 1939. Before the Depression, his father had been a typesetter on the old *New York World,* had lost his job when the paper was purchased by Scripps-McRae in 1931, and had since held a series of odd jobs, doing whatever kind of work he could get. He'd started working that summer for the ice and coal station on Second Avenue, making deliveries for them all over Manhattan. When he got home each night, filthy with coal dust, he'd strip naked in the middle of the kitchen and climb into the washtub alongside the sink. He was in the tub that night, singing about the butcher, the baker, the candlestick maker, when Jamie excitedly unfolded the plan to him.

His father said no.

He had a lot of good reasons. It would take them forever to get to City Island by bicycle. The roads would be packed with traffic on the Labor Day weekend, and therefore dangerous. Where would they get fishing poles, did they have money to rent poles, did Jamie think money grew on trees? And how could they fish from the dock there, where seven hundred *other* people would be trying to do the same thing, seven *thousand* other people. They would have to rent a rowboat, did they have money for a rowboat, did Jamie think money grew on trees? And what did they plan to use for bait, and what ungodly hour of the night did they expect to get home, and on

214

and on his father went, the wet coal dust streaking down his face, the washtub filling with blackening suds, his knobby knees poking islandlike out of the water. "The answer is no," he said, and went back to singing about this being the time to fall in love.

"I keep thinking," Jamie said now, "that maybe I've said no too often to her, that if maybe I'd said yes once in a while, she wouldn't be in Greece today, and planning to move on to India. If I could relive that phone call from her, I'd do it in a minute."

"You really do love her a lot, don't you?" Lucy said, and gently put her hand on his arm, and suddenly he recalled the woman in Louisville who'd said, "You're really a very genuinely deep nice man, aren't you?" and the way Joanna had later mimicked those words.

"But you mustn't blame yourself, really," Lucy said, her voice very much like Joanna's, higher-pitched but with the same cadences and lilt. "I wish I had a nickel for every time I gave *my* father a heart attack. It's part of growing up," she said, seemingly unmindful of the fact that she herself was only twenty-four, "something we all go through," her hand touching his arm again, resting there, "but we all get over it." She smiled, withdrew her hand to lift her wineglass, smiled over the glass as she sipped at the wine, put the glass back on the table again, and then rested her hand on his arm again, the fingers widespread.

After dinner she walked him to the Plaza, where he'd booked a room for the night, and asked if he'd like to have a nightcap in the Oak Bar. When he said he thought he'd better get some sleep before having to cope with the Skokie Marvel again, she said, "Or maybe you'd like to come to my place instead. For the nightcap, I mean. I'm right on Thirty-eighth." He thanked her, but said no again, and they shook hands and said their good nights. Narrow hips swaying, she went down the steps opposite the fountain, and hailed a taxi.

It was close to midnight. Alone in his room, he almost called Joanna.

And then he thought, No, she's forgotten me by now, she won't even remember what I look like. Lew Barker, who was the biggest swordsman Jamie knew, once told him he was constantly shocked by the infidelity of women. "Not the playing-around of married women," Lew had said, "that's not the infidelity I'm talking about. Perhaps I mean inconstancy. Yes, that's a better word, however Shakespearean. Inconstancy. I am constantly shocked by their inconstancy. I'll enjoy an affair of several months' duration with this or that delectable young thing, and then for one reason or another will not see her for a while. And then, if I call again to announce myself and my renewed intentions, why this young lady will say she's no longer *interested!* When I remind her of the joys we shared together, the ecstatic heights to which we'd been transported, the fun and the laughter, the gay madcap adventure of it all, the romance of wading in the Seagram Building's pool or waltzing with a blind man on Fifth Avenue—why, Jamie, she'll have *forgotten* it all, she'll have put it out of her mind, she'll have *dismissed* me as if I'd never existed. It's enough to break an old man's heart, I tell you. The inconstancy of women. Enough to break an old man's heart."

He lifted the bedside telephone receiver.

He knew her number by heart, still knew it, started to dial it, and then hung up. I should have taken her up on it, he thought, Lucy, I should have said, "Sure, why not, let's go to your place for a nightcap, what the hell?" Same blond hair and blue eyes, same young good looks, exactly the same, what the hell. But not the same at all. Not Joanna. Whom he loved.

He turned out the light.

It took him a long time to fall asleep.

June 29, 1970

Dear Mom and Dad,

I'm sorry to have to disappoint you, but no, our plans have not changed, that is what we still plan to do. And whereas India may seem very far away to you, it does not seem far to us, sitting here on Samos, where we can see the mountains of Turkey right across the bay, right across the sparkling water. Please don't worry, the situation is in control, and we will make our travel plans well in advance before moving on, which won't be for some time yet.

And please be assured that I will carry you with me *wherever* I go, and will be proud to carry that luggage. You are in my heart and soul and you will always be. We have all had beautiful lives together, and we are indebted to each other for a large part of it. It's funny how much I miss you both. I send my essence to you every day and wish you all the best of luck and strength. I know the feeling is reciprocated. We all need each other, but separate paths

216

we must take. I dedicate a prayer to our old age and the force which keeps us striving and experimenting. I miss you very much and of course love you as I love myself.

Lissie

July 7, 1970

Dear Lissie:

Eight days this time, which I suppose is something of an improvement. And, at least, the reassurance that you won't be moving on to India for "some time yet," whatever that means. I *hope* it means you'll be giving the idea further thought and reflection, and eventually will decide against it. I don't know what you think is waiting for you there in India, Liss. I don't understand any of this too clearly.

I only know that I love you and miss you, and worry about you constantly. I do not know this boy Paul, I know nothing about him. It pains me to think that you are living with a stranger. It pains me to think that the last time we had a conversation of any real substance was when you were in San Francisco, and then in anger over a boy I didn't know, who seems to have passed out of your life to be replaced by *another* boy I don't know. I would not like to believe that the angry words we exchanged on the telephone had anything to do with your decision to run off to Europe. I would not like to believe that your decision to go on to India has anything to do with any anger you may be feeling now.

Lissie, I wish you would decide to come home. I miss you terribly. Please write again soon.

Love,

Dad

July 14, 1970

Dear Lissie:

We have not heard from you since your letter of June 29, and even accounting for the usual postal lag, we are beginning to get very worried. We tried to phone you in Greece yesterday, but it turned out to be impossible to reach you. We finally left word with someone in the post office there, or *tried* to leave word, but we were talking English and he was talking Greek, and I'm not sure he got the message straight. But there *are* telephones there on Samos, Lissie, we found that out after all our frantic attempts, and I wish you would call us collect as soon as you receive this to let us know that you are all right.

Love,

Dad

4-027712E107002 07/20/70 ICS IMPPMIZZ CSP NVNB

1 203 784 8072 MGM TDMT RUTLEDGE CT 07-20 1243 P EST

TDMT RUTLEDGE CT 07-20 1243 P EST

MELISSA CROFT
POSTE RESTANTE
KOKKÁRI, SAMOS
GREECE

MOM AND I WORRIED AND CONCERNED. ARE YOU ALL RIGHT? PLEASE CABLE OR CALL AS SOON AS POSSIBLE. LOVE, DAD.

They had still not heard from her by the night of Jamie's birthday party. He was born on July 23, but that fell on a Thursday this year, and so Connie had planned the party for the following night. He knew there was going to be a gala celebration for his forty-fourth birthday; no one could have kept as a surprise the workmen hanging Japanese lanterns in the trees bordering the river, the caterers arriving to set up tables and chairs, the three-piece band (not *rock,* thank God!) who arrived looking bewildered at a little past seven, the leader complaining they'd been up and down the street twenty times already, searching for the mailbox. What Jamie hadn't realized was that Connie had planned a party of such magnitude.

Taking her cue from Jamie's own hanging of Lissie's pictures each year in December, she had festooned the living room with pictures of him taken at various stages of his life, pictures of him as a somewhat scrawny little boy, and later as a tall and slender teenager; pictures of him in his Army uniform and on the Yale

218

campus; pictures of him on their honeymoon, pictures of him holding the infant Lissie in his arms, even poster-size blowups of the pictures he'd taken for the first *Life* essay, so that the living room was a visual history of Jamie Croft from the first shot of him as a baby lying on a furry robe in a commercial photographer's studio to a picture Connie herself had taken only two weeks earlier, a candid shot of Jamie at his desk, typing a letter to Lissie in Greece.

But she had also (and here she acknowledged her debt to Ralph Edwards) invited not only half the town of Rutledge and most of the people Jamie worked with in New York, but also many people Jamie thought he would never in his life see again. There was his closest friend from when he was a kid on Eighty-sixth Street (Jamie's mother, who had helped Connie with the selection, stood by beaming as Jamie embraced the man), now a bit pudgy and going bald, an accountant in New Jersey. There was his old Army buddy, a rangy kid from Maine who'd trudged through the jungle by his side, and who'd once saved Jamie from an exploding grenade by tackling him and knocking him headlong off the machete-hewn trail; he was now a farmer, still living in Maine, married to a shy woman in her late thirties, who stood by uncertainly as Jamie and her husband reminisced about sudden death. There was Maury Atkins, his roommate from Yale, who had first warned him to stay away from Constance Harding, and who admitted jovially now that he'd almost made the biggest mistake of his life, embracing Connie, and surprising Jamie (Maury was now a banker in Bridgeport) by kissing him on both cheeks. There was Connie's roommate from Lake Shore Drive, the bored-looking brunette who'd been sitting with her the first time he asked her to dance at that Yale mixer, the one who'd taught Connie to swear like a sailor. There was the couple who'd lived across the hall from them when they were renting their grubby little apartment on West Seventy-eighth; he'd been a dental student at the time, and his wife had worked for an insurance company; each night, as he'd pored over his textbooks and made his drawings of molars and bicuspids, she'd listened to the radio, wearing a headset and shaking her hips in time to the music as she washed and dried the dishes. There was the man who'd been the department head at the school where Jamie had taught photography three nights a week while waiting for his big break. There was the young, soft-spoken blond (now no longer young, his blond hair sifted with gray) assistant editor at *Life,* who'd murmured over and over again, "These are very good, these are very good," before picking up the phone and asking someone named Charlie to come in and have a look. There was, under the Japanese lanterns on a surprisingly cool, clear night (it had been raining a lot this July), a steady parade of people from the past and the memories they evoked, and Jamie realized all at once just how long and how hard Connie had worked to reconstruct for him not only his *own* history, but the history they had shared together for so many years now.

In bed later that night, the partygoers gone, the Japanese lanterns extinguished and swaying in the treetops on a faint breeze that blew in over the river, the water trickling below their bedroom window, always a faint whisper in July, never the rushing torrent it became in March, she snuggled close to him and asked, "Did it make you happy, Jamie?"

"Yes," he said. "Very happy."

He did not mention that two people had been missing from his party. Two people missing from his life. His daughter Lissie. And his . . .

Joanna.

July 25, 1970

Dear Lissie:

Your three letters and the birthday collage you made arrived here today, were in fact waiting in the mailbox when Mom and I got up at noon after the party she gave for me last night. Thank God you're all right, and thank you for your thoughtfulness. The collage is really beautiful, Liss. I've hung it in the barn, over my desk, and I'll think of you whenever I look at it. I can't begin to tell you how relieved we are. Before that batch of mail arrived, I had already called Andrews Travel and booked air passage for myself to Athens, fully intending to come there to Samos personally, certain that the goddamn Greeks had thrown you in prison or something. You'd mentioned in one of your earlier letters that the police thought you'd come illegally from Turkey, and I was beginning to think the worst. Thank God you're all right, Lissie, and are still on Samos. Does this mean you've changed your mind about moving on to India? I hope so.

Do you know what I wished for last night, Lissie, when I blew out the candles on my cake? I know I'm not supposed to tell anyone, for fear it won't come true. But let it be our secret, okay? I wished I would wake up one morning soon, and go down to the kitchen, and find you sitting there at the table shoveling cornflakes into your mouth. I would say, "Good morning, Lissie," and you would look up and say, "Hi, Dad," and go back to your cornflakes. And everything would be the same as it was again. I miss you, Lissie. Please come home soon.

Love,

Dad

August 3, 1970

Dear Mom and Dad,

We arrived here in Istanbul early Saturday morning and we have been roaming it since, enjoying every moment, though alas we will be leaving tomorrow morning. Dad, I've thought of nothing but you since the minute we arrived here. What a city for taking pictures! Everywhere you look, there is something new and different to see! I'm not only talking about the tourist attractions like the Blue Mosque or the Hagia Sofia, but the streets themselves, and the people in them, so alive and vital, and so unlike anything in America. It's the only city in the world, you know, that actually straddles two continents, Europe *and* Asia, and the influence of both (continents) is felt everywhere you go. They are building a bridge across the Bosphorus right this minute, which means people will be able to *walk* across from Europe to Asia! Isn't that something?

We'll be leaving here tomorrow morning when we set out across Turkey toward Iran. I can't begin to tell you how exciting all of this is, and how much I'm looking forward to the next leg of what so far has been the most rewarding time of my life. To be experiencing and learning, to be seeing all these different cultures so different from our own in America is more thrilling than I can possibly express. Please know that I love you both dearly, and will have much to tell you when I get home.

I can't give you any address for you to answer because we will be on the road for the next several weeks, but I will write to you from time to time to let you know how I'm doing.

All my love,

Lissie

Dear Lissie:

We have not heard from you since receiving those three letters and your birthday collage. Are you still in Greece? Is there some problem? I feel as if I'm trapped in some kind of nightmarish time-warp. In effect, Lissie, your past has become our present. We never know what's happening or what you plan to do next until we receive a letter relating events that have already gone by. Please write more often, won't you? Because just now, the distance between us has made a meaningless jumble of past and present.

Love,

Dad

This is Asia.

It begins, really and truly *begins,* not ten miles outside the city. They have taken the ferry from the Galata Bridge to Üsküdar, and have hitched a ride in the back of a pickup truck piled high with ears of corn and driven by a Turkish farmer who does not speak a word of English. He drops them off at Izmit, before making a right turn onto a secondary road leading to Eskisehir, waving at them from the cab of the truck as it disappears in a cloud of dust. They walk almost half the distance from Izmit to Adapazari, at least twenty kilometers by their map. As dusk stains the western sky and a setting sun tinges the waters of the Black Sea to the north, they sit on their duffel bags by the side of the road, wearily waving their thumbs at passing automobiles and trucks. The huge trailer truck that finally stops is painted green, the legend LABERRIGUE & CIE, MARSEILLES painted in white on its side. The driver leans over toward the open window on his right. *"Où allez-vous?"* he asks.

"Nous allons à Delhi," Lissie answers in hesitant French.

"Eh bien, montez-vous et soyez à l'aise. Je peux vous conduire jusqu'à Teheran."

223

The driver's name is Jean-François Bertaut, and he is transporting a load of heavy farm machinery from Marseilles to Teheran. He tells them this, after realizing how sparse Lissie's French is (three years of it at the Henderson School, another semester of it at Brenner), in a heavily accented English that could provoke laughter were he not their benefactor on an alien road that is already succumbing to the long shadows of night.

In the roadside gloom beyond the window, Lissie sees a baggy-pantsed woman drawing water from a well, sees an ox-cart loaded with earthen jugs and driven by a man wearing a fur hat and a long mustache, sees terraced cornfields, and sunflowers growing in wild profusion and then—she thinks surely it is a mirage—a camel caravan! The laden beasts plod along in the dusk, men in turbans and flowing robes walking beside them, the dust rising to cause a further diffusion of the rapidly waning light. "Look, Paul!" she says, and he turns from where he is sitting beside her as the truck rumbles past the caravan, a dozen camels in all, she guesses. "Yeah," he says, "wow," and she thinks, *I'm in Asia.*

The driver wants to know what is happening in the United States, particularly among the young people. He is himself in his fifties, Lissie guesses, a rotund little man wearing a peaked woolen cap, a gray jacket over a green V-necked sweater, and a tan shirt. His eyes are a pale, faded blue, his nose bulbous and interlaced with thin red veins, the mark of a heavy drinker. He has a thick, blondish mustache. When he takes off his cap to mop a red handkerchief over the top of his head, Lissie is surprised to discover that he is almost entirely bald.

His frame of reference as it pertains to the young people of France is what he calls the "minirevolution" that occurred in Paris during the spring of 1968, when students took over the Sorbonne, openly smoking marijuana in the courtyard and demanding constitutional reform, chanting *"De Gaulle, adieu! De Gaulle, adieu!"* and precipitating a pitched battle with the French riot police in the Latin Quarter. Jean-François was there at the time, visiting his sister; he saw the armored trucks and water cannons, he personally observed the police firing tear-gas grenades at the students and workers, who in retaliation hurled Molotov cocktails and cobblestones they had torn up from the streets. He can understand the attitude of the *workers*—eight million of them went on strike, demanding higher wages and shorter hours—but why the *students?* What was *their* complaint? Paul and Lissie (he pronounces her name in the French manner—"Leez") are both young people, perhaps they can explain to him what is troubling today's youth, including his own son who is somewhere in Holland right this moment, *"Peut-être qu'il fume l'herbe ou pire,* eh, as I have coming to expect."

They would have sounded inarticulate at best even to English-speaking adults back home as they, or more accurately Paul—Lissie has already begun to doze as the blackness of night surrounds the lumbering truck—tries to tell about the war in Vietnam, and the way kids all over America are being dumped on, and about the stupid laws regarding something harmless like marijuana, and about the corruption of the American government, and the nine-to-five mentality of the American male, and the corporate structure that is stifling individuality, and the oppression of women back in the States, and the emphasis on materialism, and the—

"Ah, oui, oui," Jean-François says, not understanding at all.

It is, perhaps, not the best of all possible ways to be seeing a foreign country, especially one as exotic as *this* one. The road is a route traveled by caravans centuries before Christ was born, skirting the Black Sea until it angles off toward Ankara, and then never veering more than a hundred miles inland as it skewers Yozgat, Sivas, Erzincan and Erzurum, coming within fifty miles of the Russian border as it swoops down toward Diyadin and then Gürbulak, the last town on the Turkish side before entering Iran. Lissie must content herself with only glimpses of the countryside as the truck rumbles along on the relatively good road at a steady fifty-mile-an-hour clip except where there are excavations or detours (and there are many), at which times Jean-François slows down to a snail's pace that enables her to appreciate more fully the strangeness of the nation through which they are traveling.

Summer is full upon the land here in the north of Turkey. In the apricot and apple orchards, the trees are already bearing fruit. Oxen and mules, horses, and here and there a straining man, pull ancient plows as they furrow the earth. Behind them, swarthy women wrapped in long scarves knotted over the forehead, draped about the throat, hanging down the back, squat to pick their potatoes or onions. Everywhere, the voices of the muezzin summon the faithful to their prayers. She learns to tell time by the chanting voices that float mellifluously from the minarets at dawn, noon, midafternoon, sunset, and the beginning of night, a darkness that falls with a sudden hush as the voices echo and die.

The lilting voices of children rising and falling on a sloping green field as they herd cattle homeward at dusk. The Kurdish voices of the men in the coffee house at a truck stop outside Imranli, rumbling out through the open arched doorway, not a woman in the room, the men mustached and bearded, two of them smoking water pipes, their dark eyes studying blond Lissie as she pauses in the doorway, all conversation stopping; she quickly takes Paul's arm and follows Jean-François to a stand selling hot sausages and a drink that tastes like warm lemonade. The voices of shepherds calling to each other, leather smocks over cotton trousers, skullcaps and beards, a single star gleaming in the summertime sky.

The sheep are wearing blue beads around their necks—what are *they* for, she wonders. They pass farmhouses without electricity, the feeble glow of candles shining behind paneless windows. They pass fields of plants Jean-François identifies as poppies— *"Coquelicots, vous savez,"*— and vineyards bursting with young grape. As they come closer to the Iranian border, she can see in the distance the snow-covered peak of Mount Ararat, and she wonders all at once if Noah's Ark is *really* up there someplace, as promised by the guidebook she purchased in Ankara.

The distance from Istanbul to the border is some 1,200 kilometers, which she figures at six-tenths of a mile for an approximate distance of 720 miles. Jean-François picked them up outside Izmit on the evening of the fifth. By his reckoning, they will reach the border early on the morning of the eighth; he is averaging thirty-five, forty miles an hour, and sleeping only when he is utterly exhausted, pulling the huge truck over to the side of the road whenever his eyelids begin to droop, catching an hour's sleep here, two hours there, pushing on again as soon as he is refreshed.

It is four-thirty in the morning when they pass through the sleeping Turkish town of Gürbulak. Turkish customs at the border gives them no trouble at all. Jean-François knows some of the men on duty, one of whom speaks a bastard French, and they pay scant attention to his passport, his visa and his various other papers. The one who speaks French glances cursorily at Lissie's passport and visa, and then studies Paul's. Nodding, he hands the papers back and says a few words to Jean-François in French Lissie cannot understand but which she takes to be a comment about herself since the words are accompanied by a leer and a laugh she thinks is lewd. Waving, the man passes them through.

The Iranian customs barrier is a mile or so down the road.

A single light burns outside a ramshackle wooden hut painted white. The countryside around the hut is still black, the sky overcast and moonless, not a single star glowing in the somnolent night. Inside the hut, a radio is playing softly. Music. Odd-sounding stringed instruments. As the truck slows to a stop, she hears two men laughing inside the hut. Jean-François climbs down from the cab. A man in an olive-green uniform comes out of the hut. He is short and swarthy, and he is wearing a peaked cap tilted low on his forehead. He has a thick nose with a pencil-line mustache under it. Jean-François begins talking to the man in French. The man replies in a language Lissie imagines to be Persian, and then shakes his head impatiently, and goes back into the hut. A hooded light flicks on over the entrance door. When he emerges again, he is trailed by a slightly taller man wearing the same olive-green uniform but with different markings on his epaulets; his superior officer, Lissie guesses.

In English, the second man says to Jean-François, "Papers," and holds out his hand. His attention is caught by the glint of Lissie's blond hair in the cab of the truck, illuminated by the light the other man turned on. He squints his eyes, cranes his neck for a look into the cab, and still looking at Lissie, accepts the papers Jean-François extends to him. He has a cold; he keeps sniffing as he studies the papers, runs his forefinger under his dripping nose, and finally reaches for a handkerchief in his back pocket and blows his nose noisily before returning to the papers. In English, Jean-François explains that this is his passport, and this is his visa ("Yes, yes," the officer says), and this his bill of lading, and this his authority to transport farm machinery into Iran, and this his *carnet*—"Yes, yes," the officer says, "open the truck for me."

Jean-François goes around to the back of the trailer, unlocks the padlock there, and opens the doors wide. Farm machinery, just as he'd explained. A tractor and a cultivator. That is all.

"You are going where?" the officer asks.

"Teheran."

"And returning when?"

"*Aussitôt que je* . . . when I make *délivrance.*"

"When is that?"

"*J'attends arriver* . . . I expect arrive Teheran tomorrow."

"And will leave Iran when?"

"*Après-demain.* The day next."

227

"Close the doors," the officer says, and comes around the rear of the truck to the cab again. From the driver's side, he points up into the cab at Paul and says, "You. Papers."

Paul slides over on the seat and is handing down his passport and visa when the officer says, "Here. Where I can see. The woman, too. You," he says, pointing to her. "Blondie. Out of the truck."

The word "Blondie" sends a shiver of unreasoning fear up her spine. She opens the door on her side of the cab, and then starts around the front of the truck to where the officer is waiting under the light. The engine is still running; Jean-François has not turned off the ignition, expecting this stop to be as brief as the one on the Turkish side had been. The headlights pierce the darkness ahead, illuminating the lowered black-and-white-striped border barrier. She feels the heat of the engine as she passes through the headlight beams to the other side of the cab where the officer is now looking at Paul's passport.

"You have been where?" he says.

"Traveling directly here. Through Europe and then Turkey."

"Where do you go now?"

"Delhi."

"To return when?"

"I'm not sure yet."

"Visa," the officer says, and extends his hand. Paul gives him the visa they obtained at the Iranian Consulate in Istanbul. He looks at it, nods, says, "Fifteen-day transit."

"Yes, sir."

He hands the visa back. "How many cigarettes you have?" he asks.

"I don't smoke," Paul says.

"How many cigarettes?"

"None."

"Whiskey?"

"None."

"You have narcotics?" the officer asks.

"No, sir."

"Marijuana?"

"No, sir."

"Cocaine?"

"No, sir. Nothing."

"You are American, and no marijuana?" the officer says, and laughs. "Blondie?" he says, and turns sharply to where Lissie is standing near the cab fender. *"You* have marijuana?"

"No," she says. "No, sir."

"Papers," he says, and holds out his hand.

She puts her passport and her visa on his outstretched palm. He studies both, checks Lissie's picture against her face, and then says, "Where do you go now?"

"To Delhi."

"With boyfriend here?"

"Yes."

"How many cigarettes you have?"

"None."

"Whiskey?"

"None."

"Where is your luggage?"

"In the truck. In the . . . back of the truck."

"Open the door again," he says to Jean-François over his shoulder. He looks at Lissie's passport. "You were born . . . what is this?"

"December 19, 1951."

"So you are how old?"

"Eighteen," she says.

"Eighteen," he repeats. "Nice, Blondie. Eighteen. Get your luggage."

She walks around to the back of the truck, where Jean-François has again unlocked and opened the big doors. She pulls out her duffel and carries it to where the officer is now pacing under the overhead light.

"That is all?" he says.

"Yes."

"One piece?"

"Yes."

"Open it."

She unzips the bag for him. He kneels beside it, pokes at it tentatively, and then reaches into it with both hands, feeling, rummaging. She watches silently as he riffles through her several pairs of blue jeans, her dozen or more bikini panties, her blouses and sweaters, her sandals and shoes. He unzips her cosmetics kit and seems fascinated by the array of lipsticks and eye liners. He studies her plastic container of birth-control pills.

"What is this?" he asks.

"Pills," she says.

"Narcotics?"

"No, no. Birth control."

"What is that, birth control?"

"You take them so you won't have babies."

"This?"

"One every day," she says, and nods.

He looks at her skeptically, and then studies the manufacturer's name on the circular container, and then the numbers for the days of the month, and then pops one of the pills out and studies the manufacturer's colophon stamped onto the face of the pill itself. She thinks, *He's going to fuck up my cycle, the dope.* The night air is chill. She shivers again, and zips up the front of her leather fighter-pilot's jacket. He is trying now to put the pill back into the hole from which he popped it. He gives up, and drops the container and the loose pill back into the cosmetics kit. He zips it closed. He stands up.

"Inside," he says.

"What for?" she says.

"Search," he says. "Inside."

"Search? For what?"

"Narcotics."

"I have no narcotics."

"We shall see. Inside."

"Paul," she says, turning to him.

"Listen," Paul says, "she's not carrying any dope, there's no sense . . ."

"Shut up," the man says. "Inside," he says to Lissie.

"I'm an American citizen," she says, immediately thinking she has said exactly the wrong thing. The man's eyebrows arch. A smile crosses his face.

"Ah," he says, "American citizen."

"Yes," she says. She is trembling now. She wishes she could stop trembling.

"Does America not have customs?"

"What?"

"*La douane,*" Jean-François says.

"What?" Lissie says.

"Do they not search?" the man asks.

"You . . . you already *looked* through my bag."

"Inside," he says.

"What for?"

"A more complete search. Inside."

"No," she says.

A more *complete* search means a *body* search. She'll be damned if she'll allow this officious little bastard to probe her cavities with his germy little fingers.

The unlikeliest hero steps forward. Fat little Jean-François Bertaut, his peaked woolen cap covering his bald head, his shaggy mustache bristling, his jacket open over his sweatered potbelly, says calmly and with only the faintest trace of a French accent, "I will be her witness."

"What?" the officer says.

"*À Teheran, je vais raconter aux officiers tout ce que est passé ici.*"

"I do not speak French," the officer says.

"I will say all what I see and hear. To *les officiers* in Teheran."

The officer turns away from him. "Inside," he says to Lissie.

"*Pas sans moi,*" Jean-François says, moving into his path. "I will stay with the young girl."

The officer hesitates. Hands on his hips, he stares at Jean-François, their eyes locked in silent combat. Lissie, terrified now, watches them. Is the officer wondering how the officials in Teheran will react to his demand for a body search when nothing in her bag seems to warrant one? Who *are* these officials in Teheran, anyway? Does Jean-François even *know* if there is anyone in that city to whom he can report unseemly conduct at the border? He has traveled this road many times before, so maybe he knows what he's talking about. But what if he doesn't? The officer keeps staring at him. Paul, standing by, says nothing. She will remember later that he did nothing, said nothing.

"*Alors,*" Jean-François says, "*allons,*" and takes Lissie's arm, and jerks her toward the cab of the truck.

"The search will be made," the officer says, and then to Jean-François, almost under his breath, "You may attend."

She cannot at first comprehend how a body search in the presence of a courageous little Frenchman will differ in any way from one conducted in private. Reluctantly, she follows them both into the hut. Jean-François insists that the second officer go outside. His superior says something in Persian, and the man goes out to stand by the fender of the truck. He is lighting a cigarette when the senior officer closes the door.

The search, much to her surprise, is circumspect in every way. She realizes, as the officer delicately, gingerly, and cautiously pats her clothing and then looks through the shoes he has asked her to remove, that he is going through the search now only as a matter of face-saving routine. Whatever he had earlier planned or expected has been headed off by Jean-François's intervention and his threats of reporting the entire incident to some nameless officials in the capital. The search takes no longer than three minutes. She remembers having looked up at the clock on the wall when she sat down to take off her loafers; she looks up at it again when the officer says, "That is all, you may go." He turns to Jean-François then, and—with the faintest trace of a smile on his mouth—says, "Do you see, then, there was nothing to fear."

Jean-François returns the smile. *"Merci, mon capitain,"* he says, *"vous êtes très gentil."*

"I am not a captain," the man replies, suddenly understanding French, and then abruptly turns away to light a cigarette. Dragging on it, he pulls open the door and calls something in Persian to his colleague. The other man immediately raises the striped border. They are both still standing outside the hut as Jean-François eases the big truck away from the border station. The senior officer has his hands on his hips, the cigarette dangling from his mouth. It is a quarter past five, and the sky in the east is already becoming light.

The seemingly endless, intermittent diatribe Paul delivers all the way to Teheran, some eight hundred kilometers and a bit more than ten hours from the border, is wasted on Lissie; she keeps thinking that he did nothing to stop what was about to happen to her. Aside from his early, feeble attempt to dissuade the officer, abruptly aborted when the man ordered him to shut up, he stood by helplessly while all those veiled threats fluttered ominously on the still predawn air, a Persian song-and-dance designed to frighten her into submission. And then what? Disrobe for them? Had they really expected her to suffer the indignity of an internal examination she might have denied even to a *female* customs official?

Rape had been in the air last night, she is certain of that, as chilling as the cold wind that blew in over the mountains to the north. A cozy hut-enclosed rape, to be sure, complete with radioed musical accompaniment—finger cymbals tinkling perhaps, tambourines jingling, the rhythmic strumming of a *sitar*, the lyric frenzy of a flute—but rape nonetheless. The fifty-dollar rape. Two gorillas with their olive-green trousers and undershorts down around their ankles, Lissie spread and struggling, Islamically invaded while outside Paul Michael Gillis shufflingly kicked shit and mumbled something about how long it was taking them to get to India.

She can understand (oh, *sure,* she can) how frightened he must have been by the officer's inspection of his spanking-clean, brand-new passport. He is, after all, a draft dodger; he could not have called any further attention to himself once he was in the clear, even if it meant throwing Lissie to the wolves instead. But, Jesus *Christ,* couldn't he have made at least a show of support, puffed out his manly chest, said, "Now see *here,* my good fellow," clenched his fists, maybe even—if worse had come to worst—thrown both those little bastards over his shoulder in a sudden judo move?

No, not Paul. Stood by. Watched. Said nothing after he'd been told to shut up. True, those words had snapped on the dank morning air like the crack of a whip, sending a flutter of new fear through Lissie, causing her mouth to go suddenly dry. But *she* had been the one expecting imminent violation; she'd had every *right* to be frightened by that threatening little bastard with his snotty little fingers, plump fat sausages like the ones she'd seen hanging from trees in the Turkish countryside, the *thought* of those fingers touching her, poking at her, probing her—*Jesus!*

And now it is Paul who, in retrospect, is highly insulted. She pays scant attention to the Iranian landscape unfolding beyond the dust-streaked window on her right; she wants only to get through this fucking country as quickly as possible, hitch another ride the minute Jean-François drops them off in Teheran, get *out* of here, cross the border into Afghanistan and then Pakistan, keep *on* going till they reach a civilized place like India, where the people speak English they learned at Cambridge or Oxford. She pays even less attention to Paul's rambling tirade, enormously pissed off by his behavior at the frontier and determined to make him pay for it somehow, if only by denying him the conjugal rights he has already accepted as his proper masculine due. Her mind wanders as he rides his high horse to the limits of his righteous anger.

He is using the border incident as a means of clarifying for Jean-François the indignities young people everywhere are forced to suffer at the hands of ignorant, uncaring adults who consider today's youth a menace to the smug, self-satisfied, fat existences they enjoy at the expense of the poor, downtrodden masses who bear the brunt of taxation without true representation. On and on, he goes. The jails are full of blacks, Puerto Ricans, and draft dodgers, he says, all of them hippies in their own right, all of them

233

fighting in their own way for a dignity denied them by the fucking Establishment, all of them chasing the fake American promise of freedom and equality for all regardless of race, creed, color, sex—

She doubts that Jean-François understands a fifth of what Paul is saying. As he keeps up his rambling monologue, she remembers the scorn with which the boy in the Princeton sweatshirt denounced America on that Cape Cod beach last year; remembers Judd at Woodstock, and the way he called grownups "the enemy"; remembers the atrocity stories the two Carnegie Tech dropouts told in San Francisco, and Barbara Duggan's later speculation about the envy young people aroused by their mere existence. Half-listening to Paul, she wonders for the first time in months whether *young* people are as full of shit as adults are.

August 10, 1970

Dear Mom and Dad,

We arrived here in Teheran yesterday afternoon about three, and we'll be leaving here in just a little while, as soon as we've had some breakfast. I thought I'd write this and mail it before we start off again. We had a terrible experience at the border coming in, and when we start hitching again today we don't plan to stop till we reach Delhi.

It's not as noisy here as it was in Istanbul, but the city seems more confusing somehow, I don't know why, with all these automobiles and taxi cabs (they're orange here, not yellow like New York or black like London) and buses they must have *bought* in London, actually, because they're the same red double-decker ones I saw when I was there, and squares and streets all intersecting and crazy. It all looks very modern here, and not at all Asian, which is surprising after what you see on the road. I mean, that's where the *real* Asia is, not in cities like Teheran with its big apartment houses and office buildings and movie theaters and fancy shops and supermarkets and signs like on Broadway and music blaring out of speakers everywhere, you'd think you were in an American city, not New York or San Francisco, but someplace like, I don't know, some shitty little city someplace in America.

The only thing that seems remotely Asian about this place is these drains they have running in the gutters that the citizens use for washing food in, or throwing garbage in, or peeing in, or spitting in, and then they wash their *hands* and *faces* in this mucky water, can you believe it? Well, maybe that isn't Asian, but it's certainly filthy, and it sums up the way I feel about Iran in general, I guess. Here in Teheran, the Shah's done a lot of modernization, but most of the cities and towns we passed on the way here looked uniformly drab and dull—gray will do it every time, Mom, and gray seems to be the favorite color for the buildings here. The favorite *food* is (surprise!) lamb. Also rice. And cheese. And this flat bread they bake in charcoal pits.

The men are all wearing white shirts and baggy black pants, with here and there one or two who are dressed like sheiks, with the turbans and robes, you know, but for the most part the clothing, in the cities anyway, is westernized. Except for the women. A lot of them are still wearing the chador, which is this long piece of cloth, usually black but sometimes brightly colored, that they wrap around their body and drape across the shoulders and over the head. It used to be against the law here to run around without a veil over your face, but the Shah changed all that. Paul says the Shah's government is as corrupt as our own back home. Paul's beard looks marvelous now, and by the time we get to Delhi I'm sure he'll be mistaken for a guru or something. No address yet, because we're still on the move. But I'll keep in touch. Please know that I love you and respect you both very much.

All my love,

Lissie

P.S. Ooodles and ooodles of kisses to both of you.
P.S.S. Scads and scads of hugs, too. I love you both. I love you. Hugs and kisses. Love. Bye for now.

The road outside Teheran angles sharply northward at Asalak where they catch a ride in another truck, this one carrying fertilizer from a plant in Germany. The driver speaks only German. Hunched over the wheel, he carefully watches the asphalt ribbon that winds through the pass to Babol and the sea. They drive eastward along the Caspian for the better part of the day, coming at last to the town of Gorgān, where the driver indicates to them in sign language that he will be spending the night here. It is only late afternoon, but a look at their map tells them that the nearest town of any size is Meshed, which they estimate to be some five hundred kilometers away—at least a ten-hour journey over twisting mountain roads. They eat mutton and boiled rice in a roadside teahouse, and then rent a small room there for the night. The room costs them twenty cents, and is furnished with a straw mat and a small silk prayer rug that would cost $600 back in the States. As Paul rolls over toward her, Lissie—for the first time in her life—claims she has a headache.

In the morning, and quite by chance since they had made no previous arrangement with him, they are picked up by the same German driver who seems happy to see them again, and who chatters on in German as though they understand him completely. They are in the mountains now, and traveling eastward along the Russian border, never more than seventy kilometers from it, and at one point—near Shirvan—less than fifty, the equivalent of thirty miles.

The road is tortuous and difficult. The German driver stops talking and concentrates on steering. They do not reach the bustling city of Meshed until long after dark. The German driver says his farewells, and they begin hitching again at once, catching first a small Iranian van carrying a mysterious cargo that rattles and clanks in the back, and then a larger truck en route from Istanbul and driven by a man who speaks only Greek. At midnight, they pass through the Iranian town of Taybad, cross the border without incident, and come into Islam Qala on the Afghan side. It is 12:20 on the morning of August 12. They are at this moment eighteen hours away from their rendezvous with the dogs of Shahnur.

Where earlier the truck route ran through the Elburz Mountains hugging the Caspian Sea and the Russian border, here in Afghanistan it avoids the loftier impassable peaks of the Hindu Kush range, and swings far to the south to enter the pass at Herat. Their Greek driver is following the route traveled by Alexander the Great in the fourth century B.C.; he will emerge from the pass at Qala Adras, and then continue on south in a wide loop that will take them to Kandahar and then through Jaldak and Shahnur (where they will meet the wild dogs) and finally through Ghazni and Kabul and eastward through the Khyber Pass into Pakistan.

The roads are narrow; the posted speed limit is fifty kilometers, and everywhere the headlights pick out the small triangular, red-bordered signs that stand in warning on the rock-strewn edge of the road: S-curve ahead. And ahead. And ahead. And ahead. The mountain range lies upon the land like a giant twisted paw, its curved talons digging into the sandy wastes to the southwest. Lulled by the motion of the truck, Lissie dozes most of the night and awakens sometime after dawn to discover a sandswept vastness on her right, just outside the open window.

The deserts in this part of the world are linked by a topography that respects no artificially created geographical borders. On Lissie's map, the Dasht-i-Margo here in Afghanistan seems only an extension of the Dasht-i-Lut in Iran. As she squints her eyes against the eastern sun into which the truck is driving head-on, she spots upon the horizon a band of nomads riding mules, not camels, and herding before them a dozen or more beasts that look like long-horned cattle. The men are wearing turbans and smocks over baggy pants and sandals, all a dusty white, men and animals blending with the furrowed, windblown sand behind them. The small caravan shimmers like a mirage in the morning sun, and then is gone as the truck rounds a hilly curve. The shade is merciful but brief, the shadow of the hill embracing the truck for only an instant before it emerges again into full sunlight. There is only the desert now—and the unblinking sky.

The Greek driver stinks of garlic. He is prone to farting as well, and his effusive, effluvial stenches—combined with the heat and the desert dust that assail the open windows—are making Lissie a trifle ill. Ahead, she sees in the distance what appears to be a roadside bazaar, and as they approach it, another smell joins the pervasive mix in the cab of the truck: the unmistakable aroma of mutton cooking in oil. She has been sniffing this same scent halfway across Asia now. It is usually accompanied, as it is now, by the sweeter smell of rice frying with raisins and nuts, and this heady combination wafts back toward the truck now to comingle with the stench of the Greek's flatus, the Greek's halitosis, the stifling desert heat, the choking desert dust—she will vomit.

But the Greek slows the truck to avoid running down the jabbering crowd of people clustered about the jerry-built bazaar, and finally stops the vehicle altogether. Announcing in Greek, with appropriate, unmistakable, hand-to-mouth gestures, that he is going to have some breakfast, he climbs down from the truck, accompanied by the miasma of his body odors, trailing his various stenches behind him, wrapping them around him like the vaporous clinging veils on the women who crowd the meat vendor's stand.

Lissie buys herself a piece of the ubiquitous thin bread (here in

Afghanistan it is called *nan)* and a cup of hot green tea. Paul, sitting cross-legged beside the Greek driver, is eating mutton and rice. He complains the mutton is stringy. They leave the bazaar at seven-thirty that morning. The wind blowing in off the desert is hot and dry. Lissie tilts onto her face the straw hat she bought at the Covered Bazaar in Istanbul. She closes her eyes. She hears the Greek driver trying some English on Paul. He gives up after a few sentences. The desert is still again. She dozes.

Shahnur is only eleven hours away.

It must be close to noon when they approach Yakchal. Ahead, she can hear the muezzin calling as the truck slows down outside the village. She can see a dozen men touching their foreheads to the ground before a gray wall with an arched niche in it. Their feet are bare, their exposed soles dirty against the white humps of their massed backs bent in supplication to Mohammed. At a turn in the road a bit farther on, a group of silent barefooted children stand beside a peeling wooden gate in an ancient stone wall. One of the girls—Lissie guesses she is eleven or twelve—is wearing a beaded necklace around her throat; it reminds Lissie of a necklace Grandmother Harding gave her when she was nine. The driver shifts gears after rounding the curve, and the truck gains speed again. Lissie yawns. In a little while she is dozing again.

She does not catch the name of the next town; she awakens someplace in the center of it when the driver begins honking his horn. The cause of his impatience is a flock of sheep being led by a turbaned boy carrying a stick. The highway here has become a narrow dirt road pressed on either side by gray-walled buildings, and the sheep are crowding the road from curb to curb, leisurely bleating as the boy indolently flicks his stick at them and the Greek driver angrily honks his horn. Several men at the curb gesture for him to shut up.

The flock of sheep parts to let the truck through. The boy with the stick makes a gesture remarkably like that of throwing a finger back home—has he met many Americans?—and the truck eases through amid a cacophony of its own honking horn, the bleating sheep, and the shouting street merchants. Whatever the name of the town (she misses it again, craning for a look at the sign on their way out) they are through it and on the highway again by 2:00 P.M.

In just four hours, they will meet the dogs of Shahnur.

The driver and Paul both want to push on for Kabul, which is the

238

capital and which they are both sure they can reach before midnight. The roads will be less crowded after dark, they will make better time, and so on. But Lissie is exhausted, and she tells Paul she cannot spend another moment in the cramped cab of the truck; they have been driving steadily since early yesterday morning; her legs are stiff; this seems like a nice little village where she's sure they can find a room for the night. She thanks the driver in English, and climbs down from the cab, almost stumbling. Paul, behind her, is clearly annoyed that they will be spending the night here. She tells him that she's just about to get her period, which is one of the reasons she has chosen not to spend the next five or six hours in a truck with a flatulating Greek.

The village is situated in the valley through which the Arghandab River runs. As they stand on the dusty road, watching the truck rumble off northward and westward toward Kabul, she hears the first echoing chant of the muezzin calling worshippers to their sunset prayers, and sees the jagged edges of the mountaintops turning molten as though in religious response. She is desperately hungry, she realizes; she has had nothing to eat since the *nan* and tea early this morning. She is exhausted as well, and a bit irritable, and she wants only to find a place to eat, a place to stay before it gets dark. In the fields beyond, she can see the black felt tents of the nomad shepherds, glowing now in the rays of the setting sun. On the bank of the river, several women wearing black chadris—as the tentlike veils are called here in Afghanistan—pause in the washing of clothes and kneel to Mecca, their heads bowed, their hands clasped, behind a turbaned old man who similarly kneels and offers his prayers on the grassy bank. Lissie and Paul walk on the dirt road above the river. The shadows are lengthening.

She has not seen many dogs since they crossed the Bosphorus into Asia proper. She does not know if this has anything to do with religious belief (she knows, for example, that Islamic law does not permit the depiction of human beings or animals) or if it has only to do with exotic appetites; do they *eat* dogs in Muslim nations? Or is it possible that these people simply cannot *afford* to keep pets? She does not at first associate the skinny mongrel who comes around the side of the building with the black felt tents she sees just beyond, nor with the nomads' sheep grazing on the greensward. She and Paul have been following the familiar aroma of broiling mutton, and are entering a walled courtyard which, they realize as soon as they see the stacked garbage, is on the kitchen side, at the *rear* of the low flat building. They are about to turn and retrace their steps when they see the dog entering the courtyard from the opposite end.

He is a spotted animal standing some two feet high, brown and white, with a pointed snout and glittering black eyes, a mongrel who seems to be a cross between a Doberman and a Dalmatian. "Hey there, boy," Paul says, and is smiling and hefting his duffel onto his shoulder again when the dog's ears go back and he bares his teeth. A low growl starts somewhere deep in his throat. He stands rooted to the spot near the cans of garbage stacked outside the kitchen, and Lissie realizes that he is only protecting his discovered turf, this treasure trove of inedible shit he has stumbled upon, and she whispers to Paul, "Let's get out of here," and they are backing away from the dog when suddenly he multiplies himself by two, and then by four, and there are *eight* dogs in that cloistered courtyard where only the spotted mongrel speaks in his low growl and in the distance the chant of the muezzin echoes and fades.

The dogs are poised and trembling.

As taut as drawn springs, they await only the hair-trigger release that will send them hurtling across the courtyard in attack. As yet, there is no barking. Only the spotted one speaks in his low growl, and the others wait and listen to the leader of the pack, their ears twitching to the modulated notes that rise and fall like the earlier chanting of the muezzin. As the sunlight fades, there are eight pairs of glittering eyes in that courtyard, fastened on these intruders who look different and sound different (she shouldn't have spoken to Paul) and smell different from any human being they have ever known. She does not want to do anything to inspire the attack she is certain will come anyway, no sudden move, no shrill warning, especially no aroma of fear, which she is positive is seeping from every pore to pollute the air as surely as had the Greek's farts. The leader of the pack is still growling. Perhaps he is as frightened as she is. Perhaps the growl is only his macho-dog act, perhaps he is only strutting his stuff for the seven mutts behind him, all of them watching with those glittering little eyes and those twitching ears, waiting. Cautiously, she places her hand on Paul's arm. Watching the dogs, they begin backing out of the courtyard—and just then, the leader springs.

He seems propelled by the force of his own growl. He is airborne an instant after he begins his charge, his fangs bared as he lunges unerringly for the jugular. Lissie brings up her right arm and his jaws clamp on it, his fangs biting into naked flesh. She remembers

240

something about hitting for the nose, and instinctively clenches her left hand and smashes the fist at the dog's nose, remembering an instant later that it's a *shark* you're supposed to hit on the nose, a fucking *shark,* and wincing in pain as the weight of the animal knocks her flat on her back to the ground. His teeth are still clamped onto her forearm. The pain is excruciating. She smells the dog stink on him, and the putrid aroma of the garbage now scattered on the courtyard floor from the open can she knocked over when she fell. She does not know where Paul is, she prays with every religious remnant in her body that he hasn't deserted her. She will pray in Islamic if that will help; just let him *be* there, just let him not have turned and deserted her.

The dog is gnawing on her arm as if it is the sundown meal he'd been searching for here in the courtyard. The other dogs are yapping in random frenzy, and she realizes as her eyes frantically graze the courtyard walls that Paul has fled through the gate, Paul has left her behind, Paul has *run* again. It is then that the truly terrifying thought comes to her: are these dogs *starving?* It is one thing to be bitten by an angry or a frightened animal; it is another to be *eaten* by a hungry one. Someone bursts into the courtyard from the kitchen door at the rear of the building. He is wearing baggy pants and a turban and an apron, and there is an ancient musket in his hands. There is another man behind him, waving a cleaver. The gun goes off. There is another shot, and the dogs begin barking now in unison against these new intruders, these shouting saviors, these nice Afghans who make such pretty rugs, these dear lovely people. She thinks *But where the hell are you, Paul*—and then faints from loss of blood, or hunger, or fear, or exhaustion, or everything.

August 14, 1970

Dear Mom and Dad,

Well, here I am in the city of Kabul where Paul and I have spent a day resting because we were attacked by wild dogs in the village of Shahnur just two days ago. The doctor says it will be all right for us to move on to India tomorrow, which is what we plan to do first thing in the morning. I'm very tired, and my right arm hurts like hell, so if you don't mind, I'll make this postcard brief.

All my love,

Lissie

He called his attorney. His attorney said there was no
need for alarm but that it might be wise to call the State
Department in Washington to see if they might be able to help him
in locating Lissie. The man he spoke to there was named Mr.
Brothers. Mr. Brothers told him there was virtually nothing the
State Department could do. Unless they knew his daughter's
address, there was no way their various consuls in Asia could even
begin making inquiries. He suggested that Jamie contact him again
the moment he knew where his daughter could be reached. Jamie
thanked him, and then hung up. He had called the State Department because he'd wanted help in locating his daughter; he had just
been told to call back *after* he'd located his daughter.

He was a stranger to the part of the world in which his daughter
was traveling. He telephoned the India Government Tourist Office
and asked for a map to supplement the one in his 1967 Rand
McNally Atlas, and then bought a half-dozen more maps in the
Doubleday near Fifty-seventh. Some of them proved worthless
while others were so detailed and sophisticated that they listed
currency rates, time changes, temperatures and rainfalls at various

242

times of the year, and even unlighted tollgates one might expect to encounter at night. The roadmaps gave him a sense of security. The countries through which she had passed, the country in which she was now traveling (presumably) seemed more civilized than he'd imagined them to be; there were primary roads and secondary roads and even little back roads, just as there were in Connecticut.

Like an armchair general planning a fall campaign, Jamie spread his roadmaps on the long table in the barn and tried to second-guess Lissie's route.

Had she entered India at Lahore, which seemed likely, and then continued on to Delhi and eastward to Calcutta? Or had she gone up to Nepal instead? It was supposed to be beautiful there in Nepal, maybe they went right out of Delhi into Nepal, looks like maybe, what can this be, maybe nine hundred miles to Katmandu, that's where they may have headed, supposed to be terrific there in Katmandu, temples and everything, monks, whatever, would have taken them maybe, well, how many miles a day would they be averaging, oh, figure thirty miles an hour, maybe a bit more, but say thirty and play it safe. So figure two hundred, two hundred and fifty miles a day, no more than that, they'd have been in Katmandu—well, let's say they spent at least a few days in Delhi, let's say they left Delhi on the twenty-first, they'd be in Katmandu by, where's the calendar, well, I don't need a calendar, just divide nine hundred by two-fifty, that's close to four days, they'd have been in Katmandu by the twenty-fourth of August.

He made this calculation on Sunday, August 30, sixteen days after Lissie had written her last letter home. At a dinner party that night, he learned that both Reynolds McGruder here in Rutledge, and Matthew Bridges in nearby Talmadge, had a month ago received telegrams from the Defense Department stating that their respective sons had been killed in action. Apparently both young men (their lieutenants' letters to each family read like carbon copies of each other) had been engaged in dropping supplies to a beleaguered South Vietnamese rifle company when the Vietcong opened fire and blasted the hovering helicopter out of the sky. It seemed as though Charlie hadn't heard that the Americans might be pulling out. Or perhaps Charlie had simply decided that dropping ammunition and food could be considered aiding and abetting the enemy. Either way, Roger Bridges (who would have been twenty-one this month) and David McGruder (whose twentieth birthday would have come in December) would never again or respectively play drums and lead guitar in the group they had formed two years ago.

Dr. Frank Lipscombe warned Reynolds McGruder to keep a careful eye on his surviving son, lest he wrongly begin to feel that his brother had been killed in his stead, and then react hysterically to the unfortunate tragedy. This was not an uncommon wartime experience, Lipscombe explained to McGruder, witness the remarkable insights of the play *Home of the Brave,* where the hero suffered hysterical paralysis because of guilt feelings exacerbated on the battlefield. "The guilt in the case of your son Danny," he said, "may be caused by an erroneous belief that only a stroke of luck sent *him* to college and *David* to Vietnam. In which case, he could easily . . ."

"Yes, I understand," McGruder said. Tears were forming in his eyes. He turned away and went to sit quietly on the deck outside.

"How's your daughter doing?" Lipscombe asked.

"Fine," Jamie said. He never knew what to say when they asked.

"Where is she now? Home for the summer?"

"No," Jamie said, and hesitated. "She's in India."

"India?"

"Yes."

"Ah," Lipscombe said.

Jamie waited. He knew what the next question would be. It had been asked of him a dozen times or more since that last letter from Lissie. It had been asked at Rutledge parties, and outside the Rutledge post office, and in the Rutledge hardware store, and once during a shoot in New York, and once in the steam room at the New York Athletic Club—the same question each and every time. Lipscombe asked the question now.

"Where in India?"

And Jamie, as always, hesitated. He didn't *know* where in India. He had not heard from his daughter since the fourteenth of August.

"I don't know where," he said at last.

Lipscombe's eyebrows went up onto his forehead. "Haven't you *heard* from her?" he said.

"Not recently," Jamie said.

"Well, I'm sure she's all right," Lipscombe said.

They all said that. You told them you didn't know where your daughter was, and they all said, "Well, I'm sure she's all right."

Jamie was not at all sure she was all right.

He could not later remember exactly when he began to believe she was dead. It was certainly sometime in September. With a son, he thought, they draft him and the authorities know where he is at all times and if he gets killed in a rice paddy they send you a telegram like the one Reynolds got, or the one Matthew Bridges got, they send you a telegram. But with a daughter, there's no one to keep track of where she's been or where she's going, no one but herself, and if she doesn't choose to let you in on the secret, why then you are in the dark, man, you are sitting here in the autumn dark in the town of Rutledge, Connecticut, drinking strong whiskey neat on a cold September afternoon, the trees rattling, the wind wanting to know where the summer had gone? Where'd my golden girl of summer go, he wondered, where's my darling Lissie?

He would sometimes wake up in the middle of the night, and lie staring at the ceiling, wondering whether Connie was awake beside him, wondering (if she was asleep instead) whether he should awaken her to discuss the only thing that seemed to be on his mind these days, the possibility that his daughter was dead. He would lie there, certain now that Connie was awake beside him and possibly thinking the exact same thoughts, but he would say nothing to her, would lie there silently instead in the stillness of the night, and then become suddenly angry, trembling with an overriding fury that made him want to get up and knock the radio-clock off the dresser, or pick up the chair with his clothes draped over it, hurl it through the window, push his fist through plaster and lath, *kick* things, *smash* things—how could she *be* so fucking inconsiderate, didn't she *know* they were back here waiting helplessly for some word from her, hoping against hope that she wasn't—

Dead, he thought.

And the anger would vanish, and he would lie in the darkness as the grief enveloped him, the sadness touching his eyes, sitting behind his eyes but refusing him the mercy of tears, wrapping him as completely as a shroud, his face, his throat, suffocating him, constricting his chest, making it impossible for him to breathe in the dark, his daughter dead in the dark, she had abandoned his life and forfeited her own, in the dark, dead someplace in India. He mourned for her, but the tears would not come. His eyes burned with tears scalding from within and behind, but they would not come. He could not cry for the daughter he knew was dead but prayed was not.

Once, in the middle of the night at the beginning of October, he dared to cross the line he and Connie tacitly respected, dared to open the casket of horrors stored in the darkest corner of his dread, dared to whisper in the dark, "She's dead, isn't she?"

Connie sighed.

And said nothing.

Larry Kreuger called the very next day.

It was Lester Blair who found her.

He had come down from the house up on the ridge to walk his two Irish terriers through the woods near the reservoir. She was lying in the underbrush alongside the old logging road that paralleled the Blair driveway. The dogs stopped dead in their tracks. He thought at first they'd smelled a raccoon, or maybe a snake; there were lots of copperheads here near the water. One of the dogs began whimpering. Lester said, "Shh, boy," and squinted through the foliage, and saw her lying on her side with the back of her head blown away.

She was wearing what looked to be a party dress, pink and silky and spattered with blood, the hem pulled back over pantyhose she must have torn coming through the woods, ladders up the sleek shiny sides of both legs, blood on the legs, too, blood all over the ground around her, shining on the fallen russet leaves. One of her high-heeled shoes had dropped from her foot. The foot looked particularly vulnerable without the shoe on it. More than anything else, that foot without a shoe on it seemed to sum up for Lester the utter vulnerability of the young girl who lay on the ground on the shiny red leaves. The weight of a twenty-gauge shotgun crushed the wet red leaves.

The call to Jamie came at 10:00 A.M. that Sunday morning, the eleventh day of October. He was sitting at the breakfast table with Connie, sipping at his coffee as he leafed through the *Times Magazine* section, studying the photographs, commenting every now and again on the particular ineptitude of this or that photographer; he had begun to notice about himself that he rarely commented on skill anymore, but only on the *lack* of it. When the phone rang, he took another sip of coffee before answering.

"Hello?" he said.

"Jamie, it's Larry Kreuger. I'm sorry to be breaking in on your Sunday this way."

His voice sounded odd. Jamie knew at once that something was wrong. He had no idea yet of the magnitude of the wrongness.

"What is it?" he asked at once.

246

"I wonder can you come on over." Larry's voice, southern, gentle, polite, was still underscored with an ominous note.

"What's the matter?" Jamie asked.

"It's Scarlett."

"What about her?"

"She's gone and killed herself," Larry said, and his voice broke.

Two state troopers—both of them tall and strapping—were in the Kreuger living room when Jamie got there. The local police had just left, Lester told Jamie, shaking his hand at the front door, and then went on to relate how he had discovered the body in the woods while he was walking his dogs, and how he hadn't known who she was, knew she was a local kid he'd seen around, but didn't know her name. He'd run back up the hill to his house, and called the cops from the phone in the den, and then went back down to the logging road with them. In a little pink evening bag attached to a belt around her waist, they found a driver's license identifying her as Scarlett Kreuger. "The thing that got me," he said, "was her shoe was off, on the left foot, the shoe was off. That would have been the definitive shot. Bring the camera in tight on the foot and the shotgun lying beside it on the wet leaves. That would have defined it, Jamie. If we were doing it for television, I mean, where we can't show the actual violence."

Across the room, Jamie could hear the droning voice of one of the troopers. Larry looked up from where he was sitting on the couch, and signaled to him. Jamie walked across to him, aware of the whisper of his loafers on the thick carpet. Larry took his hand. "Glad you could come," he said. "Sit down, these gentlemen were just asking some questions."

"Melanie all right?"

"Yes, fine," Larry said, nodding.

"Connie's on her way over."

"Fine," Larry said. He'd been crying. His eyes were red, the lids puffed and swollen. But there were no tears on his face now; only a numbed and bewildered look. In the kitchen, Jamie could hear the hushed voices of consoling women.

"You were saying she went to this party at the country club last night," one of the troopers prompted. Blue eyes. Blond hair at the sideburns. Pad open. Big gun holstered at his side; Jamie had heard that in some states the troopers used .357 Magnums, put a hole in a man the size of a sewer lid. He did not yet know that the jagged exit wound at the back of Scarlett's head measured some six inches in diameter.

"Yes," Larry said. "An engagement party. At the country club."

"Which country club would that be, sir? The one here in Rutledge, or the . . ."

"The Talmadge Club."

"Over near the university?"

"Yes."

"Did she go alone, sir?"

"No."

"Went with someone?"

"Yes."

"A boy?"

"Yes, but not . . ."

"Would you know his name, sir?"

"Scotty Klein. Dr. Klein's son."

"Live here in Rutledge?"

"Yes. The Kleins are good friends of ours."

"Came here to pick her up, did he? This . . .uh . . ." The trooper consulted his pad. "Scotty Klein, was it?"

"Yes, Scotty."

"What time was that?"

"When he picked her up?"

"Yes."

"About seven-thirty. But . . ."

"This her steady boyfriend or something?"

"No, no, nothing like that. Rusty Klein, that's the . . ."

"Thought you said it was Scotty."

"Yes, but this is the *daughter*. Rusty. She and my . . . daughter were in the same graduating class. The class of '69. They all went together, you see. Rusty and . . . Scarlett, my daughter . . . and the Klein boy."

"Oh, I see. So it wasn't just the two of them."

"No, it wasn't."

"It was the two Klein kids and your daughter."

"Yes, that's right."

"How old is she, sir, your daughter?"

"Eighteen. She'll be nineteen in . . ." He hesitated. He looked helplessly at Jamie. "She would have been . . . would have been nineteen next month."

"And the Klein kids?"

248

"Rusty is my daughter's age. I don't know how old Scotty is. Younger, I know. I think he's a senior at Lafayette."

"Was it the Klein boy who was driving?"

"Yes."

"Would you know what kind of car, sir?"

"What difference does any of this make?" Larry asked in his mild southern voice. "My daughter killed herself. You saw her lying on the ground there, you know she put that shotgun in her mouth and blew the back of her head off. The shotgun is mine, it was in the garage, on pegs there in the garage, wall pegs, she took the gun and shot herself with it, so why do you want to know what kind of car Scotty Klein was driving, what possible difference in the world can it make *now* what kind of car Scotty was driving?"

"Well, in case he . . . you see, sir, in something like this . . ."

"They dropped her off here at the house," Larry said wearily. "At two in the morning. I heard the car in the driveway, I heard Scarlett calling good night to them, I heard the car leaving, I heard her coming in the house."

"Then the Klein kids couldn't have had anything to . . ."

"No, nothing at all."

"I'm sorry, sir. We have to . . ."

"I understand."

"After your daughter got home, did you hear her go out again?"

"No."

"Did you see her or talk to her?"

"She put on the radio in the living room . . ."

"This was at two in the morning?"

"Yes. A rock-and-roll station. I called down for her to cut it down a bit. She said, 'Okay, Dad,' and lowered the volume and . . . and . . . we . . . we didn't say anything else after that."

"Didn't hear her leave the house or anything?"

"No."

"Did you know she was gone? I mean, this morning when you got up, did you . . . ?"

"Not until the police came here. The Rutledge police. To . . . to ask if I'd come down to the . . . the old logging road near the reservoir . . . and . . . and . . . identify the body."

"I'm sorry about all this, sir."

"Yes."

"Real sorry."

"Thank you."

"We'll leave you now, sir. I'm sorry."

"Thank you."

"I'm sorry, sir."

"Thank you."

"I'm sorry."

The state troopers filed out of the room. Lester Blair closed the front door behind them, and then asked Jamie if he wanted a drink or anything. As discoverer of the body, he had obviously taken a proprietary interest. Jamie looked at his watch. It was still only ten-thirty in the morning; the call from Larry seemed to have come hours ago. He declined the drink, and Lester went out to the kitchen.

"I'm sorry I had to interrupt your weekend this way," Larry said.

"Don't be ridiculous," Jamie said, and found himself putting his arm awkwardly around Larry's shoulders.

"You were the only one I could think of," Larry said. "Because of the way Scarlett felt about you. How close you were."

Jamie looked at him, not understanding.

"Your joking with her all the time, she got such a boot out of that, Jamie. Your asking her if she was just home from Atlanta, she always repeated that to me. And if we were having a party or anything, she always asked me was Mr. Croft coming. Made me envious sometimes, the way she admired you. Do you remember the story you had in one of those magazines last year, I forget which magazine it was, Jamie, you'll have to forgive me, but it was about these runaway kids in the Village, do you remember it?"

"Yes, I remember it," Jamie said.

"Read that story cover to cover, pointed out each and every picture to me. She was art editor of the school's magazine you know, and later president of the Photography Club, which was when she became so deeply interested in your work. But it was as a man and a father she admired you most, and that was because Lissie was such a fine person and Scarlett loved her to death. Wanted to be just like Lissie in everything she did. Tried to dress like Lissie, combed her hair like Lissie's, would've changed places with Lissie in a minute if a way could've been devised. I guess that's why I called you first, Jamie. I guess I figured that as a father you . . . you might understand what I was feeling, what I'm feeling now for . . . for my little girl."

"Yes, Larry, I do."

"These times . . . I don't know about these times. The kids . . . I think she was taking some kind of pills, Jamie, I'm pretty sure she was, she seemed so . . . I don't know . . . *out* of it all the time. I kept wishing she'd go back to school again . . . she was at Risdee, you know, up in Providence for a while, studying photography there, she was always interested in photography, I guess I told you that, you've got to forgive me, I'm sort of, this happening today, all of it so . . . so sudden, you know. The cops appearing on my doorstep, Jimmy who works in the post office during the week, all dressed up like a proper cop on Sunday and ringing the doorbell to tell me there's somebody in the woods over near the reservoir, little bag on her belt has my daughter's driver's license in it, would I come have a look to identify her? *Identify* her? I said. Because, Jamie, you don't *have* to identify somebody unless she's *dead;* if she's alive she can identify herself, am I right? So if some girl was there in the woods with my daughter's driver's license in her bag, and they're asking me to *identify* her, then this has *got* to be her and she's got to be dead. Melanie was still asleep, I didn't wake her up. As I was leaving the house, she called to me, asked me what it was. I told her it was nothing, I'd be back in a minute, go back to sleep, honey, I'll pick up the *Times* in town.

"She was lying on her side in the leaves, Jamie. The leaves were all covered with blood. That was the first thing I saw, the blood. And the first thing I thought was somebody *did* this to her, somebody *killed* my daughter, all that blood shining on the leaves, the sunlight coming in over the reservoir and setting all those leaves on fire with her blood. And then I saw the shotgun on the ground beside her, and I recognized the gun, it's the gun I keep in the garage, right outside there, right on the wall in the garage, keep the cartridges in a box on a shelf beside it, that was my shotgun, the initials L.H.K. on it—Lawrence Harold Kreuger—burned into the stock, my gun, and my daughter lying dead beside it with chunks of her skull and her hair and her . . . oh, Jesus, Jamie, oh, God, oh, Jesus, oh, God . . ."

Jamie held him close, his arm tight around his shoulders. He did not truly know this man, he still could not believe this man had come to him for comfort, nor could he understand why he was offering it so freely. Had that tired routine with Scarlett really registered over the years, "Oh, lookee heah, it's Missy Scah-lutt home fum Atlanta!" and the blank, unblinking stare on Scarlett's face each and every time, her green eyes wide, and on that freckled face the certain knowledge that poor Lissie Croft's father was certifiably nuts. And yet . . . she'd admired him. As a man and as a father. Admired him most as a man and a father. Those had been Larry's words. Jamie felt tears beginning to brim in his eyes, and he blinked them back guiltily; he was not on the edge of crying for Larry's daughter who'd blown off the back of her head with a shotgun, but instead for his own silent daughter in India, who seemed not to admire him at all as a man and as a father.

"I told them yes," Larry said, "that's my daughter, that's my Scarlett. But, you know, Jamie, I'm not so sure that *was* Scarlett lying there in the forest. Oh, yes, that was Scarlett's pink party dress that girl was wearing, and her face was Scarlett's sure enough, the face hadn't been harmed, you see, she'd put the gun in her mouth and what it did was take off the back of her head, but the face was still Scarlett's, the green eyes open and looking up at the sun, wide open, way she used to stare at me when she was a little girl asking me all sorts of questions. People said she wasn't too bright, Jamie, I heard people saying that about her, but she was the most inquisitive little girl I ever knew. There . . . there were . . . she was lying there with her eyes open and her mouth open and there . . . there were flies buzzing in the . . . in the bl—"

And he began weeping.

He was a southern male, born and bred in the sovereign state of Georgia, and was not expected to break down in a time of crisis, but he turned his face into Jamie's shoulder, and wept unashamedly, clinging to him like a son in his father's arms. Jamie kept patting him, muttering sounds of reassurance, nonverbal, simply little *umms* and *ahhs* and *uhhs,* his hand constantly patting while Larry wept out his despair against his shoulder.

Melanie Kreuger came out of the kitchen not five minutes later, looking clear-eyed and crisp in a pale blue robe that fell to her ankles. She saw her husband cradled in Jamie's arms, and then came immediately to where they were both sitting on the sofa, and extended her hand to Jamie and said, "Jamie, how *good* of you. Have you had coffee? Would you like coffee? Les-tuh, bring Jamie a cup of coffee."

"Melanie," he said, "I'm so sorry for you."

"Yes, darlin'," she said, "but be sorry for my daughter. Jamie, dear, whut are we to do?"

He didn't understand her at first. He blinked at her in much the same way Scarlett had blinked each time he recited his "home fum Atlanta" line.

"We'ah both Methodists, Larry and mahself, but Scah-lutt was

252

never one to go to church, and I know it would offend her, Jamie, if we had any soht of r'ligious service for her. So whut are we to do?"

"Well, the church here in town . . ."

"Is nondenominational, I know. But Jamie, the *emp*hasis is on Jesus, and I *know* Scah-lutt would not want anythin' like that, I *know* it for a fact. Jamie, this has nothin to do with Larry and me, this has only to do with Scah-lutt. It would pain me to have a service that isn't the soht I grew up with, but I know it would pain Scah-lutt more to have anythin r'ligious. You probably knew her better than anyone on earth, includin' her own parents, so I'm sure you know that's true."

There it was again. The indication that Scarlett and Jamie had shared a deep understanding of each other, that she had looked upon him as something of a surrogate father, information that was startling and unbelievable to him. Of all Lissie's friends, he had perhaps been least close to Scarlett. Had it been Rusty Klein who'd blown her brains out in those deserted woods, he might have understood a supposition of friendship. He had enjoyed many long and mature conversations with Rusty, and had in fact written a letter of recommendation for her when she'd applied to Bennington. But Scarlett? He scarcely knew her.

"Do you think you could talk to the minister?" Melanie asked.

"Yes, surely, I'd be happy to. About . . . what did you want me to talk to him a . . ."

"A memorial service. But not at the church, Jamie. I thought someone might contact the town supervisor to see if we couldn't use the Town Hall . . ."

"I'll take care of that. When did you want . . . ?"

"Tomorrow."

"All right, I'll talk to Andy."

"And the minister, too. I'd want him to say a few words, Jamie, but I don't think Scah-lutt would appreciate a lot of Bible-thumping. If you could just explore that with him . . ."

"I will."

"And, Jamie, I'd want *you* to say something, too. Because she loved you so much, my dear," Melanie said, and put her hand over his.

"I'll go see Andy, and then I'll run over to the church."

"Thank you," Melanie said, patting his hand. "Jamie, why do you think she did this?"

"I don't know."

253

"Did your daughter ever mention anythin' about her usin' drugs?"

"Scarlett?"

"Yes. Did Lissuh ever say she was usin' drugs?"

"No, never."

"Theah's so much I didn't know about her," Melanie said, and shook her head. "I have the feelin' sometimes, Jamie, that we raised a generation of strangers. But I guess there's no lookin' back on what we did or didn't do, is there? It's just . . . your daughter kills herself on a lonely road in the woods, you've got to wunduh . . ." She shook her head again. "I guess I'll always try to imagine that last moment when she made her final decision, Jamie, when she put the barrel of that gun in her mouth and decided none of it was wuth a damn anymore. An' pulled the trigger. I'll always wonduh whut went through her mind in that very last second. But I guess theah's no lookin' back, is there? I guess things just happen, an' we deal with 'em, an' . . . an' try t'manage. That's it, isn't it, Jamie? We look ahead an' . . . an' try to rescue the future."

"Yes," Jamie said. "I guess so."

"But it'll seem so *forlorn* without her," Melanie said, and shook her head again, but did not weep.

The minister's name was Llewelyn Harris, and he had been leading the congregation of the town's nondenominational church for the last six years. His wife, Bridget, had caused a minor scandal only last year by accepting the role of Blanche Dubois in the Rutledge Players' production of *A Streetcar Named Desire*, appearing on stage in a half-slip and bra that revealed (among other things) her unshaven armpits. It had been the opinion of the congregation that she'd brought rather too much ardor to the scene in which she was raped by the brute Stanley, and Harris had been living since in constant terror of being transferred to some grubby little mining town in Pennsylvania. When Jamie came to him that Sunday afternoon, he had already heard about the suicide on the old logging road and frankly wanted no part of it. But he said nothing as yet, and simply listened as Jamie told him he was there to arrange a memorial service for young Scarlett Kreuger.

Harris cleared his throat. "But this was," he said, and cleared his throat again, "a *suicide,* am I correct?"

"Yes," Jamie said.

"Mm," Harris said. "That may be difficult."

"What may be difficult?" Jamie asked.

"The various aspects," Harris said.

"What aspects?" Jamie insisted.

"Well . . . primarily, the suicide."

"I'm afraid that's one aspect we can't ignore."

"Precisely what I'm saying. The church, as you know, does not condone the taking of one's own . . ."

"No one's asking for condonement."

"You're asking for God's blessing, are you not? You're asking me to conduct a memorial service for the dead . . ."

"No, I'm not asking for God's blessing," Jamie said. "The girl wouldn't have wanted God's blessing, she wasn't a religious person. Her parents are both devout, but . . ."

"Yes, but the victim was not. Moreover . . ."

"You've hit on the exact word," Jamie said.

"Pardon?"

"Victim."

"Of herself, yes."

"No. Of something quite outside herself. Reverend Harris, I came here to ask only *one* thing, but now it seems I have to deal with *two."*

"Shall we take them in order then?" Harris asked, and smiled thinly.

"First . . . a service that doesn't overly stress doctrine."

"By doctrine . . ."

"Church doctrine."

"Do you mean a service that doesn't stress our belief in the Lord Jesus Christ?"

"The dead girl didn't believe in the Lord Jesus Christ."

"Then perhaps you've come to the wrong church. Perhaps you should find a religious group that . . ."

"The Kreugers are part of your congregation," Jamie said flatly.

Harris blinked, and then cleared his throat again. "What is your second request?" he asked.

"I don't expect you to ignore the fact that young Scarlett killed herself . . ."

"I could not ignore it, no."

"Nor can anyone *else* who'll be at that service tomorrow. I think to ignore it would be to ignore the horror of what she did to herself. But I don't want you to condemn it, either, Reverend Harris."

"I cannot give God's blessing to a suicide," Harris said.

"Then we're back to square one," Jamie said, rising. "I'll try the church in Talmadge. Thank you for your time, Rever—"

"Mr. Croft, you're placing me in an impossible position. How can I with any conscience deliver a memorial service that ignores any mention of God, and further ignores . . ."

"No one's asking you to ignore *your* beliefs, Reverend. I'm asking only that you don't pretend they were Scarlett's."

"Well . . . maybe *that* can be managed. But how can I give blessing in a house of worship to an act specifically . . ."

"You won't *be* in a house of worship."

"Pardon?"

"The family doesn't want it in a church."

"Then what . . . I'm afraid I don't . . . why are you here if . . . ?"

"I've already talked to Andy Wilkins, and he's letting us use the Town Hall tomorrow, after the funeral. The parents are religious people, Reverend Harris. Your presence would be a comfort to them. I don't think *anyone* would be truly served—not the Kreugers, not Scarlett, not anyone—if we pretend she didn't kill herself. We'll all be sitting there tomorrow with the knowledge of how she died, the terrible knowledge that she couldn't find another way out. *Don't* ignore it, Reverend Harris. *Don't* condone it or bless it, but for God's sake don't *add* to her parents' misery by condemning it as a violation of God's law."

The rectory fell silent. Outside in the church parking lot, Jamie could hear the minister's two young daughters jumping rope in the bright October sunshine, chanting "Double-ee-Dutch, double-ee-Dutch." A trapped fly buzzed against the leaded windowpane. Harris shook his head.

"I would have to say it was wrong," he said.

"That would be condemning it."

"Mr. Croft, please, can't you see . . . ?"

"Reverend Harris, Scarlett Kreuger was out there alone in those woods with the barrel of a shotgun in her mouth. Something was *wrong*, yes, but it wasn't her putting that gun in her mouth and pulling the trigger. It was whatever caused her to go out there in the first place, whatever caused her to even *consider* such a thing. *That's* what was wrong. *That's* what was so horribly, shockingly *wrong*."

Harris was silent for what seemed a very long time. Outside, one of his daughters laughed. The fly kept buzzing in the sunlight, trapped. Harris nodded. He sighed. "Yes," he said, "of course."

"Thank you," Jamie said, and let out his breath.

"The waste," Harris said, "the utter wastefulness of it," and nodded again.

The custodian had rearranged the folding wooden chairs in the Town Hall so that they formed a semicircle around a long wooden table upon which were arranged three baskets of white lilies. The funeral was over at nine-thirty that Monday morning, and it was close to eleven when the hall began filling for the scheduled memorial service at eleven-thirty. The adults took seats on the wooden chairs; the young people wandered toward the back of the hall, and ranged themselves against the wall there. There were a great many young people. Jamie had expected there would be, but their presence unsettled him nonetheless and caused him to wonder whether what he planned to say would appeal to them. He had not written out a formal speech, had thought he would just say what was in his heart, basing an impromptu eulogy on what Melanie, dry-eyed, had said in the invaded sanctity of her home yesterday morning, and what he himself, outraged, had said in the fly-buzzing stillness of the rectory yesterday afternoon.

A tall, blond, bearded boy stood leaning against the wall at the rear of the room, his arms folded across his chest, his pale blue eyes watching Jamie as he sat behind the long table. He seemed to be taking Jamie's measure, silently anticipating what would be said about Scarlett. The boy looked familiar. Was he Scarlett's boyfriend? Someone Jamie had seen her with in town? But Larry Kreuger had said she didn't have a boyfriend. Or had he simply said Scotty Klein wasn't her boyfriend? Jamie couldn't remember. Yesterday's events seemed to have occurred in an airless, soundless vacuum that now defied true recall. The bearded, blue-eyed boy was still watching him. Their eyes met for an instant, held until Jamie turned his gaze away. More people were coming through the open oaken doors. Outside on Route 16, Jamie could see one of the town cops waving his arms at drivers wanting to park their cars. There would not be enough chairs for everyone. He wished suddenly that he had not agreed to speak today. He hadn't *known* the girl, damn it!

But that was the point.

He waited while the hall filled. Connie, who with some of the other women had made coffee and sandwiches for after the service, came up front to sit beside red-eyed Larry Kreuger and his wife.

The minister went to them, whispered some comforting words as he held Melanie's hand briefly between both his own, and then came around the long table to take the chair beside Jamie's. A hush fell over the room. The minister nodded to Jamie. Jamie got to his feet and looked out over the room. From the back of the hall, the boy with the beard and the pale blue eyes looked back at him.

"I didn't know Scarlett too well," he began. *The truth,* he thought. *Start with the truth, and stay with it.* "I wish I had. Her parents think I knew her well, shared with her a philosophy, or a view, or at least a common understanding of life that somehow transcended the difference in our ages. I wish *that* were true, too, but it simply isn't. Scarlett was one of my daughter's friends, but not a very close one at that, just a casual acquaintance really, someone who dropped by the house every now and then, another face in this town where there were, and are, so many teenage faces. I see some of them at the back of the room today, lining the wall, adults now, or almost adults, the way Scarlett was an adult or almost one. But not a person I knew, not really.

"I came late to this town. We didn't move here, my family and I, until December of 1967. That was less than three years ago, a very short time in the history of a town that can recall Hessian soldiers in the streets. So I was denied the privilege so many of you others enjoyed. I didn't know Scarlett in kindergarten, I didn't know any of these kids when they were still very young, I didn't see them performing in elementary school pageants, I didn't watch them at Little League practice, I didn't have to call parents in the middle of the night to say little Sally, who I see standing there at the back of the room, tall and beautiful, little Sally, or Annie, or Nancy, or indeed *Scarlett* if I'd known her then, had decided she didn't *really* want to sleep over and was crying to be taken home. I missed all that, I came to these kids late. My own daughter was almost sixteen when we moved here. I caught all these kids who were her friends just as they were moving into their teens, just as they were on the verge of—forgive me, I must say this—leaving. Leaving us. Before they got here."

He paused.

He looked out over the faces.

Connie sitting beside the Kreugers in the first row; behind them Reynolds and Betty McGruder whose boy had been killed in Vietnam; just behind them Frank and M. J. Lipscombe whose daughter had joined a commune out in Arizona only last week; and there was George Yancy, the postmaster, a widower whose only son Ralph had been in an automobile accident this past June, three months after he'd got home from Vietnam. And all the other townspeople, watching him, waiting for what he had to say next, the vast expanse of faces stretching toward the back wall where the young people stood, and there—the pale-eyed, bearded boy, his arms still folded across his chest, his eyes demanding to know why Scarlett Kreuger had killed herself in the woods early yesterday morning.

"We all know Scarlett shot herself," Jamie said, and saw Junie Landers in the third row open her mouth in surprise, and looked directly into her face and said, "Yes, that's the truth, we can't deny it." He looked to where the Kreugers were sitting, Larry's hand between Melanie's hands, and he said, "Nor do I think Larry and Melanie would *want* us to deny it. It's a shocking horror they're going to have to live with for a long, long time, and we can only *help* them live with it by recognizing it ourselves, and not pretending it didn't happen. Because if we say to ourselves that this was just something with *Scarlett,* you know, a problem unique to *Scarlett,* something *she* couldn't work out and had to deal with in the only way that seemed possible to her—by going out onto a deserted logging road in the middle of a lonely wood, alone with herself, alone with whatever final thoughts consumed her, and shooting herself, killing herself—well, if we can think this was Scarlett's problem alone, and allow ourselves to believe that Scarlett was only an accidental casualty and not a victim of something that has been happening for a very long time now, why then we will have done her the final disservice, we will have committed the final obscenity."

The pale-eyed, bearded boy was watching him. His arms were still folded across his chest. He leaned against the back wall, his head slightly tilted, light streaming through the long windows to burnish the beard and mustache. Long hair and skeptical eyes. Faint look of derision. A look he had seen often enough on the face of—well, his own daughter. Well, all right, I'm saying all the wrong things, he thought, they shouldn't have asked me to make this speech, anyway, I'm not a public speaker, I don't now how to *do* such things. The Kreugers shouldn't have asked me to talk about Scarlett as though she were my . . . own daughter. He looked again at the pale, blue-eyed bearded boy at the back of the room. My own daughter, he thought. Arms folded, cold dead eyes, watching, challenging.

"There was a little thing I used to do whenever Scarlett came to the house," Jamie said. "Not recently. My daughter and Scarlett

259

haven't seen too much of each other in recent months. I mean when Scarlett was younger, sixteen, seventeen. Whenever she came to the house, I used to say 'Oh, lookee heah, it's Missy Scah-lutt home fum Atlanta!' and she'd look at me and blink—I don't know what she was thinking, her parents tell me now she used to get a kick out of it, but maybe she was thinking, Well, here's this baffling little joke again from Lissie's dumb father, I just don't know. But the point, the thing I'm trying to say is, is . . . that was *it,* that was the extent of our communication. 'Hello, Mr. Croft' and 'Oh, lookee heah, it's Missy Scah-lutt home fum Atlanta!' That was *it,* do you see? That was *all* of it. And I wish now just once I'd have said, 'Hey, Scarlett, what's new in your life, what's important to you, what would you like to talk about?' Just once. And I wish that just once Scarlett would have asked me why I had a worried look on my face, or why I, why I . . . you see, I think we could have *talked.* I think we could have prevented what happened. It's too late now, I guess."

The bearded boy against the wall was still watching him, his blue eyes unwavering, his arms still folded across his chest. It seemed to Jamie that he wanted something more from him.

"But maybe it isn't too late for the rest of us," Jamie said, and then nodded, and gave a small, embarrassed shrug, and turned to the minister where he was sitting with his prepared notes in his lap.

There was silence in the room.

Jamie sat down and the minister took his place behind the long table with the lilies on it. Jamie scarcely listened to what he was saying, but he knew the man was keeping his promise, toning down the Jesus stuff and expressing no official church condemnation of suicide. Jamie was thinking he'd made a complete fool of himself. He hadn't even *known* the girl, they shouldn't have asked him to say anything. In retrospect, Melanie had said it better anyway, had said in a single sentence everything he'd hoped to say today: *We look ahead and try to rescue the future.*

The bearded boy with the blue eyes was still standing at the back of the room when the Crofts left. He said nothing to Jamie as they passed him on their way out. In the car, when Jamie asked Connie whether it had been all right, she said, "Yes, fine, darling," but he knew she was thinking he should have prepared a talk, the way the minister had.

13

He could never understand why he thought of New York City in medieval terms, as if it were cobblestoned and turreted when it was neither—well, yes, a vestigial cobble here and there. But Jamie saw it always as one of those magnificent old towns perched high above the Rhine or the Loire, commanding the surrounding countryside, a fortification to which the peasants could scurry whenever barbarian hordes threatened. The metaphor became strongest during the winter months, when grim gray armies attacked, crouching beyond the river-moats, laying icy siege.

In November, the faces became pinched and withdrawn. Men walked briskly, their unaccustomed overcoats bulky and cumbersome, one gloved hand clutching a dispatch case, the other thrust deep in a pocket. The Hare Krishna kids in their saffron robes and topknots walked Fifth Avenue indifferent to the wind, shaking their tambourines and chanting. Loonies of every persuasion bundled themselves in sweaters or shabby overcoats, carrying signs that promised doom or redemption. The bag ladies searched assiduously through the experimental concrete garbage bins on every corner, hampered by the intransparency of the new containers, wishing perhaps for the old wire-mesh types that had been too easy to steal in a city where stealing was almost an honest profession diligently pursued. The ladies were cold and unsmiling. They wore woolen gloves cut off at each of the fingers and thumbs.

Despite the cold, the three-card-monte sharks were busy at work, cruising the avenue with their folding stands, setting up shop on the windswept sidewalk, the shill watching the actor as he manipulated the cards on the table top, "Follow the red ace, man, just tell me wheah the red ace is, watch it now," or swiftly moving the three whiskey bottle caps, "Where's the pea, thass all you got to tell me, man. Pea's under one of these heah caps, you see it now?"

The street musicians were out, too, discreetly plying their trade, their hand-lettered cardboard signs beseeching STRUGGLING THROUGH JUILLIARD or HELP ME MAKE BEAUTIFUL MUSIC, while behind the signs sat the supposedly embryo violinists or accordionists or—on the corner of Fifth and Fifty-sixth, outside the Hallmark store—a young blond girl playing a flute.

His heart stopped.

Her face came into his mind.

Everywhere around him, while the girl sitting cross-legged on the sidewalk played her flute and the silvery notes splintered on the brittle air, the beautiful women of this city rushed past, gorgeous New York faces unlike any others in the world, gloved hands clutching the collars of cloth coats, mufflers trailing, long hair blowing in the wind, fast, moving fast, high heels clicking on the sidewalk, chin and nose and breasts and flashing instep cleaving the crystalline air, lovely—but none of them Joanna.

There was a telephone booth on the corner.

He realized with a start that he had forgotten her number.

The opera company had begun its fall season, he had seen their full-page ad in the *New York Times* several months back. But would she be rehearsing today? From past experience, he knew that her rehearsal schedule was erratic. She probably wouldn't even remember him.

He looked up her number and dialed it.

He let it ring four times and was about to hang up when he heard her voice.

"Hello?"

She sounded as if she'd been sleeping. *Jesus,* he thought, *I've woken her up.*

"Joanna?" he said.

262

"Yes."

"Jamie," he said.

"Yes, Jamie, how are you?" she said.

"Jamie Croft," he said, as though certain she had mistaken him for someone else.

"Yes, I know."

"I didn't wake you, did I?"

"Wake me? It's almost twelve o'clock."

"I know, but I thought . . . you sounded . . ."

"No, I was practicing. What is it, Jamie?"

"I . . . uh . . . was wondering how you're doing."

"Ah. Were you?"

"Yes."

"I'm doing fine. How are you doing?"

"Fine."

"Good."

Silence. There hadn't been anger in her voice, not quite, just an edge of . . . wariness? Distance? Indifference? The silence lengthened.

"What is it you want, Jamie?" she said.

"I thought . . . I thought I might like to see you."

"Ah."

"If you were free."

"Ah."

"I'm right here on . . ."

"Just like that, huh?" she said.

"I know it's been a long . . ."

"Six months on the first of November."

"Yes, I . . ."

"But who's counting?"

Another silence.

"Joanna," he said, "I'm . . ."

"After six months, you call out of the blue and tell me you want to come over. What do you expect me to . . . ?"

"I said I'd like to *see* you. I didn't say anything about . . ."

"What you said, in fact, was you *might* like to see me. Didn't you hear the word *might* in there, Jamie? I'm sure I heard the word *might* in there."

"I guess I said might."

"I *know* you said might."

"I guess I was afraid you'd . . ."

"What? Hang up?"

"Well . . . yes."

"Gee, why would I hang up?" Joanna said. "Man drops a person off on her doorstep six months ago, says he'll call her, and is never heard from since, why should a person hang up? A person should instead go dancing in the streets with delirium, *nu?* You've got *some* fucking chutzpa, mister. You know what means chutzpa? You've got it. In spades."

"I guess so."

"Take it as a fact."

"Okay."

"He admits it."

"I admit it."

There was another silence. He thought surely she would hang up this time. He felt he should say something before she hung up, but he could not find any words. It was she who broke the silence.

"Are you very old now?" she asked.

"What?"

"Have you gotten very old?"

"No. Old? What do you . . . ?"

"Is your hair all white? I keep thinking your hair is all white now. I don't know why. I keep thinking it all the time."

"It's still brown, Joanna."

"You hurt me badly," she said. "Do you realize that?"

"I'm sorry."

Silence.

"I'm truly sorry."

Silence.

"May I come there?" he said.

Silence.

"Joanna?"

"Come," she said, and hung up.

"Sit down," she said.

His heart was pounding. He took a chair near the fireplace. A log was smoldering on the hearth. The room smelled faintly of smoke, more faintly of Joanna's perfume.

"I want to say something to you," she said. "Would you like a drink or anything?"

"No, nothing, thank you."

"Are you sure?"

"Yes."

"Jamie," she said, "I love you. I've loved you from the moment I met you, I've loved you since then." She took a deep breath and then said, "You hurt me very badly."

"I know that. I'm sorry."

"I don't want you ever to hurt me again, Jamie. I love you very much, but if you plan to walk out of here again in another month or so . . ."

"No, I—"

". . . then please do it now, walk out now and spare me the pain later."

She was wearing much the same clothing she had worn the first time he came to this apartment, a man's tailored shirt with the tails hanging loose over a pair of blue jeans. Her hair was caught in a pony tail at the back of her head. There was lipstick on her mouth, but she wore no other makeup. Her eyes looked somewhat faded. She was barefooted. On the grate, the log continued to smoke.

"I've been seeing Mandelbaum again," she said.

"Yes?"

"I told him all about what happened. He said he thinks I'm a daughter substitute. He said you go to bed with me because you really want to go to bed with your daughter, and I'm the one who takes the curse off it." She paused. She studied his face. "He said you would have hung onto me if your daughter *really* had been coming home because then you'd be safe, you see, you'd have me and you wouldn't have to worry about jumping in bed with your daughter one night . . . Jamie, please don't make that face, this is Mandelbaum talking, not me. He said that the minute you knew your daughter *wasn't* coming home, you threw me out because you didn't need me anymore, you didn't need an insurance policy against incest. Those were his words. An insurance policy against incest. That's supposed to be me, Jamie. The insurance policy."

"Joanna, with all due respect for Mandelbaum . . ."

"Well, I think maybe he's right this time, Jamie. For once in his entire life, maybe he's right."

"I never thought of you as—"

"The point, Jamie, is I don't want to be an insurance policy. I don't *want* our relationship to depend on whether your daughter's *here* or *there* or wher*ever* the fuck she is. I'm really not all that interested in your daughter, Jamie. I don't even *know* your daughter, Jamie, and I'm not sure I ever *do* want to know her. All I—"

"Joanna . . ."

"No, don't 'Joanna' me, okay? Just listen to me. This is what I'm saying. I'm saying I love you, and I want you very much, I'm aching for you just sitting here opposite you and remembering what it was like. But, Jamie, if you called me today because your daughter's back home again and your insurance has lapsed . . ."

"My daughter isn't home, Joanna. My calling you today had nothing to do with my daughter."

"Then, Jamie, why did you call?"

"I guess because I missed you," he said. "I guess because I love you."

"Ah. Guess. Don't guess, Jamie. Love me or don't love me, but please don't guess."

"I love you," he said.

"And when your daughter comes home? What happens then? Do you still love me?"

"I don't think she's coming home," he said. "I think she's dead, Joanna. Joanna, I think she's dead," he said, and began weeping. She went to him. She cradled his head against her breast. She sighed heavily.

She took his hand then, and led him up the remembered steps to the third floor of the house, and then down the corridor to the small library with the Persian rugs and the Franklin stove and the red leather chairs and the music stand and the open flute case, silver against green velvet, and through the library into her bedroom, where she undressed again without artifice or guile, revealing herself to him as once she had. Holding her, he felt a gladness he thought he would never know again, a sheer soaring joy that had nothing whatever to do with the sexual act they were about to perform, nothing to do with her flesh warm against his, her lips soft against his, but only with the happiness of being with her again, and knowing that she loved him, and knowing that this time he would never let go of her again. He said to her later, clear-eyed this time, holding her in his arms, "I really do think she's dead, Joanna. I don't think I'll ever see her again."

But then, early in December, he opened the mailbox one day and found in it an undated letter from India. It began:

Dear Mom and Dad,

Many, many incredible things have happened since the last time I wrote . . .

In Delhi, what she thought at first was just a case of *la turista* turned out to be dysentery (she spelled it "dysenterry" in her letter) requiring medication and hospitalization for the better part of a week. She had arrived in that city on August 18, after a 750-mile journey from Kabul.

She mentioned nothing about Paul in her letter home. She went into detail she might have spared about the dysentery and her subsequent stay in the hospital, and she wrote a nice little haiku about having seen the Taj Mahal by moonlight the day after she was discharged (that would have been August 25), the little poem set apart from the rest of the letter and adorned with a tiny sketch Lissie made of that imposing structure.

> *Mumtaz Mahal died*
> *To inspire Shahjahan*
> *To glorious heights.*

They were relieved to learn that she'd rid herself of the dysentery that had assailed her and was feeling well enough to visit the memorial on the day after she'd got out of the hospital. She seemed happy enough at this point (they had only come partly through the first page of her two-page letter, standing side by side near the mailbox where it had magically appeared, Jamie holding the letter in both trembling hands, both of them reading it in the waning December light) and they were delighted to learn that she was in a part of India called Goa, which seemed to be warm and sunny now that the monsoon season had ended, the temperatures hovering in the high eighties, with lovely palm-lined rivers leading to the Arabian Sea and the magnificent beaches on its eighty-two miles of coastline. *I have $10 left, and am living on a beach. It's fairly cheap here and very warm, but I want to go to the U.S.A. very soon.* Those words were the last ones at the bottom of the page. Jamie turned the letter over:

I have an idea I would like you to consider. I want you to make an investment in me so I can make some money and in the end pay you back. With $200 I can mail enough things in $10 parcels (Indian shirts, jade, ivory, beads, silk, etc.) legally and sell it in the States for much much more. Enough so that I could pay you back and have enough money for myself to pay for school, housing, etc. I think, after much contemplation on my survival, especially when we were walking in the Himalayas (20,000 feet high) and living in caves and whatnot, that this method of making some money on my own is a good one. It would enable me to start making my own money. I am capable and very willing to do this work.

I would need $450 to $500—$200 for the merchandise and the rest to get me to Brussels and from there back to New York on Icelandic. I can complete everything and be home for Christmas if you send money immediately to: Telex code, THISTLE, State Bank of India, Panjim, Goa. We must work fast if I am to be home with my family for Christmas which is something I want very much. Finished Tolkien's trilogy, great book. Am now reading *Siddhartha*. The world is so exciting, really. I went to Bombay, Chundigargh, Mundi, many very primitive villages. If Telex doesn't work, use INTERNATIONAL BANK DRAFT to STATE BANK OF INDIA, PANJIM, GOA. My address is Melissa Croft, % Poste Restante, Calangute, Goa, India. I will check at the bank and the post office around December 10 for your communication. Much love to everyone. If you don't send money at least telegram a few of your thoughts.

Love,

Lissie

The thoughts she had solicited were somewhat confused. Jamie and Connie were, first and foremost, grateful that she was alive, delighted at long last to have an *address* for her, a true and proper *address,* even if it was only a General Delivery address, a bona fide *address* (not to mention a Telex code) to which they could write or cable! Jesus! He could *write* to her again! He could actually write "Dear Lissie" and "Love, Dad." He had an *address!* But there were some disturbing things in her letter that caused them to wonder, once again, what was happening to her, and whether or not they could trust her. The letter-from-camp syndrome was immediately apparent, although this time she had treated them gratuitously to each of the bowel movements caused by the dysentery infection, forsaking not even the attendant mucus and blood. Okay. At least they knew she'd been sick, and was now all right again.

But what was this about "Many, many incredible things" happening, and then no elucidation of just *what* those incredible things might have been? Was one of those incredible things "walking in the Himalayas (20,000 feet high) and living in caves and whatnot"? Were more of those incredible things her visits to "many very primitive" villages like Chundigargh and Mundi, if indeed those *were* the villages she'd had in mind when writing her letter, the syntax seemed sometimes rather odd and disjointed.

Why, for example, had she told them she needed money for an adventure into the world of commerce, something new, something they had never before heard from her either in person or in her infrequent letters, and then idly reported that she'd read *Lord of the Rings* and was reading *Siddhartha,* before continuing with the details of how they could get the money to her? Why, all of a sudden, was she so intent on paying for her own "school, housing, etc."? And could she be trusted with "$450 to $500" ostensibly needed to purchase the merchandise and then to come home? Or would she use that money (as she had used the money she'd received for the Venice–New York ticket) for travel further into the unknown? Would her *next* letter come from Outer Mongolia? Siberia? The moon?

They had no way of knowing that Lissie had been stoned out of her mind on the day she wrote her letter from Calangute.

It's like Woodstock all over again, Lissie thought. No, it's *better* than Woodstock. Woodstock was vague at first, indecisive, kids not realizing there'd be no busts, sneaking their joints, cupping their hands around roaches, eyes cocked for troopers. No troopers here. Everything cool here. Even *opium* is legal here. It's Woodstock in Europe, Portuguese influence, churches, Catholics, it's Europe in Asia, Woodstock in Europe. What were their names? she wondered. The twins who took us to Elysium, Robby's friends, the *Dutch* girls, come on, what were their *names?* Elisabeth and Ida, yes, Verschoor, yes, Robby's friends, where was Robby now, and whatever has happened to Barbara Duggan, so long ago my goodness.

Voices drifted everywhere around her, shards of sunlight splintered on the water, naked bodies, laughter, she drifted, she splintered like sunlight, she giggled and heard her own giggle. Woodstock playing in Amsterdam. Ida said it, yes, the prettier of the two girls, Ida, but Woodstock my ass some Woodstock, what a place *that* was, girl sitting in her own shit, some Woodstock all right,

Jesus! Never in my life poke a needle in my body, never, voices drifting someone splashing out of the water cock dangling swaying cute like a pendulum running up the beach to where the palm trees fringed Paul lying beside her. Woodstock playing in Asia, more like the tropics though, islands Mom and Dad used to take me to when I was small, silver sunshine hot summer sun whitewashed buildings, ocean sparkling hot summer sun higher than a fucking kite listen to Paul listen to the dope, she giggled.

". . . split for Katmandu the minute I get the money," always talking about what he was going to do when the bread got here, Daddy's hard-earned loot. Daddy, you are on the wrong train, she thought, here is where you *should* be, Daddy, taking pictures of marvelous hippie bodies naked unashamed in the sun Portuguese Catholics frowning under parasols trouble in Paradise too much skin for the locals brown like the natives brown all over tiny tits all brown Paul's cock brown everything brown in the sun like the good brown hash we smoke smoke smoke, she giggled again.

". . . then bring the hash back over the border, shouldn't be any trouble doing that, do you think?" talking to a boy with a heavy black beard and a minuscule cock. She checked out the cock, heard more laughter up the beach, glanced away into the splintering silvery sun, girl with melon breasts approaching, Lissie shaded her eyes, suck his sweet cock here on the beach, raise some Portuguese eyebrows, always makes me horny this fucking hash too fucking good this fucking hash makes me want to *do* things suck his crazy tiny cock the stranger's black beard, "and then to Turkey for the hard shit."

The hard shit Paul was talking about had to be heroin or opium or morphine or something you shot in your arm, never poke a needle in my body, she thought. The hard shit had to be something Paul was going to buy in Turkey when he came back from Nepal with the hash he would sell, "profit on the hash has got to be something like five, six hundred bucks, don't you think?" he was saying, his voice drifting like the clouds overhead blue-bellied the sun blinking out for a moment. "Take that plus the original five to Turkey and spend it on the hard shit. I can get it raw for twenty-five a kee, that means I can buy me forty kees. Then all I'll need is a connection to get the shit to Marseilles," talk talk talk, shit shit shit, the cloud drifted like the talk, the sun blinked on again, *pop!* She giggled. She was so happy she was so high she was so fucking loose and free and high and happy she would *never* go home. All she wanted was the five hundred from Daddy, all she wanted to do was spend the rest of her life here on the profit Paul would make on the hash he bought in Katmandu—but he'd just said, hadn't he just said he wanted to go to Turkey for the hard shit tough shit it's *my* money, she thought, it's *my* daddy's money he's sending here to his darling little girl so high so happy so fuck you.

"What's this about Turkey?" she asked.

"Yeah, for the hard shit," Paul said.

"What do you mean? You mean heroin?"

"No, no. Opium. Raw opium."

"That's heroin."

"Well, it's opium, is what it is. I mean, opium's opium, and heroin's heroin. You can't call oranges apples and . . ."

"Let me get this straight," she said. "Are you telling me you're going to push *heroin?*"

"No, I'm going to buy the raw stuff and sell it at a profit, that's all."

"That's pushing heroin," she said. All she could think of was the girl at Elysium sitting in her own shit. Paul was saying he wanted to buy and sell heroin, that's what he was telling her, he wanted to buy and sell hard drugs to kids who sat on the floor in their own shit. No way, she thought. "No way," she said aloud, shaking her head. "Not with my money."

"Why the fuck not?" he said.

She blinked at him. Up the beach, someone began strumming a guitar and the words to "Blowin' in the Wind" drifted languidly on the air, the voice almost a whisper. The naked boy with the black beard and the tiny cock rolled over onto his side and propped his cheek on his hand, elbow bent, a faint smile on his face, as if he was enjoying a two-character, one-set play starring a pair of extremely good actors.

"You told me," she said, *started* to say, but Paul waved this away impatiently as if what he'd once told her was of absolutely no consequence now that there was the possibility of a very large deal involving the purchase and resale of Nepalese hash and then the further purchase of some forty kees of opium which, for Christ's sake, would bring two hundred grand in Marseilles, that's exactly what he said to the bearded boy now, "two hundred grand," sounding like a New York gangster.

She stopped listening to him. She didn't really care anymore. She knew only that he was a stranger who planned to make money

271

selling raw opium to someone in Marseilles who would convert it to heroin which might or might not be sold later to young kids in America—she didn't know and she didn't care, she wanted only to be *rid* of this fucking little pusher who'd done nothing to help her in Iran or with the dogs, the fucking dogs.

"I'm going home," she said.

It was a decision made as easily as that.

Silence.

New Year's Eve.

He was sitting in the living room adorned with the matted pictures of Lissie he'd hung when he'd still expected her home for her birthday. It was three hours to midnight, three hours to 1971, and his daughter was not here, and he was beginning to believe again that she was dead. He sat in his new tuxedo, sat in his new ruffled blue shirt and his blue velvet tie and cummerbund to match the blue velvet on the tuxedo lapels and cuffs, sat in tuxedo and ruffled shirt, and the Schlumberger cuff links Connie had bought for him on his twenty-eighth birthday, too many years ago and he wondered where his daughter was, and he thought again that she was dead.

He had not felt this since receiving the undated letter she'd written from Goa, but now he was beginning to believe it again. The State Department didn't know where she was, Mr. Brothers had called to say they'd had no luck contacting her on the beach at Goa, so Jamie could only believe that somehow the $500 he'd sent hadn't reached her, or possibly she'd been slain on some Iranian road, or was being tortured in some Turkish prison, he didn't know *where* she was, or *if* she was, if she still even *existed*. She was his daughter, and she'd been gone since April, and this was now the thirty-first of December, and he didn't *know,* he simply didn't *know,* and he wanted to weep. He brought the glass of Scotch to his lips and then hesitated. He had taken to drinking it stronger these days, a *lot* of Scotch and just a few ice cubes.

The toast did not come immediately to his mind or to his lips. He looked around at the pictures of Lissie, not too many taken this year, not too many at all, the tradition somewhat strained, but plenty of others from the years before. The one of Lissie kneeling to pluck the dandelion in Central Park, and the one of her in the rowboat at Martha's Vineyard when she was almost fourteen, five years ago, Jesus. And there, near the post, the picture of her

272

tangled in her skis at Stratton, and there, his favorite, the lollipop shot, Lissie in the second year of her life, looking down in consternation at the sand-covered lollipop, blue eyes squinted, her blond hair catching the sun for a dazzling halo effect. He lifted the glass in a toast.

"Fuck it," he said.

When he heard the car outside, he thought at first it was the booze he'd ordered from Ritchie's Wine & Liquor in Talmadge. He'd discovered earlier, when he'd come downstairs to pour himself a solitary drink while Connie was still dressing, that he'd run out of Courvoisier and Grand Marnier both, and he'd been worried that someone might want to come back tonight after the party at the Blairs', and he'd seem ill-appointed—though who gave a fuck? Really, who *gave* a fuck? He glanced at his watch, and realized that he'd placed the order only fifteen minutes ago. Still, he'd asked them to deliver as soon as possible as he and his wife would be leaving the house at nine-thirty, ten. Though it seemed too early for Ritchie's to be making delivery, he thought it might just *possibly* be them after all, and he went to the drape in the living room, and pulled it back, and looked out to the curb.

It had been snowing on and off for the past week, and the snow was piled high in the front yard, creating a wall of white that protected the house from the street. Above the banked snow, he could see the yellow roof of a taxi cab, its exhaust fumes puffing on the brittle silent air. He heard the door of the cab slamming shut. A guest arriving for the big party across the street, he thought. He knew the Sammelsons were having a big party, but in Rutledge, Connecticut, neighbors never invited neighbors who lived just across the street. He let the drape fall. He walked into the kitchen and was pouring himself a fresh drink when the doorbell rang.

His heart stopped.

He knew, he knew before he took the twenty steps, thirty steps from the wet-sink in the kitchen to the entry hall, he knew, his heart was pounding, he knew this was his daughter. He fumbled with the lock, he tried to twist the old brass key in the lock that had been here when the mill was converted to a house in the year 1910, his hands were trembling on the key, he could not twist the fucking key, he knew this was his daughter standing outside the door, and he could not open the door, he could not, "Just a minute," he said, and at last twisted the key, and threw the door wide.

He did not recognize her at first.

This could not be . . . this was not his daughter.

The snow was falling behind her. She stood just outside the door with a tentative smile on her face, illuminated by the globe to the right of the door, slanting down onto cheekbones that were higher than he remembered them, deeper hollows beneath them than he remembered, her face altogether thinner than he remembered, her hair stringy and oily, plastered to her skull, an Indian band, *American* Indian, across her forehead—she looked sallow and dirty, this was not his daughter. She was barefooted. There was snow banked eighteen inches high in the front yard, but she was barefooted. The temperature outside was thirty-four degrees Fahrenheit, but her feet were naked and dirty below the hem of the tent dress patterned with lilies of the valley. She was wearing a leather fleece-lined jacket. The jacket was unzipped and open. Beneath it, he could see a black velvet vest.

"Dad?" she said.

He took her into his arms. He was too crushed by the weight of the moment to find the strength to call to his wife upstairs, too overwhelmed by the sudden tears in his eyes to call up to her where she was applying her lipstick at the bathroom mirror, too suddenly relieved and grateful and tremblingly weak to inform his wife that their daughter was home, their daughter was at long last home. He held Lissie close, he kissed her hair, he kissed her face, her nose, her cheeks, he said, "Lissie, Lissie," and only then did he find the voice to shout, exuberantly, "Connie! She's home!"

1971

At the breakfast table on New Year's Day, Lissie casually mentioned that she was infested with crabs, and that maybe they should all get something to wash with or whatever, because they'd all been doing a lot of hugging and kissing the night before. Jamie went immediately to the phone and called Harry Landau, who'd been their family physician ever since they'd moved to Rutledge. It was 1:00 P.M. but Harry was still asleep. Alice Landau asked if this was an emergency. Jamie said No, it wasn't, but he'd appreciate it if Harry could get back to him as soon as possible. Harry returned the call at two-thirty.

"Happy New Year," he said.

"Happy New Year," Jamie said. "I need some help, Harry."

"What with? A hangover?"

"I only wish. Crabs," Jamie said.

"Crabs?"

"Yeah. And head lice, too."

"Where you been sleeping, Jamie?" Harry said, and laughed.

"Well, it's—" He felt suddenly embarrassed. Crabs were associated with . . . well . . . with sexual intercourse. He felt suddenly as if his daughter had come home from India with a venereal disease. "What should we do for them, Harry?"

"Put 'em on a long leash, and take 'em for a walk," Harry said, and laughed again. "Are you serious about this?"

"I am," Jamie said.

"Crabs," Harry said, and Jamie could visualize him shaking his head. "Well, here's what you do."

What you did, Jamie discovered, was you went to the Rutledge drugstore for two bottles of lotion (one for Lissie, one for himself and Connie) only to learn that the drugstore was closed on New Year's Day, and *then* what you did was you drove to the Talmadge alternate listed on a card hanging in the window, and you listened to the Talmadge pharmacist warning you about getting any of this stuff in your eyes, "Because what it is, you see, is an in*sect*icide, you understand? I mean, this is just as strong as anything you'd go spraying on a cockroach or a spider, you understand? I mean, those are *insects* you've got crawling around on your body, and if you want to get rid of 'em you've got to use an in*sect*icide. So be careful of your eyes." Jamie itched all the way home.

The directions said that they were to apply the lotion to every patch of hair on their bodies and then wash it off the next day. In the tub the following night, vigorously scrubbing her groin, Connie said, "I haven't had such action down here in a *long* time," a comment Jamie let pass. He simply nodded and waited his turn at the tub.

The crabs, as it turned out, were the least of the joys she'd brought home from India. They did not learn until the Tuesday after her return that there was an open sore the size of a half-dollar on the instep of her right foot. Jamie rushed her over to Harry's office that same morning. Harry glanced at the festering sore, said it looked like a cut that had got infected, examined it more carefully and told them exactly how lucky they were: the wound was on the verge of becoming gangrenous; another week or so, and Lissie might have lost the foot. In the car on the way home, Jamie dared to say, "You didn't take very good care of yourself in India, did you?" Lissie shrugged and replied, "I got that cut in Brussels, on the way home." Jamie was silent the rest of the way to the house, trying to understand his own feelings.

In Harry's office, he'd initially felt only embarrassment. "You remember, Liss, don't you, Harry? She's just back from India, I thought you ought to take a look at that sore on her foot." Harry scanning her from top to bottom, the realization in his eyes that *here* was the crab-carrier: "Yes, how are you, Lissie, good to see you." Jamie's embarrassment heightened by her appearance, the threadbare jeans, the unpressed blouse she'd bought in India, the black velvet vest she'd been wearing on New Year's Eve ("Turkish," she'd told them. "Cost only four lira"), the tattered sandals she'd insisted on wearing without stockings or socks even though there was a pus-dripping sore on her right foot and the temperature outside stubbornly refused to budge higher than eighteen degrees. The embarrassment dissipated to be replaced by fear when he learned how dangerously close to amputation her foot had been, and then anger at the thought of her allowing this to *happen* to herself, didn't she *know* there was a foot attached to her body, hadn't she *realized* the sore was badly infected, hadn't she even *thought* of going to a doctor, weren't there any *doctors* in India?

"Weren't there any *doctors* in India?" he asked, as they went into the house.

"I told you I got it in Brussels," she said, and hung her fighter-pilot's jacket ("Railway Lost in London," she'd told them, "cost only eight pounds") on the rack in the entrance hall, and then went directly upstairs to her room.

Having her home was, in many respects, rather like not having her home. She spent a great deal of time in her room, listening to the rock-and-roll records she'd missed all the while she was abroad. "It's like having friends you can always come back to and understand," she told them at dinner one night. She was eating vegetables and *only* vegetables, and whereas she rarely told them much about her travels—she still had not revealed all the details, for example, of the Iranian border incident, or the attack of the wild dogs in Shahnur, or the "living in caves and whatnot" in the Himalayas or any of the other "many, many incredible things" that had happened to her in the eight months she'd been gone—she *did* tell them why she'd decided to become a vegetarian.

"It was after coming through Iran, and then Afghanistan, and Pakistan, where all we were eating day and night was this broiled mutton. Well, it suddenly occurred to me that what I was eating was *sheep!* I mean, this was 'Mary Had a Little *Lamb!'* I was eating—and besides it tasted lousy. So I figured I could do without it entirely, I mean without the kind of meat you could get over there. But I haven't had an urge for any *other* kind of meat, either, I mean I'm not desperate for a steak or a hamburger or anything like that. Besides, it makes me feel a lot cleaner inside."

To her parents, she continued to look . . . well . . . there was no other word for how they thought she looked: dirty. On the *outside,* at least. She rarely combed her hair, and even after she'd showered it seemed a tangle of knots, a mare's nest sitting on top of her narrow face, and framing it in tatters. She wore no makeup except the kohl she'd brought home from India, and this she applied in heavy black outline around each eye for a rather spooky effect. Her tent dresses were never pressed, her jeans were worn straight from the dryer, her feet were invariably bare and invariably dirty. But *inside,* she claimed to be immaculate, and often went into rapturous explanations of her sanitary routines, reminding them of the letter that had detailed all the symptoms of her dysentery.

"When I get up each morning," she said, "I go to the toilet first thing. That's something I learned from this girl I met in India after I split with Paul, Marjorie Kildare, who's buying and shipping the stuff I'll be selling here. You've got to get all the shit and piss out of your system first thing in the morning, otherwise it remains in your body poisoning you. There's no sense avoiding meat or other unclean foods, if you keep all the shit and piss inside, do you see? So what you do, you empty your bladder and move your bowels first thing in the morning, to get all the poisons out of your system. Then you shower to wash off any residue that's clinging to your anus or your vagina, and then you're clean both inside *and* out."

(So how come you get crabs? Jamie wondered.)

These conversations usually took place at dinner, the one meal at which Lissie joined them with any regularity. She invariably slept till noon, sometimes later, on occasion not rising till two or three in the afternoon. She would eat a "breakfast" of raisins and skim milk, and then would walk out in her robe, barefooted, to check the mailbox, eagerly awaiting word from her partner in Bombay, who, Jamie was sure, had absconded with the money left in her trust. He knew better than to mention such a thought to Lissie, nor did he or Connie ever comment on the lingering smell of stale marijuana in her room. Her friends came and went, most of them girlfriends, every now and then a boy the Crofts knew. In a rare intimacy one night at the dinner table, Lissie told them that Sally Landers was "doing speed." When Jamie said he was going to the phone right that minute to call her parents, Lissie warned him that she'd never tell him anything again as long as she lived if he did such a terrible thing.

When Lissie received the long-awaited letter from Marjorie Kildare, listing the various items of merchandise she'd purchased with their modest, joint hundred-dollar investment, and advising her that the shipments, in separate parcels, would be going out of Bombay that same day, she was ecstatic. She immediately got on the phone to Rusty Klein, who was home on a long weekend from Bennington, and told her the good news. "Rusty's very depressed these days," she later told her parents, but again did not amplify. Her parents were by then used to these mysterious allusions, the letter-from-camp syndrome that Lissie seemed to have adopted as part of her normal life-style.

In the beginning, they used to question her further, hoping for elucidation, but she'd only go into rather long and (they suspected) deliberately convoluted stories that obfuscated rather than illuminated. Eventually, they'd given up. Similarly, Connie—toward the middle of the month—gave up preparing special salads or cooking additional vegetable dishes for Lissie. She told her flatly, and not without sympathy for her daughter's dietary preferences, that she worked too hard every day of the week to have to come home and worry about what *Lissie* would be eating that was different from what the *rest* of the family was eating. This was not a restaurant she was running here, and if Lissie wanted to maintain a diet that was not necessitated by any physical ailment, then she herself would have to—

"I *do* consider it a physical need," Lissie said.

"I said physical *ailment.*"

"Eating meat would make me physically *ill,*" Lissie said.

"I'm not suggesting that you eat meat."

"You're telling me you won't cook for me if I insist on eating only vegetables."

"I'll cook only the vegetables I would normally cook with each meal," Connie said.

"Fine, that'll be a fucking starvation diet," Lissie said.

"Whatever *other* vegetables you want, you can cook for yourself," Connie said. "And watch your language."

The embarrassment lingered like a fever.

It was an embarrassment lessened in intensity for Jamie only because Lissie was a *girl.* Even if she refused to put on a proper dress and stockings and shoes when they took her out to dinner, even if her hair looked dirty and uncombed most of the time, even if her ridiculous eye makeup made her look like a braless bride of

Frankenstein, there was still something *less* embarrassing about her and all the other girls than there was about the *boys*.

One afternoon, alone with Joanna in her apartment, he tried to explore this with her. She had, at first, and in direct contradiction to Jamie's unbridled joy, been exceedingly wary about Lissie's homecoming, suspecting at once that her reappearance in his life might cause changes Joanna was not prepared to accept yet another time. He had stilled her fears. He was here to stay, he'd told her, a declaration she'd found a trifle overstated since the length of his stay each week varied from between two to three hours, after which he caught the train home to his loving wife and resurrected daughter. Count your blessings, Joanna had cautioned herself. He loves you, he keeps saying he loves you, don't rock the boat. But he rarely discussed his daughter with her—seeming in his mind to have created dichotomous territories, one exclusively Connie's and Lissie's, the other Joanna's—and she was surprised when he began talking about her that afternoon.

"Maybe I'm kidding myself," he said. "I am, after all, the father of a daughter, and maybe I *want* to believe she doesn't look as ridiculous as the boys do. But I think it's true, Joanna. And I think it's because women have always been the ones who wore the feathers and paints."

"Tell that to Geronimo," Joanna said.

"Well, *isn't* it true that women are the style-conscious ones?"

"So?"

"And that they'll wear outlandish clothes . . ."

"Thanks."

". . . until a style catches on and becomes a *fashion?*"

"So?"

"So if Lissie chooses to run around looking like a freak . . . that's what she's begun calling herself, you know. No more hippie. Now it's freak."

"I *hate* that word," Joanna said.

"Freak," Jamie said, and sighed.

When Lissie's merchandise arrived from India, she spread it on the living room Bokhara, squatting cross-legged behind it like a merchant realized, the Oriental rug lending credence to her trade, holding up each garment and artifact, slipping bangles over her wrists, fastening earrings to her ears, babbling all the while in a rapid monologue that sounded almost Persian, words tripping over words as she excitedly described how she would begin selling all of this stuff as soon as she'd inventoried it and figured out a proper markup, popping a little ivory pipe into her mouth, grinning around the stem and puffing imaginary smoke like an imaginary pasha. Two days later, a letter arrived from Brenner University, surprising both Jamie and Connie, but not Lissie, for she was the one who'd written asking for information about reenrolling in the fall. She had been home for almost two full months by then, and Jamie was beginning to believe that everything was going to be all right.

Even Lissie's initial disappointment over the New York reaction to her Indian merchandise proved to be temporary. She had cruised the shops along Lexington Avenue, had decided they were selling only stuff for plastic hippies, and had then walked down to Grand Central and shuttled over to Times Square, where she'd caught an express downtown. She was carrying a suitcase filled with items similar to the ones she herself was wearing (and still wearing at the dinner table that night as she related her story), an embroidered, long-sleeved blouse over her jeans, silver bangles, a mirrored vest, a turquoise necklace. The response had been the same all over the Village. She'd sold one or two items, but for the most part the shop owners had dealers with whom they did business regularly on a volume basis, and they weren't interested in buying odds and ends from what one shopkeeper called "itinerant peddlers."

Disappointed but undismayed, she left for Boston at the beginning of March, determined to sell her goods to the head shops in Cambridge.

The day was very cold, but she found herself working up a good sweat nonetheless as she carried the suitcase up the steps from the Harvard Square station, emerging from the kiosk into a wintry sunlight, blinking against it, zipping up her fighter-pilot's jacket, and then beginning to walk up Mass Ave.

Her hope was to sell all the merchandise to a single shop, find a little place that specialized in fine imported stuff, unload all the goods at once, even if it meant making a smaller profit than a shop-by-shop, door-to-door sort of salesmanship might bring. The important thing was the turnaround. *Make* the small profit, send the money to Marjorie in India so she could buy *more* stuff this time, and then make a larger profit next time around because of the increased volume, and so on until they had a going business that would practically run itself.

But if she couldn't find any one shop that would take all the stuff, there was really quite a variety, then she planned to lug this damn suitcase all over Boston, selling bits and pieces of the goods wherever she could, and unloading it all before she went home at the end of the—

"Carry your bag, honey?"

The voice startled her. She had been looking into the far distance, scanning the shop signs up the street, searching for a suitable prospect, and hadn't noticed the young man who sidled up beside her and who was now reaching for the handle of her suitcase. She pulled away instinctively.

"Hey, come on," he said, "lemmee hep you with that."

He was tall and slender and black. He was wearing blue jeans, brown desert boots, and a brown leather car coat. A patch of black hair hung under his lower lip. Not quite a beard, it sat like a small upturned isosceles triangle pointing downward to a square chin. Above the hairy patch, his smile was a dazzling white.

"I can manage," Lissie said.

"The name's Sparky," he said, grinning.

"Goodbye, Sparky," she said, and he burst out laughing. "I *mean* it," she said. "Disappear."

"Ony want to hep you with your burden," he said.

"I don't *need* any help," she said, and stopped before a shop window brimming with just the sort of merchandise she was carrying in the valise—a wide assortment of silver and turquoise jewelry, brass bells and bowls, leather sandals, pouches and belts, cotton shirts and vests, an Oriental bazaar right here in Cambridge.

"Gonna buy yourself some gear?" Sparky said.

Without answering, Lissie opened the door. A bell tinkled over it as she hefted her suitcase into the shop. Through the plate-glass window, she could see Sparky still standing there on the sidewalk, grinning in at her. She turned away from him abruptly. A pair of hanging green curtains at the rear of the shop parted, and a dumpy little bald-headed man stepped through them, beaming, his blue eyes twinkling in a moon face, a fringe of brown hair over each ear. As he approached her, she realized that the baldness and the roly-poly waddle created a mistaken impression of advanced age. He could not have been much older than Lissie herself, perhaps twenty-one or -two. He was wearing baggy brown pants and a long-sleeved, white shirt, the cuffs rolled up. A *square,* she thought. *Running a head shop, no less.*

"Hi," she said, "I'm Melissa Croft, and I . . ."

"What are you selling, Melissa Craft?"

284

"Croft," she said.

"Croft, Craft, let me hear it."

His voice had a good rich timbre, surprising for someone so short—she guessed he was five eight, five nine, certainly no taller than that. She'd always associated deep voices with tall men, but maybe they came with the stout ones, too. He was definitely overweight.

"Who's your friend outside with the evil eye?" he asked.

"I don't know," Lissie said. "He wanted to carry my bag."

"He looks like a pimp."

"That's just what I thought."

"Saw the suitcase, probably figured you stepped straight off a bus and headed for the street life in Cambridge." He paused. "You *didn't* step straight off a bus, did you?"

"No."

"I didn't think so. You're selling something, am I right?"

"Right."

"Are you selling what's in my window?"

"Well, not *exactly* what's in your wind—"

"But *similar* to what's in my window?"

"Similar, yes."

"I don't want it."

"Why not?"

"Because if you're selling what's not selling, why should I buy it?"

"I've got some beautiful stuff here," Lissie said.

"Save your breath."

"Don't you even want to *see* it?"

"Is it from India?"

"Well . . . yes."

"No way," he said, and shook his head.

"Why? What's wrong with Indian merchandise?"

"Nothing's wrong with it."

"Then why won't you look at it?"

"You want to waste your time? Okay, open the bag, waste your time, show me the stuff."

"What for? You said you won't buy any of it."

"I *may* buy some of it, okay? Out of pity, okay?"

"I don't *need* pity."

"What *do* you need? A cup of coffee? Come on, I'll lock the shop and buy you a cup of coffee."

She looked at him.

285

"What do you say?"

She kept looking at him.

"Fat men are very light on their feet," he said, and grinned. "Terrific dancers," he said, and snapped his fingers in the air on either side of his head, like a flamenco dancer. "Besides, if you have a cup of coffee with me, I'll tell you why you're going to have a hard time selling your stuff. Okay?"

"Deal," she said, and nodded.

He extended his hand over the counter. "Matthew Hobbs," he said, "nice to know you." He came around the counter, and reached for a coat on a wall hook. "You can leave your bag here if you like," he said.

Sparky was still waiting on the sidewalk outside. He glanced at Lissie as Matthew was locking the door, muttered, "Ain't no accountin' for taste," and then put his hands in the pockets of the leather coat and went slouching off up the street, affecting the sort of cool, hunched-over, shit-kicking style the street-gang kids used to use back in the fifties.

At an espresso joint on Ellery Street, they sat close to a blazing fire and ordered two cappuccinos from a blond waitress wearing a black leotard. "Where are you from?" Matthew asked.

"Connecticut."

"You don't sound Connecticut."

"What do I sound?"

"New York."

"Well, I was *born* in New York. And grew *up* there, actually."

"You grew up nice," he said, and grinned. "What do *I* sound?"

"Boston."

"I do? Shit," he said.

"Like the Kennedys sound."

"Is that good or bad?"

"It's good, I guess. I don't know," she said, and shrugged. "You said you'd tell me . . ."

"Okay. First of all, the shirts don't fit right."

"What do you mean? I'm wearing one of them right now. It fits fine."

"You're very slender, Melissa."

"Call me Lissie, will you?"

"Why? What's wrong with Melissa?"

"Nothing's wrong with it, I just happen to prefer Lissie."

"What are you sore about, all of a sudden?"

"I'm not sore. Well, yes, I *am* a little annoyed. You don't know a *thing* about the kind of shirts I've got, and you're telling me they don't *fit* right."

"*Most* of them don't, okay? Especially on the men. The shoulders are too narrow. We've got husky *brutes* here in America," he said, and raised both arms in a weight-lifter's pose and flexed his muscles and grinned again. "And the madras stuff needs special care which nobody today is interested in; they want to throw it in the washer and dryer and if you do that you *ruin* madras. And the little pipes for holding roaches, and the bigger ones for smoking opium or whatever turns you on, we can get cheaper here in the States, made in Korea, so who wants to spend additional loot for fancy Indian ones? The silver jewelry is cheaper and better from Mexico, and the turquoise . . ."

"I happen to have *fabulous* turquoise."

"Ah, you're a turquoise expert?"

"No, but I've seen the stuff they're selling here in Cambridge, and I know mine . . ."

"What makes you think hippies care about quality?"

"What?"

"Good turquoise is expensive, Lissie, I'm sure you know that. The best stones . . ."

"I've got some *very* good stones, and they didn't cost a fortune."

"Unpolished stones?"

"Yes."

"You've got to be a good judge to appreciate an unpolished stone."

"My partner's had experience."

"Where's your partner?"

"In Bombay."

"How'd you and her like to buy a store?" Matthew said, and grinned again.

"What do you mean?"

"I'm going out of business next week."

"You're kidding!"

"Would I kid a beautiful girl like you? Don't look so glum, here's the coffee."

"Yeah," she said.

"You're thinking 'Where am I going to sell my stuff,' right?"

"Yeah."

"You'll sell it, don't worry."

"Sure. The way *you're* selling it."

"Maybe my location isn't a good one," he said, and shrugged. "I don't know, I just don't know what's happening. Everybody today is into the Sergeant Pepper shit. Costumes, you know? Civil war uniforms and opera capes, like that. Took awhile to catch on, but here it is, folks. The Beatles could've ruled the world if they wanted to. Instead, they went out of business . . . the way *I'm* going out of business next week."

"Wait'll I tell Marjorie about this."

"Who's Marjorie?"

"My partner in Bombay."

"It's not the end of the world. Would you like to go to a movie or something?"

"What? Oh. No. No, thanks. I've got to . . . I guess I've got to . . . I don't know. I'll just keep lugging that bag around, I guess, until I sell what's in it. This is some letdown, I've got to tell you. I thought we'd make a fortune, I mean it."

"Easy come, easy go," Matthew said. "What's your number, can I call you sometime?"

"Well . . ."

"Will you be here in Boston for a while?"

"What I planned to do was sell the stuff and head right home."

"Where are you staying?"

"I'm crashing with a friend of mine. A junior at Brenner."

"Male or female?"

"Female."

"Want to go to a movie with me sometime?"

"Maybe."

"Light on the feet," he said, and again brought up his hands and did his flamenco-dancer finger-snaps.

"Her name's in the book," Lissie said. "Brooke Hastings."

"Okay. Maybe I'll give you a call."

"What are you going to do now?" she asked. "I mean, if you go out of business."

"*When* I go, not *if* I go. Maybe go back to dental school."

"*Dental* school?"

"Yeah, I dropped out to start the business. Have you ever seen a fat dentist? I've never seen a fat dentist in my life. I figured nobody would go to a fat dentist, so I dropped out and opened the business. My draft number also had something to do with it—three-twenty-seven out of a possible three-sixty-five, not bad, huh? So I dropped out. Fuck my father." He leaned conspiratorially across the table and whispered, "My father's a dentist."

"So now you'll go back to school."

"Sure. Maybe. I figure if I can't become a multimillionaire *merchant*, I might as well become a multimillionaire *dentist*. Matthew Hobbs, D.D.S. Dr. Matthew Hobbs. It doesn't sound too bad, does it?"

"If it's what you want," Lissie said.

"Who *knows* what I want? Does *anyone* know what he wants anymore?" he said, and shook his head. "Would you like another cappuccino?"

"No, thanks."

"I don't know *anybody* who knows what he really wants," Matthew said. "My father knew he wanted to be a dentist from the minute he saw an oil-drilling rig outside Tucson, Arizona. Do *I* want to be a dentist? Who the hell knows? Do *I* want an air-conditioned Cadillac like my father's got? Probably. Do *I* want a two-hundred-thousand-dollar house in Lexington, swimming pool in the backyard, membership at the golf and tennis club? Again, probably. But it'd be so nice to *have* all those things without having to *become* what those things *force* you to become. Am I making any sense? Do *you* know what *you* want?"

"I thought I'd make a little money, you know, and then go back to school in the fall."

"Okay."

"But now I don't know."

"Do you *want* to go back to school?"

"Oh, sure. Well, I guess so. I mean . . . what else is there to do? I guess I could go back to India. But . . . I don't know," she said, and shrugged.

Sparky was waiting on the sidewalk when they got back to the shop. "Thought you'd never get here," he said, and grinned. "I'm about to freeze my *ass* off."

They tried to ignore him as Matthew unlocked the door, but the moment the shop was open, he stepped inside and began studying the various pieces of jewelry in the display case.

"Can I help you?" Matthew asked.

"Just lookin'," Sparky said.

Lissie picked up her suitcase.

"Thanks for the coffee," she said.

"Stick around awhile," Matthew said.

"No, if I'm going to sell this stuff, I'd better get . . . ."

"Whut you sellin, honey?" Sparky said at once, and turned from the counter.

"You're beginning to annoy me, you know?" Lissie said.

"Annoy you? I hear you're sellin', so I may be buyin', so how is that annoyin'?"

"I'm not what you think. I didn't just get off the bus, so fuck off, will you?"

"Nice talk on the lady," Sparky said. "Who said you're off any bus?"

"You're a pimp, am I right?" Lissie said.

"Whut? Me?" He clenched both fists over his chest. *Me? a pimp? Do I look like a pimp?*" he asked Matthew.

"Yes," Matthew said.

"I am not no pimp," Sparky said. "Is that why you been runnin' from me, honey? 'Cause you think I'm a pimp? I am *not* no pimp, cross my heart an' hope to die," he said, spitting on the pressed-together index and middle fingers of his right hand, and then making an *X* over his heart with them. "Whut you got in that valise there? If it's somethin' you want to sell, then maybe I'd be innerusted in buyin'. So whut is it? You gonna open that bag for Sparky?"

Lissie looked at him.

"Well, whut is it *now*, honey? Was I goin' to rip it off, it'd be easier closed than open. Now come on, open it for me."

Lissie looked at Matthew. Matthew shrugged. She knelt before the suitcase, laid it flat on the floor, and unfastened the clasps.

"Well, well, *whut* have we here?" Sparky said, kneeling beside her. There was the smell of strong cologne on him. She was worried he would stink up the fabrics in the bag.

"Just don't touch it, okay?" she said. "Anything you want to see, I'll show it to you."

"Still afraid I'm gonna rip it off, huh?" he said and shook his head. "First she thinks I'm a pimp," he said to Matthew, "and now I'm some kinda thief. My, my. How much you want for this whole bag of shit here?" he asked.

"What?" Lissie said.

"The whole bag. Whut was you hopin to get for it door-to-door?"

"Well . . . what difference would that make to you?"

"Name a price," he said, and reached into his pocket.

"For the . . . the whole bag here? The whole . . . ?"

"The whole bag of shit, raaaht," Sparky said, and pulled out a thick roll of bills fastened with a rubber band. *A pusher,* she thought, he's a *pusher.* "So?" he said, taking off the rubber band and sliding it over his hand and onto his wrist, "how much?"

"Three hundred," she said.

A hundred percent markup would have brought $200 for the lot. After listening to Matthew, she realized she'd be lucky if she and Marjorie made a $50 profit on their $100 investment. She was now asking for three times what they'd paid for the stuff.

"Sounds steep," Sparky said, raising his eyebrows.

"That's the price," Lissie said. "Take it or leave it."

"You just sold a whole bunch of shit," Sparky said, and began peeling off $50 bills from the roll. His hand stopped. He looked up from the roll and grinned. "Provided," he said.

"Here it comes," Lissie said, and nodded knowingly to Matthew. "What's the catch?"

"*Two* catches," Sparky said. "First, the price includes that ratty suitcase."

"Okay."

"And second, you let me take you to lunch. To celebrate."

Lissie hesitated a moment. Then she nodded and said, "Deal."

They ate in a hamburger joint near the Harvard Coop, the suitcase on the floor beside the table, the $300 in fifties tucked into the right front pocket of Lissie's jeans. Every now and then, she ran her hand over the bulge of the money; she was certain Sparky was a pusher who might try to pick her pocket or else later send a confederate to mug her on the way home. Lissie ordered a salad. Sparky spread relish and ketchup on his hamburger, and then looked up at her and said, "So whut's your name?"

"Lissie," she said.

"For Melissa, right? Got a cousin named Melissa down home. Melissa whut?"

She hesitated. "Melissa Green," she lied.

"Green. Is that Jewish?"

"No."

"Green," he said. "Where d'you live, Melissa?"

"Connecticut," she said. "New Canaan, Connecticut." Another lie. Chewing, she looked up from her salad to check his face. He seemed to have bought both lies.

"Food okay?" he asked.

"Yes, thanks. Yours?"

"Fine. Melissa Green of New Canaan, Connecticut, huh?" he said, and grinned. "How about that?"

"What's the Sparky for?" she asked.

"Spartacus."

"You're kidding."

"Spartacus Marshall, uh-huh. He was a slave, you know, Spartacus. So was my great-granddaddy."

"Where are you from?"

"From?"

"You said 'down home' a minute ago . . ."

"Oh, that's where my *momma*'s from. Down home, Shiloam, Georgia, population three hundred and nineteen. Me, I was born and raised right here in Boston."

"*Are* you a pimp?" she asked suddenly.

"Nope."

"Cross your heart?"

"An' hope to die," he said, grinning.

"What then? A pusher?"

He looked at her. His eyes were intensely brown, his hair formed a tightly knit woolen cap over his skull, his nostrils flared, his lips were thick, he was altogether black and altogether handsome. She lowered her eyes, refusing to meet his. Her gaze lingered on his hands, the huge knuckles of a street fighter, the contradictorily slender fingers of a pianist.

"You want an answer?" he asked.

"Yes," she said. Her eyes were still on his hands.

"Then look at me."

She raised her eyes.

"An' ask me again."

"Are you a pusher?"

"I'm a pusher," he said.

She nodded.

"Why you want to know? You doin' some kind of shit?"

"No."

"You sure?"

"I'm sure."

"Then why you so innerusted in if I'm a pusher. You lookin' for some quality grass?"

"No."

"You smoke grass, don't you?"

"I do," she said simply.

"Sure you don't want to buy some fine grass with all that money you got for your goods?"

"Positive."

"Where'd you *get* all that stuff, anyway?"

"India."

"What's the dope scene like over there?"

"Wide open."

"But you never done none, huh?"

"Only grass."

"Want a hit of something stronger?"

"No."

"You sure?"

"I'm sure."

"Want to come smoke some grass with me?"

"I don't think so."

"Why not? I thought we were celebratin'."

"We are, but . . ."

"Paid you five times what *you* paid for that shit, least you could do is smoke some grass with me."

"*Three* times," she said.

"Whut?"

"Three times what I paid."

"Well, sheee-it!" he said, and burst out laughing. "What *are* you, some kinda honest mother honkie? I really dig you, Melissa. Whut's your real name?"

"That's it. Melissa."

"Ain't no honkie in the whole *world* named Melissa, that's a nigger name if ever I heard one. Whut's your real name? Come on, if I can tell you I'm a pusher, you can at least give me your real name."

"That's it. Melissa. But most people call me Lissie."

"Lissie."

"Uh-huh."

"Lissie Green, huh?"

"Well . . ."

"That ain't it, is it? That's the name to fool the big bad nigger pusher, ain't it? So he don't come hangin' 'roun your doorstep peddlin' his dope."

"It's Melissa Croft," she said. "And I don't live in New Canaan, I live in Rutledge."

"Where you stayin here in Boston?"

"With a friend of mine."

"Whut's *her* name?"

"Brooke Hastings."

"Where's she live?"

"Near Brenner."

"Maybe I'll give you a call, tell you how much I appreciate bein' charged three times whut . . ."

"If you think I overcharged you for that stuff . . ."

"Well, you *did,* didn't you?"

"Fine, then I'll give you your money back."

"Ha!" he said.

"I will."

"Okay, give it back," he said.

"Okay," she said, and reached into her pocket.

"You try to give that money back, I'll break your arm," he said. "A deal's a deal."

"You have no use for any of that stuff," Lissie said.

"I'll give it to all my friends as presents. Throw a party, invite all my friends, and lay this stuff on 'em. How long you gonna be here in Boston?"

"I don't know. Why?"

"Give you a call, invite you to m'party."

"No, I'd rather you didn't."

"Why? 'Cause I'm black?"

"That's part of it, yes."

"What's the rest of it?"

"You're a pusher," she said. "That's the rest of it."

"I coulda said I was a civil engineer."

"But you didn't."

"I'll tell you a story, Liss," he said, and somehow his use of the diminutive put them instantly on a more familiar basis. "When I was in the third grade, teacher went out the room for a coupla minutes, an' when she come back she ast the class, 'Who was talkin' while I was out the room?' Well, *ever'body* was talkin', but nobody raised their hand. 'Cept me. I'm the dummy raised his hand. So teacher—her name was Mrs. Rosen, she taught me the biggest lesson I ever learned—she says to me, 'All right, Spartacus, you may stay after school for a half-hour today.' You dig? For bein' *honest,* I'm the one gets the heavy shit laid on him. Never again. Never. Never *confess* to nothin' an' never *volunteer* for nothin'. When I was in Nam—"

"Vietnam? You were in the Army?"

"Yeah."

"When was that?"

"Got out six months ago."

"And started pushing."

"Listen, Mrs. Rosen, I'm sorry I opened my fuckin' *mouth,* okay? It was a way to make a quick buck, okay, get me back on my feet again. Ain't too many patriotic Americans eager to *hire* us war vets, you know, even if we're lily-white pure, which I don't happen to be, as you already pointed out," he said, and grinned.

"I've got a thing about pushing dope, okay? Let's leave it at that."

"'Fraid I'll try to turn you on? Hook the honkie from Connecticut?"

"No, I'm not afraid of that. I'd never stick a needle in my body as long as I live."

"They's other than needles, Lissie chile. You best beware the mean ole pusher," he said, and cocked his head to one side and curled his hands into a witch's claws.

"I really don't think that's funny," she said.

"Anyway, I'm plannin' on gettin' out of it," he said.

"Sure you are."

"I mean it. Maybe go to India like you did. See the world. I got me quite a bit of money stashed away . . ."

"I'll bet. The blood of innocent . . ."

"Hey, lay *off* that shit, okay?" he said, and reached across the table and grabbed her wrist.

"Let go of me," she said.

"Just lay off, okay?"

"Just keep your hands off me."

"Black nigger hands, right?"

"No, black fucking *pusher* hands, let *go* of me!"

"Okay, okay," he said, and released her wrist. "Man, you really *do* have a thing, don't you?"

"I said I did."

"I'm hearin' you, I'm hearin' you."

"Don't ever do that again. I don't like to be . . . to be . . . I just don't like it."

"Okay."

They were silent for a moment.

"I meant what I said about maybe gettin' out."

"Sure."

"Maybe go to Spain. You ever been to Spain?"

"No."

"Want to come with me?"

"Sure, when do we leave?"

"You mean it?"

"Don't be ridiculous."

"Then how about comin' up to my place instead? Have a little smoke together."

"No."

"Why not?"

"I don't want to."

"You smoke, you tole me you . . ."

"Yes, but I don't want to."

"Come on," he said.

"No."

"Come on."

"No."

"I'll call you sometime, okay?"

"No."

"I'll call you."

"No."

"I'll call you."

Sparky Marshall was a black man in his mid-twenties, Jamie guessed, wearing just under his lower lip an ornamental patch of hair Jamie had learned to call a "Dizzy kick" when Gillespie was turning the music world around with his bop in the late forties. Above the miniature spade beard (*No pun intended,* Jamie thought) Sparky's smile was a dazzling white. His eyes were intensely brown, his hair formed a tightly knit woolen cap over his skull, his nostrils flared, his lips were thick, he was altogether black and altogether handsome, and he was, moreover, fucking Jamie's daughter.

"The Sparky is for Spartacus," he said, extending his hand and taking Jamie's in a firm grip. "Spartacus was a slave. So was my great-granddaddy."

Jamie was wondering whether Lissie expected Sparky to sleep in the same room with her that night. He discussed this privately with Connie. Then they discussed it with Lissie.

"We feel Sparky should sleep in the guest room over at the barn," Jamie said.

"What for?" Lissie said. "We're sleeping together in Boston, what kind of hypocrisy is this?"

"I don't care *what* you're doing in Boston," Connie said. "This is Connecticut, and this is my house, and in my house Sparky sleeps in the barn."

"You don't know how funny that is," Lissie said.

"I'm glad you think it's funny."

"What you just said. About in your *house* Sparky sleeps in the *barn.*"

"I think you know exactly what I mean, Liss."

"Okay. *He* sleeps in the barn, *I* sleep in the barn. Does that take the curse off?"

"I don't know what curse you're talking about," Connie said. "It simply seems to me that if you were visiting *Sparky*'s parents for the weekend, as he is visiting *us* for the weekend, then I'd expect them to find a room for you while you were there, a private room of your own, and that's what I intend to provide for Sparky. In the *barn.*"

"You're not at all concerned about his privacy," Lissie said. "This is sheer hypocrisy. And I wouldn't be surprised if it had something to do with his being black."

"That has *nothing* to do with it," Jamie said.

"Some of my best friends are black, right?" Lissie said.

"As a matter of fact, some of them are," Jamie said.

"Sure, Dad."

"Lissie, he sleeps in the *barn,*" Jamie said flatly.

"Then so do I."

"What you do is your business," Jamie said. "If you want to go creeping over there in your nightgown in the middle of the night, that's up to you. But while Mom and I are both awake, then *you're* in your room in the *house,* and Sparky's in *his* room in the *barn.*"

"Hypocrisy," Lissie said, but she was smiling.

Connie's parents were in Rutledge that weekend for their usual monthly visit; they would be leaving soon for two weeks in the Caribbean. At the dinner table that Friday night, Jamie tried to explain (to a less than fascinated audience) an idea he had for something he thought he might call "The Face Book."

"I'd start with the premise that there are only two or three dozen *perfect* facial types in the entire world," he said, "and then I'd find the definitive example for each type, and then start looking for people who resembled whoever it might be, Lena Horne, let's say," and he glanced at Sparky. "I'll take their pictures and then do a sort of color-spectrum thing, string them all out, maybe fifty or so photographs on facing pages. It'd be like they did in *Jekyll and Hyde,* the way Spencer Tracy changed—"

"Who's Spencer Tracy?" Lissie asked.

"—on the screen from Jekyll to Hyde or vice versa. Like that, a gradual metamorphosis, an evolution. Here's the *crudest* example of this particular facial type, and here it is getting a little more refined, and here it is getting closer to perfection and *here's* perfection itself, this is what we in this day and age consider perfection."

Connie's father, surprising Jamie (he was, after all, a retired businessman), said it sounded somewhat like the action photographs Muybridge had taken as a guide for artists, the frame-by-frame pictures of a man running or leaping or climbing or whatever. Jamie said that wasn't the idea at *all,* and used the color-spectrum concept as a metaphor once again, the subtle gradation from white to red, if they could visualize that, with each of the intervening shades of pink in between.

"The idea sucks, Dad," Lissie said, and everyone at the table laughed, except Connie's mother, who thought Lissie had said something dirty. Sparky was quiet all through dinner. He might just as well have not been there. Early the next morning, he caught a train into the city, "to handle some business in Harlem." He did not specify what the business was. They all took a long walk by the river, and when they got back to the house Jamie laid a fire and mixed some Bloody Marys. The fire was still crackling in the living room when they sat down to lunch. The day was crisp and clear. Slanting rays of pale March sunlight streamed through the dining room windows, the kind of light Jamie loved for black-and-white shooting. It was one o'clock in the afternoon. There was no indication of what was about to happen. It simply happened, all at once, startling all of them.

Whenever Connie's mother or father were visiting, Jamie invariably drank too much, the better to dull their numbing effect on him. He had, as usual, drunk one too many Bloody Marys before lunch, and there was a glazed look on his face even before they sat down at the table together. But Lissie's unspeakable behavior should have penetrated even the thickest of alcoholic hazes. From time to time during the unexpected outburst, as Connie was drawn more deeply into the argument, Peter Harding virtually forgotten in the heat of the daughter-mother exchange, Connie found herself turning to Jamie for support, her eyes flicking to his face, her daughter's sharp words yanking her back again, Jamie giving nothing. Not support, not admonition, not even seeming *notice* of anything that was happening there in the harsh wintry sunlight. Silence. Only silence in the midst of a storm as frightening as it was sudden:

PETER: Where'd your young man go, Lissie?
LISSIE: Into the city, Grandpa.
PETER: Ah, the city.
LISSIE: Could you please pass the stringbeans, Mom?
PETER: Is he enjoying his visit with us?
LISSIE: Yep.
PETER: I can imagine.
LISSIE: What does *that* mean?
PETER: What?
LISSIE: That you can *imagine* he's enjoying his visit with us?
PETER: Well, isn't he?
LISSIE: Of *course* he is.
CONNIE: Lissie, I don't like the tone of your voice.
LISSIE: Really? Well, *I* don't like the tone of Grandpa's voice.
PETER: Me? What did I say?
LISSIE: Implying that because Sparky's black, he should be tickled to death we're offering him our—
CONNIE: Lissie, that's your *grand*father you're—
LISSIE: So what? He's talking like a goddamn *fool!*
CONNIE: Lissie!
LISSIE: Well, he *is!*
CONNIE: Lissie, shut *up!*
LISSIE: Okay.
CONNIE: I *said* shut up.
LISSIE: And *I* said okay.
PETER: What did she think? That because her young man's black . . .?
CONNIE: Let it go, Pop.
PETER: No, what did she mean? Is she saying I'm . . .?
CONNIE: Pop, please let it—
LISSIE: He knows damn *well* what I thought.
PETER: And what's that, Melissa?
LISSIE: Fuck it!
CONNIE: Lissie!

PETER: That's all right. I've heard the word before.

LISSIE: I'm just sick and tired of this family thinking I'm some kind of *six*-year-old who doesn't know what she wants or needs. I'm just sick and *tired* of it. And of all the innu*endo*es about Sparky because he's black.

PETER: Is he black? I hadn't noticed.

LISSIE: Very funny, Grandpa.

PETER: There's a black lady in our building—isn't there, Stephanie?—who'd enjoy knowing how I . . .

LISSIE: Some of my best friends . . .

CONNIE: Oh, for God's sake, Lissie, get *off* that tired old line!

LISSIE: Okay, tell me something.

CONNIE: Finish your—

LISSIE: No, tell me. Are you glad, or are you *not* glad that Sparky isn't here today?

CONNIE: Me? Are you asking me?

LISSIE: I'm asking *all* of you.

CONNIE: I'm glad he's not here, all right?

LISSIE: Ah! Why?

CONNIE: I don't like him.

LISSIE: Ah! *Why* don't you like him?

CONNIE: Because he accepts our hospitality without a word of thanks, which may be etiquette down home in Shiloam, Georgia . . .

LISSIE: His *mother's* from Shiloam. Sparky was born in Boston. And that last remark was *racist,* in case you don't know it.

CONNIE: Rudeness is rudeness in any color.

LISSIE: You just can't forget he's black, can you?

CONNIE: Can *you?* You're the one who keeps—

LISSIE: Oh, *fuck* this! Just fuck it! I don't have to sit here and listen to this shit, I really don't. I'm going upstairs to pack, fuck it.

PETER: What did I say, Connie?

CONNIE: Go talk to her, Jamie.

JAMIE: What?

CONNIE: Go upstairs and *talk* to her, goddammit!

She was in her room on the top floor of the house, hurling clothes into a suitcase when he climbed the stairs. She looked up angrily, and said, "Doesn't anybody *knock* in this house?"

"I'm sorry, the door was open, I thought . . ."

"You're *still* supposed to knock."

"Sorry," he said, and sat on the edge of one of the twin beds. "Are you really leaving?"

"I am."

"What about Sparky? He said he'd be back . . ."

"I've already called him. He's meeting me in Boston."

"I really don't think there's any need to—"

"Well, I think there is."

"Lissie, you surely can't believe that whatever Mom and I feel about Sparky has anything to do with the color of his skin."

"That's *just* what I believe."

"And in *any* case, you had no right talking to your grandfather that way."

"Didn't I? When he was insinuating that Sparky's a watermelon-eating nigger who should be *thrilled* to be in white massa's house? Come on, Dad."

"He wasn't suggesting anything of the sort. In fact, I think he likes Sparky."

"How about you? Do *you* like Sparky?"

Jamie hesitated. "No," he said.

"Why not?"

"Because he seems distant and remote, and I can't shake the feeling that inside he's sneering at us. If you think that's racist, I'm sorry. I *do* happen to work with a great many blacks, Lissie, and no one has ever accused me of racist attitudes. And if you knew how many black children Mom patiently helps and teaches . . ."

"The white man's burden, right?"

"Lissie, you're being particularly dense. I'm trying to say that neither Mom nor I—and *certainly* not your grandfather, who innocently stepped into a buzz saw—was trying to put down your friend Sparky."

"It seemed that way to me."

"We've always welcomed your friends in our home, but whenever you bring guests here . . ."

"Oh? When did your daughter suddenly become a guest?"

"I didn't say that. *Sparky's* the guest, *Sparky's* . . ."

"Sparky's a person I love and admire, and if you could for a moment see past the fact that's he black, then you might be able to share my feelings, which apparently you're unwilling to do. It seems the *only* thing that'll please you and Mom would be a goddamn Harvard graduate, knowing how much education means to you, even if the only reason it's important is as a means of making money. Money doesn't mean very much to me, Dad. I was living in India on thirty cents a day. The important thing to me is experiencing life and living it to the fullest, and also loving someone with whom I can completely *share* that fulfilling experience. I'm trying to make it clear that I won't tolerate any unkind remarks about a person I love deeply. I don't consider Sparky a *guest* in my house. I don't consider Sparky . . ."

"I do," Jamie said.

"Well, I don't."

Jamie sighed.

"When are you coming home, Liss?" he asked.

"Not for a while. I'm going back to Boston, and I'll . . ."

"That's not what I meant. I meant when are you coming *back* from wherever you disappeared to last April?"

She looked at him steadily for a moment, and then said, "I'm back, you know I'm back."

He shook his head. "Someone's back," he said, "but I'm not sure it's Melissa Croft."

"It's Melissa Croft," she said and nodded emphatically.

He sighed again. "Two things," he said.

"Yes, what are they?"

"First, I don't think your grandparents appreciate the kind of language you use with such frequency these days. Nor do I. It makes you sound cheap, Lissie, and if you had any respect for . . ."

"The way I talk is the way I talk," she said. "What's the second thing?"

"I'd like you to go downstairs and apologize to your grandfather."

"No way," she said.

Jamie was parked several buildings up the street from Dr. Mandelbaum's building, sitting behind the steering wheel of the Corvette and reading a copy of *House Beautiful* in which there was a layout of pictures he'd taken of a poet's house in Katonah. When someone knocked on the curbside window, startling him half out of his wits, he threw up his hands and the magazine as if a gun had just been thrust in his back. The face that materialized in the car's window frame was round and beaming, with brown eyes magnified behind thick-lensed glasses and a gray Freudian beard clinging to the jowls and chin of none other than Dr. Frank Lipscombe, Rutledge's own psychological seer.

Jamie rolled down the window. "Hello, Frank," he said.

He knew Lipscombe worked on this street, had in fact cautioned himself a thousand times to be careful of Ninety-sixth Street where Dr. Frank Lipscombe dispensed psychological tidbits cheek by jowl with Dr. Marvin Mandelbaum. But if Lipscombe *worked* here then what was he doing in the *street* here at a quarter to two in the afternoon, instead of upstairs making some schizophrenic patient whole and sound again? What the hell are you doing downstairs,

Jamie wondered, five minutes before Joanna is due to come out of number sixty up the block?

"What brings you to Nightmare Alley?" Lipscombe asked, smiling through the open window.

Jamie could not immediately think of a lie. He smiled back at Lipscombe, hoping desperately that a lie would miraculously appear on his lips, flow mellifluously from his mouth—"What am I doing here? Why, what I'm doing here is is is is"—but not a single lie would come, not a single fabrication to explain why a man would be sitting in a parked automobile reading *House Beautiful* at 1:45 P.M. on a bitterly cold winter's day. He pulled an old psychiatric trick: he asked a question in answer to a question.

"What are *you* doing here?" he asked. "Shouldn't you be working?"

"Came down for lunch," Lipscombe said. "One to two every day. Late lunch. My last appointment is at six, which means I'm through at six-fifty and home in Rutledge at eight-thirty. If I eat a late lunch, I can wait for a late dinner. How about you?" He said all this hunched over, his arms folded on the frame of the window, his smiling face peering into the car, the blustery March wind gusting around him.

"I'm waiting for my assistant," Jamie said.

"Assistant?"

"Guy who works with me," Jamie said. "Had to drop off some lenses."

"Ah," Lipscombe said.

"And pick up a strobe."

Snow him with jargon, Jamie thought.

"Should be down any minute now, in fact," he said, and looked at his watch.

The little hand was almost on the two and the big hand was almost on the ten, which meant that in about thirty or forty seconds, Joanna would leave Mandelbaum's office, and take the elevator down seven floors to the street, and come sashaying out of number sixty up the street and right over to the car where Frank Lipscombe was leaning in the window, oblivious to the cold. But no, she was smarter than that; if she saw Frank, she'd walk right on by, she'd know better than to—

Still looking at the watch, he saw the minute hand lurch perceptibly. It was now exactly one-fifty. Joanna was bidding Mandelbaum goodbye and perhaps handing him a check for his deep perceptions during the month of February.

"Mind if I sit down?" Lipscombe said, opening the car door.

"What?"

"Sit for a minute?"

"Well, uh, sure, but he's, uh, he'll be down in a minute, he . . ."

"I just wanted to say," Lipscombe said, opening the door and sliding onto the front seat beside Jamie, "that you did a hell of a job at that memorial service." The door slammed shut behind him. He rolled up the window. Jamie glanced into the rear-view mirror. Up the street, he could see the green awning over the door to Mandelbaum's building. No Joanna yet. The dashboard clock read five minutes to two, but it always ran fast. He looked at his own watch again. Only a minute had gone by. She was probably still up on the seventh floor, pressing the button for the elevator.

"A very nice job," Lipscombe said.

"Thank you," Jamie said.

"With more insight into what's troubling today's kids than one might expect from a layman."

"Well, thank you, Frank."

"The entire concept of *leaving* before they ever *got* here. I liked that. It created an instant image, almost a double-exposure, coming and going at the same time, a concept of *speed* . . . perhaps an unconscious association with drugs, eh? I'll bet any amount of money you see the entire world through a viewfinder, am I correct, Jamie, you don't have to answer me."

Through the viewfinder that was the rear-view mirror, Jamie saw a blonde in a blue overcoat coming out of Mandelbaum's building. His heart leaped. No, she was too short, her walk was different, her hair—

"I'll tell you something I've never told to anyone else in the world," Lipscombe said, and stretched out, leaning his head back against the seat. Oh, Jesus, Jamie thought, he's making himself comfortable, he's going to be here for the next fifty minutes, unburdening himself. How much should I charge? What does Mandelbaum charge Joanna? Please, honey, *please* notice him sitting here in the car before you pull open the door and say hello, okay? *Please!*

"Are you interested?" Lipscombe asked.

"In what?" Jamie said.

"In what I've never told anyone else in the world."

"Yes . . . certainly."

"I love my work," Lipscombe said.

"Uh-huh."

"That's what I've never told anyone else in the world."

"Uh-huh."

"Love it," Lipscombe said. "Do you love yours?"

"Yes. I do. Yes."

"I knew you would."

"Uh-huh."

"Because our work is similar, you see."

"Similar? Photography and psychiatry?"

"Voyeurs," Lipscombe said.

"Ah."

"We're both voyeurs."

"Ah."

"*You* look in a viewfinder, *I* look into somebody's mind. All day long they tell me stories, Jamie. I sit in my big leather chair, with my hands folded over my belly, and they lie on the couch looking up at the ceiling and they tell me stories. It's like going to the movies every day but Sunday. My job is like going to the movies, can you beat a job like that? I close my eyes and listen to their voices, and I see the motion pictures they've produced for me, all these wonderful movies they've written and directed and are starring in for me. What's even better, most of the movies are pornographic.

"I sit there with my hands on my belly, and a patient tells me how she's cheating on her husband by running downstairs every morning the minute he's gone, to apartment 3C on the floor below, where a bachelor is living, she runs down every morning the minute her husband leaves for work and she sucks this guy off while he's eating his cornflakes, can you believe it? She tells me this, and I see the movie in my mind. I hear the cornflakes crunching, I hear the zipper as she pulls it down, I hear her slurping around on his cock, a movie."

In the tiny movie that appeared in the rear-view mirror, Jamie saw Joanna step out through the door of Mandelbaum's building, hesitate for a moment under the awning, look up the street and down the street, first toward Madison, and then toward Park where she spotted the Corvette and began moving swiftly toward it. She was wearing purple that clashed violently with the overhead green of the awning as she stepped out like a filly breaking from the gate, long legs flashing, trotting rather close to the brick wall of the

306

building as though wanting to stay on the inside rail, and then sidestepping toward the curb in a quick glide, thirty seconds away from the car, twenty seconds, ten seconds, in an instant she would open the door and trip over Lipscombe.

He lost her in the rear-view mirror.

He caught his breath, jerked his head sharply to the right, and saw her gliding past the automobile, high heels clicking on the pavement, purple slacks and short purple coat, blond hair caught in a streaming purple scarf, not so much a glance at the car she knew so well—she had spotted Lipscombe.

Jamie let out his breath.

"Or sometimes," Lipscombe said, "they'll tell me dreams or fantasies that are even more marvelous than the true stories, the work of a Fellini or a Bergman, for example, as compared to the shlock shit of a Brooks or an Altman—passions exploding in colors unimaginable, described to me in Technicolor brilliance, the senses heightened. I can *smell* the musk, I can *taste* the juices, I can *hear* the pounding of a heart in the stillness of the theater of my mind."

Silence.

Lazily, Lipscombe looked at his watch.

"I'd better get upstairs," he said. "I have a patient at two."

"They should charge *you*," Jamie said, and smiled.

"Hmh?"

"Admission."

"Oh. Yes," Lipscombe said and, chuckling, opened the car door. "But don't suggest it to them."

"I won't," Jamie said, chuckling himself. He looked toward Park Avenue. Joanna in full purple sail was crossing the street against the light, glancing toward the Corvette to see if Jamie's visitor was still in it. A Cadillac honked its horn at her and then almost ran her down, the son of a bitch!

". . . saw you on Ninety-sixth Street," Lipscombe said.

"What?" Jamie said.

"I won't tell Connie I saw you on Ninety-sixth Street."

Jamie looked at him.

"She may think you're seeing a shrink on the sly," Lipscombe said, and winked, and slammed the door shut.

Jamie's heart was pounding.

He watched Lipscombe go into his building, tempted to follow him, make sure he got on the goddamn elevator. Instead, he alternated his attention from the doorway to the steady progress of

Joanna approaching on the opposite side of the street. She stopped just across from his car, looked to make sure the visitor was truly gone, and then crossed against traffic again, dodging cars until she reached the safety of the curb. Yanking open the door, she said at once, "Who was *that?*"

"Lipscombe."

"Who?"

"The Rutledge shrink."

"Oh, my *God!"* Joanna said.

At a party that Friday night, in the center of a circle of men and women, Frank Lipscombe began holding forth on adultery and its effects on marriages of long-standing. It was the doctor's learned opinion that middle age was a particularly dangerous time for the survival of marriages that had until then "weathered the storms of conviviality," especially during this very confusing epoch when the young people of America were setting examples that seemed to encourage every fantasy entertained by any male beyond the age of forty.

"Who among the men here," Lipscombe asked, "has not been tempted by the sight of nubile nipples puckering naked beneath paper-thin T-shirts? Who among us . . . ?"

"Oh, Frank, be *serious,"* his wife said.

"I wish I were being *less* serious," Lipscombe said, a faintly offended look on his bearded face. "Who among us has not considered the thought of flight to a commune, no more catching of the commuter train at eight-oh-seven, no more mortgages to worry about, or tax bills or fuel bills, or kids to send through college . . ."

"Well, there's the crux of it," Jeff Landers said, clearing his throat. "Once the kids are gone, the tendency is to relax a little, loosen the restraints of the moral code, consider entertaining the fantasies that . . ."

"Precisely my point," Lipscombe said.

"Well, maybe that's the way *men* begin feeling when their children go off to school," Diana Blair said, "but I don't think *women* get the urge to wander, or even *begin* to consider entertaining . . ."

"Yes, their fantasies," Lipscombe said.

"I just don't think so," Diana said, and smiled.

"Well, perhaps the inclination toward straying *is* strongest in the male," Lipscombe conceded, and here he glanced at Jamie with what seemed more than casual interest. "And in the case of the middle-aged man who's been married half his lifetime and who can hardly be considered a novice in the field of connubial stress, we've got to assume that before embarking on a philandering course he has taken into consideration the risks involved and the possibility that a marriage of considerable duration may be severely undermined should the relationship with the intruder force—"

"The what?" Diana asked.

"The intruder force."

"Oh."

"Should the relationship with the intruder force become something more than casual and in fact assume dimensions that might eventually destroy the existing marriage."

"Oh," Diana said again.

"In short, the middle-aged man can be forgiven for ogling the pair of teeny-bopper tits thrust at him by every highway hitchhiker he passes—and excuse me, ladies, if you have teenage daughters, as I know some of you have—and can be forgiven further for assuming these young ladies are not entirely blameless for arousing . . ."

"Oh, for Christ's sake, Frank," his wife said, "you sound like a fucking sexist *pig!*"

"I do? Forgive me, darling. I'm only saying that there really isn't much danger in the menopausal male's fantasies or even his acting-*out* of those fantasies with an occasional partner—usually younger than he is, I might add—provided the relationship doesn't *take.*"

"Take?" Connie said.

"*Take,*" Lipscombe repeated. "As with an inoculation for smallpox. We inquire whether or not it has *taken,* whether or not the toxin-antitoxin has been *effective.* In the same way, a middle-aged man's philandering can mean everything or nothing at all. If the romance *takes,* it will oftentimes result in the dissolution of a marriage of many years' duration. End of lecture, and I would like another martini."

"Jamie?"

"Mmm."

"Are you asleep?"

"Mmm."

"What did you think of Frank?"

"Frank?"

"Lipscombe."

"What about him?"

"What he said."

"What'd he say?"

"Always talking about male menopause and middle-aged men running around after . . ."

"He's boring and he's full of shit."

"Always the same stuff, isn't it?"

"Always. But tonight he had a new audience."

"Do you believe any of the things he says?"

"Not a word," Jamie said.

"Not any of it?"

"None of it. Why? Do you?"

"Well, maybe it's just that he keeps *saying* it over and over again. After a while . . ."

"Connie, I've got a nineteen-year-old daughter. When I hear Frank talking about teeny-bopper tits . . ."

"What's she got to do with it?"

"Lissie? Well, if you can't see what *she* would have to do with . . . with . . . with . . . with whatever it was Frank was implying . . ."

"He was implying, he was *stating,* actually, that men past the age of forty . . ."

"Well, I certainly would qualify for that, I guess."

"Yes, you would, Jamie. Are *prone* was what he said. To having affairs."

"Mm. Well, I'm sleepy, honey, so if you don't mind . . ."

"But you don't think so, huh? That middle-aged men are susceptible to having affairs."

"I guess *some* middle-aged men are susceptible and others aren't."

"How about you, Jamie? Are *you* susceptible?"

"I told you . . ."

"Do you find younger women attractive?"

"Younger than whom?"

"Than *meem,* for example."

"No. Besides, it wouldn't matter. If you're asking me . . ."

"Yes, whether you'd be susceptible."

"The answer is no."

"Because your nineteen-year-old daughter in Boston would magically prevent . . ."

"I didn't say that."

"What did you say?"

"That it wouldn't be *seemly* for a man with a nineteen-year-old daughter . . ."

"Ah, *seemly.*"

"Yes, what's wrong with *seemly?*"

"It's just that it's such an old-fashioned word."

"Well, maybe I'm an old-fashioned person."

"Do you find Diana Blair attractive?"

"Diana?"

"Yes, Diana Blair. Remember Diana? She's the one with the big tits who said women don't fuck around when their kids go off to school. When Frank was explaining how middle-aged men . . ."

"Connie . . ."

"Yes?"

"I'm not sure I like being pounded over the head with all this middle-aged shit. I'm forty-four years old . . ."

"Yes, I know how old you are."

"I'll be forty-five in July, and I'm not sure I really *enjoy* being *reminded* of it so *vigorously.* I mean, if there's some *reason* you're *harping* on that asshole's dissertation . . ."

"No reason."

"Then if you don't mind . . ."

"But you haven't answered my question."

"What was the question?"

"Do you find Diana attractive?"

"Yes, all right? In a cheap sort of way."

"What does that mean, a cheap sort of way? Does that mean you'd like to screw her?"

"No."

"I think you *are,*" Connie said. "Screwing her."

"Don't be ridiculous."

"*Are* you?"

"No."

"Then who *are* you screwing?"

"Nobody."

"Because it sure as hell isn't me," Connie said.

"Connie, I'd like to go to sleep now," he said. "Really. If that fucking dope Lipscombe can provoke this kind of discussion between a man and his wife . . ."

"Jamie?"

311

"Mm?"

"You *are* having an affair with someone, aren't you?"

"No."

"Because if you are, you can tell me. Really. It won't be the end of the world."

"I am *not* having an affair."

"Okay, Jamie."

"That's the truth."

"Okay."

"I'm not."

"Good night, Jamie."

"Good night."

They were silent for several moments.

"I'm not," he said again.

She did not answer.

Lying in the dark beside her, listening to her breathing, he wondered why he hadn't told her the truth. She suspected the truth, she obviously suspected it, so why hadn't he told her? Why hadn't he been able to find the courage to tell her he was in love with another woman? How long could he continue living the lie?

"Connie?" he said.

"Yes?"

"Are you asleep?"

"No."

"Connie," he said, and hesitated. "I love you," he said.

She was silent for a moment.

Then she asked, "Why are you telling me this now, Jamie?"

"I don't know."

"Why now?" she asked again.

"I don't know."

"All right," she said, "go to sleep."

"I love you," he said.

"All right," she said.

He could not fall asleep. He lay in bed beside her, thinking of what Lipscombe had said at the party, thinking of the conversation he had just had with Connie.

He had known her almost half his life.

She was his history.

She was bonfires in the streets of New York on election night, and Alf Landon buttons, and Mayor La Guardia reading the comics during the newspaper strike. She was the Lindbergh baby being kidnapped, and the Dionne quintuplets, and the Duke of Windsor abdicating his throne for Wally Simpson. She was *radio*, lines like "Who's Yehudi?" and "One of these days I'll have to clean out that hall closet," shows like "Grand Central Station" and "The Green Hornet," she was Woody Herman coming from the roof of the New Yorker Hotel, she was the Japanese attack on Pearl Harbor and the death of Franklin Delano Roosevelt, the conquest of polio, the McCarthy hearings on television when Lissie wasn't born and Joanna was only six. She was his *past,* she was *himself,* so how could he leave her? He loved her. How could he possibly leave her?

Ah, but he loved Joanna more.

Ah.

He got out of bed, went into the bathroom to take a robe from the hook behind the door, and then tiptoed back to Connie's side of the bed and turned off the burglar alarm. He did not put on any outside lights. In the dark, he made his way barefoot over the flagstone path to the barn, and unlocked the studio door, and then turned on only the light over his desk. It was almost two o'clock in the morning. He dialed her number and waited.

"Hello?" she said.

"Joanna?"

"Jamie?" she said, surprised, instantly awake. "What is it?"

"Honey," he said, "I had to call, I don't know what to do. I want to tell her about us, but . . ."

"Why?" she asked, suddenly panicked. "Are you about to—?"

"No, no . . ."

"Jamie, don't walk out on me again. Please don't do that."

"No, that's not . . ."

"You said you wanted to tell her."

"Yes."

"Then . . ."

"I want to leave her," he said, and paused. "Joanna, I want to marry you."

There was a long silence on the line.

"Joanna?"

"Is that a . . . a proposal?" she said.

"Yes, I think it's a proposal."

"Because . . . Jamie, please don't fool around at two in the morning, okay? Because . . ."

"Joanna, will you marry me?"

". . . because I cry very easily when people I love ask me to marry them."

"Will you, Joanna?"

"Jamie, you don't *have* to marry me, you don't *have* to tell her, no one's *forcing* you to . . ."

"It doesn't make any sense this way, Joanna."

"Jamie, darling . . ."

"I want to marry you, will you marry me?"

"Jamie, Jamie, please, I *will* cry."

"Please say you'll marry me."

"Yes, Jamie, I'll marry you. Jamie, do you mean it? Do you really . . . ?"

"I mean it."

"Jamie, you're not going to call me in the morning and tell me . . ."

"No, I'm not going to do that."

"Because then I'd shoot myself, or stick my head in the oven. So please don't do that to me."

"I won't, darling, I promise."

"Jamie, I love you."

"I love you, too," he said.

"What time will you be in on Monday?"

"I'm seeing Lew at ten. I should be through at eleven, eleven-thirty. Give me ten minutes after that."

"Make it five."

"I'll make it three."

"I love you," she said again.

"I love you, too."

"Call me tomorrow."

"I will."

"Sleep well, darling."

"You, too," he said.

He put the receiver back on the cradle. He took a deep breath, and rose from his chair at the desk. He was turning to walk toward the door when he saw Connie standing there in her nightgown. He did not know how long she'd been standing there, just inside the door, did not know how much, if any, of the conversation she'd overheard. As with most important events in his life, he had the feeling that this one, too, would happen by accident.

"Who was that?" she asked.

"A friend," he said.

"A friend you call at two in the morning?"

"Yes," he said.

"What friend?"

No more lies, he thought.

"A . . . woman I know," he said.

"A woman you call 'darling'?"

"Yes," he said. "A woman I call 'darling.'"

"Who? Diana Blair?"

"No," he said, and shook his head wearily. "Not Diana Blair."

"Then who? Tell me who she is. This woman you call 'darling.'"

"Her name is Joanna Berkowitz."

"Do I know her?"

"You've met her."

"When? Joanna . . . ? Oh. The Vineyard. The one in the gold top."

"Yes."

"But that was . . ."

"Yes."

"Almost two *years* ago, wasn't it? Wasn't that the summer of . . ."

"Yes."

"How old is she? She's just a child, isn't she? She can't be much older than Lissie."

"She's twenty-six."

"Twenty-six."

"She'll be twenty-seven in . . ."

"How long has this . . . did this *start* on the Vineyard?"

"Yes. Connie . . ."

"So what . . . so what does . . . what does . . . you said . . . I heard you say you . . . you . . . you loved her. You said you loved her. So what does . . . what do you plan to . . . what?"

"Yes, I do," he said.

"Love her?"

"Yes."

"*Love* her?"

"Yes."

"Then what . . . ? Jamie, what does . . . Jamie, what do you . . . ?"

"I think we . . ."

"No."

"Connie, I would . . ."

315

"No, don't say it."

"I would like a divorce."

"No. The answer is no."

"Connie . . ."

"No!"

"Connie, I want . . ."

"No, I'm *not* going to give you a divorce so you can run off with a . . . with a . . . girl who . . . who . . . you son of a bitch."

"Connie . . ."

"No older than your *daughter,* you son of a . . ."

"She's—"

"You son of a bitch."

"Connie, please try to—"

"Get out," she said.

"Connie—"

"Get out, you fucking son of a bitch."

On the way from Logan International to the address she had given him in her last letter home, he kept remembering a springtime not too long ago, in 1968, several months after they'd moved into the Rutledge house. They had brought their big black tomcat with them when they moved from the city in December, and he'd run away while they were still unpacking the cartons. One weekend in March as Lissie, home from school, was telling them for the hundredth time how much she missed Midnight the cat, there was a sudden scratching at the back door, and there he *was!* Sitting there and meowing, just as if he'd never been gone for almost four months. "Well, now, hello," Jamie had said, and Lissie had scooped poor bewildered Midnight up into her arms and danced around the kitchen with him and then called Scarlett Kreuger to tell her the cat was home, it was a miracle. He was killed the very next weekend, running across the road to escape a big Labrador who was chasing him. Lissie was back at Henderson by then, and her parents were afraid to tell her at first; it was Jamie who finally broke the news to her.

He was about to break the news to her now.

"You're the one who left," Connie had told him bitterly on the phone, "so *you* go tell your daughter."

He paid the cabdriver and got out of the taxi. He was expecting worse, he supposed. The three-story house she was living in with Sparky was on a residential street lined with trees still bare from the onslaught of winter. A white picket fence surrounded the clapboard

316

building, forsythia bushes tentatively budding against it, jonquils and crocuses timidly beginning to patch the brown lawn. He went to the front door and studied the name plates under the bell buttons. None for either a Croft or a Marshall. He rang the one marked SUPERINTENDENT, and a black woman answered the door and told him his daughter lived on the third floor, in apartment 3B. He climbed the stairs and knocked on the door. It was eleven o'-clock in the morning, he hoped Sparky would not be there. He did not want to talk to her in Sparky's presence.

She was wearing a long granny nightgown when she opened the door. Her hair was sleep-tousled. Her eyes blinked open wide the moment she saw him.

"Jesus!" she said. "Dad! What . . . ?"

"Hello, darling," he said, and stepped into the apartment, and hugged her. There was the aroma of stale marijuana in the air. The living room was modestly furnished with thrift-shop stuff. A psychedelic poster hung on the wall behind the couch. Beaded curtains separated the living room from the bedroom beyond, where he could see an unmade bed with no one in it. He hoped Sparky was already gone for the day.

"What are you doing in *Boston?*" she said. "You want some coffee? What time is it, anyway?"

"Eleven," he said. "Where's Sparky?"

"Must've left early," she said, and shrugged. "Gee, Dad, this is *really* a surprise. Wow! I can't get *over* it. Come on in the kitchen. Jesus," she said.

There were dirty dishes in the kitchen sink. The refrigerator was a relic that had been painted white over its original baked enamel. She took a container of orange juice from it, and then poured a jelly glass half-full. "You want some of this?" she asked.

"No, thanks," he said.

"Sit down," she said, "I'll make some coffee. How's Mom?"

"Fine," he said, and pulled a chair out from the kitchen table. The table was covered with a patterned oilcloth. It felt sticky to the touch.

"So what are you doing up here?" she asked. She had taken a can of coffee from the wooden cabinet over the sink and was searching for a spoon in one of the drawers. Her back was to him.

"There's something we've got to talk about, Liss," he said.

"I'll bet I know what," she said. "That letter from Brooke, am I right? Asking you to pay my half of the expenses from before I moved out."

"Well, I've already paid those, Liss. It's . . ."

"Then what? The long-distance calls Sparky made to Georgia?"

"No, no."

"Well, it must be something pretty important to drag you all the way up to *Boston*," she said, and put the pot on the stove, and struck a match. The gas jet ignited with a small pop.

"Lissie," he said, "your mother felt I should be the one to tell you this."

She turned from the stove.

"What is it?" she said.

"Lissie . . . Mom and I are separated."

"What do you mean?"

"Living apart from each other," he said.

"What? Come on," she said, and smiled. He was watching her intently now, like a scientist gauging the reactions of a laboratory rat. She felt suddenly embarrassed, as if she had done something unspeakably horrible, when really she had done nothing at all. She waited for him to tell her this was just a little joke, he'd come up here to spring a little joke on her, they were still living happily ever after. He said nothing.

"Well . . . when did . . . when did this happen?" she asked, and sat at the table beside him.

"Two weeks ago," he said.

"Gee," she said. She was no longer smiling. She realized her hands were trembling, and she clenched them on the oilcloth-covered table top. "Well . . . where are you living? I mean, if you're separated . . ."

"Mom went out to California. To see her sister."

"Why didn't she call me first? I mean, *Jesus* . . ."

"She wanted me to tell you."

"And . . . where are you living, Dad? Are you still living at the house?"

"No, the house is closed. Your mother'll be living there when she gets back."

"So . . . so where are *you?*"

"In New York."

"Where?"

"I'm living with someone, Liss."

"Someone? Who?"

"A woman."

"What?" she said.

"I'm sorry, Liss, but . . ."

"No, what do you mean? A *woman?* Who?"

"Her name is Joanna."

"Well . . . well, who the hell is Joanna?"

"Joanna Berkowitz."

"Do I know her?"

"No."

"I'm not sure I understand, Dad. When did you . . ."

"Lissie, there's still a lot we have to talk about."

"Yeah, it would seem so. Are you getting a divorce? I mean, is this just a separation, or are you getting a divorce? Can you tell me that?"

"I've asked for a divorce, Liss."

"And is Mom giving it to you?"

"Our lawyers are already negotiating. Jerry Warren's handling it for me, your mother's hired a law firm in New York. We're hoping it'll all be settled before too long."

"And then what?" Lissie said.

"Joanna and I plan to get married." He paused. "Lissie, the important thing for you to know is that divorcing a woman doesn't mean divorcing a child as well. I think you're old enough at nineteen to accept the fact that whereas I'm your father, I'm also a man in my own . . ."

"What does that mean, Dad?" she asked. "Does that mean you don't love Mom anymore?"

"I guess that's what it means."

"Well, don't you for Christ's sake *know?* You left home, you're talking about *marrying* this Joanna person, *whoever* the hell she is . . ."

"Joanna Berkowitz," Jamie said.

"Great, she's Joanna Berkowitz, who *gives* a shit? You're telling me you're going to marry her, and in the same breath you're telling me you *guess* you don't love Mom anymore. *Do* you love her or don't you? It seems to me that's the only important thing you've . . ."

"Lissie, I'm not sure I want to go into all that with you."

"No? Who would you *like* to go into it with? *Joanna?* I'm your fucking daughter, I get out of bed one morning and I find out my parents are getting a divorce, who would you *like* to discuss it with? Shall we get the landlady up here, ask *her* how she feels about all this?"

"I'm trying to say . . ."

"You're trying to say it doesn't matter *what* I think about any of this. Isn't that what you're trying to say?"

"I'm asking you to understand, Lissie."

"Understand what? That you're abandoning your family?"

"I'm doing no such thing!"

"No? What do *you* call it?"

"People *do* get divorced, Lissie. I didn't invent it, it's been around for . . ."

"Oh, come *on*, Dad."

"Honey, I love you, but this has nothing to *do* with you, it has only to do with . . ."

"Nothing at all, right," Lissie said. "My parents are breaking up, it has nothing to do with me."

"It has to do with your mother and . . ."

"Yeah, and Joanna Berkowitz or whoever, but not me."

"That's right, Lissie."

"No, it's *not* right, Dad. Don't try to tell me it's *right,* okay? Because I think it's *wrong,* I think it *stinks.* I think when your father runs off with another woman . . . how old is she, anyway?"

"Twenty-six."

"Great! The girl you plan to marry is only seven years older than I am."

"Well, eight. Almost eight."

"How old are you, Dad?"

"You know how old I am."

"You're forty-four, forty-five, whatever the hell you are . . ."

"I'll be forty-five in July."

"Forty-five, and she's twenty-six . . ."

"Almost twenty-seven."

"Well, if that doesn't tell you something, Dad . . ."

"What should it tell me, Liss?"

"You're the grownup, you figure it out yourself, okay?"

"I thought you were a grownup, too."

"Right now, I don't feel like one," she said, and her voice broke, and suddenly she began crying.

"Honey," he said, "honey, please . . ."

"Jesus, Dad, why'd you . . . ?"

"Honey, honey," he said, and pulled his chair closer to hers, and took her in his arms.

"Why'd you have to do this?" she said, sobbing. "Why are you *doing* this?"

320

"Because I love her," he said.

"I thought you loved Mom."

"I did."

"I thought you loved me."

"I still do, darling."

"Does Mom want this divorce?"

"I don't suppose she does."

"So that leaves only you and this woman who want it."

"I guess so."

"What did Grandma say about it?"

"She said I should do whatever makes me happiest."

"Grandma said that? Jesus!"

"Honey, this has nothing to do with anyone but your mother and me. This isn't something we take a *vote* on."

"I *want* a vote!" she said, and began sobbing again, pressing her face against the rough fabric of his jacket, her nose running, the tears streaming down her face, her shoulders heaving uncontrollably. "I have feelings too, you know," she said, sobbing.

"I know that, darling."

"I know you're a man in your own right . . ."

"I am."

". . . what you said before, but here's a situation that's suddenly *thrust* upon me . . ."

"Yes, I'm sorry for that. But, Lissie, you had to be told sooner or later, and your mother and I thought this would be the best way."

"Without my knowledge, I mean all of this was happening without my knowledge."

"That's true."

"I have plans of my own, you know."

"There's no reason for you to change any of your plans."

"Where will I live?"

"That's a strange question, coming from you, Lissie," he said, and brushed her hair away from her face, and smiled.

"I mean . . . where will *home* be?"

"Wherever you want it to be."

"I want it to be where it's always been," she said, and began sobbing again. "With you and Mom."

"That isn't possible anymore, Lissie."

"It *could* be possible. If you just told Mom . . ."

"No, I don't want to do that."

"I want to see Mom," she said, sobbing. "I want to go to California. Can you give me some money to get to California?"

"Yes, if that's what you want."

"Life goes on, I know that."

"Yes, Lissie, it really does."

"It's just . . . I'm going to need time to get used to this. I'd like to go to California, is that all right? Would you mind if I went out there to see Mom?"

"If that's what you want."

"It's what I want. Could we go to the airport now?"

"What?"

"I'd like to go now. I have Aunt Janet's address, I'd like to pack and catch a plane as soon as I can, and go out there to see Mom."

"Lissie, don't you think you should give this a few days, talk to her on the phone, see if she *wants* you out there in . . ."

"No," she said flatly. "I want to go *now.*"

He looked at her.

"Okay," he said, and sighed.

"Good," she said, and nodded, and then sniffed, and wiped her hand across her nose, and went into the bedroom to pack.

April 12, 1971

Dear Dad,

It was very nice of you to call out here yesterday to wish me a happy Easter, but I think if you had known beforehand what anguish it would cause Mom, then maybe you wouldn't have done it. I have now had a lot of time to talk to her and to get *her* viewpoint on what you plan to do, and I am more than ever convinced that it is not the right thing, Dad. You are absolutely destroying her, Dad, and I don't think you realize that. She is a woman of forty, she was just forty last week, as you well know, and you are leaving her to take care of herself after twenty years of marriage, it was twenty years in February, Dad. Are you sure you really want to do this?

Are you sure you want to destroy a woman who has loved you all these years, and destroy your family as well? I did not think you were that kind of a person, Dad. I hope I am right about you, and that you will reconsider and perhaps give Mom a call here to discuss it. I know your attorneys frown upon private communication, but that seems extremely silly to me, especially when there is so much

322

at stake here. So if you feel like calling Mom to discuss this, why don't you? I'm sure she would be receptive. You know Aunt Janet's number, but please remember that there's a three-hour time difference out here, three hours *behind* New York. When it's noon in New York, it's only 9:00 A.M. out here.

We spent a very quiet and lovely Easter together here with Aunt Janet and Uncle Dave and the boys, and were just sitting down to dinner when your phone call came. When Mom realized who it was, she burst into tears, and it took us an hour to get her back to herself again. Holidays are a very bad time, I guess you know that, Dad. Or maybe you don't, since you've got Joanna whereas Mom and I have no one. We are spending a lot of time on the beach together, getting to know each other all over again. She is really a fine and wonderful person, and I'm so proud to have her for one of my parents. The weather here has been wonderful these past few weeks, sunny and in the mid-seventies. Mom has rented a car while she's here, and we're using it to full advantage, driving wherever the mood takes us, all up and down the Pacific Coast Highway, and chattering away to each other all the while.

I'm not sure exactly when I'll be back in Boston. Mom plans to leave here in a few weeks, and then she will go back to Rutledge. It's her plan to rent the house after the divorce and find a small apartment in New York. It will be very difficult for her to live in Rutledge with the shame of everyone knowing you left her for another woman. Well, that will pass, I suppose. Still, it will be better for her to be in New York, and maybe I'll go back when she does, and try to help her find an apartment. Or maybe I'll run up to San Francisco first to see my friend Barbara Duggan, who is back from Europe and who is now living with this very nice boy she met in London. Anyway, there are a lot of options open. Please call me out here to say hello, and at the same time, if there's anything you might feel like saying to Mom, you could do it then. Shanti.

Your daughter,

Lissie

April 20, 1971

Dear Lissie:

I'm sending this to you at the address you gave me when you

323

called from San Francisco, and I'm hoping you're still out there with Barbara and haven't yet started east. I am writing to tell you that the lawyers feel a settlement won't be reached until next month sometime, but at least your mother and I have agreed that one of us will go down immediately afterward to Haiti or the Dominican Republic for what is virtually an overnight decree.

Considering the fact that Joanna and I plan to get married as soon after that as we can (we're hoping it will be June sometime), I really think it is time you met. Do you think you will be back by the first of May? We would love to have you spend the weekend with us. Please say yes, Lissie, as this is very important to me.

Love,

Dad

May 6, 1971

Dear Dad,

I'm sorry I haven't been in touch with you, especially about your invitation to come see you last week, but there were things I had to work out, and I decided to come here to Boston instead, which has always been a city that's been good to me, and try to make some sense of what has happened to my life. I *do* have a life of my own, you know, and whereas I can understand how important it must have seemed to you for me to meet the woman you plan to marry, it was a bit more important that I come here instead to work out my own future, which has been thrown into such a turmoil by changes I had no part in making, just as Mom's future has been.

Mom told me on the phone last week that she expects to be signing the separation agreement on the twentieth, and will be going down to Haiti that weekend to get the divorce. She tells me this is the way *she* wants it, her going down there instead of you. I guess this is her way of taking the curse off the shame you have caused her. Well, this seems a pretty abrupt way of ending a twenty-year marriage, don't you think, Dad? I still hope you know what you're doing with your own life and with the lives of those who love you deeply.

I don't think I'll be coming down to New York anytime soon, though I may be going to Rutledge to spend some time with Mom

324

after she gets back from Haiti. I have a feeling she is going to need me. Please do not hesitate to write to me at the address on the envelope, which is where I expect to be for the next couple of months. I want you to know that I love you and think about you often. Keep the good faith.

Your daughter,

Lissie

P.S. The address is Sparky's new one. I am still living with him. I know you never liked him, Dad, but I want you to know that I plan to continue our relationship. He is the most meaningful person in my life just now.

It wasn't until the beginning of June that she went to meet the woman her father was about to marry. She went to the New York apartment only because the wedding had been set for the end of the month, and she knew she would have to attend, and felt it might be less awkward if she met Joanna Berkowitz beforehand. Otherwise, she had no interest whatever in the woman her father had chosen to replace her mother.

Late afternoon sunlight reflected in the upper-story windows of the brownstones as she walked up East Sixty-fifth Street, searching for the address her father had given her on the phone two days earlier. She was wearing a wide flapping tent dress printed with a paisley design, and knee-length red socks tucked into workman's high-topped shoes. When she'd left Boston early this morning, her landlady said, "You look like Katrinka, miss." She didn't know who Katrinka was, but the landlady was smiling so she took it for a compliment.

She found the address in the middle of the block, a three-story brownstone with green drapes showing in the ground-floor windows. She took a deep breath, climbed the front steps to a door the same color as the drapes, and rang the brass bell set into the frame. She could hear nothing beyond the thick front door. She rang the bell again, and almost before she took her finger off the push-button, the door jerked open.

The woman standing there, smiling out at her, was truly beautiful, taller even than Lissie was, with straight blond hair falling to her shoulders and framing an oval face with lovely blue eyes and a patrician nose sprinkled with freckles that spilled over

325

onto one cheek. Extending both hands to her, smiling radiantly, she said, "Lissie? Please come in," and took Lissie's hand between both her own, and urged her gently into a living room dominated by a huge fireplace. Her father was sitting in a chair near the hearth. He got to his feet at once. Smiling, he came toward Lissie.

They hugged. He kissed her on the cheek, she returned his kisses. They hugged again. She broke away gently and he went to hang her shoulder bag on a wall peg inside the front door. Everything seemed to be moving in slow motion, her father turning from where he'd hung the bag, June sunlight streaming through the frosted glass panel above the front door, touching his face and his hands, his words coming from his mouth as though at a wrong speed on a broken turntable, he was asking her if she wanted anything to drink and the woman behind him, the beautiful woman named Joanna was saying Lissie might prefer some pot instead, would you like some pot, Liss?

"No, thanks," Lissie said.

"Something to drink then?" her father said.

"If you have some Scotch . . ."

"Yes, sure."

"With a little soda."

As her father went out to mix the drink, she marveled that only a moment ago this beautiful woman with whom she was now alone had offered her *grass!* Did her father smoke grass in the privacy of his little Blond Bimbo's boudoir? That was what her mother called Joanna: "Your father's Little Blond Bimbo."

"How was the weather up in Boston?" Joanna asked.

"Hot," Lissie said. *Oh, great,* she thought, *we're going to talk about the weather.* "This is a nice place," she said.

"Thank you."

"Have you got the whole house, or what?"

"Yes," Joanna said. "Dining room, kitchen and guest room on the second floor, our bedroom on the third."

Our bedroom, Lissie thought. *You cheap cunt.*

"Everything all right in here?" Jamie asked, coming down the stairs with the fingers of both hands spread around three tall glasses. "Lissie?" he said. "Yours is the one on the outside here, you want to just take it? Ah, thank you, honey. Joanna, here's the two cents plain," he said, handing her the second glass. He lifted his own glass. "Here's to all of us," he said.

"I'm not supposed to toast with this," Joanna said.

"Why not?" Jamie asked.

"Nonalcoholic."

"What's two cents plain, anyway?" Lissie asked.

"Seltzer water," Joanna said. "Don't you know the story about Harry Golden and his books?"

"No. Who's Harry Golden?"

"A writer," Joanna said. "He had a big hit with his first book, which was called *Only in America,* and then he wrote another one called *For Two Cents Plain,* which didn't do as well, and then a third one called *Enjoy, Enjoy!,* which did even worse, and finally someone suggested to his editor that the next one should be called *Enough Already!"* Joanna laughed and Jamie laughed with her. Lissie sipped at her Scotch. "Those are all Jewish expressions," Joanna explained, and shrugged.

"You're Jewish, right?" Lissie said.

"Yes. Uh-huh."

"There was a kid at Brenner named Berkowitz, Carol Berkowitz. Do you know anybody by that name?"

"No, I'm sorry."

"I thought she might have been related."

"It's a common name."

"She was a pain in the ass, anyway," Lissie said.

"Maybe she *is* related, after all," Joanna said, and laughed.

"How long will you be staying, Lissie?" Jamie asked.

"What do you mean? Here in the city, do you mean?"

"Yes. With us, actually. If you like."

"My bag's already at Mom's."

"Oh."

"She's all alone in the new apartment, I thought I'd spend a few days with her."

"Well, fine, fine," Jamie said. He nodded, glanced at Joanna, and then took a swallow of his drink. "Are you hungry, Liss? I made a dinner reservation for seven-thirty, but if you're getting hungry . . ."

"I already told Mom I'd be having dinner with her."

"Oh," he said. "Well, I guess I'll . . . uh . . . have to . . . uh . . . change the reservation. I'll do that later," he said, as if talking to himself aloud. "Meantime, let's catch up on what we've been doing, it's been a long time, Liss. How'd you like California?"

"It was fine."

There was a silence.

327

"You're still seeing Sparky, huh?"

"Well, I really don't want to discuss that, Dad."

"I was just wondering whether or not he'll be coming to the wedding."

"No, I don't think so."

"He's more than welcome."

"I'll be coming alone."

"But you *are* seeing him, is that right?"

"What difference can that possibly make to you?"

"Well, your . . . your life *is* of some interest to me, Lissie. I guess you realize your happiness . . ."

"Uh-huh."

"It is, darling."

"Uh-huh."

"Would anyone like some cheese puffs?" Joanna said, pushing herself up out of her chair. "I'll put some in the oven." She smiled at Lissie, patted Jamie's shoulder as she passed his chair, and then moved swiftly out of the living room and up the stairs.

"She's very pretty," Lissie said.

"Thank you," Jamie said.

"So," Lissie said.

"So," Jamie said.

"Where's the wedding going to be?"

"In Rutledge."

"You're not getting married in *church,* are you?"

"No, no."

"Then where?"

"At the Kreugers' house."

"I didn't know they were such good friends of yours."

"They're not, really. They're repaying a kindness, Lissie."

"Uh-huh. To who?"

"Well, to me."

"But not to Mom."

"No. Not to your mother."

"I wish you wouldn't keep calling her 'your mother,' Dad. She's still *Mom* to me, okay? You can still call her *Mom,* it won't threaten anything you've . . ."

"Lissie . . ."

"Aw, shit," Lissie said, and shook her head, and took another swallow of Scotch. "So that's who you're marrying, huh?"

"Yes, that's who I'm marrying."

"Trading Mom in for a new model, huh?"

"Is that what your mother said?"

"No, that's not what *Mom* said, it's what *I'm* saying."

"I love her, Lissie."

"Good, I hope so. You're fucking up everybody else's life, I should hope you're doing it for a good—"

"Lissie, please lower your voice."

"Why do you have to get married in *Rutledge,* for Christ's sake? Must you, must you . . . *advertise* to everybody in that *town* that this is the woman you were fooling around with while you were still married to Mom? Jesus, Dad, don't you have any decency at *all?*"

"Lissie, I wish you'd try to understand. Joanna and I . . ."

"Forget it, I don't want to hear about you and Joanna. Let's talk about the weather again, okay? It was very hot in Boston. The forecasters said it was going to be hot tomorrow, too. What time is it, anyway, I lost my watch. I told Mom I'd be back by six. What time is it now?"

"Four-thirty."

"So soon? Shows how the minutes fly when you're having a good time, doesn't it? I'll just finish this and run along, I'm sure you and Joanna have a lot you want to talk about, big wedding coming up, you must have millions of things to discuss. So," she said, and swallowed the Scotch remaining in her glass, and put the glass on the coffee table, and stood up. "You put my bag in the hall, didn't you, I'll get it, Dad, you don't have to bother . . ."

"Lissie . . ."

"Say goodbye to Joanna for me, will you, I'll let myself out."

She went into the entryway, and took her bag from the wall peg. She shrugged it onto her shoulder, tossed her blond hair, and started for the door. She had one hand on the doorknob when she turned to him, and hesitated, and then said, "I love you, Dad," and went out of the house.

16

The sky was overcast on that twentieth day of June, and whereas the forecasters had promised sunshine for sometime later in the afternoon, Melanie Kreuger was certain her decision to hold the wedding indoors had been the right one.

The house looked glorious.

There had always been in this house a sense of coziness, the massive beams and posts throughout, the huge brick fireplace in the kitchen, the small, bright pantry with the shelves of china Melanie had brought up from Atlanta, the fine mahogany furniture in the living room and wood-paneled dining room, and in all the bedrooms the canopied beds with their butternut head- and foot-boards and the framed photographs of Civil War soldiers who had been the Kreugers' ancestors. But today, and this was the Kreugers' gift to Jamie and Joanna, the house was massed with flowers, the several buckets of riotously blooming daisies on the front doorstep serving only as casual invitations to a profusion of bloom within. The moment they stepped into the house, Jamie and Joanna broke into wide grins.

Larry Kreuger led them into the kitchen where he plucked a

bottle of champagne from the tub of ice at the bartender's feet and popped the cork from it. The bartender looked annoyed as Larry took four stemmed glasses from the row he'd lined up on the wet-sink counter, poured generously into them, and then said, "Before the others arrive. A private toast." He lifted his glass. "Jamie," he said, "you're a good and decent man, and you've found yourself a beautiful and gracious woman, and I wish you both every happiness in the world."

"Amen," Melanie said, grinning.

"Thank you," Jamie said, and hugged Joanna close.

There had been talk in the town that it was too early for the Kreugers to be hosting such a celebration; Scarlett had killed herself last October, and this was now only June, barely eight months later. But the occasion was for them, and Melanie told this to Jamie the first time she proposed it on the telephone, a way of coming to terms with life again, of shaking off the persistent grief that seemed threatening to bury her and her husband along with their daughter. Only this past February had the Kreugers been able to spend an entire evening in the company of friends without one or the other of them bursting into tears. Melanie, her voice soft but determined, told Jamie on the phone that she really wanted to do this for him, and that it would be a kindness if he accepted. She did not mention that the first time she'd laughed since the death of her daughter was at a story Joanna told the first time they'd met, in April.

The guests Jamie had invited from his side of the family, so to speak—in addition to his mother and a dozen or more couples from Rutledge and Talmadge—were mostly photographers and their girlfriends or wives, and one might have thought from the number of cameras in evidence that this was a convention of photographic equipment retailers. Even Lew Barker had brought a camera. "First pictures I'll be taking since I got myself off the street and behind a desk," he confided to Jamie, and then kissed Joanna on the cheek and said, "There's still time to get out of this, darling." The women accompanying the photographers were usually people they'd met in their line of work, which meant that many of the wives and girlfriends were models Joanna instantly recognized from the pages of *Vogue* and *Harper's Bazaar*.

Joanna's father, a jolly little man who had liked Jamie the moment he'd met him, commented that he had never seen so many beautiful girls in his life. Joanna's Uncle Izzy Berkowitz, who used to play first desk with the Philharmonic and who had first engendered in her a love for the cello, idly wondered which one of the bearded young men was the rabbi. When Joanna informed him that a Christian minister would be performing the nondenominational ceremony, Uncle Izzy rolled his eyes heavenward and said, "My mother will die." Joanna's grandmother, the spry old lady who had first taken Joanna to see *Lucia di Lammermoor,* whereat Joanna had fallen in love with the lady flute player and the instrument itself, and who had just overheard every word her two no-good sons had exchanged, said, "I haff no intention uff dyink b'fore my dollink iss merrit!" and Jamie suddenly realized upon whom Joanna Jewish patterned her voice. But in addition to Joanna's many *real* relatives—and there were many; this was her first marriage—she had also invited "relatives" from her large *musical* family, all the musicians and composers and conductors and teachers she'd known since starting her lifelong love affair with music in general and the flute in particular. If, like the photographers, all these musicians had brought the tools of their trade with them, there'd have been no room in the house for the people.

The guests kept coming through the front door.

Jamie kept expecting Connie to arrive.

The wedding was set for three o'clock sharp. At five minutes to three, Larry Kreuger asked if he might have everyone's attention, please, and then he signaled to the minister, and to Jamie and to Joanna, and to Lew Barker who was Jamie's best man, and to Linda Strong, who played second flute with the New York City Opera Orchestra and who was Joanna's maid of honor, and to Lissie who'd been standing near the Welsh dresser in the dining room, talking to some kids from Talmadge, and they all went together into the living room.

The words that served as the basis for the simple ceremony were those the minister had suggested, later amended and amplified by Jamie and Joanna to say what they felt should be said about what they were doing here today, in this place, in the company of their fellowmen. (He kept expecting Connie to walk through the door.) As they stood before the young pastor whose pregnant wife was sitting just near the window which, open just a crack, billowed the sheer curtains into the room, they each and separately recognized the importance of the vows they would be taking within the next few moments, but Jamie perhaps more than Joanna: he had already taken similar vows once in his lifetime, and he was about to take them again.

332

Standing just behind them, watching, listening, Lissie thought the same thought that had passed through her father's head at several different times today. She stood there behind this woman her father was marrying, waiting to hear the words this woman and father had concocted between them to sanctify what they were about to do, looked at this woman, and could think only that somebody was missing here, somebody who *should* have been here was *not* here. As the minister began to speak, she realized who was missing. Her mother. She had been expecting her mother to walk into this house from the moment she'd got here this afternoon. Her father was getting married. But some stranger was standing by his side.

"Dearly beloved," the minister said, "we are gathered together here in the sight of God and these witnesses to join this man and this woman in holy matrimony, which is an honorable estate not to be entered into unadvisedly, but reverently and discreetly. Into this holy estate, these two persons now come to be joined. I charge you both," he said, "to remember that love and loyalty alone will avail as the foundation of a happy and enduring home. No other human ties are more tender, no other vows more sacred than those you now assume.

"James," he said, "wilt thou have this woman to be thy wedded wife, to live together in the holy estate of matrimony? Wilt thou love her, comfort her, honor and cherish her, in sickness and in health, prosperity and adversity, and forsaking all others, keep thee only unto her, so long as ye both shall live?"

"I will," Jamie said.

"Joanna, wilt thou have this man to be thy wedded husband, to live together in the holy estate of matrimony? Wilt thou love him, comfort him, honor and cherish him, in sickness and in health, prosperity and adversity, and forsaking all others, keep thee only unto him, so long as ye both shall live?"

"I will," Joanna said.

"The rings, please," the minister said, and Lew Barker promptly handed him the two gold bands. "The wedding ring is the outward and visible sign of an inward and spiritual bond which unites two loyal hearts in endless love," the minister said, and gave one of the rings to Jamie and the other to Joanna. As Jamie slipped the ring onto her finger, he said, "In token of the vow made between us, with this ring I thee wed." Joanna slipped the second ring onto his finger and repeated the same words.

"Forasmuch as James Croft and Joanna Berkowitz have consented together in holy wedlock," the minister said, "and have witnessed the same before God and this company, by the authority committed unto me by the church and the laws of this state, I declare that James and Joanna are now man and wife." He grinned broadly and said, "May God bless your union and grant to you the wisdom, strength and love to nurture and sustain it forever. Amen."

"Amen," the assembled guests murmured.

Lissie kissed her father on the cheek. "Congratulations," she said. As Joanna offered her cheek to her, she extended her hand instead. Their eyes met. Joanna took the hand.

"Good luck," Lissie said.

With so many musicians in attendance, it would have been surprising if no one played the piano. There were, by Joanna's count, six *genuine* pianists at the wedding and at least a dozen other musicians whose second instrument was piano. Politely but pantingly, they waited their turn at the Kreuger piano bench, and the wedding guests were treated in succession first to Scriabin's *Sonata No. 1 in F Minor* (in its entirety), next to the Allegro and Adagio sections of Mozart's *No. 17 in D Major,* then to Lanner's *Valse Viennoises* and finally to a melody composed on the spot in honor of the bride and groom, the pianist using a system of note-for-letter substitution wherever a letter actually signified a note—as it did with F, A, C, E and E, G, B, D, F.

As the piano-playing and musical hijinks continued in the living room, the caterers—cleaning up the debris of the wedding feast—tried to be as quiet as mice in the kitchen. After-dinner drinks were still being served, and now that the sun had finally come through, the French doors that led from the living room were open to the sloping vastness of the lawn outside. As sunset stained the western sky, some of the guests wandered out onto the grass, drinks in hand. Cameras clicked every thirty seconds. Professional models, even though they were not the stars here today, seemed to sense the exact instant before a shutter-release button was pressed: the smile magically appeared, the hair was tossed, the champagne glass lifted to just the proper height. Looking at the developed prints later, Joanna was astonished to see how many *background* people automatically leaped into the foreground with dazzling white smiles and sparkling eyes.

In the dining room and in the living room, in the kitchen and on the lawn, the conversation and the wine and the music flowed. And in what the architect had called the "milk room" and what Melanie still referred to as the playroom, the Rutledge kids gathered together as they did at most parties where there were grownups and kids, isolating themselves from the adults and filling each other in on what was happening where. What they talked about mostly that afternoon and evening was the five-part series the *New York Times* had begun publishing the Sunday before, under the modest headline VIETNAM ARCHIVE: PENTAGON STUDY TRACES 3 DECADES OF GROWING U.S. INVOLVEMENT.

The kids had not been surprised by the immediate response from the Nixon administration. As soon as the second installment was printed last Monday Attorney General John N. Mitchell fired off a telegram to the *Times,* citing the espionage law and ordering the newspaper to stop publication of this highly classified material. The *Times* had responded with a flat refusal, claiming the government was acting in violation of the First Amendment by invoking prior restraint where freedom of the press was concerned.

The kids all felt it was about fucking time the Establishment, as represented by no less stately a symbol than the *New York Times,* was getting a small taste of the same kind of shit *they'd* been getting for years. It seemed ironic to them that the issue revolved around the Vietnam war, which all of them had been yelling about *forever,* only to have *their* First Amendment rights violated—if not through open suppression, then certainly through ridicule, contempt or intimidation—each and every time they opened their mouths. But oh what a lot of yelling and hollering when the *New York Times* turned champion of the First Amendment now. As far as they were concerned, this was simply a matter of Establishment vs. Establishment, and whoever won the battle it was *still* all a lot of bullshit.

Somebody idly asked if anybody was holding.

One of the kids said he was, and they all went out on the lawn together.

Lissie went out on the lawn with the rest of them.

The plan was to spend the night at the Rutledge Inn, an authentic eighteenth-century coaching house, and then drive Lissie back to New York with them in the morning. They had left the reception at six o'clock, checking first with Esther Klein, who assured them Lissie was sleeping over with Rusty that night, and then slipping out the side door while someone in the living room was playing Schumann's *No. 2 in G Minor.* At the inn, they made clumsy love

335

in a huge old fourposter bed, called down for drinks and a snack at ten-thirty, watched the eleven o'clock news on television, and then turned out the lights. In the dark, they both agreed that if their marriage lasted ·as long as the reception that had followed it, which for all they knew was *still* going on, they'd be doing pretty well.

"Nobody there gives us a year," Joanna said, suddenly very solemn.

"Who says?"

"I *know,*" she said.

"They're wrong," he whispered, and kissed her gently. "It'll last forever."

He was awake earlier than Joanna the next morning, and had showered and shaved even before she began stirring. He went to the bed, gently nudged her, and asked if she wanted him to order breakfast. He called down to room service, and then looked up the Klein number in the directory, and dialed it. It was 9:00 A.M. by then, and he wanted to make sure Lissie was up and around; they had told her yesterday they'd be picking her up sometime between ten and ten-thirty.

Rusty answered the phone.

"Hi," Jamie said, "this is Mr. Croft."

"Hi, Mr. Croft," she said.

"Lissie awake yet?"

"Uh . . . yeah," Rusty said.

"Could you call her to the phone, please?"

"Well . . . yeah," Rusty said. "Just a second."

He waited. There had been something strange in Rusty's voice, a hesitancy, a wariness. No, he was imagining things. He waited. Across the room, Joanna sat up, stretched lazily, yawned, and then plunked her head down on the pillow again. Jamie waited.

"She awake yet?" Joanna murmured into the pillow.

"Well . . . I guess so."

"I didn't get enough sleep," Joanna said.

"Better get up, hon. Breakfast'll be here in a minute."

"Okay," Joanna said.

"Honey?"

"Okay."

She sat up, blinked into the room, sighed, and then got out of bed and padded to the bathroom. Jamie waited. He looked at his watch: "Come on," he said, under his breath. A knock sounded on the door. "Just a minute," he said. Into the phone, he said,

"Rusty?" He put down the phone and went to the door. "I'm on the phone," he said to the waiter, "just put it down anyplace." He went back to the phone, picked it up, said, "Hello?" and got no answer. The waiter put the breakfast tray on a coffee table between two wingback chairs, and then brought the check to Jamie to sign. Jamie added a tip to the total, and then signed the check. The waiter went out of the room. There was still no one on the other end of the line. "Hello?" Jamie said. "Rusty? Hello?" In the bathroom, he heard the toilet flushing, and then the sound of water splashing into the sink. He waited. Joanna came out of the bathroom.

"Did you get her?" she asked.

"No, not yet," he said.

"Well, what . . . ?"

"Hell-o?" a voice said.

"Lissie?" he said.

"Hell-o, Dad," she said.

The voice sent a sudden chill up his spine. It was the voice of . . .

"Lissie?"

"Hell-o, Dad."

"Are you all right?"

"I'm o-kay, Dad."

"Then . . . then why are you talking that way?"

"What, way, Dad?"

It was the voice he had heard people affecting whenever they told the joke about the idiot painting the horse's legs. It was the voice of a moron.

"Lissie," he said, "are you drunk?"

"No, I'm o-kay, Dad."

The same moronic voice, deep and slow, the word "okay" broken in two, with what seemed an interminable pause between the halves.

"What . . . what took you so long to get to the phone?" he asked.

"Did, it, Dad?"

"Yes, it took very long."

"Gee, Dad."

"Lissie . . ."

"Gee."

"You'd better put Rusty on."

"O-kay, Dad."

"Get Rusty, will you?"

"O-kay."

He waited.

"What is it?" Joanna asked.

"Hello?" Rusty said.

"Rusty, what's the matter there?"

"What do you mean, Mr. Croft?"

"What's the matter with Lissie?"

"Well . . . I don't know, Mr. Croft."

"Where are your parents? Let me talk to one of your parents."

"They both left for work already."

"I'll be right there," Jamie said. "Tell Lissie I'm on the way over."

He hung up without waiting for Rusty's reply. Across the room, Joanna was watching him, alarmed. "What is it?" she asked again.

"I don't know, honey. She sounded . . . strange. I want to run over there, I'll be right back."

"Drive carefully," she said, and went to him, and kissed him on the cheek.

He did not drive at all carefully. He screeched the car around every familiar backroad curve, driving the mile and a half to the Klein house in less than three minutes, racing up the gravel driveway, yanking up the hand brake and turning off the ignition in almost the same swift motion, and then walking quickly to the front door and ringing the bell. Rusty answered the door. She was wearing a long granny nightgown and she was barefooted.

"Where's Lissie?" he said at once.

"In the bedroom," Rusty said.

"Where?"

"Upstairs."

He had been in the Klein house before and was fairly familiar with the layout. He took the steps up to the second floor, walking past the Kleins' treasured collection of clocks ticking on every wall, filling the corridor with a sound that seemed ominous in the otherwise silent house. One of the clocks chimed a single note. He looked at his watch. Nine-thirty. Another clock sounded. And then another. As he glanced through the open doorway to the master bedroom, the bed unmade, Marvin Klein's pajamas in a heap on the floor beside it, the corridor reverberated with the sound of all the clocks ticking and chiming. The chiming stopped abruptly. Now there was only the ticking. He opened the door at the end of the hall.

Lissie was lying on the bed, on top of the covers, one hand over her eyes. She was wearing a long granny gown, similar to the one Rusty had on. A shaft of morning sunlight angled through the window like a laser beam.

"Lissie?" he said.

"Mm?"

"Lissie? It's Dad."

"Mm?"

"Are you all right?"

"Oh, yes, Dad."

The same slow, deep voice. The moron's voice.

He took her hand from where it lay covering her eyes. She allowed him to move it. She looked up at him. Her pale blue eyes were glazed. Her face was beaded with perspiration.

"Lissie, what's the matter with you?" he said.

"I'm o-kay, Dad."

"What'd you take?" he asked at once.

"Take, Dad?"

"Lissie, damn it, what did you *take?*"

"Nothing, Dad."

"Get dressed," he said. "Can you dress yourself? Rusty!" he shouted. "Damn it," he said, "what'd you do to yourself? Rusty!" he shouted again.

He heard Rusty running up the corridor. She stopped in the doorframe, as though afraid of entering her own room.

"Help her get dressed," he said. "Where's a phone I can use?"

"In the kitchen," Rusty said. "Or in my parents' bedroom, if you . . ."

"Get her dressed," Jamie said, and went out of the room. As he walked down the corridor, the clocks ticking all around him, he heard Rusty whisper behind him, "Liss? Come on, Liss, we've got to get you dressed," and his daughter answering in her moronic voice, "O-kay, Rust."

He found the wall phone in the kitchen, looked up the number for the Rutledge Inn, and dialed it at once. He asked for Room 412, and when Joanna came on the line, he said, "Honey, there's something wrong here, I don't know what it is, I think she's taken something."

"Taken?"

"Some kind of drug. I really don't know, Joanna, I'm only guessing. I want to run her over to Harry's."

"Harry's?"

"Our doctor. Harry Landau. I'll call you later, honey. I'm worried about her, I want to get her over to Harry's right away."

"All right, darling."

"Love you," he said, and hung up. "Rusty?" he yelled. "How's it going?"

"I need some help," Rusty called back.

He went up the stairs and through the clock-lined corridor. His daughter was sitting on the edge of the bed, wearing only panties. Rusty was struggling to tug a pair of blue jeans over her knees. "Don't you have a *dress* she can wear?" Jamie said. "Something she can just pull over her head?"

"Well, yeah, but I thought . . ."

"We'll be here all *day* with those fucking jeans," he said.

Rusty looked at him, and then went swiftly to her dresser. She found a tent dress in the middle drawer and carried it back to the bed, where Lissie sat motionless, looking down at her feet. "Liss," she said, "let's slip this over your head, okay?"

"O-kay, Rust," Lissie said.

Rusty dropped the dress over Lissie's head, and then pulled first one arm and then the other through the armholes. "You want to put on her shoes?" she asked Jamie.

"Where are they?" he asked. "What shoes?"

"The ones she had on at the wedding."

"Heels?"

"Yes."

"No, she'll . . . haven't you got something low she can put on? Sandals or . . . ?"

"I've got some clogs that should fit her."

"Yes, good." Rusty went to the closet. As she rummaged around for the clogs, Jamie said, "What'd she take?"

"I don't know," Rusty said.

"But she took something, didn't she?"

"I don't know."

"Was there anything there she *could* have taken?"

Rusty came back with the clogs. As she stooped to put them on Lissie's feet, she said, "Well, some of us were smoking, but . . ."

"I'm not talking about grass, Rusty."

"Well, there was some other stuff, too, I guess."

"What kind of stuff?"

340

"I really don't know, Mr. Croft. But I saw some pills going around."

He went to his daughter.

"Liss," he said, "let's go now."

"O-kay, Dad," she said.

She rose unsteadily, wobbled, pushed out her arms for balance, and then clutched at his arm for support. He suddenly realized why it had taken her so long to get to the phone. Looping her left arm over his shoulder, putting his own right arm around her waist, he struggled down the corridor with her, their shoulders brushing against the ticking clocks, Rusty hurrying along behind them, straightening the clocks. As he went out the front door, all the clocks began chiming again, a sustained chiming this time, clock after clock going off and chiming the hour with deep rumbling *bongs* and high tinkly *dings*. It was 10:00 A.M. on the morning after Jamie's wedding, and his daughter looked and sounded and moved like a fucking vegetable.

The Stamford neurologist to whom Harry Landau immediately sent them examined Lissie in private and then told Jamie that she had undoubtedly taken a massive dose of some kind of drug, most likely a barbiturate, which was causing the sluggishness and lethargy. There *were* laboratory tests that could isolate barbitu- rates, but he rather suspected the effects of the drug would wear off in a day or so, and that Lissie would most likely come through the episode relatively unaffected by it.

"What do you mean by 'most likely'?" Jamie asked.

"Well, I don't know how much of the drug she's ingested," the doctor said. "I'm fairly sure it wasn't injected by syringe, I could find no puncture marks on her arms or legs. But she may have swallowed more than one tablet, perhaps even more than *several* tablets, in which case . . . does your daughter have a history of drug abuse?"

"No," Jamie said, offended by the words "drug abuse." His daughter was not a goddamn addict. She had, in fact, told him on many occasions that she would never stick a needle in her body.

"Perhaps she decided to experiment," the doctor said, "like so many other kids these days. And . . ." He spread his hands wide, and shrugged. "She may just have been unlucky. Whatever she took, it's had a serious effect on her. Just how serious remains to be seen."

"What do we do now?" Jamie asked.

341

"Take her home and put her to bed. Sleep is the best possible thing for her right now. That shouldn't be difficult, she's almost out on her feet as it is. My guess is she'll sleep all day today, and through the night, and part of the morning as well. When she wakes up, you'll most likely be able to tell."

"Tell *what?*" Jamie said.

"Why . . . how well she's cerebrating."

"And if she . . . if she still sounds the same and . . . and moves the same?"

"You'd better call me."

He was embarrassed as he walked her out of the waiting room and down to the car, leading her like one of the handicapped children Connie worked with, Lissie mumbling over and over again "I'm sorr-ee, Dad, I'm sorr-ee, Dad" in that same moronic voice, helping her into the car where she sat still and silent, her hands folded in her lap, all the way back to the inn. He was further embarrassed when he led her into the lobby and asked the desk clerk if they could find a room for her, she was his daughter, and she wasn't feeling too well, she needed a room for the night. The desk clerk, a pimply-faced kid in his early twenties, took one look at Lissie, and sized the situation up for exactly what it was: the chick was on some kind of bad trip. But he found a room for her, nonetheless, just across the hall from Jamie's and Joanna's. It was Joanna who undressed her and washed her hands and face, and then got her into bed, and pulled the covers to her throat.

"Good night, Mom," Lissie said, and the words caused a new wave of despair in Jamie.

As the neurologist had promised, Lissie slept all that day, and through the night, and most of the next morning. She was stirring when he went into her room again at 11:00 A.M. He raised the shade. June sunlight spilled onto the shag rug. Lissie opened her eyes. He went to the bed and sat on the edge of it.

"Good morning," he said. "How do you feel?"

He waited.

Lissie smiled.

"Are you feeling any better, darling?"

She nodded.

"Good," he said. "Would you like some breakfast?"

"Has, Sant-a, come, yet?" she asked, and his heart sank.

He was forced to call Connie in New York.

"Connie, it's me," he said. "Jamie."

"What is it, Jamie?" she said curtly.

"Connie, please," he said. "We've had enough yelling and screaming to last us a long time, don't you think?"

"I wasn't aware that anyone was yelling or screaming," she said in her V.S. and D.M. voice. "What is it you want, Jamie?"

"Lissie is sick," he said.

"Sick? What do you mean, sick?"

"She's taken something," he said. "Some drug. She's not . . . not quite out of it yet."

"Out of it? What do you mean, Jamie?"

"Well, she's not behaving quite like herself, Connie. Her . . . her speech is . . . is . . . you know . . . hesitant and . . . and . . . she . . . she sounds retarded, Connie, that's the way she sounds. She slept all day yesterday, and she's sleeping again now, she sat up for a little while this morning, and had some orange juice, but her eyes are still glazed, Connie, and when I called the doctor, he . . . he said . . . it may . . . well, we'll have to wait a bit longer, to . . . to see what happens."

"What did he say may happen?"

"He didn't know. He doubts if the damage will be permanent, but he simply can't say yet."

"Where is she?" Connie asked.

"Here at the inn."

"What inn? The Rutledge Inn, do you mean?"

"Yes. We've taken a room for her. The doctor advised . . ."

"What doctor? Harry?"

"No, a neurologist Harry sent us to."

"What's his name, I want to call him."

"It's Steven Loesch, he's on Strawberry Hill in Stamford, I have the number here if you want it."

"Yes, please."

He read off the number to her, and then said, "I'll call you when I know what's happening."

"Do you think I should come up there?" Connie asked.

"Well, that's up to you."

"I could open the house and . . ."

"She's comfortable here, Connie," he said.

"Still. She might want to be home."

The words hung there.

"I think it might be best not to move her," he said.

There was a long pause on the line.

"How was your wedding?" Connie asked.

"Fine, thank you," Jamie said.

"Congratulations," she said.

"Thank you," he said. He hesitated, and then said, "I'll call you as soon as there's any change."

"Call me anyway," Connie said. "Even if nothing . . ."

"Yes, I will."

"What drug was it?" she asked.

"I don't know, hon . . ." He cut himself short. He had almost called her "honey" through force of habit. Graciously, she did not comment on the slip.

"Thank you for letting me know," she said, and hung up.

By noon the next day, Jamie was convinced she would never recover. Last year, when she'd disappeared from the face of the earth, he was forced to believe at last that she was dead. Now, he believed again that she was dead, the Lissie he'd known and loved was dead, and in her place there was a paler image, a blurred one, an imperfect casting from the Lissie mold. He had looked in on her at nine, and again at ten and eleven, and as he opened the door now, he realized he was hoping she would be sitting at the dressing table combing her hair, or else singing at the top of her lungs in the shower, or brushing her teeth and spitting foam into the sink— anything to indicate life, anything to indicate his daughter was back.

She was still in bed.

As he closed the door behind him, her eyes opened wide. She turned her head toward him.

"Lissie?" he said, tentatively, cautiously. "How do you feel?"

"I've got a very bad headache," she said.

He sat on the edge of the bed, and listened to her telling him—in her normal speaking voice, and at a somewhat breathless pace— that she really hadn't taken anything at the wedding although there was all kinds of shit to be had, uppers and downers and speed and green flats and white Owsley and even some smack, but really she hadn't done anything but smoke a little pot.

What she thought was that maybe somebody had dropped something in her drink as a joke, you know? Kids sometimes did that, like they dropped something in somebody's drink just for the fun of seeing the person get off. This was usually some goody two-shoes they did it to, so maybe somebody decided she was a bit square and figured they'd do a number on her. But she swore to God she hadn't taken anything on her own, and she was sorry for any trouble she'd caused him over the past several days especially since it was right after his wedding and all.

Jamie held her close and said he'd only been worried for her, that was all, and he was glad she was back, he was glad his darling girl was back again.

Dear Lissie:

When Joanna and I returned from the Hamptons after the long Fourth of July weekend, there was a message from your mother on the machine. I called her back and she told me she's concerned about whether or not you'll be returning to school in the fall. As I'm sure she mentioned to you, one of the snags in reaching a settlement sooner was that she insisted I pay for your education until you got your degree, however long that might take you. I refused to do this. The agreement now is that I will pay for your education until you get your degree but *only* if you begin school at an institute of higher learning this September and "diligently and without interruption pursue a legitimate course of study."

What that means is that I'm legally (and willingly, I might add) bound to pay for the rest of your college education but only if you start school in September and continue school without any more side excursions. I think you can understand your mother's concern about this. I don't normally enjoy talking to her on the phone because it always seems to turn into a screaming contest these days, but this time she was level and calm, and wanted only to know whether you'd discussed your plans with me. Apparently, the last time you talked to her, you sounded somewhat vague. So if you get a chance, would you please drop her a line and tell her what you plan to do in the fall?

And while you're at it, how about sending *me* a nice long letter, too?

Love,

Dad

July 12, 1971

Dear Lissie:

The letter I sent to your Boston address was marked "Return to sender." Does this mean that you and Sparky have moved and neglected to give the post office a forwarding address? I'm trying again, but without much hope. If you do receive this, please write or call home, won't you?

Love,

Dad

July 14, 1971

Dear Lissie:

On the off chance that Rusty would have a new address for you, I called the Kleins in Rutledge yesterday and spoke to her. I still don't know why one of your friends would have your address when your father doesn't, but she gave it to me when I asked for it, and I'm hoping this will reach you. You seem to change your address as often as you change your underwear.

What do you plan to do about returning to school? Please let me know as I'd like to arrange for an automatic transfer of funds from my bank to yours each month once you begin. There's still time, this is still only the middle of July. But, come to think of it, the summer will soon be over, won't it, and I would appreciate knowing what the situation will be. Rusty didn't have a phone number for you. If you have a phone now, would you please give me the number in your next letter? It's been too long since I've heard your voice.

Love,

Dad

July 19, 1971

Dear Dad,

I'm sorry I haven't written sooner, but Sparky and I were in the process of moving to this new apartment, which now turns out to be a bummer because our neighbors are bringing up all kinds of shit about the "mixed couple" on the fourth floor. It turns out now we should have stayed where we were, even though the place was overrun with roaches and rats. I don't know how long we will be in *this* horrible place, because human roaches and rats can be worse than the other kind. In fact, we are thinking of maybe going abroad again. I am eager to introduce Sparky to all the places I traveled through last year, where it doesn't matter what the color of your skin is. I know he will be accepted in India, where we will most likely end up, if that is what we decide to do.

I thought I ought to discuss this entire school situation with you, since it seems to be a matter of such importance to you and Mom. I have met a girl here who was studying at the Boston University of Fine Arts, but who dropped out after this last semester, and who is planning to go to India in the fall, to study there, to study Hindu and Buddhist painting. Sparky and I have been talking to her, which—combined with the shitty situation here in this new environment—has caused us to consider making the trip, stopping first in London and then Greece for a little while, and then moving on to join Sondra, her name is Sondra, in India.

This is still indefinite, of course, but the plan would be for me to finish studying in India and then either work and paint or go to another school. With my training in Indian art, I should be able to bring much more insight and concentration into my life. In short, when you ask what my plans for schooling will be, those are my tentative plans at least. I would also study yoga while I'm there, *really* study it, and not just fool around with it the way I did when I was in Greece last year. Anyway, that's the plan. So you don't have to worry about sending money to a bank in Boston. I don't *have* a bank in Boston, anyway. All my love to everyone.

Your loving daughter,

Lissie

P.S. Happy birthday!

July 22, 1971

Dear Lissie:

I can't say I'm tickled. Neither is your mother. I called her the minute I got your letter, and we discussed this completely, and it seems to us that you'd only be running off again, shirking your real responsibility, which is to become an educated, self-respecting and—one day—self-supporting woman. Asking me to pay for an art school in India, where you would be studying yoga and Hindu and Buddhist painting and whatnot is not my idea of a sound preparation for the future. If you choose to make this decision, then please understand that your tuition and expenses will be your own responsibility. Before you leave for India, if indeed that is your choice, I hope you will have enough money to get you there, to keep you there safely and well, and to get you back home when you choose to return. I really thought you would have had enough of India by now, Lissie. I hear the crabs there are the size of the cockroaches in the apartment you just left.

Love,

Dad

July 25, 1971

Dear Dad,

I was extremely disturbed by your last letter. I was under the impression that my education would be paid for until I graduated, no matter *where* or *what* I chose to study. That is my understanding of the settlement agreement. If I am mistaken, please correct me and I will adapt to this situation. But if I am correct, then I honestly feel you should reconsider your position. The settlement you signed is binding in the laws of your society, particularly if it is signed by both partners in a dissolving marriage. That is what a law student here in Boston, a former law student, told me.

In other words, I consider your agreement to send me to school until I graduate a valid and binding contract and if you will not respect this agreement then I will begin thinking of you in an entirely radically different light, and I will also consider taking action to compensate me for my loss. Please allow me to continue my trust in you. This shit depresses me.

Love,

Lissie

July 29, 1971

Dear Lissie:

Croft's First Law. Never—and I mean *never*—threaten to sue your own father. I hate to upset your karma this way, but I think there are some things you should understand, and I'll try to explain them as briefly and as fully as I can. The first thing you should know is that I am well aware of my responsibilities, as I've always been. I don't need legal threats (and will not stand for them in the future) from a daughter whose welfare has always been a matter of great concern to me.

Secondly, your understanding of what constitutes a college or a university or a legitimate course of study seems to be in conflict with mine. I am flatly saying "no" to your studying art in India, unless you pay for it yourself. A few flower pressings and collages aside, this is the first I'm hearing about a talent no one seems to have noticed or commented on before, and I certainly do not intend to encourage it at my expense.

One day you are going to learn that the laws of "my" society are the laws of "your" society as well, and that you can't run off to Timbuktu to escape them or your problems. I love you a great deal, but legal threats from daughters are for Gothic novels, not real life. You could just as easily have come in here and held a pistol to my head. The effect would have been quite the same. I have no desire to discuss the matter further.

Love,

Dad

350

August 4, 1971

Dear Dad:

Since you seem so *positive* about not financing my further studies in India, then perhaps you would like to consider an alternate proposition. Marjorie Kildare is still in Bombay, and I've been corresponding with her, and we think we now know the sort of things we can buy to make a business work here in America. Three hundred dollars would be enough for me to do what I have to do. The Icelandic air fare (this is tourist on propeller-driven plane) is only $182.40, which means once I get the $300, I'd have $117.60 left over for investment. We plan to start with fifty dollars each, like we did last time, which will give us a total of a hundred dollars, more than enough to buy a variety of things, all very legal, which we will then send back to another friend of mine here in Boston, for selling here to the better stores. Buying the goods is the important thing, and I will do that with Marjorie in India, and then use my share of the profits to study art with Sondra. Sparky will be doing his own thing over there, so you don't need to worry that any of the money you send will find its way into his pocket.

So now you see my plan and my motive. I'm trying to make an all-important, well-thought-out stab for my final break. My own life is before me, and I'm ready to start. I will be glad to hear and respect your thoughts. You are still my father, and with that honor you have my love and respect. But I'm in control now and very excited, and it really doesn't matter if you like my plan, it will happen anyway. Love to everyone who cares to hear it.

Your daughter,
Lissie

August 9, 1971

Dear Lissie:

The answer is still no.

Love,

Dad

She called her mother at once to complain, asking Connie for *her* interpretation of the separation agreement, arguing that studying in India was the same as studying any place *else*, wasn't it?

351

Connie told her she agreed completely with the interpretation Jamie had made, and then went on to say that studying art in India was hardly what she expected of a daughter as intelligent as Lissie was (Here we go with the *Vassar* shit again, Lissie thought), a person who should instead be taking advantage of the many opportunities currently available to young women all over the United States.

"Well, that's not the point," Lissie said.

"What *is* the point, Liss?"

"The point is, if I'm such an *intelligent* young woman, as you say . . ."

"Yes, you are, Liss."

"Then I should be able to make up my own mind about *what* I want to do and *where* I want to do it."

"Not with your father's money," Connie said.

"What do you mean? When did you all at once get to be on *his* side?"

"This isn't a war," Connie said.

"I don't see *you* refusing his money," Lissie said. "Those alimony checks that come in every . . ."

"That's quite another matter," Connie said.

"How's it any different?"

"I was his wife," Connie said.

"And I'm his daughter."

"You're still his daughter. I'm no longer his wife. The alimony is small enough compensation for . . ."

"You'll *always* be his wife," Lissie said. "You can't just chalk off . . ."

"You're wrong," Connie said. "It's over and done with. He's made a new life for himself, and that's exactly what I intend to do."

"Talk about fast recoveries," Lissie said.

"Lissie, this is very difficult for me. Please don't make it any harder than it has to be."

"Are you crying?" Lissie asked.

"No, I'm not crying."

"You sound . . ."

"I'm *not* crying, Lissie. Would you like it better if I were?"

"Well, no, of course not."

"In fact, I'm feeling pretty good about myself these days. I've cut my hair, I've bought myself a new wardrobe, I'm going to Europe sometime in October . . ."

"Europe?"

"Yes."

"Alone?"

"Lissie, you sometimes say things that are much funnier than you realize they are. Yes, alone. Europe. In October. Alone."

"Well . . . gee," Lissie said.

"Honey, I have some people coming for dinner tonight, I've really got to get things started. Can we continue this conversation tomorrow?"

"Well, sure, I guess so."

"I'll call you in the morning, okay?"

"Sure, Mom. Fine."

"Goodbye, darling."

"Goodbye, Mom."

She hung up feeling rotten. *However* her mother looked at it, Lissie saw her father's obstinacy about paying for her studies in India as only another example of his refusal to come to her assistance when she needed him most. The thing she desperately wanted (the one thing she could never tell to either of her parents) was to get Sparky away from Boston, show him a world he'd never been privileged to see because he was black and shit upon in this country, and therefore had turned to the only thing he could possibly do to support himself. She had tried on too many occasions to get him to quit dealing, but after all their arguing she was forced to conclude that he was right. What else *could* he do? He'd been born poor, had been forced by this country's prejudice to learn the ways of the street, how to survive in the street, and then had been shipped to a Vietnam jungle where he'd learned that the only people fighting that dumb war were either poor or black or both. If she could only get him away from *here,* into a climate of acceptance, into an environment that was totally color-blind, why then she felt he could finally realize his full potential as a man and as a human being.

She recognized, of course, the danger the East represented. When Paul was planning his big narcotics coup (God, that seemed centuries ago!) he'd had all the statistics at his fingertips, reeled them off to her the minute she told him she was splitting for home, trying to convince her to stay. Afghanistan produced some 100 tons of heroin annually, most of which was exported to Iran, a country that was one of the largest consumers of narcotics in the world. ("Four hundred thousand addicts there!" Paul had told her. "Why would I have to sell to *Americans,* if that's what you're so fucking worried about?") Pakistan produced something between 30 and 150 tons of opium a year, much of which also found its way into Iran. Opium was legal in India, and India produced more of it than any other nation on earth, but most of it was for home consumption. All told, the buying and selling of dope was a common practice in Asia and, yes, Lissie recognized the danger of introducing this free-and-easy trade to someone who was *already* a pusher.

But the danger here was greater.

The reason they had moved from their old apartment, which had really been a great one, despite the roaches and an occasional rat— actually, she'd seen only one rat in all the while they'd lived there— was that they couldn't afford the rent on it anymore. And the reason they couldn't afford the rent was that Sparky was taking the profits he made in his brisk college-student trade and using them to buy dope for himself. He had denied this vehemently at first, told her he'd have to be some kind of real sucker to get himself hooked like the jerks he was selling to. But she knew all the signs, had seen them often enough in Goa, knew he was a junkie even before she came upon him in their bedroom one night, cooking smack in a spoon, and threatened to leave if he stuck that fucking needle in his arm. That was the first time he'd hit her, slapped her backhanded across the face because she'd knocked the spoon out of his hand and spilled his precious shit all over the floor. He cooked up another batch. She watched despairingly as he shot up.

Which was why if only her father could see his way clear to sending her the three hundred she'd asked for, well, then, she could combine this with what she'd been able to hide from Sparky, put aside from her waitressing and baby-sitting, and get them both over to Europe. The way she figured it, he'd *have* to go over there clean because the customs officials would naturally tear apart any young person's luggage, *especially* if he was black, and would find whatever he was holding, and Sparky certainly was smart enough to realize that spending his life in a foreign prison wasn't worth the risk of trying to carry shit off an airplane. So he'd *get* to London clean, and since England had pretty strict laws about dope even though they gave it to you free if you were an addict and a subject of Her Majesty the Queen, he'd *stay* clean in England till they got on the road to Greece, and she'd make damn sure he stayed clean there, too. You couldn't *help* but stay pure in body and mind and spirit on those beautiful beaches in Greece, she had Samos in mind again, she had been very happy there with Paul. She wouldn't even mind if Sparky smoked a little grass every now and then, there was nothing wrong with grass. The thing was to get him away from the needle.

Once he'd kicked it cold turkey in London and later in Greece—she figured they'd spend, what, two, three months on the beach, that was *surely* enough time to kick a habit—then they'd move on to India where she'd get him involved in buying and selling the goods she'd be shipping back to Boston; Sparky was a good businessman who just happened to be in the wrong business. And once she started school there, she'd get him interested in *that,* too, get him to enroll in a few classes, and with the climate of acceptance there, the knowledge that there he wouldn't be just another of America's shit-upon blacks, why then there'd be no problem. Her *father* was the goddamn problem. She was thinking of her father on that night in August when Sparky tried to turn her on.

He had been in the bedroom for an inordinately long time. Her constant fear was that he would O.D. on bad shit, there was a lot of bad shit floating around Boston. She never watched him after that first time, the time he'd slapped her, because she couldn't bear seeing him poisoning himself that way. But tonight, when he went in the bedroom to shoot up, and when he was gone so goddamn long in there, she thought she'd better see what he was up to.

The windows were open wide, this was the hottest summer she could ever remember. He was lying on the bed. The charred spoon, the syringe, the empty glassine packet were on the table beside the bed.

"Hey," he said when she came into the room, and then grinned and waved open-handed at her, his fingers spread like a fan.

"You okay?" she asked.

"Oh, *yeah,*" he said.

"You've been in here a long time."

"Cain't *move,* is what it is. Fuckin' potent stuff Jimmy laid on me."

She kept looking at him. He was wearing only undershorts. His eyes were glazed. The grin perched on his mouth like the monkey on his back.

"Whut?" he said.

"Nothing."

She was thinking that if her father sent her the three hundred

355

dollars they could leave here in a week, pack all their stuff, get the hell *out* of here.

"Y'look too gloomy," he said. He was still grinning vacantly.

"You *make* me gloomy," she said.

"Not now," he said, and waved the argument aside before it could begin. "Feelin' too good, cool the bullshit, Liss."

"If I didn't love you, I wouldn't *give* a damn what you . . ."

"Then love me, an' shut up."

"You're killing yourself," she said.

"Here it comes."

"Yes, here it comes. Sparky . . ."

"Whyn't you jess go on over there to the dresser, Liss . . ."

"What?"

". . . fine yourself that other bag of shit . . ."

"What?" she said again.

"Best fuckin' shit Jimmy ever laid on me. Cook yourself some an' shut up, Lissie. Do me a goddamn favor."

She thought suddenly of that day back at Henderson, when Jenny was smoking pot in the locker-room toilet.

"No," she said.

"Y'*really* loved me," Sparky said, "you'd *join* me, 'stead of fussin' at me all the time."

"No," she said again.

"Go fine it," he said. "Top drawer of the dresser. I'll cook it up for you, darlin', show you how to . . ."

"Not for you, not for anybody," she said, and walked out of the room.

The couple on the third floor were sitting on the stoop outside the building. They said nothing to her as she went by. She knew they were trying to force the landlord to evict her and Sparky. They'd told the landlord there was drug traffic on the fourth floor of the building. She knew it was because Sparky was black, this fucking country. The streets were miserably hot. Her tent dress clung sweatily to her thighs as she walked the three blocks to the bus stop. It was almost nine o'clock when she got to Cambridge. She wandered Harvard Square for another half-hour or so, and then bought a ticket to see a movie, anything to get out of the heat. The movie was a foreign film called *Blow-Up,* they brought back a lot of foreign films in Cambridge, made sure the college kids were up on their culture. It broke at about eleven-twenty, and she was coming out of the theater, into the suffocating heat again, moving past the cashier's booth, when a voice at her left elbow said, "Hey, look who's here."

She did not recognize him at first. He seemed only another of the faceless squares she'd learned to avoid over the years, a dumpy little bald-headed man, blue eyes twinkling in a moon face, a fringe of brown hair over each ear. Then suddenly he brought up his hands and snapped his fingers on both sides of his head like a flamenco dancer.

"Matthew Hobbs," he said. "Light on my feet."

"Oh, hi," she said.

"How's business?" he said. "You want a cup of coffee?"

"Well, I . . ."

"Come on, you won't turn into a pumpkin till midnight."

She looked at her watch. "Well, okay," she said, and they began walking up toward the square.

"So tell me, *did* you ever get your business going?" he asked.

"I gave it up."

"Wise move," he said. He was puffing. "Slow down a little," he said. "Are we running a foot race?"

"I'm sorry, I . . ."

"I've got to lose some weight, I know," he said. "My love life is suffering, I mean it. My roommate asked me yesterday how I had the *nerve* to undress in front of strangers. He wasn't talking about himself, he's not a stranger, I've been sharing the room with him since I started summer school. I'm making up courses, you know? He meant *strangers*. Girls. People of the female persuasion. I'm too fat, I know it. How tall do you think I am?"

"I don't know."

"Five eight. How tall are you?"

"Five nine."

"You seem much taller," he said, and looked down at her feet. "Are you wearing heels?"

"No, I . . ."

"No heels. You're tall. I'm short and fat. Spencer is right. My roommate. Spencer Larsson, he's Swedish."

"Your roommate where?"

"Tufts. I'm gonna be a fucking *dentist,* would you believe it? Listen, do you *really* want coffee? It'll only keep us awake."

"Well . . ."

"You want to walk instead? I can use the exercise."

"Sure, but I have to get home before long."

357

"Mother waiting up?"

"Well . . . not exactly."

"Man in your life these days? I remember when I met you . . ."

"Yes, the situation has changed."

"Brooke Hastings," he said.

"What?"

"You were crashing with a girl named Brooke Hastings."

"Yes, that's right."

"Tempus fugit," Matthew said. "The Charles okay?"

"The Charles is fine."

They walked by the river. A semblance of a breeze was blowing in off the water.

"Spencer cuts his toenails once a week," Matthew said. "How often do you cut your toenails?"

"Whenever they get long," Lissie said.

"Big muscular Swede," Matthew said, raising his arms and flexing his muscles. "Built like a marble statue. Spencer Larsson, where'd a Swede get a name like Spencer? Cuts his toenails every week. Saturday morning. Every Saturday morning. I didn't even know I *had* toenails till I began rooming with him. Well, that's not exactly true. Did you used to chew on your toenails when you were a kid?"

"No."

"I did."

"How'd you get your feet in your mouth?"

"I mean the parings. After your mother cut your nails. Didn't your mother used to cut your nails?"

"Sure."

"After your bath, right?"

"Right."

"So? The parings. Nice clean parings. Toenail soup," he said. "How'd you like the movie?"

"It was good."

"Do you know what it was about?"

"Sure. I mean I *think* so."

"It was about witnessing the primal scene."

"What's that?"

"The primal scene? It's your mother and your father fucking."

"Oh."

"Do you remember the part in the film where he's enlarging the pictures he took in the park?"

"Yes. My father's a photographer, you know."

"No, I didn't know that. Of the couple hugging and kissing in the park, do you remember?"

"Yes."

"And he's trying to dope out what happened? By blowing up the pictures, remember? That's where the title came from, *Blow-Up.*"

"Well, it was also a play on words."

"Oh, sure. But the key scene in the movie is the enlarging of those black-and-white pictures. What's your father's name?"

"James Croft."

"Never heard of him. I thought he might be Steichen or somebody."

"No."

"Does that bother you? That I never heard of him?"

"Me? No. It might bother *him,* though."

"When I meet him, I'll tell him how much I admire his work, how's that?" Matthew said.

Lissie said nothing.

"Anyway, the photographer keeps blowing up all the pictures, bigger and bigger, trying to find out just what the hell those two people were *doing* there in the park. Because he's a kid trying to dope out the primal scene he's just witnessed, you understand? And finally, after all the enlargements, he zeroes in on a big blowup of a *pistol.*"

"Ah," Lissie said. "Yes."

"You know what a *pistol* stands for, don't you?"

"Sure, a cock."

"Right, a penis. So there you are."

"Well, I think that's an interesting way of looking at it," Lissie said, "but I'm not sure that's what the movie was *really* about."

"Did *you* ever witness the primal scene?"

"No."

"Are you sure?"

"Positive."

"No lech for your daddy, huh?"

"None at all."

"What does your mother do? You said your father . . ."

"She's a speech pathologist." Lissie paused. "They're divorced. My father got married again two months ago."

"Yeah, me, too."

"Your father remarried?"

"No, my mother. And not two months ago. Two *years* ago."

"How do you feel about it?"

"About what? The divorce? The remarriage? I don't think about it anymore."

"But when you *did* think about it."

"I hated them at first. *Both* of them. My mother and my father both. I tried everything I could think of to get them together again. That's because I was afraid I'd try fucking my mother now that the competition was out of the way."

"Come on," Lissie said.

"I'm serious. Listen, Freud knew what he was talking about. I never even *liked* my father, I mean there wasn't the slightest bit of communication between us *ever*. But all of a sudden my mother was leaving him for this tennis player . . ."

"Tennis player?"

"Yeah, a pro on the over-forties circuit. Actually, he's not a bad guy. The point is, my mother was leaving my father, and all of a sudden I was desperate to keep the marriage together. I practically got down on my hands and knees, *begging* her to give up this adolescent fling of hers." Matthew shrugged. "I used to be a ninety-seven-pound weakling. The minute my parents separated, I started eating like a pig. You know how much I weigh now? A hundred and eighty-four pounds. That's a lot. I'm only five eight, did I tell you that?"

"Yes, you told me," Lissie said.

"How do you like his new wife?"

"She's okay, I guess."

"How old is she?"

"She was just twenty-seven."

"And you?"

"Nineteen."

"When will you be twenty?"

"In December."

"Close. I mean your ages."

"Yes," Lissie said.

"Makes matters worse," Matthew said. "Listen, you'll get over it."

"Get over *what?*"

"Your resentment, or whatever it is you're feeling."

"I'm not feeling anything at all."

"I thought maybe you might be. *I* sure did. But you'll get over it, believe me. I play *tennis* with the son of a bitch now. Whenever they invite me over, I try to whip his ass in tennis. They live on Long Island, he's got his own court—naturally. I try my best to beat him. It's like I have another father all at once. With my *real* father, I'm going to dental school and trying to whip *his* ass that way, and with my stepfather, I try to beat *him* at tennis. What does your stepmother do?"

"I don't think of her as that."

"Well, that's what she *is,* you know. You know what they call a stepmother in France?"

"No, what?"

"A *belle-mère.* That's kind of nice, don't you think. *Belle-mère?* Beautiful mother? A mother you don't have to take shit from. Very different from the American concept of the *wicked* stepmother. *Belle-mère.*"

"My mother calls her the Little Blond Bimbo."

"Wicked Witch of the West, right?"

"The *East.* They live in New York."

"So what *does* she do?"

"She's a musician. She plays the flute."

"Yeah? Hey, cool."

"Mm," Lissie said.

"You play any instrument?"

"No."

"I used to play guitar," Matthew said. "With a rock group. Well, who didn't?" he said, and shrugged again. "Amateur Night in Dixie, you know, rehearse in the garage, all that shit—Hey, kids, let's put on a *show!* I was the world's worst guitar player."

She thought suddenly of Judd, and wondered where he was these days. And then she wondered if Paul was still in India, and felt suddenly as though time were rushing by too quickly. Across the river someplace, a bell tower tolled the hour. It was midnight. She was about to turn into a pumpkin again.

"I've got to get home," she said.

"Sure. Hey, listen, I'm sorry I talked your ear off."

"No, I enjoyed it."

"I'm not usually so garrulous. Spencer calls me the 'Mummy's Curse.' That's because I'm usually so quiet when I'm with that fuckin' marble statue. Do you like horror movies?"

"Yes. Well, sort of. If they're not too scary."

"Want to go see a horror movie with me sometime? I'm an

361

expert on horror movies. I mean, lady, if you think I know all about the primal *scene,* you ain't heard nothing till I give you my theory on the horror-movie monster as a metaphor for Death."

"I'd love to hear it sometime," Lissie said.

"You just heard it," Matthew said, and grinned. "So how about it? Can I call you?"

"Well . . ."

"See a movie, catch a bite to eat." He shrugged.

"Well, you see . . ."

"Go dancing?" He brought up his hands and snapped his fingers. "Very light on my feet, lady."

"It's just that I'm sort of involved with someone right now."

"Oh, sure, right."

"I'm sorry."

"Will you let me know when you get *un*involved?"

"I don't think that'll be any time soon."

"Everything ends sooner or later," Matthew said.

"I'm not so sure of that."

"Everything," he said, and nodded solemnly.

"Well, *if* it ends . . ."

"Yes, he said breathlessly?"

"I'll call you," she said, and smiled.

"I'm at Tufts."

"Yes, I know."

"So call me," he said.

"If it ends."

"When it ends. Promise?"

"I promise."

"Good," he said, and looked at her, and nodded. "Good," he said again.

August 17, 1971

Dear Lissie:

I've had no word from you, and I'm wondering if you've received my last several letters and the few little things I picked up at Saks and Doubleday for you? I called Rusty Klein in Rutledge yesterday to ask if she had a phone number for you, and she said she did but that you'd requested her not to give it to anyone. I was sure this didn't apply to *me,* but Rusty seemed adamant about it, and when I spoke to her father later, he said he didn't know where she kept her private directory, so I'm afraid her secret (and yours) is still inviolate.

I would call your mother to ask her for the number, but I really don't enjoy talking to her, Lissie, and it would be so much easier if you were to send it to me yourself. Besides, if Rusty won't give me the number, I'm sure your mother has the same instructions, and she'll also refuse to give it to me. Why don't you just call here collect some night, and we can have a long talk and fill each other in on what's been happening, okay? Hope to hear from you soon.

Love,

Dad

August 23, 1971

Dear Lissie:

Well, in desperation, I finally *did* call your mother last night, and she told me she does indeed have a number for you, and has been talking to you regularly but—just as I'd expected—she would not give me the number because you asked her not to.

Lissie, I don't know what's going on, I really don't. Are you still sulking over my refusal to give you the $300 you wanted for your trip? If not, why haven't you answered any of my letters, and why have you given your phone number to everyone but your own father? I really don't understand. Won't you please contact me soon?

Love,

Dad

August 30, 1971

Dear Lissie:

Your mother wrote to tell me you were in New York to see her last week, and that you seem well and happy. Couldn't you have called while you were in New York? Your mother said you had decided not to go back to Brenner in the fall. What *do* you plan to do, Liss? I'm worried about you, and wish you would call or write. I would love hearing from you.

Love,

Dad

P.S. Please call collect.

September 7, 1971

Dear Lissie:

Joanna and I were in Rutledge for the Labor Day weekend, and Mr. Landers gave me a sweater you left when you were there visiting Sally. I am sending it under separate cover. I haven't heard from you in quite some time, and am worried about you. Please call. I miss you.

Love,

Dad

September 12, 1971

Dear Lissie:

It has now been a very long time since we've seen each other. I have no quarrel with you, and I'm not sure even now that I understand your quarrel with me. I know only that if the breach continues very much longer, we are in serious danger of losing touch completely. I cannot believe that's what you want, Lissie. I can assure you it's not what I want. Again, I extend our love and our invitation to you. Our house is open, we would like to see you. How about next weekend? You should have this letter in a day or two, so can we count on the weekend of the eighteenth? Please call or write to let us know.

Love,

Dad

He missed her desperately.

He missed her debris: the shoes and sweaters she used to leave in the dining room or on the hallway stairs of the old Rutledge house, the bathrobe or nightgown draped over a banister; the books strewn all over the house like the discarded pillage of a barbarian army; the unwashed pots and spoons in the kitchen after she'd made popcorn or fudge; the mysterious little seedlings in glasses full of water she'd left on every windowsill; even the bathpowder footprints that trailed across the dark wooden floors after each of her hour-long showers, during which she used every drop of hot water in the house.

He missed her noise: the banging of screen doors; the shouting down three flights of stairs; the blaring of her bedroom record player, the bass turned up full so that all anyone could hear was the insistent thrum of the electric guitar chords; her single-fingered pounding at the piano as she tried to master a tricky passage from this or that latest rock hit, her foot stubbornly nailed to the loud pedal; the sudden jubilant shriek whenever she received a telephone invitation to a party or learned that a movie she wanted to see was playing in Greenwich. He missed her silences as well: Lissie sitting on the deck, staring at the river, sunlight in her golden hair; Lissie chewing a pencil as she pondered a translation from her French textbook; Lissie sitting cross-legged on the floor in front of the usually off-limits living room stereo equipment, earphones on her head, her eyes closed, listening; Lissie's dark and dangerous sulks at the dinner table whenever she felt she'd been crossed, especially by *him.* He missed Lissie's presence and her essence; he missed having his daughter *home,* if only for a brief visit.

He wrote to her again at the beginning of October. He read the letter several times before putting it in the envelope, and then asked Joanna to read it, and finally he retyped it, making a few changes Joanna had suggested, and mailed it off to her:

October 4, 1971

Dear Lissie:

I am feeling bewildered and hurt just now—a deep personal hurt I wake up with every morning of the week. The distance between us now seems longer than when you were in India, primarily because you are now only a phone call away and refuse to pick up the receiver. Can't you see how hurtful your silence is? If it's

365

deliberately designed to inflict pain, then it's unforgivable. If it's simply the result of carelessness or thoughtlessness, then it's immature. You can't expect people to continue caring about you when you show every evidence that you don't care about them.

Lissie, my darling, I feel more and more often that you *never* came back from India. Somebody came back, but I'm not sure it was you. The last time I saw you was just after the wedding, all that horrible mess after the wedding. That was the last time I saw you. In June. And this is now October. But Lissie, I'm beginning to think the last time I *really* saw you was just before you left for Europe without telling us, when you came home from San Francisco just before Easter last year and apologized for all that business with Judd and the argument on the telephone, and then went back to Brenner to live in the dorm, and then disappeared from the face of the earth. I feel as if you've disappeared again. Or perhaps you've only *extended* your disappearance.

I tried to explain to you a long time ago that a man does not divorce his children, he only divorces his wife. I tried to explain that there would be *two* families in the future, Liss, the one you share with your mother, and the one you share with me. Lissie, my dearest, I have only one family now, and it consists of you and Joanna and Grandmother Croft, that is all the family I have. The only connection I now have with your mother is the alimony check I send her every month. You're behaving as if I divorced *you* as well, Liss—or worse, as if *you've* divorced me. What is the matter? What have I *done* to you?

You are my daughter, and I love you. I would like to make a strong effort to restore some honesty and harmony to our relationship. There is much to be said. I do not know whether a more open communication and a renewed, true and valid family relationship rank high enough among your priorities to merit your giving of your time and yourself. That is something you will have to let me know. Our home is open to you. Will you please come to see us? I miss you, Lissie. I love you.

Love,

Dad

She called her mother on the day before she was scheduled to leave for Europe.

"Are you all packed and everything?" she asked.

"Hardly," Connie said. "I'm sure I'm taking too much. I'll only be gone for three weeks, but you'd think it was a year."

"Well, just don't decide to go on to India or someplace," Lissie said, and was pleased when her mother laughed.

"No chance, don't worry. Just London, Paris, Rome . . ."

"Try not to get pinched on the ass, okay?" Lissie said.

"I wouldn't *mind* a pinch on the ass," Connie said, surprising her.

"And be sure to write me, okay?"

"Every day."

"I'd hate to think it runs in the family. Not writing, you know."

"Every day, I promise. If only a postcard."

"Well, some letters, too."

"Letters, too, I promise."

"You sound good, Mom."

"I feel good."

"Does . . . uh . . . Dad know you're going?"

"I haven't spoken to your father since . . . God, I can't even remember. August sometime."

"Yeah, me, too," Lissie said.

There was a silence on the line.

"What do you mean?" Connie said.

"I haven't talked to him," Lissie said.

"Your *father?*"

"Yeah."

"You haven't talked to him since August?"

"Well, actually, I guess maybe longer than that."

"When, Lissie?"

"Well . . . since after the wedding, I guess."

"The wedding was in June."

"Yeah."

"This is October. Are you telling me you haven't talked to your father in all that time?"

"Yeah. I guess. Well, he writes to me, you know."

"Do you answer his letters?"

"Well . . . no, not really."

"Lissie, what *is* this? When you asked me not to give him your phone number, I thought it had something to do with Sparky, your not wanting him to know you were still living with Sparky. Now you tell me . . ."

"Well, let's just skip it, okay, Mom?"

"No, let's *not* just skip it."

"Come on, Mom, I really don't want to talk about it."

"Why haven't you spoken to him?"

"I just haven't felt like it."

"He's your father, Liss."

"Sure, he is."

"What does that mean? That . . . *sneer* in your voice."

"It wasn't a sneer."

"It sounded like one."

"It's just that I find this boring."

"He's your father, Liss. He loves you, he . . ."

"Then he shouldn't have left me. He shouldn't have . . ."

"What's done is done, there's no changing it now. I want you to call him."

"No, I don't want to."

"Then *I'll* call him. And I'll give him your number."

"I wish you wouldn't do that, Mom."

"Lissie, can't you see how *wrong* this is?"

"Mom, I called you to say goodbye, I knew you were leaving tomorrow, I just called to say goodbye. I didn't want to get into a long thing about Dad, really, Mom."

"I want you to call him."

"No."

"Lissie, please do me that favor."

"I can't, Mom, I'm sorry."

"Why not?"

"I'd . . . feel funny."

"Lissie, you *owe* it to him."

"I don't owe him a goddamn thing!" Lissie said.

There was a long silence on the line. Then, in a very low voice, Connie said, "Don't you ever say that again, Liss. Not to me, not to anyone. You owe him a great deal more than you may imagine. You're his daughter. Call him, go to see him. That's all I'm going to say about it."

"I can't understand you, Mom, I really can't . . ."

"Can't you? I'm trying to *breathe* again, Lissie. And I suggest you start doing the same."

She thought she heard her mother sigh.

"I'll write to you from London," Connie said, "as soon as I get there. Take care of yourself, darling."

"I will," Lissie said. "And Mom . . ."
But she had already hung up.

The doorbell rang at ten minutes past midnight.
This was New York City.
"Who the hell?" Jamie said.
Joanna was already sitting up in bed.
"Don't answer it," she said.
The doorbell kept ringing.
"It's another burglar," Joanna said.
"Burglars don't ring the doorbell," Jamie said.
He got out of bed, put on a robe, and then walked through the small library, Joanna's flute lying in its black leather case, silver against green plush, the tiled Franklin stove and Oriental rugs, out into the corridor with the window at the end of the hall where the burglar had come in that time long ago and down the stairs to the second floor of the house, guest bedroom off to the right, kitchen and dining room just beyond the stairs, and down into the living room and past the fireplace and into the tiny entry hall with its wall pegs and the narrow frosted glass window over the front door. He looked through the peephole. "Jesus," he said, and took off the nightchain and unlocked the door.
"Hi, Dad," Lissie said.
She was standing in the doorway with Sparky Marshall. She was wearing a blue paisley tent dress, high-topped workman's shoes, blue knee-length socks and her fighter-pilot's jacket. The leather was cracked and peeling at the elbows, and the fur collar had been worn raw around the neck. The fleece lining was a dullish gray color now; he doubted she had ever had the jacket cleaned. Sparky was wearing blue jeans, brown boots, a brown leather coat and a ten-gallon hat tilted rakishly over one eye. His smile, as usual, was dazzling.
"We didn't wake you, did we?" he asked.
"No, I had to get up to answer the door, anyway," Jamie said.
Sparky laughed. "Thaass a good one," he said.
"Well, come in, come in," Jamie said, and took their coats and hung them on the wall pegs just inside the door, and then closed and locked the door again. He was tempted to tell Lissie that people didn't normally drop in at midnight without calling first, but she was here at last, and he said nothing, simply hugged her close and kissed her cheek while Sparky stood by grinning. She broke

away suddenly, as though embarrassed, and then said, "You remember Sparky, don't you?"

"Yes, sure. Come in, don't stand in the doorway."

Joanna was coming down the stairs in a baby doll nightgown. She saw Sparky putting down a duffel bag just inside the front door, and immediately backed up the steps again.

"Well, come in, please," Jamie said, "would you like a drink? Something to eat? Are either of you hungry?"

"I wouldn't mind some Scotch over ice," Lissie said.

"You got anythin' sweet?" Sparky asked, and Lissie glanced at him sharply. "Some chocolate or somethin'?"

"I'll see what's in the kitchen," Jamie said. "Joanna," he called as he started up the stairs. "It's Lissie!"

"Hey, hi," Joanna yelled down from the top floor. She had put on a bathrobe and was starting down the stairs again. "What a surprise!" As she moved past Jamie on the second-floor landing, she whispered, "Who's that with her?"

"Sparky Marshall."

They were sitting in the easy chairs before the fireplace when Joanna came into the room. Sparky got to his feet at once.

"Joanna, I don't think you've met Sparky," Lissie said.

"Pleasure," Sparky said.

"My father's wife," Lissie said. "Joanna."

Joanna extended her hand.

"Sparky Marshall," Lissie said.

"For Spartacus the slave. My great-granddaddy was a—"

"Oh, lay off the slave shit, will you?" Lissie said.

"Well . . . please," Joanna said, "sit down. Is your father getting you something to drink?"

"Is that a television I see there in the bookcase?" Sparky said. "Mind if I catch a little Carson?"

"Well, no, go right ahead."

Jamie came back with the Scotch for Lissie and a bag of chocolate chip cookies. "All I could find," he said, handing them to Sparky who had turned on the television set, and was now sitting cross-legged on the floor in front of it. "You *did* want ice in this, didn't you, Liss?" Jamie said.

"Yes, thanks," she said, and took the glass. In front of the television set, Sparky dug into the bag of chocolate chip cookies, and then laughed at a joke Johnny Carson told.

There was a long silence.

"Well," Jamie said, "this is certainly a surprise."

"You said I was welcome any time," Lissie said.

"Well, of *course* you are, darling."

"Mom's in Europe, and we felt like spending a few days in New York, so here we are," she said, and spread her arms wide, almost spilling some of the Scotch in her glass. "Oops," she said, and grinned, and brought the glass swiftly to her lips.

"You look great, Liss," Jamie said. "Doesn't she look great, Joanna?"

"Yes," Joanna said, and smiled.

"This guy kills me," Sparky said, laughing.

"So how's it going up in Boston?" Jamie said.

"Colder'n a witch's tit up there," Sparky said. "Ony October an' I'm freezin my ass off."

"Are you still living in the same . . . ?"

"Yeah, well, you know," Lissie, "it's tough to find a decent apartment in Boston. Unless you have tons of money, of course."

"Sure, all those college kids up there," Joanna said, nodding.

"Yeah, that's just it. The nice places are pretty scarce."

"'Specially when you're doin' a black-on-white number," Sparky said, and dug into the bag of cookies again.

Lissie glanced at him again, and then—in needless explanation, it seemed to Jamie—said, "Sweet tooth," and smiled nervously.

"This's real nice here," Sparky said, digging into the bag, looking around. The bag was empty. He crumpled it, and tossed it at the fireplace, missing. Joanna got up from where she was sitting, picked up the bag where it lay on the hearth, and placed it on the grate.

"Listen,'' Sparky said, getting to his feet abruptly and turning off the television set, "you mind if we continue this in the mornin'? I'm really whacked out." He turned to Joanna. "Where you want us, Joanna?"

"Well . . . I guess one of you can use the couch here," she said, "and . . ."

"There's a guest room, isn't there?" Lissie said at once.

"Well, yes, but . . ."

"I think it'll be okay if they use the guest room," Jamie said.

Joanna looked at him.

Lissie smiled.

Sparky went to where he'd dropped the duffel just inside the front door, hefted it by its strap onto his shoulder and said, "Just lead the way."

"It's upstairs," Jamie said.

Joanna was still looking at him.

"G'night, Joanna," Sparky said over his shoulder.

"Good night, Joanna," Lissie said.

"Good night," Joanna said. She picked up the glass Lissie had left on the floor, and then watched them as they went up the stairs behind Jamie. As she carried the glass into the kitchen, she saw Lissie and Sparky down the hall, just outside the guest-room door. Lissie peeked in, and then whispered something to Sparky. Sparky giggled. Together, they went into the room.

"Good night, Dad," Lissie said, and closed the door.

"Good night," Jamie said, and turned to see Joanna standing just outside the entrance to the kitchen. He went to her and said, "You okay, honey?"

"Sure," Joanna said.

In bed again, she was silent for a long time. Then, at last, she said, "How long will they be staying?"

"I don't know."

"You *did* ask her to call first, didn't you? In your letter, I mean."

"I don't remember."

"I mean, you didn't tell her it would be okay to just . . ."

"Honey, she's *here.*"

". . . barge in at midnight, did you? Most people are asleep at midnight, unless they're . . ."

"Honey, I haven't seen her since June . . ."

". . . night watchmen or . . ."

"Joanna," he said. "Please."

The bedroom went silent.

"She's my daughter," he said. "We haven't seen each other or talked to each other in four months. She's here now. I'm glad she's here, and I hope this'll be the start of a better . . . a better relationship between the two of us."

"I hate that fucking word *relationship.*"

"Well, whatever you want to call it," he said.

"What are we supposed to do about tomorrow?"

"I don't know."

Tomorrow—or rather *today,* since it was already ten minutes to one on Sunday morning—was the tenth of October, and Joanna's grandmother had invited them to her house in Great Neck to be with the family on Yom Kippur. Joanna wasn't religious, and had no intention of spending any time at all in the synagogue with her

372

relatives, listening to the cantor intoning "Kol Nidre," and then fidgeting through the subsequent prayers and the Confession with its fifty-six categories of sin (*all* of which she was certain she'd committed at one time or another) and its attendant breast-beating. But sundown and the call of the *shofar* signaled—at her grandmother's house, anyway—the start of a feast of enormous proportions, the end of a long day of fasting, prayer and introspection. If there was one day in the Jewish calendar that spoke most strongly to the Jewish conscience and sensibility, it was Yom Kippur. They had planned to leave the apartment sometime around four tomorrow afternoon. But now Lissie and Sparky were here.

"Damn it, I *wish* she'd called first," Joanna said.

"I don't see any problem," Jamie said. "We'll spend the day with them, and then just . . ."

"Just what?"

"Well, she can just run over to her mother's," Jamie said.

"No, her mother's in Europe, you heard her say her mother's in Europe. You also heard her say they felt like spending a few days in New York. Suppose they want to spend them *here?*"

"I still don't see any problem."

"The problem is I don't want to leave them here alone."

"Why not?"

"I just don't want to."

"She's my daughter."

"Sparky isn't."

"Well, then I'll . . . I'll just have to tell Lissie we've made other plans, and we're sorry, but we'll have to leave."

"And *they'll* have to leave when we do."

"Yes," he said, and hesitated. "That's what I'll have to tell her."

Oddly, he thought immediately of Lissie's restriction to campus when she was still a student at the Henderson School, and Connie's refusal to cancel her plans for the weekend.

"You sound uncertain," Joanna said.

"No, no, I'll tell her, don't worry," Jamie said.

Joanna hugged him close.

"Maybe I married a *mensh,*" she said.

At nine the next morning, Jamie knocked on the guest bedroom door.

"Mm?" Lissie said.

"Honey, it's Dad."

"What is it, Dad?" she asked sleepily.

373

"Time to get up," he said.

"What?"

"Time to get up."

"What time is it?"

"Nine o'clock."

"That's the crack of dawn, Dad."

"I know it's early, but we've got a busy day planned, and I'd like you to get up now, okay?"

"What kind of busy day?"

"Lissie, honey, just get up, please, we'll discuss it over breakfast."

"Well . . . okay," she said. He waited outside the closed door. "Sparky," she said gently. "Honey. We have to get up."

"Whut the fuck *for?*" Sparky mumbled.

"They've got plans for us."

"*I* got plans for us, too, baby," he said, and began laughing.

"No, not now, honey, really, we have to get up."

"Whyn't you just bring that sweet l'il mouth down here?" he whispered.

"Sparky," she whispered, "we *really* have to . . ."

"Come on down here," he whispered.

Jamie turned away from the door and walked back down the hallway to the kitchen. The coffee was perking. The toaster popped up two slices of bread as he came through the door.

"Did you wake them?" Joanna asked.

"Yeah," Jamie said, and nodded.

"Better tell them this coffee's ready."

"Well . . . not just now," Jamie said.

She looked at him.

He nodded.

They did not come out of the bedroom until a quarter past ten. Jamie and Joanna were still sitting at the kitchen table, finishing their second cups of coffee.

"Good morning," Lissie said. "Mm, that coffee smells good."

"Got any orange juice?" Sparky asked, pulling out a chair and sitting beside Joanna.

"In the refrigerator," Joanna said.

"Liss?"

Lissie opened the refrigerator, took out the container of orange juice, and poured some into two glasses. She carried them to the table and then sat down beside Sparky.

"Some eggs would really hit the spot, Joanna," she said.

"We're just having a light breakfast," Jamie said. "You see, what I thought we'd do . . ."

"Yeah, what *are* all these big plans you've made for us, Dad?"

"Well, I thought we'd all go out to an early lunch together, twelve-thirty, something like that, and then go over to the Modern, if you like . . ."

"What's the modern?" Sparky asked.

"The museum," Lissie said.

"Oh, terrif," Sparky said, and rolled his eyes.

"Spend a little time together walking, whatever," Jamie said. "It's like a spring day outside, you won't even need your jacket."

"Wisht it was springtime in Boston," Sparky said, and rolled his eyes again.

"Get off the nigger act, will you, please?" Lissie said.

"The thing is," Jamie said, glancing at Joanna, "we'll have to cut our visit a little short. I don't know whether you planned to spend the night here or not, but we've made other plans, you see."

"Oh? What other plans?" Lissie asked.

"We're going out to Great Neck. To spend Yom Kippur with Joanna's folks."

"That's when they blow the chauffeur, ain't it?" Sparky said, and grinned.

"We'll be leaving here about four," Jamie said, and hesitated. "So . . . I . . . I guess you and Sparky'll have to make other arrangements for tonight."

"What do you mean, other arrangements?" Lissie said.

"Some place else to stay."

"Great," Sparky said. "We come all the way down from Boston . . ."

"Well, we can still spend the entire afternoon together . . ."

"Sure, till four o'clock, when you'll be splitting."

"We were hoping we'd, you know, see a lot of you over the next few days," Lissie said. "We hitched all the way down . . ."

"I'm sorry about that, Liss."

"Hey, don't sweat it, really," she said. "We'll just have to make the best of it. I'm sorry we got here so late last night, but we had a tough time catching rides. Anyway," she said, and shrugged and went back to the stove. She came back with the coffeepot, poured some into the cups on the table, returned the pot to the stove, and then sat down beside Sparky again.

"If we're going for an early lunch," Joanna said, "I'd better get started. Excuse me," she said, and went out of the kitchen.

"I'll be skippin' lunch, if you don't mind," Sparky said, and Lissie quickly looked at him. "Got some business uptown," he explained to Jamie. "Have to take a rain check." He looked at his watch. "Fact, I better get crackin'," he said, and pushed back his chair.

They were alone in the kitchen.

"So," Lissie said.

"I'm really sorry about this," Jamie said.

"The thing of it is Mom's not here, either, you know. I came down here just to see *you*. Now it's turning into a big *lunch* type thing." She shook her head. "I thought we'd have a chance to talk, you know."

"Well, if . . ."

"Instead, it'll be, you know, polite chitchat. I think we've got more to say to each other than just polite chitchat, Dad."

"Would you like me to ask Joanna . . . ?"

"No, no, I don't want to upset Joanna."

"I'm sure she wouldn't mind if we had lunch alone. Just the two of us."

"Well, that's what I'd *like*, really, but if it'll upset Joanna . . ."

"I'll ask her."

"I'd appreciate it, Dad," she said, and suddenly hugged him.

Over tempura and sukiyaki in a Japanese restaurant on West Fifty-fifth Street, she told him how truly sorry she was not for having been in real touch with him since June, but she'd had her own life to work out, she'd been in the midst of trying to pick up the wreckage of her own life. And then, startling him because she seemed to be in the midst of an apology, she said, "But I guess you don't much care about other people's lives, do you, Dad?"

"Lissie," he said, "peace," and smiled and covered her hand with his own. "I'm sure you didn't come all the way to New York to argue with me."

"Well, I wasn't aware we were arguing," she said. "I'm trying to have a meaningful discussion here. That's what you asked for in your letter, isn't it? A more *open* communication? Okay, I'm trying to communicate."

"Well, it's not really communication when you accuse me of . . ."

376

"I didn't *accuse* you of anything," Lissie said. "I simply *asked* whether you cared much about other people's lives."

"I care about *your* life, yes, Lissie."

"How about Sparky's life? Do you care about his life?"

"I hardly know Sparky."

"You could get to know him better . . ."

"Lissie . . ."

". . . if you'd make any kind of effort. I mean, we're both decent people, Dad, you don't have to . . ."

"I know you are. But, Lissie, I really don't want to talk about Sparky just now."

"What *do* you want to talk about, Dad?"

"I want to know what's happening to us. I want to mend whatever . . ."

"It's a little late to be asking that, isn't it?"

"No, I don't think so. If I thought it was too late, I wouldn't have written that letter to you."

"Okay, then," she said. "Let's start all over again."

"Please," he said, and squeezed her hand.

"Let's get it all out of our systems, let's clear the air."

"That's just what I want to do."

"So," she said.

"So," he said, and paused. "I've always leveled with you, Liss . . ."

"I know you have."

"Not because you're a decent person, which I've never doubted, by the way, but also because you're my daughter. And I love you."

"I love you, too, Dad."

"It's just that each and every time we've tried to communicate recently . . ."

"I know."

"You've misunderstood my concern and interpreted it instead as anger or . . ."

"No, I . . ."

". . . or reprimand, or scorn . . ."

"Well, guilt-ridden was what I thought."

"Whatever."

"Yes," she said, and nodded.

"When all I was trying to do was understand what was happening to us."

"Yes."

"I'd like to correct that situation, Liss. I really would."

"So would I."

"If you love me as much as you love your . . . as much as you love *Mom* . . . then *my* happiness and welfare should at least be of some concern to you."

"It is, Dad."

"I'm very happy with Joanna, Liss."

"I'm glad about that. Really I am."

"And I hope to stay married to her for the rest of my life."

"Good, I hope so, too, Dad."

"I've been trying to keep a dialogue open between us, Liss, you know I have. I've invited you here repeatedly without response, I've sent gifts without your acknowledgment . . ."

"Well, I've been going through a lot, you know. Sparky . . ."

"Yes, I know that. But still . . ."

"Anyway, that's what we're trying to put behind us, isn't it? I mean, I'm here, we're together again . . ."

"But shouldn't we discuss this, Liss? I mean . . ."

"Sure, let's get it all out in the open."

"I really *do* want you to be a part of this family."

"That's what *I* want, too."

"But it won't work if you continue to believe your mother . . . *Mom* . . . was unfairly treated. Isn't that what you really believe, Liss?"

"Well, yes, Dad. Sort of. But I'll get over it."

"But *why* do you feel that way, Lissie? It wasn't your mother who rushed up to the Henderson School every weekend when you were confined to campus, it was me. It wasn't your mother . . . Mom . . . who nursed you through that drug episode in June. When you tell me . . ."

"Yeah, Dad, but *you're* the one who *left,* not Mom."

"Okay, I admit that. But in people's lives . . ."

"And you know, being great in tragedies doesn't necessarily mean a person's good at other things, too, you know what I mean?"

"I didn't mean that to sound . . ."

"No, I know. But, like, what am I supposed to say to that? Gee, too bad there weren't *more* tragedies? I mean, do you see what I mean?"

"Yes, Lissie. But I've *tried* to be a good father in other ways as well. I wasn't saying that rushing you to the doctor . . ."

"Oh, I know that. I meant . . . like . . . well, for example, I had to learn from *Mom* just how long this thing with Joanna had been going on. You expect your welfare to be of some concern to me, but you never *tell* me anything. So how can you expect . . . I mean, it was going on for two *years,* Dad. And God knows how many other women . . ."

"There were never any other women."

"Well, Mom doesn't seem to think that was the case."

"Mom is wrong."

"She thinks you had an affair with Mrs. Blair, for example."

"I didn't."

"Well, she thinks so."

"Your mother . . ."

"It doesn't really matter, anyway, does it? I mean, who *cares* about that, that's not the point. The point . . ."

"The point is I wasn't."

"Okay, you weren't, let's say you weren't. The point is you didn't choose to tell *me* any of this, I had to hear it from Mom. *She's* the one who tells me things, she's the one who accepts me for what I *am,* Dad."

"What are you, Lissie?" he said. "Please tell me what you are."

"You know what I am, Dad. I'm a hippie."

"A hippie," he repeated, and nodded.

"A hippie, yes, Dad."

"Well," he said, and sighed. "I guess it's okay to call yourself a hippie and go running around the street in secondhand clothes when you're only nineteen. But if you're *still* running around the street that way when you're forty, then you're not a hippie anymore, Liss, you're a *bum.*"

"What are you saying, Dad?"

"I think you know what I'm saying."

"You're calling me a bum, right?"

"No, I'm not. But, Liss, have you reenrolled at school, for example?"

"You know I haven't."

"Have you made any plans at all for the future?"

"Not yet."

"What kind of work are you doing now, Liss?"

"Baby-sitting. Waitressing. Like that," she said, and shrugged.

"And when you're forty?"

"My life-style doesn't have to change simply because I get older.

I don't *need* as much as you do, Dad. I don't *need* an apartment with a dozen rooms in it . . ."

"Six, Liss."

"I don't *need* vacations in the Caribbean . . ."

"You never seemed to complain about them when you were . . ."

"I don't *need* a goddamn fancy sports car . . . what are you driving these days, Dad? What's Joanna driving?"

"Is that your quarrel with us? Our life-style?"

"I don't have any quarrel with you."

"Then why haven't you written? Or called?"

"I've been busy making my own life. You kicked me out of your life, so now I'm trying to make a life of my own. Is there anything wrong about that?"

"Only the part about kicking you out. Nobody's done that, Lissie."

"No. Then what was marrying Joanna?"

"Marrying Joanna was . . ."

"Was kicking out me and Mom, that's what it was."

"No, Lissie."

"No? Then what's today? The same thing all over again, isn't it?"

"What do you mean?"

"We come all the way down from Boston to see you, and you go running off to Long Island. Okay, maybe Yom Kippur is important to Joanna . . ."

"It's *the* most important Jewish—"

"When did you get to be Jewish, Dad? The point is, do you have to kick us out into the street? Do you know what checking into a hotel tonight'll mean for Sparky and me? Do you have any idea what kind of white-black shit we get dumped on us all the time?"

Jamie glanced at the waitress hovering near one of the screens shielding the kitchen.

"Oh, *fuck* her," Lissie said, "this is your daughter here."

"What do you want me to do, Lissie?"

"What time will you be back tonight?"

"Late."

"So can't we stay in the apartment while you're gone? I mean, will that be such a big deal? If we spent another night with you?"

"I'm not sure how Joanna would feel about that," he said, even though he already knew *exactly* how Joanna felt about it.

"Well, yeah, Joanna," Lissie said.

"But I'll ask her," he said.

"It *would* be a big help, Dad," Lissie said. "You've got no idea what we go through, I mean it."

"Let me ask her," he said, and covered her hand with his own. "I'm sure it'll be all right."

She put her hand over his, and suddenly grinned across the table at him. "Do you know what I used to love with all my heart?" she asked.

"What's that, Lissie?"

"When you used to hang my pictures in the living room. On all my birthdays. Do you remember that, Dad? When you used to hang my pictures?"

"Yes, I remember," he said, and turned away to signal for the check because he did not want her to see the sudden rush of tears to his eyes.

Joanna was sitting in half-slip and bra at the dressing table, putting on her face, when he came into the bedroom at three that afternoon.

"How'd it go?" she asked.

"Fine, I think."

"The *talk,* I mean, not the lunch."

"The talk especially," he said, and went to her and put his hand on her shoulder.

"Well, good, darling," she said, and smiled at him in the mirror. "Is Sparky back yet?"

"No, not yet."

"Well, what are we . . . ?" She turned and looked at the clock on the bedside table. "We'll be leaving in an hour, Jamie."

"Lissie asked if they could spend the night."

"What'd you tell her?" Joanna said, and looked up at him.

"That I'd discuss it with you."

"The answer is no."

"Why?"

"Because I don't like the idea."

"If you didn't mind the idea of them sleeping together in the guest room *last* night . . ."

"Who *says* I didn't mind the idea?"

"Joanna, she's nineteen years old. That's old enough to be treated like a grownup. When *you* were nineteen . . ."

"When *I* was nineteen, I didn't bring *men* home to my father's house. I spared him at *least* that, Jamie."

"I'd like to do her this one favor," Jamie said.

"One favor? Jesus! You've been running yourself ragged over her ever since I've known you. A *million* and one favors, you mean."

"I don't want her to have to check into a hotel, Joanna. I think that would be difficult for her."

"Fine, then, do what you like."

"I want your okay on it."

"Why? You live here, too, don't you?"

"Then I'll tell her she can stay, okay?"

"Sure."

"Joanna?"

"I said sure."

"Okay, that's what I'll do."

"Fine."

"I'll tell her," Jamie said, and went out of the room.

It was almost two in the morning when they got back to the Sixty-fifth Street apartment. The weather had turned cold again; he fumbled with stiff fingers to insert the key into the lock, and then opened the door, and turned on the table lamp in the entryway. There was the smell of marijuana in the air, Joanna detected it at once. Jamie went into the living room, snapped on the lights, and then stopped dead in his tracks, as though unexpectedly struck in the face by an unseen intruder. Joanna, turning from where she was hanging her coat on a wall peg beside Lissie's fighter-pilot jacket, opened her eyes wide, and then went to stand speechlessly beside him. Aghast, they looked into the room.

A trail of debris stretched from the bay window fronting the street to the staircase leading to the upper stories, the flotsam and jetsam of what seemed to have been a wild party. Empty whiskey bottles lay scattered on the floor, glasses were on every table top. The ashtrays were bulging with butts and marijuana roaches, and someone had ground out a cigarette on the polished marble top of the mail table just inside the entrance door. A fire had been started in the fireplace, a log still smoldered there. But the screen had not been replaced afterward, and there were blown ashes and several large scorch marks on the Oriental rug just beyond the hearth. Someone had spilled a drink on one of the red plush-velvet easy chairs that flanked the fireplace. A white sweat sock was draped over one of the lampshades. A pair of panties, the crotch stained with what appeared to be menstrual blood, was crumpled on the floor near the big brass wood bucket.

Like hunters tracking a wild beast loose in their midst, they followed the spoor up the carpeted steps to the second floor of the building. The refrigerator door had been left ajar; its light cast illumination into the kitchen, revealing the stack of dirty dishes in the sink even before Jamie snapped on the overheads. A loaf of bread, an open box of cornflakes, a container of milk, a melting slab of butter were on the kitchen table. The mate to the sweat sock in the living room was on the range top, alongside a copper kettle that had been blackened because the flame under it had been allowed to burn too long and too hot. Down the hall, in the guest bedroom, the bed was unmade, and there were blankets and pillows on the floor. Whoever owned the stained panties in the living room had left her track upstairs as well, her menstrual blood ripening one of the white monogramed bath towels that had been a wedding gift from Joanna's grandmother. Popcorn, matchsticks and newspapers trailed an uneven path across the carpeting. On the night table beside the bed, there was a syringe with a broken needle. A torn glassine packet lay beside the syringe, and beside that was one of Joanna's sterling tablespoons, a wedding gift from her father, its bowl blackened.

In the library upstairs, the music stand had been knocked over and the charred remains of a manuscript were under the grate in the Franklin stove, where the pages had been used to start another fire. One of the stove's tiles was cracked. Joanna's flute case lay open on the floor. Someone had used the flute as a poker. The end opposite the mouthpiece was black, the hole clogged with ashes. It was the sight of the violated flute that infuriated them most, Joanna because the flute was her life, Jamie simply because he loved her. Eyes blazing, nostrils flaring as though she had at last caught scent of the elusive *something* they'd been stalking, Joanna threw open the bedroom door. Lissie was asleep on their bed, wearing only a T-shirt and cotton panties. In the ashtray beside the bed, there was a used condom.

"Wake up, Goldilocks," Joanna said.

She sat up at once, blinked into the room, and then smiled and said, "Oh. Hi."

"What the hell happened here?" Jamie said.

"Well, we invited some friends in, you know . . ."

"You had no right to do that."

"It was just some . . ."

"Get off that bed!" Joanna said.

"This is where we *live,*" Jamie said. "This is our *home . . .*"

"We were going to clean up," Lissie said.

"When?" Joanna said. "We told you we'd be home tonight, we told you we'd be home around midnight, it's two in the morning, *when* did you . . . ?"

"You've made a pigsty of our home!" Jamie said. "Goddammit, Liss, what's the *matter* with you?"

"Nothing's the matter with me," Lissie said, suddenly defiant. "We had a *fight* is what, okay? Sparky and his friends ran out of here . . ."

"I don't *give* a damn about your fight," Jamie said, taking a step toward the bed. "You're not six years old, you had no right to . . ."

"Who the hell gave you permission to use this room?" Joanna said.

"That was Sparky's idea."

"Was it Sparky's idea to leave a rubber in the ashtray? What was *that?* A little souvenir of your tender romance?"

"He left in a hurry."

"Which is just the way *you're* gonna leave!" Joanna said.

"Listen, you," Lissie said heatedly, "why don't you shut the fuck up? My father . . ."

"*Lissie!*" Jamie shouted.

"Where'd you get this rotten kid?" Joanna asked.

"My father and I are trying to talk here," Lissie said. "If you'd . . ."

"Get dressed," Joanna said. "Pack your things and get out. Take your boyfriend's scumbag with you."

"I don't *have* to do what you . . ."

"Lissie, darling," Joanna said sweetly, " you almost spoiled our wedding day, but that's the last thing you're *ever* going to spoil. Get out. And don't come back till you've learned a little common decency and respect. If not for me, at least for your father."

"I *do* respect my father."

"And I respect Adolf Hitler! Get rid of her," Joanna said, and stormed out of the room.

"You heard her," Jamie said.

"Dad, you don't know how terrible it was," Lissie said, and suddenly began sobbing. She got off the bed, and went to him, and hugged him close, her face pressed against his chest, her tears wetting his shirt, and all at once he felt his anger dissolving. He held her tightly and said, "What happened, Lissie?"

"He was a junkie, Dad," she said in a rush, sobbing, catching her breath, "half the kids *here* tonight were junkies. I didn't know that, Dad, I wouldn't have allowed him to invite them if I'd known. He said it would just be for a few drinks, they tried to turn me on, Dad, it wasn't the first time, Dad, I just wouldn't do it, I'd *never* stick a needle in my body as long as I live, you know that, Dad."

"Yes, darling, I know that."

She moved away from him abruptly, as though remembering she was still wearing only T-shirt and panties, and went quickly to the chair across the room, and took her dress from it, and pulled it over her head. Searching for her shoes and socks, she said, "I'll clean up before I leave, Dad, I promise, it's just that it happened so suddenly, the fight with him, and he . . . he was gone before I . . . before I knew what was happening." She burst into tears again, and he went to her and embraced her again, and then brushed her hair away from her face, and she nodded, and sniffed, and then, still sobbing, said, "I guess everything has to end sooner or later, doesn't it, Dad, but oh, God, oh, *God!*"

"Stop crying, Liss," he said, and handed her his handkerchief. "Here. Blow your nose."

"Thanks, Dad," she said, and took the handkerchief. "God, I'm going to miss him, Dad."

"You'll get over it," he said. "Dry your eyes."

"I hope so, Dad. I mean, you don't *know* what a trauma this is for me, Dad, He was the only one I had. When I realized I didn't have a father anymore . . ."

"Didn't have a *father?* Lissie . . ."

"You know what I mean, Dad. The distance between us and all." She sat in the chair beside the dressing table, and pulled on her blue socks, and then began lacing the high-topped workman's shoes. "Sparky was always there," she said, "he was at least always *there*. And he respected me, Dad. I know that may sound strange, him hitting me and all . . ."

"*Hitting* you?"

"Yes, Dad," she said, and looked up at him.

"Jesus, Lissie, why didn't you *tell* me any of—?"

"I'm sorry, Dad but it wasn't the kind of thing I *could* tell you, not when there were all those hard feelings between us."

"Did you tell your mother?"

"Please don't call her that, Dad, *please!* You have no idea how it hurts me to hear you calling her 'your mother' instead of 'Mom.' If you had any idea . . ."

"Lissie, it wouldn't be right for me to refer to her as 'Mom.' We're divorced now."

"Yes, I know that, Dad, but couldn't you *please* make the effort?"

"Lissie . . ."

"Knowing how much it means to me?"

She got up from where she was sitting, went to the dresser, and picked up Joanna's silver hairbrush. As she began brushing her hair, she said, "Do you think Joanna would mind my using this?"

"You've used everything else," Jamie said, "I think it's a little late to be asking whether . . ."

"God, she didn't have to say all those terrible things to me," Lissie said, standing before the mirror and brushing her hair. "I mean, shit, it's not as if I *wanted* any of this to happen, it just sort of got out of control."

"You shouldn't have invited those people here in the first place," Jamie said.

"*I* didn't invite them, *Sparky* did."

"You're my daughter, not Sparky."

"If I'm your daughter, then how could you allow Joanna to say all those horrible things to me? Without once standing up for me. I mean, *Jesus,* Dad, how could you do that to your own *daughter?*"

"Lissie . . . Joanna's my wife."

"So she's your *wife!* I'm your *daughter!* Doesn't *that* count for anything? I'm your flesh and blood! A *six*-year-old, great, that's what she called me, a *six*-year-old."

"*I* was the one who . . ."

"Not that it should have come as any surprise. I mean, you've been telling me *forever* how immature I am. Or how thoughtless or careless or inconsiderate or whatever the hell. I guess it's just never occurred to you how hurtful that can be. I mean, Dad, did it ever *once* occur to you that maybe you owe me a sincere apology? I mean, if you ever expect me to *really* forgive you."

"Forgive me? For *what?*"

"For everything."

"Everything? Honey, I'm not sure I know what you're . . ."

"Well, for example, you never *really* helped me, no matter what you say now, when Holtzer restricted me to campus that time."

"I came up to see you every—"

"Sure, but you didn't get the restriction lifted, and it got into my files, and that's why I didn't get accepted at Vassar."

"Lissie, you don't know that for a—"

"And then, right after graduation, you ran off to Italy . . ."

"We'd planned that trip months in advance."

". . . and shipped me off to the Cape while you were having a good time over there. Well, so what? I'd been left alone before. But then you raised that terrible fuss when you found out I was living with Judd . . ."

"I think you can understand how—"

"And you wouldn't even trust me with *cash* when I got stranded in Venice that time."

"But Lissie, you *did* cash in the ticket I . . ."

"And again in India, it took *forever* to get the five hundred dollars I asked for . . ."

"I sent it the minute I received your letter. Lissie, I don't see the point . . ."

"The point is . . . and Sparky, all that business with Sparky . . . the *point,* Dad, is you never seem to think about how *I* might be feeling about anything. Can't you for once wake up in the morning feeling a little happier for *me?* Mornings are a beautiful time. Can't you try to dig them?"

"All right, I'll try to *dig* them," he said, and smiled.

"Well, you don't have to make fun of the way I talk, Dad."

"I'm sorry, I didn't . . ."

"I mean, that's just *another* sign of disrespect, isn't it? You keep telling me there are *two* families now, but until I can become a respected member of this new *family,* as you call it, then how can I respect you in return? Or Joanna, either."

"Let's go back just a bit, okay?"

"Sure."

"You said you wanted a sincere apology. What kind of . . . ?"

"I don't want a superficial apology, Dad."

"You just told me . . ."

"How the hell can anyone apologize for all the hurt that's been done to me? Jesus, why do you keep trying to make *me* feel guilty? What did *I* do, would you mind telling me?"

"Lissie, let's try to *hear* each other, okay? I don't think we're hearing each other just now."

"Maybe 'cause you're not listening. I thought I was making myself perfectly clear."

"You said you wanted an apology. All right, I think I'm adult enough to—"

"Meaning *I'm* not, right?"

"I didn't say that."

"When are you going to accept me for what I *am*, Dad? Mom accepts the real *me!* I don't *care* how generous you are, Dad, I mean *fuck* the little gifts from Saks or Bonwit's. It only matters how *honest* you are. And if you think going to bed with a dozen other women while you were still married to . . ."

"Lissie, I did *not* go to . . ."

"Oh, fuck it, who *cares?* But it wasn't *honest,* can't you at least admit that?"

"If it isn't true, why should . . . ?"

"Well, I happen to think it *is* true. Can't you even *discuss* it with me? I'm almost twenty years old, I'll be twenty in December, I'm not a kid sucking lollipops anymore. You should be able to discuss anything under the sun with . . ."

"Not what's private and personal between me and . . ."

"Joanna, right, Joanna. Everything's private and personal between you and Joanna, with nothing left over for your daughter. What the hell do you *see* in her, anyway?" Lissie asked abruptly, turning from the mirror. "Would you mind telling me? What the hell did *she* offer that none of the *others* did? All *I* can see . . ."

"What I see in Joanna is none of . . ."

"What is it you share with her, Dad? Your enormous ego?"

"My *ego?* What . . . ?"

"Yes, your goddamn *fame* and your financial *success* and your fucking ego, *yes!* Where the hell's the *substance,* Dad? Jesus, don't you see what I'm saying?"

"No," he said tightly. "Why don't you tell me what you're saying, Liss?"

"Here comes the anger again, right? I can see it in your eyes, I can hear it in your voice."

"Yes, here comes the anger again," he said.

"What the hell have *you* got to be angry about? You've moved on to greener pastures, haven't you? It's Mom and me who were abandoned."

"Lissie, I really don't want to hear . . ."

"Oh, fuck, who cares *what* you want to hear? How the hell can you *possibly* expect me to accept this new family of yours, this *fake* fucking family you've created, when you . . ."

"Lissie, I think we'd better . . ."

"Am I supposed to accept Joanna simply because *you* love her?"

"You're making it imposs—"

"Why *should* I communicate with . . ."

"All right," he said, and nodded.

". . . people who think I'm a worthless shit?"

"All right," he said again, very quietly, and she fell suddenly silent.

They stood staring at each other.

He took a deep breath.

"How'd you ever get to be *this?*" he said, almost to himself.

"Blame it on the times," she said, and suddenly and surprisingly smiled.

"No."

"Then blame it on yourself."

"I blame it on *you,*" he said. "You should be ashamed of yourself."

"For what? For telling you the truth about . . . ?"

"I'm your *father!*"

"Then why the fuck don't you try *acting* like—"

"Damn you, shut up!" he said.

Her eyes opened wide.

"How *dare* you?" he said. "What *else* have you got for me in that sewer of a mouth? What *else* do you expect me to invite, and accept, and *apologize* for?"

It took her only a moment to recover.

"I don't have to take this kind of shit from you or anybody *else!*" she shouted, and slammed the hairbrush down on the dressing table, and then turned and walked out of the room. He heard her moving angrily through the library, heard her hurried footfalls going down the three flights of stairs and across the living room, heard the front door of the house slam as she went out. The last glimpse he had of her was from the bedroom window as she walked past the lighted lamppost outside the house, her blond head ducked against the wind, her tent dress flapping about her legs, her hands thrust deep into the pockets of the fighter-pilot jacket.

She must have written her letter that same Sunday night. It was undated, and written on YWCA stationery. He received it on Tuesday morning. It repeated much of what she had said to him in anger in the empty hours of the night, as though she wished to give her words the final stamp of permanency:

Dear Dad,

You've leveled with me, so now I'll level with you.

I appreciated (and curiously so) your attempt to settle all this, but was immediately insulted by your error in assuming that I am still a child who can be pushed around and led around by the nose. Yes, I *am* angry with you. You offer many things, oh yes. Gifts and guilt. Everything under the sun except real love. You have never confronted the facts as Mom knows them, and as she has told them to me, you have never admitted that not only were you committing adultery with the woman you later married, but almost certainly with Mrs. Blair as well. You left this family because you were no damn good. Plain and simple. I can see why you don't like Mom, and honestly why you will never like me. Because we both are reminders of your treachery and betrayal.

Where does that leave us? It leaves your daughter many bad places. It leads me to equate financial success and some measure of fame as being a place devoid of love and responsibility, of endless ego gratification with little real substance. Your daughter *does* love you as much as her mother, she just doesn't *like* you as much. To be blunt, again, my mother's well-being is of concern to me because we're in a similar position; we're both alone and facing the many problems of life. You and I do not share a common position right now. It's not that I have consciously taken sides. I am simply seeing things clearly and with my own eyes. I am not convinced that the distance between us is the only thing you're confused about. Mom served you long and well, and you repaid her by abandoning her. I can only believe this was the act of a man who *was* and probably still *is* very confused indeed. I'm sincerely glad that you seem to know exactly where you are in this matter, because no one else knows where you are. I am also glad that after screwing around for so long, you married the woman you "loved." At least you've got a family.

391

There are two reasons why I haven't accepted your new marriage. First, I had to learn from Mom how long your little romance had been going on. And secondly, I don't *like* your new wife, okay? And I will *not* accept her simply because *you* love her. I would not accept *anything* rotten simply because *you* love it. Anyway, I'm not sure I know what love means in your book. You seem to be a superficial father who gives everything but honesty and love. My instinct tells me to give consolation where it is needed most. You think Mom poisons me against you. But that's your *own* poison. It is *you* who have poisoned me against you. I don't believe anything you say about the divorce. Anyway, who gives a shit?

Once again, I'm glad you have a new life with a new woman you love. I can't help but wonder for how long. I am not *invited* to Mom's house, I am *accepted* whenever I choose to go there. I am her blood. You don't treat blood relatives as guests, and you don't embarrass them later by telling them about their bad behavior. Family is supposed to be stronger than that. I am *me*. Take it or leave it! I give you the same love I give Mom, only she—by accepting the real me—offers a more comfortable environment for honesty. Not brainwashing, just honest observation. I love my parents equally, I just don't like them or respect them equally. It doesn't matter how generous you are to me, it only matters how *honest* you are, and you were *not* honest by going to bed with other women when you were still married to Mom. That was not being honest, that was being a crook! I don't see how you can possibly talk to me of truth.

There is really nothing for us to talk about and hasn't been for a long time, even *before* you started your new family. The reason I broke off with you in the first place was because I ended *all* relationships that were founded on lies and guilt. So now you know what I really think. I am really curious to see if your heart and your home are as open as you profess now that you get a clear view of Melissa Croft the woman. As always, *my* heart and *my* home are really open to you—but not to the members of my "new" family.

Love,

Lissie

P.S. Joanna is a cold fish, and I really don't *want* any relationship with her, thanks!

P.P.S. Anyone for seconds? No, thanks, I'm full!

P.P.P.S. My trust *can* be regained, even if the road is a hard one—

but only with honesty and love. Do you even know what love means? *Love,* Dad!

He read her letter again, and then another time. He sat very still in his chair for a very long while. Then he lumbered to his feet, and went upstairs to the guest room she had shared only Saturday night with Sparky, and went to the closet there, and took from it the several cartons in which he had stacked her photographs. He carried the cartons downstairs to the living room, one at a time, and spread the pictures on the floor around the fireplace in a widening circle, as though he were dropping pebbles into a still lake the exact center of which was the hearth, watching their ripples move out, overlapping, to touch a distant shore.

Here was the picture he'd taken of her in Central Park when she was six years old and stooping to pluck a dandelion from the ragged lawn. Here was the one he'd taken at Martha's Vineyard in 1965, Lissie almost fourteen and sitting in a flaking, rusting rowboat. He moved back from the hearth, dropping pictures on the floor at his feet, the ripples widening.

Lissie at the age of twelve, tangled in her skis at Stratton. Lissie by the river in Rutledge when she was sixteen, the secret shot taken from the deck above. Lissie at the Jacobsons' Fourth of July party that same year, grinning around a hot dog dripping mustard. Pictures of her, widening circles, pictures of his daughter.

Lissie in her graduation gown, the mortarboard rakishly tilted, the zoom shot across the lawn. And here . . . ah . . . his favorite, Lissie at Jones Beach in the second year of her life, looking down in consternation at a sand-covered lollipop, her blue eyes squinted, her blond hair catching the sun for a dazzling halo effect. She had known who she was on her second birthday. When she'd seen the poster-sized shot of herself squinting at the lollipop, she'd squealed with glee, remembering, and then ran to him and hugged his knees. He'd lifted her into his arms and kissed her plump little cheek and whispered into her hair, "Daddy loves you."

He picked his way among the photographs, gingerly treading through them as though he were walking a minefield sown with memories. He stood back from them then, surveying the panorama of pictures, the floor covered with them, the room bursting with Lissie. He stood looking at the pictures for a long, long time. Then he went to the dropleaf desk in the corner opposite the fireplace, and lowered the front of it, and took a sheet of stationery from one

393

of the cubbyholes, and picked up a pen. Sighing deeply, he began writing:

October 12, 1971

Dear Lissie:

You've reviled my wife, you've called me an adulterer, an egomaniac, a loveless and dishonest person, a worthless father. I think, Lissie . . .

He crumpled the sheet of paper, and dropped it in the wastebasket under the desk. He took another sheet from the cubbyhole, looked at it blankly for several seconds, and then began writing again:

Dear Lissie:

I'm sorry I'm not the father you want or need. That is my apology. I am sorry for that. But Lissie . . .

Tears were beginning to form in his eyes.
He took a deep breath. His hand began trembling:

. . . no father in the world can be expected to take such abuse from a daughter and still offer friendship to her, no less love. You have made it impossible, finally, to offer you anything at all. If this is the freedom you've wanted all along, then, Lissie, you may have it, you may have your freedom from me.

He looked up sharply, as though she were standing immediately behind his shoulder silently reading every word as he set it down on the page, the pen moving slowly, the tears coursing down his cheeks:

You do not know how it pains me to say this, my daughter, but please understand that you are no longer welcome in my home or in my life. Lissie, my darling, good luck—and goodbye.

Dad

He read the letter over again, and sat at the desk, crying openly, while across the room the clock ticked away the fleeting minutes.

Then he put the letter into an envelope, and addressed it, and sealed it, and went out to mail it.

It was bitterly cold in the street outside.

1979

"The thing of it," Lissie says, "is that I was *there*, I was actually *there!* So when I see the television pictures of all these Iranians shaking their fists outside the American Embassy, all I can think of is that man at the border, the one who wanted to do an internal search."

The two women are sitting at a table in an Italian restaurant called Il Menestrello on East Fifty-second Street. Barbara Duggan is the one who suggested the place; until this past September, she was working as an editor at Harper & Row across the street, and sometimes dined here with writers she hoped to impress. Today is the Friday before Christmas, and Barbara has been invited by her former boss to the company's annual Christmas party. She has asked Lissie to join her for lunch first.

Both women are dressed for their pregnancies and for the unusually mild weather that has wafted into New York for the holiday season. Barbara, in her eighth month and rather larger than Lissie who is in her sixth, is wearing dressy black slacks with medium-heeled black pumps, a white silk blouse with a Peter Pan collar open at the throat and long sleeves cuffed at the wrist. A massive turquoise-and-silver pendant is hanging between her breasts. Her thick black hair is swept up severely onto the crown of her head and fastened there in a small neat knot. Her slanting brown eyes (she still looks marvelously and inscrutably Oriental to Lissie) are touched with fawn-brown shadow and a darker liner. Her lips are tinted with a berry-colored gloss.

Lissie is wearing a navy blue wool jersey dress with an Empire waist, its drawstring tied in a bow just below her breasts, the pleated front cascading over her belly. A flamboyantly patterned Gucci scarf is knotted at her throat, and her straight blond hair is styled in a blunt shoulder-length cut, somewhat longer in the front, and parted in the middle. She wears a frosted peach-colored lipstick and smoke-gray shadow with no liner.

"I know it's chic to hate Iran these days," she says, "but I hated it even then. I couldn't *wait* to get out of that country, Barb. They had these ditches, you know? These little drainage canals, whatever you call them? Running through the gutters? And the people would wash their *food* in those ditches, and throw *garbage* in them, and *spit* in them, and—" her voice lowers—*"pee* in them, you know? And then they'd wash their hands and *faces* in the same water, you had to see it to . . ."

"Please, not while I'm eating," Barbara says, and grins.

"What *is* that, anyway?" Lissie asks.

"Sausage with mushrooms. It's delicious. How's yours?"

"Marvelous."

"This used to be Le Mistral, you know."

"Ah, right. I *thought* I recognized it."

"The murals are still the same. The French Riviera."

"Is that what it means? *Menestrello?* Is it *Mistral* in Italian?"

"I don't think so. I think it means 'minstrel.' *You* should know, you spent much more time in Italy than I did."

"No, we just passed through, actually. God, that seems like a million years ago. When I was traveling with Paul, I mean," she says, and shakes her head. "I don't even know *now* if I was truly in love with him. But I felt something with him I'd never felt with anyone else. I just wanted to be *with* him all the time, *near* him all the time."

"I know just what you mean," Barbara says.

"We never budged from that bed all the while we were in Amsterdam."

"Heavenly," Barbara says, and rolls her eyes.

400

"On the train to Paris, and later on the Orient Express to the Swiss border . . . do you know what he said just before we got on the train?"

"What?"

"He said, 'It was five o'clock on a winter's morning in Syria.' That's the first line of the Agatha Christie novel. He used to quote first lines all the time. But all the way across Switzerland to Milan and Venice, I couldn't keep my hands off him. I guess even before we left Paris, I'd already given up any thought of going back to school. It was craziness, I know. But it was *so* damn exciting."

"All of it," Barbara says, nodding.

"Even the trouble at the border. *Even* those fucking dogs trying to kill us."

She glances immediately at the table nearby, to make certain the matron there hasn't overheard her obscenity. She turns back to Barbara, and wiggles her eyebrows at her. Both women begin giggling like teenagers. Now the matron *does* look at them. They sober immediately.

"What are you hoping for this time?" Lissie asks.

"Another girl. How about you?"

"A boy, I think."

"Boys are a handful."

"Yes, but you have to worry more about girls," Lissie says. "Besides, I think Matthew would like a boy."

"Matthew won't have to take care of him."

"Neither will I, for that matter. Not after the first year, anyway. We've already discussed it. I'll be going back to work again after the first year. You should see him, Barb, it's miraculous! He weighed three thousand pounds when I met him in that Cambridge head shop . . ."

"Just like us," Barbara said.

"Exactly! But he's been on a diet, and I can't believe it's the same man. He keeps looking at himself in the mirror. So do I, as a matter of fact. Looking at *myself,* I mean. I feel like a horse by comparison!"

"Do you plan on having any others?"

"I don't think so. I really had the agency going pretty well, you know, when this happened. I'm not sure *how* I'd feel about leaving it again. I'm not even sure if taking a year's leave *now* won't, you know, ruin everything I've been trying to build for the past *three* years."

"Sure, the personal . . ."

"That's right."

"Especially with travel."

"That's *exactly* right. Where they have to, you know, trust the agent's taste and judgment."

"Your personal taste."

"And judgment, right. So I hope Matthew doesn't get any *more* romantic ideas like he had last July on Fire Island."

"Is that when it happened?"

"That's when I figure it happened." She lowers her voice again. "Did you ever do it by starlight on a sandy beach?"

"In Greece I did," Barbara says.

"Yeah, well, the sand is *finer* there," Lissie says, and both women burst out laughing. The matron looks at them again, and then signals for a check.

"Do your parents know you're pregnant?" Barbara asks.

"Well, my mother does, naturally."

"Is she still living in New York?"

"No, no. She went to Paris almost immediately after the wedding."

"What's he do?"

"My stepfather? He has a perfume company over there."

"And she lives there full-time now?"

"Well, she comes to New York for a few weeks every fall."

"How'd she meet him?"

"Skiing. In Switzerland."

"Where?"

"Davos."

"Never been there."

"Me neither."

"It sounds romantic."

"Davos?"

"No, meeting a man on the slopes."

"Yeah. Actually, he's very nice."

"What about your father?"

"What about him?"

"Does *he* know?"

"That I'm pregnant, you mean? How would he know?"

"I thought you might have . . ."

"I haven't heard a word from him in more than eight years," Lissie says, and hesitates. "It was eight years in October."

"Since you've seen him?"

"Or talked to him. Or heard much about him, in fact. I don't mean his professional life, I guess he's busier than he ever was, I see his stuff all over the place. But otherwise . . . well, my mother used to fill me in every now and then, but that was when she was still living in New York."

"He had a child with her, didn't he?"

"Mm-huh."

"A girl, wasn't it?"

"Yes, mm-huh."

"How old is she now?"

"Who?"

"Your sister."

"My *sister?* Hey, come on, Barb."

"Well, she . . . I mean, she's your *half*-sister, anyway."

"Mm-huh."

"So how old is she?"

"I don't know. Five or six, who knows?"

"What's her name?"

"I don't know."

"Ever try to look her up?"

"What for?"

"Well . . . I think if *I* were in a similar situation . . . well, I'd be curious to see what she looked like."

"Mm, well."

"Anyway," Barbara says and grins. "Would you like some dessert?"

"What time is it?"

"Almost two-thirty."

"What time are you due up there?"

"Three."

"Maybe we ought to skip it then. I've still got to pick up a few more things for Matthew, none of his clothes *fit* him now that he's lost so much weight."

"Where are you heading?"

"Saks."

"Don't you miss Bonwit's not being here anymore?"

"Desperately," Lissie says, and rolls her eyes.

They say goodbye to each other outside the restaurant and promise faithfully to keep in touch and to try to see more of each other in the new year. Barbara wishes her luck with the baby. Lissie hugs her tight and says, "Oh, yes, Barb, and *you,* too."

She watches as her friend waddles across the street to enter the Harper & Row building, and suddenly visualizes her as she looked nine years ago in San Francisco when they strolled along Castro Street, Barbara wearing a brightly colored caftan, her thick black hair falling in a cascade to the middle of her back—*I remember once, when I was in L.A., I went to meet this guy in MacArthur Park, he had an ounce of good pot I wanted to buy. And this pregnant lady was walking toward me in the park . . .*

She smiles and begins walking toward Fifth Avenue.

On the corner of Fifty-second and Fifth, there is a Salvation Army band playing "Silent Night." Lissie drops a quarter in the kettle. The air is not quite balmy, but after Wednesday's snow and wind, it seems almost springlike today. She heads downtown with her big belly jutting, listening to the carols coming from someplace across the street, hearing the jingling of Santa Claus bells, savoring the *feel* of this city at Christmas time, the *pace* of it, the sheer *momentum* of it even when it's springtime in December and there is no need to rush against the brittle cold. She surveys the windows of Saks, and then walks into the store through one of the Fifth Avenue entrances.

She isn't quite sure what she hopes to buy for Matthew in addition to the mountain of gifts she's already purchased. She thinks it odd that he's begun *losing* weight in direct ratio to the speed with which she's been *gaining* weight, and isn't certain she enjoys him looking so slender and trim while she herself is beginning to resemble, more and more each day, the entire state of Rhode Island. She loved him when he was fat, so why the double-cross now? Idly, she wonders if the baby will indeed be a boy. If it's a boy, they've already decided to name him Jeremiah, after Matthew's father, Jeremiah Hobbs, D.D.S.

She wanders the first floor of the store, casually shopping the counters, hoping to find something spectacularly smashing to reward Matthew for his damn perseverance in pursuing his latest diet so conscientiously, twenty pounds in two months, that is a lot of fat down the drain while old *Melissa* Hobbs is ballooning. She stops at the sweater counter, remembering that Matthew's sweaters are getting a bit threadbare, recalling in fact that he dropped a hint only last Wednesday, his day off, about coming through the elbows of his favorite cardigan. There is a cardigan on the countertop, green, with a lovely shawl collar. She checks the label, sees that it's a medium, and wonders if a medium will be too small for Matthew, even in his trimmed-down reincarnation. "Excuse me," she says, signaling to the salesclerk, who rushes past breathlessly and says over his shoulder, "In a minute, miss."

"Shit," she mutters, and the man standing beside her turns to her, smiles, starts to say, "It's always this way at . . ." and then abruptly stops talking.

He is a man in his early fifties, she supposes, with brown eyes and a full head of dark brown hair, worn rather long. A thick beard covers his jowls and his chin. The beard is partially the color of the hair on his head and partially white. A hooded green loden coat hangs open over wide-waled tan corduroy pants and a plaid flannel shirt. A camera is hanging around his neck.

He is, she realizes, her father.

Neither of them speaks at first.

They simply stare at each other.

He is seeing a well-groomed and obviously pregnant young woman wearing a smart cloth coat over an expensive maternity dress, he is seeing his daughter as he has never been privileged to view her before. She is seeing a bearded, casually dressed man who seems very much at ease with himself, more relaxed than she's ever known him.

Still, they say nothing.

"It *is* Lissie?" he ventures.

"Yes," she says. She almost adds the word "Dad." She does not.

"How are you, Lissie?"

"Fine, thanks. And you?"

"Living in New York now, are you?"

"Yes."

"Me, too," he says. "Joanna and I are down in the Village now. Where are . . .?"

"Well, not actually the city," she says. "Larchmont. My husband has his practice in Larchmont."

"Ah. Nice there."

"Yes."

"So," he says.

"So," she says.

"You're married and everything now, huh?"

"Yes."

"I see you're . . ."

"Yes."

"When are you expecting?"

"April sometime."

"Ah." He pauses. "You look wonderful, Lissie."

"Thank you."

"So," he says again. "It's been a long time."

"Eight years."

He hesitates. Then he says, "You broke my heart."

The words pierce her to the core. She feels herself crumbling inside, and thinks for a moment that these are the first honest words he's ever spoken to her in as long as she's known him, and answers with equal honesty, "And you broke mine."

He nods. He says nothing. It almost seems the conversation will end with this brief exchange. Everywhere around them, shoppers are rushing past.

"You shouldn't have written that letter," she says, and her eyes seek his. Clear-eyed, they face each other. In her heels, Lissie is almost as tall as he is; their eyes meet at almost the same level. While everywhere around them shoppers hurry past, and clerks ring up sales or reach for ringing telephones, they search each other's eyes.

Gently, he says, "You left me no choice, Liss."

She hesitates. She takes a deep breath, and at last says, "Maybe I didn't." It is a fierce admission; it is almost a beginning. The clerk suddenly appears behind the counter. "Yes, miss," he says, "I can help you now."

She turns away from her father. "Would you gift-wrap this for me, please?" she says.

"The cardigan, miss?"

"Yes, please."

"Will this be cash or charge?"

"Charge," she says and opens her handbag and then her wallet and begins searching for her Saks card. Her father is watching her. She is aware of his eyes on her.

"Well," he says, "it was good seeing you again."

"Yes, here, too," she says, searching for the card.

"Have a merry Christmas, Liss . . ."

"You, too," she says quickly.

"And if you ever find yourself in the city . . ."

"Yes, Dad?" she says, and looks up from the handbag.

He hesitates. "I'm in the book," he says, and extends his hand to her.

She takes it.

They shake hands politely, like strangers.

He continues holding her hand.

She feels her eyes beginning to dissolve, and releases his hand at once, and hurries off into the milling crowd of shoppers before she can find the courage to ask him how her little sister is coming along.